NOVELISTS

Presenting the life and work of fifty of the most influential novelists in Britain today, this collection of review essays offers an excellent guide to the contemporary literary scene.

It covers a vast range of talents, styles and themes, from the gritty urban world of *Trainspotting* to the magic realism of *Midnight's Children* and the wartime drama of the *Ghost Road* trilogy.

Featured writers include:

- Martin Amis
- Louis de Bernières
- Sebastian Faulks
- Nick Hornby
- Ian McEwan
- Caryl Phillips
- Salman Rushdie
- Will Self
- Rose Tremain
- Sarah Waters
- Irvine Welsh
- Jeanette Winterson

Engaging and stimulating, this is the ideal guide for students, reading groups and anyone interested in contemporary British fiction.

Nick Rennison is a freelance writer, editor and bookseller.

You may also be interested in the following Routledge Student Reference titles:

CONTEMPORARY BRITISH NOVELISTS

Nick Rennison

Routledge
Taylor & Francis Group

LONDON AND NEW YORK

First published 2005
by Routledge
2 Park Square, Milton Park, Abingdon, Oxfordshire, OX14 4RN

Simultaneously published in the USA and Canada
by Routledge
29 West 35th Street, New York, NY 10001

Routledge is an imprint of the Taylor & Francis Group

© 2005 Nick Rennison

Typeset in Bembo by Taylor and Francis Books Ltd
Printed and bound in Great Britain by
TJ International Ltd, Padstow, Cornwall

British Library Cataloguing in Publication Data
A catalogue record for this book is available from the British Library

Library of Congress Cataloging in Publication Data
A catalog record for this books has been requested

ISBN 0–415–21708–3 (hbk)
ISBN 0–415–21709–1 (pbk)

CONTENTS

ACKNOWLEDGEMENTS

Many people have helped in the writing of this book, some of them, perhaps, without knowing it. My chief debt is to those friends who, over the years, have recommended novels to me, shared their enthusiasm for particular novelists or argued amiably (and, very occasionally, not so amiably) with me about the merits and demerits of books and their authors. Susan Osborne and Travis Elborough are both far better read in modern fiction than I am and I am very grateful to them for sharing with me their knowledge, without which many of the entries would have been the poorer. Sean Martin provided much help with a number of the entries. Lucinda Rennison, John Magrath, Kevin Chappell, Hugh Pemberton, Richard Shephard, Andy Miller, Honor Wilson-Fletcher, Gordon Kerr, Roger Bratchell and Andrew Holgate have all, over the years, given assistance. Roger Thorp first commissioned this book from me more years ago than I would choose to admit. At Routledge Rosie Waters, Milon Nagi and Susannah Trefgarne have been the most supportive and patient editors that any author could wish for and I owe them far more than the paltry box of chocolates so far delivered. Finally, I wouldn't have finished the book without the love and support of Eve Gorton.

PREFACE

The novel in Britain, we are confidently and regularly told, is not what it once was. Whenever commentators attempt to assess the current state of the English novel, nostalgia for some presumed golden age is almost certain to appear at some point in the discussion. One of the most enduring, if not endearing, characteristics of English cultural criticism appears to be the belief that nothing written in the present can possibly match what was written in the past. In an essay published in the mid-1930s, George Orwell felt that 'it hardly needs pointing out that at this moment the prestige of the novel is extremely low' and that 'the novel is visibly deteriorating'. In the seventy years since, his views have been echoed in a thousand articles and think-pieces heralding the Death of the Novel, a demise that has either just taken place or is, inevitably, just about to take place. If readers of British fiction are not being invited to look to the past for glories no longer attainable, they are being pointed in the direction of other countries (usually America) as the home of mind-stretching, expansive novels that put our own parochial narratives, limited and unambitious as they are, into the shade. If the message is not 'they did this better fifty years ago', it is likely to be 'they do this better 5,000 miles away'. The argument that the contemporary British novel is a poor relative of its historical and geographical counterparts is so familiar that it has become an unexamined truism. It's easy to forget that there is an alternative case to be made. It's easy to forget that at the time Orwell penned his jeremiad about the novel Virginia Woolf was still alive, D. H. Lawrence had been dead for less than a decade and Evelyn Waugh, Graham Greene, Anthony Powell, Jean Rhys and Christopher Isherwood (to name only a few) were all launched upon their careers. The vast majority of novels published in America are no more ambitious and startling than the average British novel. Orwell's pessimism was not justified in the 1930s and any unthinking, downbeat dismissal of British fiction in the last twenty years is similarly misguided. Nor need we look across the Atlantic with shamefaced embarrassment. There is actually far less need for British critics to adopt an immediate position of cultural cringe when faced by American fiction than there was, say, in the 1950s or early 1960s.

Certainly there are tasks for which the novel in Britain may no longer be suited. To attempt to use the novel as a means of undertaking a grand, sweeping analysis of society and its ills, for example, is a temptation to which British novelists continue to succumb, but the results are never very successful. In theory the undertaking should be a valuable one. No one could deny that the 1980s and 1990s saw enormous changes and upheavals in British society, from the social deconstruction of the Thatcherite years to the emergence of New Labour. Traditionally, fiction has provided a prism through which such change can be reflected and refracted. The great Victorian 'state of the nation' novels such as *Middlemarch*, *Our Mutual Friend* and Trollope's *The Way We Live Now* stand as permanent reminders that writers once felt able to embrace the largest of subjects, to offer a microcosmic reflection of a macrocosmic reality. 'There was a time', as V. S. Naipaul has lamented, 'when fiction provided discoveries about the nature of society, about states, which gave those works of fiction a validity over and above the narrative element'. Yet the nature of society and the state in the last twenty years have proved mostly beyond the reach of fiction's grasp. Britain in the last twenty years of the twentieth century and the first few years of a new millennium has shown itself too diverse, too protean to fit within the straitjackets of fictional forms that have outlived their usefulness. Some novelists, still wedded to the fictional ambitions of the past, have tried to conduct the kind of grand analysis that was once common, self-consciously writing their own versions of the 'state of the nation' novel, but the fiction that has emerged has been dead on the page, its contemporaneity transmuted into the *passé* in the short time between writing and publication.

Many of the best novelists of the last twenty years, aware of the growing impossibility of providing the kind of discoveries to which Naipaul alludes, have turned to the past as a means of obliquely reflecting the present. One of the commonest criticisms directed at recent British fiction is that it is obsessed by the past. Just as our 'heritage' society has an unhealthy obsession with departed glories, so our novelists turn away from today's realities to wallow in nostalgia and the literary equivalent of retro-chic. Some of the criticism is undoubtedly justified. There are historical novels that look back to the supposed simplicities of the past in order to avoid the messy demands of the present. For many novelists, however, the backwards gaze becomes liberating, freeing their imaginations to refashion experience in ways that a blinkered concentration on the contemporary would not allow. Historical narratives of all kinds – and they are far more various than the standard criticism suggests – use the past not as some kind of literary security blanket but as a mirror in which their narratives catch reflected glimpses of the present and the competing circumstances that have formed it. In *Chatterton* and *Hawksmoor*, Peter Ackroyd, using his own versions of seventeenth- and eighteenth-century prose with mimetic brilliance, draws readers into narrative mazes which lead them eventually to climactic revelations of the bonds between the centuries. Rose Tremain takes court life in Charles II's England (*Restoration*) and seventeenth-century Denmark (*Music & Silence*) as the setting for richly orchestrated stories that explore very contemporary ideas about love and power and the value of art.

Novels like Robert Edric's *The Book of the Heathen* and Barry Unsworth's *Sacred Hunger* use events from colonial history to illuminate issues of oppression and exploitation which are no less relevant in a post-colonial world. In *The Passion* and *Sexing the Cherry* Jeanette Winterson invents her own idiosyncratic versions of the past that can encompass both the real and the fantastic. These are all very different novels, often using very different narrative techniques, but they do have one thing in common. They are fiercely resistant to any idea of the past as a playground for those seeking the cosy pleasures of rose-tinted retrospection. All of these novels, and very many more described in this book, engage with the contemporary through the historical rather than evade it.

To argue that the 'state of the nation' novel no longer provides a viable template for contemporary fiction and that the past has often proved more amenable to fictional analysis than the present is not, of course, to argue that the best novels of the last two decades have turned away from social and political questions entirely. (Such a retreat would not be possible, in any case. Novels necessarily reflect the society in which they are written. Even the most apparently uncomplicated fantasy fiction has some kind of disguised relationship with social reality.) For British novelists in the last two decades the dramatic changes in politics and society have demanded some response but the response has best been made in a dialogue with changes in specific cultural arenas. The first is gender. It was in the 1970s that the renascent women's movement began to find new voices in fiction, but it was in the 1980s that these voices began to move closer to centre-stage. The 1970s saw the rediscovery of voices from the past (the women writers published and championed by Virago, for example), the first novels of writers like Michèle Roberts and Sarah Maitland, and influential work by Angela Carter and other female fabulists. The 1980s saw the consolidation of writing careers and a proliferation of ongoing debates in fiction about the status of women in society and the dynamics of sexual relationships. In the 1990s the pendulum may have seemed to have swung back towards the kind of gender stereotyping that characterised fiction in the past. The media obsession with the artificially created sub-genre of 'chick lit', novels filled with young female protagonists almost entirely defined by their relation-ships with men, may have waned slightly in the last two years but any cursory examination of the features pages of the broadsheet papers shows that it still exists. Yet there is no going back to the old unreconstructed images of masculinity and femininity. Many of the concerns of women writers who felt themselves culturally marginalised in the 1960s and 1970s have now filtered into the mainstream. Writers as diverse as Pat Barker, Sarah Waters and Helen Dunmore have produced novels that revisit subjects and issues raised in earlier decades while seeing their works given a level of attention in prizes and media coverage that they would not have had as little as fifteen years previously. Acclaimed male writers, at the heart of the literary 'establishment', have addressed themes that would, in earlier decades, have escaped their notice. A major part of Ian McEwan's literary project, certainly in his work of the late 1980s and early 1990s, has been a series of attempts to answer his own question, posed in the libretto for a Michael Berkeley oratorio he wrote in 1983: 'Shall there be womanly times or shall we die?' There may be no more place for those 1970s and 1980s novels memorably dismissed by the critic and novelist D. J. Taylor as books in which 'the cast sits around having contrived discussions about the nature of patriarchy', but the finest British novelists of the 1980s and 1990s, male and female, have woven more subtle explorations of feminist concerns into their work. The danger that was suggested by Michèle Roberts when she expressed the hope that eventually there will be 'male writers and female writers, rather than as at present "feminist writers" and "writers" ' still exists. Pigeonholed and typecast, the 'feminist' novelist still runs the risk of being sidelined, but the voices of a wide variety of women writers are heard more clearly than at any earlier period in the history of British fiction.

The idea of the all-inclusive 'state of the nation' novel may have been consigned to the dustbin by the best British novelists but, paradoxically, the geographic range of British fiction has, in one sense, expanded. Voices other than those of the once-dominant metropolitanism are increasingly heard. The belief that nothing much of sufficient value to be memorialised in fiction ever happens outside London may still lurk in the hearts of many novelists but it now remains unspoken. Just as the political arena has seen devolution and, in the late 1990s, the creation of new parliaments for both Scotland and Wales, so in literature there has been a resurgence in fiction set outside the narrow ambit of London and its satellite states (North Oxford, Tuscany, the Home Counties). The 1970s saw the decline of the kitchen-sink realism that, in the late 1950s and 1960s, provided new voices, often speaking with northern accents. As these have faded, their successors have arrived without the same media fanfare, but the very absence of this is suggestive. The value of non-metropolitan fiction is now so immediately acknowledged that it merits no arm-waving demands for attention.

Some of the most exciting and challenging fiction in the last ten years, in particular, came not just from outside London but from outside England. In Wales writers as different as John Williams (noir crime fiction set in Cardiff), Niall Griffiths (deracinated twenty-somethings in pursuit of connection to the world) and Trezza Azzopardi (familial dysfunction among an immigrant community in South Wales) have emerged to expand ideas of what Welsh fiction might be. In Scotland, always the home of a rich tradition of fiction, there has been a remarkable renaissance in the last two decades. The ur-text of this Scottish renaissance was Alasdair Gray's *Lanark*, but the sons and daughters of *Lanark* have proved a diverse family. Irvine Welsh has been the most visible of the new Scottish writers and his work, from *Trainspotting* onwards, has spotlighted a generation which earlier novelists ignored, but Alan Warner, Janice Galloway, A. L. Kennedy, James Kelman, Jeff Torrington and others have also made important contributions to the renewal of fictional vitality in Scotland.

Perhaps most significantly of all, British fiction has finally woken up to the realities of the post-colonial world, to the ongoing fallout from the dissolution of empire. In most instances it is forty, fifty, even sixty years since independence was granted to the colonies of the British Empire, but the political and economic consequences of this continue to shape Britain and the wider world. In the last twenty years the realisation that Britain is a multicultural society has finally been fully acknowledged by the book industry and by the publishing trade. There have been black writers and Asian writers responding to their experience of Britain since, at least, the 1950s (Samuel Selvon, for example), but it is only in the last twenty years that novelists like Caryl Phillips and Hanif Kureishi have been able to stake their claims in the mainstream of British fiction. Both of these writers (and others who have appeared in the last few years, like Andrea Levy, Hari Kunzru, Monica Ali and Zadie Smith) have given a voice to multicultural Britain. Other writers, most notably Salman Rushdie, have fused the storytelling traditions, the mythologies and the popular cultures of East and West into narratives that are as adventurous and imaginative as any being written in the rest of the world.

In the last twenty-five years the older idea of the British Novel (or, more often, the English Novel), carefully capitalised in its spelling and drawing on a recognised historical tradition, has disintegrated and fragmented. In truth, the monolithic notion of the British Novel was always something of a mythical beast. Even as the tradition was being constructed, there were other voices – those in righteous rebellion against it – that demanded to be heard. Certainly, in 2004 there is no such strange creature as the British Novel (or English Novel). Making sweeping generalisations about British fiction or about the alleged decline of British fiction has always been a perilous pastime, but now it seems more than ever counterproductive. There is no great tradition of the English novel any longer. There are only individual novels.

It is in this context that the fifty novelists discussed in this book have been chosen. The criteria I have used in choosing them have been simple, some might even say simplistic. The first defining parameter has been one of time. Any starting point for a survey like this is necessarily arbitrary, but early in the process of writing I settled on 1980 as my opening year. We like the capricious demarcations that decades provide, however misleading they can sometimes be, and this gave me two such chunks of time, the 1980s and the 1990s, to consider, as well the first few years of not only a new decade but a new millennium. Choosing 1980 as a starting point does not mean that all the books described were published after that date. All fifty of the novelists have produced their best and most characteristic work in the years since 1980, but a significant proportion of them had published fiction before that date and any general assessment of the work of these writers needed to include their earlier books. The result is that some of the novelists here categorised as contemporary were born in the 1930s, some in the 1960s. The majority of those included are of the generation born in the late 1940s and 1950s, those writers who began publishing in the years between 1975 and 1985. The youngest writers are Nicola Barker and Sarah Waters, both born in 1966. Other, younger writers (Zadie Smith, Trezza Azzopardi, Andrew Greig) might press claims to inclusion and I am sure that any future editions will need to find room for them, but I wanted each of the fifty to have a significant body of work behind them. I decided, again with an unavoidable arbitrariness, that the requirement was three full-scale novels. Only a few have that minimum requirement. Most, whatever their age, have written more than three novels.

The second parameter was provided by the (often artificial) boundaries of genre. There can be no doubt that in terms of commercial success, influence and media attention some of the most significant novels of the past twenty-five years have been books that have been categorised (with varying degrees of descriptiveness or dismissiveness) as 'genre' fiction. In addition, the barriers erected between genre fiction and 'mainstream' fiction have become more permeable in the last quarter of a century. Writers like Iain Banks move easily and uncontentiously between science fiction and 'literary' fiction. Crime novelists and thriller writers are reviewed on the same pages as more overtly 'literary' novelists and their works judged by the same critical standards. There is a case to be made that the most significant writers of fiction in the last decade have been two novelists (J. K. Rowling and Philip Pullman) whose works would in the past have been twice sidelined. Not only are they fantasy, but they are fantasy aimed, at least primarily, at children. Despite all these caveats, I believe that a worthwhile distinction can still be made between 'genre' fiction and what is usually described as 'literary' fiction. Writers of crime fiction and science fiction work within different conventions and traditions to the novelists in this book. Genre fiction has its own pleasures and its own validity but I wanted to resist any temptation, open to the accusation of tokenism, of casting a handful of crime novelists and a handful of SF novelists into the mixture. They deserve their own, separate guidebooks.

This introduction to contemporary novelists nonetheless reveals the diversity of British fiction in the last two and a half decades. The British novel is not dead, despite the attempts of many commentators to place it in its grave. There is much to celebrate in contemporary British fiction. Any art form that includes works as different as the biliously satirical novels of Martin Amis, the offbeat and laconic fiction of Beryl Bainbridge, the tangled conflations of history, mythology and philosophy written by Lawrence Norfolk, Alan Hollinghurst's witty comedies of gay manners and mores, the seductive and sensuously lyrical explorations of sexual relationships by Helen Dunmore and the subtle, understated narratives of Kazuo Ishiguro must still be alive and well. The fifty novelists whose works are briefly surveyed in this book provide the proof that both nostalgia for an indeterminately defined

golden age of British fiction and an automatic assumption that the
novel thrives better in other climes are equally misplaced.

FIFTY CONTEMPORARY BRITISH NOVELISTS

PETER ACKROYD (born 1949)

Peter Ackroyd's writings – as novelist, poet, biographer, historian and critic – have been enormously diverse but two subjects have dominated his work in all fields. One is the city of his birth – London. The other is his sense of the connection – numinous and unashamedly mystical – between past and present, and his sense that our reality is but one of myriad realities which fiction can explore.

Ackroyd was born in West London in 1949 and was brought up as a Catholic. Educated at Cambridge and Yale, he became a literary journalist and worked for the *Spectator* for a number of years. In 1986 he joined *The Times* as chief book reviewer. Ackroyd's earliest publications were volumes of poetry (*London Lickpenny* and *Country Life*) but he published his first novel in 1982 and has since written eight more. He has also published biographies of T. S. Eliot, Blake and Sir Thomas More (among others) and an epic portrait of his native city, *London: The Biography.*

Ackroyd has written widely on Dickens's fiction and its use of London. The Victorian novelist's books are, in Ackroyd's telling words, 'deeply invaded by the city'. The same is true of his own novels. London, both in its reality and in its metaphoric power, has been a notable presence in most of them. The past and present of the city are skilfully interwoven in his books. In *Hawksmoor*, still his most powerful and original novel, a contemporary detective (the namesake of the eighteenth-century architect) moves towards a mystical encounter with forces from the past as he investigates a series of murders in London churches. History reaches out to seize Hawksmoor in the shape of Nicholas Dyer, an eighteenth-century Satanist. A good part of the novel is told in the voice of Dyer, whose credo is in stark contrast to both the emerging rationalism of his age and the belief in a logical explanation that fuels any murder investigation like Hawksmoor's. 'This *mundus tenebrosus*', states Dyer, 'this shadowwy world of Mankind is sunk in Night, there is not a Field without its Spirits, nor a City without its Daemons, and the Lunaticks speak Prophesies while the wise men fall into the Pitte. We are all in the Dark, one with another'. At the conclusion of the book the barriers between the past and the present, and Dyer and Hawksmoor, seem to dissolve in a mystical transformation that few contemporary novelists other than Ackroyd would attempt. 'They were face to face, and yet they looked past one another at the pattern which they cast upon the stone . . . and who could say where one had ended and the other had begun?' In his less successful novels (*First Light* or *English Music*) this kind of reliance on the metaphysical and the mystical in his plots and on elaborate congruences between centuries becomes irritating. The parallels and recurrences are predictable rather than originally conceived and Ackroyd's apparent endorsement of some kind of enduring, ahistorical 'Englishness' appears facile. In *Hawksmoor* and his finer novels the supernatural elements slide seamlessly into the plot and the reader is more aware of Ackroyd's extraordinary ability to mimic and revivify the language of the past for his own purposes.

Hawksmoor had been preceded by *The Great Fire of London*, about an ill-fated attempt to film Dickens's *Little Dorrit*, and by *The Last Testament of Oscar Wilde*. The latter novel, if nothing else, showed the extent of Ackroyd's self-confidence. To write a first-person narrative in the voice of the most legendarily witty conversationalist in English literary history is a tightrope act which requires a strong head for heights. Ackroyd carried it off with some aplomb. He followed *Hawksmoor* with *Chatterton*, another book which ranged back and forth in time and used different narrative voices. *Chatterton* was also an exploration of another subject which clearly fascinates Ackroyd – the intertwined ideas of authenticity and inauthenticity. The eighteenth-century poet Chatterton, who became an icon of the Romantic movement in the years following his suicide at the age of seventeen, wrote poems that he claimed were the work of a medieval monk, Thomas Rowley. The nineteenth-century writer George Meredith playacted the role of Chatterton for his friend Henry Wallis's well-known painting of the poet dying in his garret room. In the present day Ackroyd's hero, Charles Wychwood, becomes obsessed by a portrait dated 1802 which may or may not be genuine and may or may not show that Chatterton didn't die his romantic death but lived on into less romantic middle age. Ackroyd's novel moves subtly back and forth through the centuries as he interlinks these stories and raises questions about forgery and pastiche in art that reflect his own style of creating fictions. In an autobiographical manuscript that comes into Wychwood's possession, Chatterton boasts:

> I set myself to write the Memoirs of a sad dog (a gentleman pursewed by Bailiffs), of a malefactor chain'd in Newgate, of an old Relict thirsting for a Man, and of a young ripe Girl about to be pluck'd. And these I related in their own Voices, naturally, as if they were authentick Histories: so that, tho' I was young Thomas Chatterton to those I met, I was a very Proteus to those who read my works.

In his own ability to adopt the narrative voices of his characters from both past and present, Ackroyd himself becomes 'a very Proteus' to those who read his novels.

First Light, following the fortunes of a heterogeneous group of caricature characters who come together at the site of a supposed ancient monument, and *English Music*, in which a spiritualist and seer visits, in his dreams, iconic figures from the English cultural tradition, see Ackroyd at his least convincing. There are moments in both books (a wonderful passage in *English Music*, for example, in which Hogarth leads the central character through the cityscape of his engravings) but the overall effect of these novels is stagey. And the stage effects are very often those not of a slick West End production but of slightly embarrassing amateur dramatics.

In *The House of Doctor Dee* and *Dan Leno and the Limehouse Golem* Ackroyd returned to something approaching his best writing. In the first book Matthew Palmer inherits a house in Clerkenwell once owned by the Elizabethan magus Dr John Dee. Once again, as in *Hawksmoor* and *Chatterton*, Ackroyd refuses to treat time as the arrow of conventional metaphor. Events are circular in their effects. Past influences present but the present also works retrospectively to influence the past. The twentieth-century researcher Matthew Palmer is haunted by voices and visions that surface again from the house's history – so much so that he fears for his sanity. Yet Ackroyd also writes in the narrative voice of John Dee, who glimpses Palmer in his crystal ball and senses his presence in the house. *Dan Leno and the Limehouse Golem* evokes the world of late-Victorian music-hall in a story centred once again (as in *Hawksmoor*) on a series of killings. Real individuals like Marx and Gissing interact with Ackroyd's inventions; fable and murder mystery mix with Gothic comedy; different narrative voices combine and contend in a characteristic blend.

For much of the last decade Ackroyd has concentrated his considerable energies on non-fiction, producing biographies of Thomas More and William Blake, and a monumental portrait of London through the centuries. He has published novels – *Milton in America*, *The Plato Papers*, *The Clerkenwell Tales* – but they have seemed less challenging in their explorations of time and identity. In *Milton in America* he played again with the idea of alternate realities which he had used in *Chatterton*. In the more recent work the question is: 'What might have happened, had the republican John Milton, not yet the author of *Paradise Lost*, fled to America when Charles II was restored to the throne in 1660?' The answer turns out to be that the puritanical Milton founds a community of devout, bigoted co-religionists who come into conflict both with the Native Americans and with a nearby Catholic township. In a search for contrasting patterns and motifs in his book, Ackroyd strays well into the territory of stereotype and cardboard characterisation. The Puritans are uniformly intolerant and pleasure hating, the Catholics cheerful yea-sayers to life and its ambiguity. *Milton in America* is often entertaining as a speculative narrative but has none of the power of Ackroyd's fiction at its best. *The Plato Papers* is, by some way, Ackroyd's oddest novel, if indeed it is best described as a novel at all. Half-fable, half-treatise, it seems much more a vehicle for Ackroyd's ideas about aesthetics and the relationship between science and religion than it does an attempt at sustaining a convincing narrative.

Ackroyd continues to publish fiction regularly but it is arguable that his creative energies are not as fully engaged in his novels as they once were. *The Clerkenwell Tales* (2003) takes him back further into London's history than he has usually gone (the novel is set, with many a nod in the direction of Chaucer, in the fourteenth century) but is otherwise content to travel along thematic paths he has traversed before. A novel based on the lives of the early nineteenth-century essayist Charles Lamb and his sister Mary, scheduled for publication in autumn 2004, seems likely to revisit familiar territory. It may be that Ackroyd has reached a point in his career where he believes that fiction does not provide him so effectively with the form he needs for innovation and invention. In the past he has believed otherwise, and novels such as *Hawksmoor, Chatterton* and *The House of Doctor Dee* stand as impressive testimony to that belief.

Ackroyd's major works

The Great Fire of London, Hamish Hamilton, 1982.
The Last Testament of Oscar Wilde, Hamish Hamilton, 1983.
T. S. Eliot, Hamish Hamilton, 1984 (biography).
Hawksmoor, Hamish Hamilton, 1985.
Chatterton, Hamish Hamilton, 1987.
The Diversions of Purley and Other Poems, Hamish Hamilton, 1987 (poetry).
First Light, Hamish Hamilton, 1989.
Dickens, Sinclair-Stevenson, 1990 (biography).
English Music, Hamish Hamilton, 1992.
The House of Doctor Dee, Hamish Hamilton, 1993.
Dan Leno and the Limehouse Golem, Sinclair-Stevenson, 1994.
Blake, Sinclair-Stevenson, 1995 (biography).
Milton in America, Sinclair-Stevenson, 1996.
The Life of Thomas More, Chatto & Windus, 1998 (biography).
The Plato Papers, Chatto & Windus, 1999.
London: The Biography, Chatto & Windus, 2000 (history).

Albion: The Origins of the English Imagination, Chatto & Windus, 2002 (cultural criticism).
The Clerkenwell Tales, Chatto & Windus, 2003.
The Lambs of London, Chatto & Windus, 2004.

MARTIN AMIS (born 1949)

A competition in the *New Statesman* magazine once invited entrants to provide the authors and titles of unlikely books. One of the winners suggested *My Struggle* by Martin Amis. The assumption on which the joke relies – that Amis's career has been made easy because he is the son of a famous novelist – is, however unfair, one that many people have made and one that has fuelled at least some of the quite disproportionate critical malice (as well as the hyperbolic praise) that he has attracted over the years. Like his father, Amis has had to bear the burden of being the voice of a particular (male) literary generation and, again echoing the experience of his father, critics have often found it difficult to assess his career dispassionately. Martin Amis was born in Oxford in 1949, the second son of Kingsley Amis and his first wife Hilary. After a peripatetic childhood and education, including a short period in America when his father was teaching at Princeton and an even shorter period in the West Indies appearing as one of the young adolescents in the film version of Richard Hughes's book *A High Wind in Jamaica*, Amis read English at Oxford. After graduation he worked as an editorial assistant on the *Times Literary Supplement* before his first novel was published. In the three decades since his debut Amis has been regarded as one of the most original and influential writers of his generation. He has written nine further novels, as well as volumes of short stories, a memoir and a collection of critical essays.

Amis's first novel, *The Rachel Papers* (1973), like his father's *Lucky Jim*, won the Somerset Maugham award for the best first novel by a writer under the age of thirty-five. This self-consciously precocious account of the self-consciously precocious teenager Charles Highway's pursuit and seduction of an older woman, Rachel, set the tone for Amis's fiction for the next decade. Highway, as overt narrator, is both intensely self-aware and self-examining ('I will not be placed at the mercy of my spontaneous self', he says at one point) and blind to much that we, the readers, are allowed by Amis, the hidden narrator, to intuit about his life and his interactions with others. Amis followed *The Rachel Papers* with two further novels which used his mordant wit and linguistic exuberance to explore self-absorption and self-obsession (it is no accident that one of his most famous characters is called John Self) amidst lovingly described decadence. *Dead Babies* (1975) (the book appeared in an early edition under the less overtly provocative title of *Dark Secrets*) follows the progress of its characters' weekend-long descent into a maelstrom of sex, drugs and drink. Old-fashioned English upper-class depravity in the shape of Quentin Villiers and his friends meets American counter-cultural amorality, represented by Marvin Buzzard, a kind of guru of self-gratification, in the unlikely setting of a country rectory owned by Villiers. Nemesis, hinted at throughout the book, arrives through an enigmatic avenger called 'Johnny', who turns out to be an unexpectedly familiar figure. *Success* (1978) is a brilliantly schematic satire on the meaning of the word that provides the book's title, structured around the lives of two foster brothers who share a London flat. As the novel opens, Gregory Riding is the apparent embodiment of success, a paragon of effortless superiority as he moves seductively through a world of glamorous parties, envious men and willing women. Terry Service, by contrast, 'a quivering condom of neurosis and ineptitude', represents failure writ large. As the book progresses, the roles are dramatically reversed. Gregory's life slides out of control just as Terry's begins to move upward and onward. Both *Dead Babies* and *Success* are dark morality tales in which Amis never allows readers the comfort of knowing for certain where the moral centre lies.

Amis's most ambitious and successful novels belong to the 1980s. After *Other People* (1981), a disorienting narrative of a woman waking in some kind of an institution and endeavouring to reconstruct the narrative of her life and the events which led her there, he was at the peak of his powers in *Money* (1984) and *London Fields* (1989). In many ways *Money* is the archetypal 1980s novel. The central character, John Self, is willing to sell what remains of his soul if only he can receive the immediate gratifications that consumer culture offers. Excess is what the culture teasingly offers, if you have the money to pay for it, and excess – of booze, drugs, sex and food – is what Self craves. Yet, beneath this absorption in the now, he senses the weight of future retribution. 'Something is waiting to happen to me. I can tell. Recently my life feels like a bloodcurdling joke. Recently my life has taken on *form*. Something is waiting. I am waiting. Soon, it will stop waiting – any day now. Awful things can happen any time.' *Money* is subtitled *A Suicide Note*, and the suicide is that of a culture. Steeped in Amis's deeply ambivalent reactions to America – at once 'moronic inferno' and epicentre of all that is energetic and vibrant – the story of John Self's crisscrossing of the Atlantic in search of funding for his film, and of his ultimate downfall at the hands of those more in tune with the *Zeitgeist* and with the almost mystical, underpinning influence of money, becomes a grotesquely comic voyage into a world that both fascinates and disgusts the writer.

Much of the elaborate verbal stylisation of *Money* illustrates the extent to which those who object to Amis's fiction – and they are as numerous as his admirers – seem to miss one of its fundamental qualities. Amis is not, in any sense, a 'realistic' writer and to apply the same criteria to his hypercharged satire and self-consciously manipulated characters as one would to a work of social realism is, rather drastically, to miss the point. He is a comic writer and his own brand of apocalyptic comedy is built around the imaginative power of exaggeration. In *London Fields* his astonishing linguistic invention (something even his critics are willing to allow him) is used to summon up a London that is not a real city so much as a fantastic conglomerate of everything he despises in contemporary culture. The Black Cross is not just a thoroughly dodgy pub on the Portobello Road. It is an amalgam of all that is worst in all the dodgy pubs of West London, some kind of weird platonic epitome of the dodgy pub. In the same way, Amis's characters have escaped the confines of realism. Keith Talent is not just a darts-playing slob; he is the darts-playing slob in his most purified, grotesque form.

> The face itself was leonine, puffy with hungers, and as dry as soft fur. Keith's crowning glory, his hair, was thick and full-bodied; but it always had the look of being recently washed, imperfectly rinsed, and then, still slick with cheap shampoo, slow-dried in a huddled pub – the thermals of the booze, the sallowing fagsmoke.

The 'unreal' city that is Amis's London, teetering forever on the edge of some kind of apocalypse, peopled by the likes of Keith Talent, is the backdrop for a multilayered, characteristically schematic narrative of murder and millennial unease.

Amis's books of the 1990s and since have been less decade-defining than his 1980s novels. In many ways the most successful work he has undertaken has not been fiction. For six years Amis's energies were primarily directed towards non-fiction and, particularly in the case of his memoir *Experience* (2000), they were energies well spent. *Experience* is especially remarkable for its portrait of Kingsley Amis, which manages to combine, with delicate finesse, truthful acknowledgement of his father's contradictory and difficult nature and a loving, generous exploration of the relationship between them. By contrast Amis's three novels of the decade seem, in their different ways, to fall away from the twin triumphs of *Money* and *London Fields*. *Time's Arrow* (1991) is built around a literary conceit, and the effectiveness of the novel depends, almost entirely, on the reader's willingness to accept the conceit and its appropriateness to the subject matter Amis is treating. For at the centre of the book is the central event of twentieth-century history – the Holocaust. As German-born American doctor Tod Friendly lies dying, his soul undergoes a reversal of time's arrow and travels backwards to the years when Tod, in an earlier incarnation, worked as a doctor of death in a Nazi camp. Watching present move into past, like a film reel winding backwards, the soul radically and poignantly misreads the events at Auschwitz – the doctor sees himself as creator restoring life to the gassed Jews. The book was shortlisted for the Booker Prize – the only one of Amis's novels to have been so – but it remains his least characteristic fiction.

The Information (1995) recapitulates many of the themes of *Success*, made even darker by the approach of middle age and mid-life crisis. Richard Tull is a sensationally unsuccessful hack reviewer and would-be great novelist who is obliged to watch the rise and rise into bestsellerdom of his friend Gwyn Barry. His attempts to even the score with the unforgivably successful Gwyn begin as highbrow slapstick but move into more familiar Amis territory with the arrival of Scozzy, a violent criminal whom Tull hires to beat up his rival. *Night Train* (1997) makes a conscious move out of familiar territory but, despite this, is, by a long way, the most disappointing of Amis's novels.

> I am a police. That may sound like an unusual statement – or an unusual construction. But it's a parlance we have. Among ourselves, we would never say I am a policeman or I am a policewoman or I am a police officer. We would just say I am a police. I am a police. I am a police and my name is Detective Mike Hoolihan. And I am a woman, also.

This leaden, half-ridiculous opening paragraph suggests that Amis has lost his unnerving sense of the rhythms and structure of his sentences. In *Night Train* his central character, Mike Hoolihan, is not convincing as a police, as a woman or as an American. As she investigates the mysterious suicide of a young woman her character fails to emerge from the restrictions of the narrative voice Amis employs, and the novel itself, uneasily balanced between pastiche of noir fiction and a crime narrative that demands a convincing resolution, falls flat.

Amis's most recent novel, *Yellow Dog* (2003), divided critics even more radically than his previous works. Some hailed it as proof of his enduring virtuosity. Others, most acerbically fellow novelist Tibor Fischer, accused him of ploughing the same fields he had worked for years without harvesting anything fresh. In many ways, certainly, *Yellow Dog* covers familiar Amis territory. An actor enters a North London bar and is the victim of a sudden assault that robs him of much of his personality and plunges him into a world of powerful and transgressive desires. A tabloid journalist called Clint Smoker, trapped in a nightmare of bachelor squalor and sleazy investigations, is drawn into an internet relationship with someone who seems his fantasy woman. Meanwhile Henry IX, king of an alternative but recognisable England, is harried by his wife's descent into a coma, by his Chinese mistress and by the possibility that his teenage daughter, Victoria, has been filmed in compromising circumstances. And, further afield, an exiled gangster called Joseph Andrews dreams of revenge and American porn stars aspire to thespian grandeur, renaming themselves, anglophilically, as Sir Phallic Guinness, Sir Bony Hopkins and Sir Dork Bogarde. This is the kind of world Amis has created before and, at its worst, *Yellow Dog* seems a tired rehash of material that has become hackneyed through his regular revisiting of it. At its best – and it is often more rewarding than its harshest critics allowed – it showed that Amis was still capable of channelling his appalled fascination with the excesses of contemporary culture into uniquely memorable fiction.

Amis's major works

The Rachel Papers, Cape, 1973.
Dead Babies, Cape, 1975.
Success, Cape, 1978.
Other People: A Mystery Story, Cape, 1981.
Money: A Suicide Note, Cape, 1984.
The Moronic Inferno and Other Visits to America, Cape, 1986 (essays).
Einstein's Monsters, Cape, 1987 (short stories).
London Fields, Cape, 1989.
Time's Arrow, Cape, 1991.
Visiting Mrs Nabokov and Other Excursions, Cape, 1993 (essays).
The Information, Flamingo, 1995.
Night Train, Cape, 1997.
Heavy Water and Other Stories, Cape, 1998 (short stories).
Experience, Cape, 2000 (memoir).

The War Against Cliché, Cape, 2001 (collected essays and reviews).
Koba the Dread: Laughter and the Twenty Million, Cape, 2002 (history/memoir).
Yellow Dog, Cape, 2003.

KATE ATKINSON (born 1951)

From her first novel onwards, Kate Atkinson has shown an originality and individual style that have marked her out as a significant talent. She writes quirky, tightly plotted novels, peopled with eccentric characters and laced with a darkly comic wit. Her novels are family sagas with a difference, mordantly funny chronicles of secrets kept and secrets, eventually, revealed. Complicated narratives dart back and forth in time, unfolding laterally rather than sequentially until Atkinson ties together all the loose ends and illuminates the meanings of the hints, clues and allusions she has strewn through the text.

Kate Atkinson was born in York in 1951. She took a master's degree in English Literature at Dundee University and went on to do further postgraduate work in American literature. While raising her two daughters she did a wide variety of jobs, from university tutor to home help. She began to have short stories published in an assortment of magazines in the early 1990s and *Behind the Scenes at the Museum*, her first novel, was published in 1995. It won the Whitbread Book of the Year Award.

Behind the Scenes at the Museum is the story of Ruby Lennox told in her own funny and feisty voice from the moment of her conception, heralded by a few grunts and groans from her father while her mother feigns sleep – a kind of welfare-state *Tristram Shandy* narrated from a female point of view. Ruby and her family live above their pet shop in the shadow of York Minster. Theirs is a story of humdrum family life in the 1950s – endless housework, minor peccadilloes on the part of Ruby's father, homework, weddings and funerals. Interwoven with Ruby's story (in a series of footnotes) are those of her great-grandmother, her grandmother, uncles, aunts and cousins as they struggle through two world wars. But there are small gaps in the narrative, hints of something amiss. Family secrets, long hidden, begin to surface – one so devastating that it overwhelms Ruby even as it explains much that has been puzzling in her life.

Given the tremendous critical and commercial success of *Behind the Scenes at the Museum* Kate Atkinson could have been forgiven had she kept to the same formula for her second, but *Human Croquet* (1997), although recognisably the work of the same offbeat sensibility, was a very different book. The Lennoxes in the first novel have the quirkiness, exaggerated for effect, that is inherent in all families. The Fairfaxes in the second are characters only possible in fiction. Once the family were the grand owners of Fairfax Manor, deep in the Forest of Lythe, but they are reduced to living in 'Arden', at the end of Hawthorne Close, a suburban house built on the foundations of the manor which burnt to the ground in 1605. They seem to inhabit an almost mythical world. People disappear, then reappear as someone very different; events replay themselves repeatedly. The title refers to a game (never played in the book) in which a blindfolded player is directed through human hoops by other players, a metaphor for the way in which many of the characters seem to treat each other, and the allusion to *Alice in Wonderland* is appropriate. At the centre of all this, young Isobel Fairfax (the narrator) is trying to discover what happened to her flighty mother, Eliza, whose disappearance years before was closely followed by that of her father, Gordon. Gordon reappeared seven years later, with a new wife, having forgotten all about Isobel and her elder brother Charles, who is obsessed with time travel and parallel universes. As Isobel's sixteenth birthday unfolds she finds herself visiting various points of the Fairfax past. She meets the very first Fairfax, whose young wife's disappearance resulted in a curse on the Fairfaxes, and spends time in the 1920s and the Second World War. The dangers of all this English 'magic realism' descending into twee whimsy or utter narrative confusion are skilfully avoided. Brilliantly, Atkinson manages to keep control of all the balls she has thrown into the air, and as the novel reaches its conclusion all the many and varied pieces of the jigsaw, no matter how small and seemingly insignificant, fall neatly and satisfyingly into place.

Emotionally Weird (2000) is the least successful of Atkinson's novels. On a small island off the coast of Scotland, in their rundown ancestral home, Effie and her mother Nora tell each other stories. Nora's are old family stories, all of which neatly avoid the issue uppermost in Effie's mind, the name of her father. Effie's are of life at Dundee University and her Star Trek-obsessed boyfriend, Bob, to whom 'Klingons are more real than Luxemburgers'. Effie's creative writing course leads her to experiment with various methods of storytelling and the novel includes extracts from many other characters' writing efforts. This allows Atkinson to spoof a variety of narrative styles and genres (magic realism, Tolkienesque science fiction, overblown romance, nihilistic drama). Effie's own work-in-progress is a murder mystery that runs through the book. There are lost dogs, down-at-heel private eyes and lots of convincing 1970s period detail in Effie's narrative of student life, while Nora's stories quietly unfold until the secret of Effie's identity is finally revealed. The major difficulty with the book, which again has the virtue of ambition to move beyond the first two novels, is that too many of the parodic diversions seem forced and out of place. Unlike the first two novels, in which all the loose ends are brought together with consummate skill, *Emotionally Weird* too often appears a ragbag of disconnected exercises in style. The exercises are all undertaken with wit and energy but they never come together to form a coherent novel.

Not the End of the World (2002) is a set of twelve linked short stories loosely inspired by Ovid's *Metamorphoses*. Framed by two stories, at beginning and end, in which two female characters, Trudi and Charlene, dream of the delights of consumerism as apocalypse explodes around them, the book once again shows Atkinson's daring willingness to let her imagination take her into territory where so many other contemporary writers would fear to tread.

Atkinson's major works

Behind the Scenes at the Museum, Doubleday, 1995.
Human Croquet, Doubleday, 1997.
Emotionally Weird, Doubleday, 2000.
Not the End of the World, Doubleday, 2002.
Case Histories, Doubleday, 2004.

BERYL BAINBRIDGE (born 1934)

For those who like neat compartmentalisation, Beryl Bainbridge's novels can be divided easily into two categories. There are the earlier novels, which draw upon her own upbringing in Liverpool and her personal experience to create laconic, blackly comic dramas in which the mundane and the unsettling sit side by side on the page. Then there are her historical novels of the last ten years, in which she provides her own oblique and offbeat perspective on iconic events and individuals in English history from the sinking of the *Titanic* and Scott's voyage to the Antarctic to the Crimean War and Dr Johnson. Yet tidy categorisation can be misleading. Her earlier novels include books like *Young Adolf* (1978), which takes as its starting point the possibility that Hitler spent a brief period in Liverpool before the First World War, and *Watson's Apology* (1984), a fictional account of murder among the respectable Victorian middle classes. And her recent historical fiction gains much of its strength from the ways in which

Bainbridge views larger events through the lens of the small-scale and domestic lives of those caught up in them.

Beryl Bainbridge was born in Liverpool in 1934 and left school at the age of fourteen. In her teens and early twenties she worked as an actress. Her experiences in rep were to provide her, nearly forty years later, with the material for one of her best novels, *An Awfully Big Adventure*. She married in 1954 and had two children. The marriage ended soon after the birth of her second child. Bainbridge had been writing since her teens – one of her teenage novellas appeared in a 1980s collection of shorter work – but it was in 1967 that her first novel, *A Weekend with Claude*, was published.

Her early novels – *Another Part of the Wood*, *Harriet Said*, *The Dressmaker* and others – all showed her gift for deadpan dialogue (which reveals much more than it seems initially to do), for spare, economic narrative and for a darkly comic vision of the world, in which the everyday and the horrific are randomly partnered. Much the best of these early works is *The Bottle Factory Outing* (1974). Memorably described by William Trevor, in a review on first publication, as reading 'as though Muriel Spark had been prevailed upon to write an episode of the Liver Birds', the novel is about two women, Brenda and Freda, who work at unrewarding jobs in a wine-bottling factory. Together with their largely Italian co-workers, they look forward, with different hopes and ideas, to the works outing. The outing, unexpectedly and haphazardly, is interrupted by death and black farce.

An Awfully Big Adventure is the last of her novels to draw on her personal experience and is set in a rep company in the 1950s. The heroine Stella is an unworldly teenager, nursing the memories of a traumatic childhood experience (only fully revealed in the last few pages of the novel), who is adrift amid the emotional chaos of the theatre company and its actors. Fancying herself in love with Meredith, the company's director, but blithely unaware that he is gay, she decides that, while waiting for him to acknowledge her love, she will go to bed with O'Hara, one of the actors. This decision, lightly taken, leads to tragedy and to the bizarre, blackly comic resolution of mysteries which have been lurking in the background throughout the novel.

In at least one interview Bainbridge has claimed that she turned to writing historical fiction because 'I had used up all my personal past'. More specifically, she was moved to write *The Birthday Boys* when, reading about J. M. Barrie and Peter Pan for *An Awfully Big Adventure*, she discovered that Barrie and Captain Scott were close friends. It's entirely typical of Bainbridge's ability to make odd and oblique connections that she should have seen a link between the 'Lost Boys' of Barrie's story and the men who accompanied Scott on his doomed march back from the South Pole. At less than 200 pages *The Birthday Boys* is as economical as her fiction always is. In the five different voices of Scott and his men she gives a new resonance to the familiar story of the journey to the Pole, the discovery that Amundsen had beaten them to the glory and the deaths of all five men in struggling to get back to their base camp. She succeeds in giving a modern perspective on the myth of untarnished heroism – the reader is made well aware of the personal and emotional failings of Scott, in particular – without losing its inherent drama and pathos. A measure of this success is the scene of Oates's death – parodied and pastiched so many times – which, in Bainbridge's telling, regains its power to move.

The Birthday Boys was followed by two further historical novels. *Every Man for Himself* takes another event which has attained a kind of mythic significance – the sinking of the *Titanic* – and uses it for Bainbridge's own purposes. In popular imagination the sinking of the *Titanic* holds a place as a prime example of man's hubris in the face of the power of nature. In Bainbridge's version of events there is no such portentous message. We are occasionally nudged in the direction of allegory – the *Titanic* as a Ship of Fools reflecting Edwardian society heading towards the iceberg of the First World War – but the focus is largely on the individuals aboard, particularly the callow narrator, Morgan.

In *Master Georgie* the setting is one of those large-scale historical events – the Crimean War – in which a more pompous novelist might place a self-consciously epic narrative. Bainbridge, however, continues to work more as a miniaturist. The most famous events and characters of the war are well off stage. The Charge of the Light Brigade gets one reference so throwaway it's easy to miss it. Florence Nightingale is conspicuous by her absence. The emphasis is on the experiences of one small group of Liverpudlians. George Hardy is a prosperous surgeon and enthusiast for the new art of photography who volunteers his medical services to the war effort. Accompanying him to the Crimea are his adoring adopted sister, Myrtle, his brother-in-law Dr Potter and an ex-street urchin called Pompey Jones who has a mysterious hold over Georgie. Structured around the notion of six photographic plates and told in the voices of several of the characters, *Master Georgie* chronicles the party's disintegration in the face of the death and disease they find in the Crimea and the gradual emergence of hidden truths about their personal and erotic entanglements.

Bleakly unreassuring about sex and mortality, the novel is also another example of Bainbridge's sensitivity to the foibles and oddities of human behaviour.

Her most recent novel, *According to Queeney*, jumps back further in time than any of her other historical novels. It also takes as its central character one of the most iconic and familiar figures in English literary history – Dr Johnson. That Johnson is such an iconic figure is, of course, the result of Boswell's biography, but the Johnson of *According to Queeney* is not the figure the hero-worshipping Boswell created. Bainbridge's Johnson is a much darker and more troubled man. Guiltily obsessed by sin, sex and death, he has troubling visions of 'a Black Dog crouching on the landing, the shadow of its lolling tongue lapping the staircase wall. The stench of its hateful breath seeped into his chamber'. He fears he is going insane. He is partially rescued from his torments by his virtual adoption into the Thrale family and by his intense relationship with Hester Thrale, fraught with suppressed sexuality and undercurrents of sadomasochism. The novel is very cleverly constructed. Vignettes of Johnson's life and his progressing relationship with the Thrales alternate with letters written years after Johnson's death by the Thrales' daughter, known as Queeney, who as an adult reflects, often sharply, on her childhood memories of the great man. Frequently the version 'according to Queeney' conflicts with the version we have been given in the preceding chapter.

Beryl Bainbridge's public persona, increasingly revealed in interviews and newspaper profiles during the last ten years, is that of a quirky and lovable eccentric, pardonably over-fond of wine and cigarettes. Whatever value this persona has for Bainbridge as a private individual, it does a disservice to her fiction. It makes it easier to sideline her work, to characterise it as offbeat and oddball. It sometimes disguises the fact that she is one of the most skilled of contemporary novelists – ruthlessly unsentimental, darkly funny and possessed of her own unique vision of the variety and vanity of human nature.

Bainbridge's major works

A Weekend with Claud, Hutchinson, 1967 (revised edition entitled *A Weekend with Claude*, 1981).
Another Part of the Wood, Hutchinson, 1968.
Harriet Said, Duckworth, 1972.
The Dressmaker, Duckworth, 1973.
Sweet William, Duckworth, 1973.
The Bottle Factory Outing, Duckworth, 1974.

A Quiet Life, Duckworth, 1976.
Injury Time, Duckworth, 1977.
Young Adolf, Duckworth, 1978.
Winter Garden, Duckworth, 1980.
Watson's Apology, Duckworth, 1984.
Filthy Lucre, or The Tragedy of Andrew Ledwhistle and Richard Soleway, Duckworth, 1986.
An Awfully Big Adventure, Duckworth, 1989.
The Birthday Boys, Duckworth, 1991.
Something Happened Yesterday, Duckworth, 1993.
Collected Stories, Duckworth, 1994 (short stories).
Every Man For Himself, Duckworth, 1996.
Master Georgie, Duckworth, 1998.
According to Queeney, Little, Brown, 2001.

IAIN BANKS (born 1954)

Very few writers succeed in combining real bestseller status with 'literary' credibility. Mass-market sales of hundreds of thousands of copies *and* respectful attention from the critics are rarely the reward of the same writer. Iain Banks is one of the few who have managed to achieve this difficult double. Not only that but, writing as Iain M. Banks (adding the initial of his middle name to his identity), he has also gained enormous success in science fiction, pleasing a huge audience of the demanding fans of that genre with novels in his so-called 'Culture' series – *Consider Phlebas* (1987), *The Player of Games* (1988), *The Use of Weapons* (1990), *Look to Windward* (2000) and others. Banks, clearly, is no ordinary writer, but the secret of his success is not hard to pinpoint – just hard for other writers to duplicate. When his early books were first published they gained notoriety for their bizarre content and graphically described violence, but this superficial and passing controversy tended to obscure the fact that Banks is, in many respects, a rather old-fashioned storyteller with a commitment to drawing his readers into well-crafted plots, peopled by characters about whom they want to learn more. He has won his large readership because, in his non-SF books, he tells stories that are recognisably contemporary in their interest in obsession, in alienated and disturbed individuals and in the difficulties of late twentieth-century urban life but does so in narratives that have the same strengths (and weaknesses) of most popular fiction of the last hundred years.

Banks was born in Fife in 1954 and attended Stirling University. He moved to London in the late 1970s and began writing while he was working as a computer programmer. His debut novel was *The Wasp*

Factory, published in 1984. Selected as one of Granta's Twenty Best Young Novelists in 1993, Banks has had increasing success with his fiction and moved back to his native Fife in the 1990s. *The Wasp Factory* won attention largely because, in telling his story of a boy obsessed by macabre ritualistic practices, Banks employed very precise, cool descriptions of blood, death, violence and the torture of animals. Reviewers were divided between those who were immediately impressed by the power of Banks's imagination and those who were apoplectically outraged by the book's subject matter and the prose he used to describe it. *The Wasp Factory* tells the story, in his own words, of Frank Cauldhame, a teenage boy living with his father on a Scottish island. Word reaches Frank and his father that his mentally unstable older brother has escaped incarceration and is returning home, news for which Frank has been prepared by the enigmatic messages given him by the Wasp Factory, the divinatory device he has constructed from old bric-a-brac, consultation of which involves the use of dead wasps. Indeed Frank has mapped out the whole island through a series of rituals and sacrifices, creating a fantasy kingdom with private meaning and significance that he regularly patrols. As father and son await the return of the brother (and Frank undertakes ritualistic preparations for this) the book uses flashbacks to illuminate the bizarre family history. Frank has been told by his father that he was castrated accidentally as a child but, with the murder and mutilation of animals heralding the brother's arrival on the island, he discovers secrets about his past and a startling revelation is made about his real identity. A plot outline can indicate how strange and macabre *The Wasp Factory* is, but only reading it (not recommended to the squeamish) can reveal Banks's remarkable control over his material, the black humour with which he suffuses all his descriptions and the sheer power of his wayward imagination. The book is one of the most original first novels in the last thirty years.

Banks's second novel, *Walking on Glass* (1985), a rather self-consciously Kafkaesque story in which three parallel narratives gradually converge and an unexpected revelation overturns the readers' assumptions about what has 'really' been happening, was something of a disappointment after his astonishing debut and remains one of the least successful of all his novels. His third novel, *The Bridge* (1986), is, however, one of his finest achievements and Banks himself has said in interviews that it is his own favourite among his books. A man, known only as Orr, has a car crash while crossing the Forth Road Bridge, and spends most of the novel living in a surreal world on a bridge, a sort of dream version of the site of his accident. The Bridge of his hallucinations is a gigantic, perhaps infinite structure, a vast alternative reality to the messy, restricted reality of his own past life and relationships, which slowly return to him. *The Bridge* succeeds on several levels – as satire, as a fantasy that prefigures Banks's SF world of the Culture to come and as an affecting story of one man reviewing the not very satisfactory course of his own life.

Espedair Street, published in 1987, is very different to Banks's other earlier novels, an often very funny story of the rise and fall of a 1970s rock star. Fiction about the music world is rarely convincing and often embarrassingly not so. The story of Daniel Weir, told by the man himself, and his journey from Glasgow poverty through international success to reclusive retirement, works so well because, although unafraid of Spinal Tap-like mockery of the farcical excesses and mania of the rock world, it is rooted in Banks's obvious knowledge of, and delight in, popular music. Weir himself becomes a convincing and likeable character and, as the novel moves towards a surprisingly powerful climax, the reader cares about his fate.

Canal Dreams (1989), in which a famous female cellist is caught up in terrorist activity in the Panama Canal and undergoes a rather unlikely metamorphosis into a weapon-toting warrior, is not one of Banks's most successful books. Banks fleshes out his story with flashbacks to the protagonist's past and explorations of her dreams and nightmares, but even the characteristic energy and liveliness of his prose fail to disguise the fact that the plot falls uncomfortably between realism and fantasy and that Banks never seems to decide which he would prefer it to be. It was followed by *The Crow Road* (1992), which returned him to the familiar territory of Scotland and wildly dysfunctional families and their secrets. 'It was the day my grand-mother exploded. I sat in the crematorium, listening to my uncle Hamish quietly snoring in harmony to Bach's Mass in B Minor, and I reflected that it always seemed to be death that drew me back to Gallenach.' So begins the story of Prentice McHoan, returning to the midst of his extended and eccentric family in search of a sense of his own identity and the truth about the fate of his Uncle Rory, who went missing when Prentice was a boy. The book, as the first lines suggest, is a funny and engaging account of Prentice's homecoming, told with a good-humoured black comedy and a relish for oddity and subversive individualism. Mixing what at first seems an offbeat coming-of-age story with a slowly developing mystery, Banks creates what is, in many ways, his most immediately appealing novel.

Banks is a prolific writer and throughout the 1990s he was producing a mainstream novel one year and an SF novel the next.

Complicity, published in 1993, uses the plot of a thriller to investigate the nature of responsibility and the corruptions of contemporary society. Journalist Cameron Colley, addicted to cigarettes, drugs and computer games, is put on the trail of a killer by a series of phone calls from an anonymous informant. Interspersed with the narrative of Colley's search for his story are sections in which the murders are described in brutal and unsparing detail (written in the second person, these seem designed to accentuate the readers' sense of 'complicity' in the crimes). Banks is as skilful as any genre writer in creating a plot that leaves his readers mystified until his chosen moments of dénouement, but he is also interested in exploring how greed and violence fuel the ways modern urban society runs. *Whit* (1995), ironically subtitled *Isis Amongst the Unsaved*, is the story of Isis Whit, a member of the 'Elect of God', an isolated religious community in Scotland. Told by Isis herself – Banks has a fondness for the opportunities offered by first-person narratives – the book follows her Pilgrim's Progress through the spiritual wasteland of late-1990s London as she journeys in search of a lapsed member of the flock, her cousin Morag. Very funny, cynical about the pretensions of religion yet generous in its portrait of the naïve Isis, *Whit* is one of Banks's most immediately entertaining books.

A Song of Stone (1997) is one of his strangest, like 'Mad Max transplanted to the Scottish Highlands', as one reviewer described it, and the working out of the story never quite matches the imaginative boldness of the landscape and characters he creates in the first few chapters. Actually set in a kind of parallel world to our own – 'this could be any time or place', we are told – *A Song of Stone* follows the story of an aristocrat whose world is invaded by a group of marauding guerrilla fighters and traces a descent into savagery and violence. *The Business* (1999) is Banks's clever satirical take on globalisation. The Business is the ultimate multinational, older than the church and infinitely more corrupt, and is now attempting to buy its own state, a principality in the Himalayas, in order to gain a seat at the UN. Kathryn Telman is one of the Business's high-flyers, groomed for great wealth and power, who suffers a *crise de conscience* when she is despatched to the Himalayan state and begins to uncover the Business's secret agenda.

Banks's most recent mainstream novel is *Dead Air* (2002). The book's central character is a ranting shock jock – given to ranting about events from a left-wing perspective rather than a right-wing one, but a shock jock nonetheless – who becomes involved in an intense sexual relationship with a gangster's wife. *Dead Air* is not one of Banks's finest achievements. Surprisingly in a work by a novelist who has, in the past, been interested in cramming as much into his plots as possible, there is a sense of insufficient material being stretched to fill the pages. There are vivid set-pieces – the early scenes of escalating frenzy as guests at a wedding breakfast begin to hurl things down from a loft apartment – and the atmosphere of a London world where media types flaunt their hollowness is well evoked but the plot never seems to take the reader anywhere. And there is a kind of shanghaiing of the events of September 11th into the narrative that, at best, seems irrelevant. Banks remains, however, one of the most consistently inventive and daring of contemporary novelists and we can assume that he will, in the future, continue to write books with the challenging and imaginative scope of his best work so far.

Banks's major works

The Wasp Factory, Macmillan, 1984.
Walking on Glass, Macmillan, 1985.
The Bridge, Macmillan, 1986.
Consider Phlebas, Macmillan, 1987 (science fiction).
Espedair Street, Macmillan, 1987.
The Player of Games, Macmillan, 1988 (science fiction).
Canal Dreams, Macmillan, 1989.
The Use of Weapons, Orbit, 1990 (science fiction).
The Crow Road, Scribners, 1992.
Against a Dark Background, Orbit, 1993 (science fiction).
Complicity, Little, Brown, 1993.
Feersum Endjinn, Orbit, 1994 (science fiction).
Whit, Little, Brown, 1995.
Excession, Orbit, 1996 (science fiction).
A Song of Stone, Abacus, 1997.
Inversions, Orbit, 1998 (science fiction).
The Business, Little, Brown, 1999.
Look to Windward, Orbit, 2000 (science fiction).
Dead Air, Little, Brown, 2002.

NICOLA BARKER (born 1966)

One critic has described Nicola Barker as having 'a determinedly perverse and ungovernable imagination', and certainly her novels and stories, and the characters that inhabit them, have an unmistakable weirdness and quirkiness that are all her own. Usually set in the less scenic and chic parts of contemporary Britain – Palmers Green, the Isle of Sheppey, Canvey Island – her books present sharp contrasts between the mundane, if vaguely sinister, topography and the oddballs who people it: pornographers, a teenage giantess, stalkers and pseudo-religious sages, a man who feeds his right hand to an owl. 'The world now is all about being normal, fitting in', Barker has said in an interview, 'so I like my characters not to be like this, yet to be loveable as well'. Few of the people in her books fit into society. Whether or not they are loveable is open to debate. They are certainly memorable, as is the elaborate prose style – rich in blackly comic metaphor and simile and packed with punning playfulness – that she has devised to tell her baroque stories.

Nicola Barker was born in 1966 in Ely, Cambridgeshire. She spent five years of her childhood in South Africa, returning as a teenager to Home Counties Britain with her mother after her parents split up. She was educated at King's College, Cambridge (writing a dissertation on the fiction of Martin Amis), and then undertook a series of low-paid, often part-time jobs which, nonetheless, allowed her to make time for her writing. Her first collection of stories, *Love Your Enemies* (1993), won the David Higham Prize for fiction and the PEN/Macmillan Award. Her second collection, *Heading Inland* (1996), won the Mail on Sunday/John Llewellyn Rhys Prize and her third novel, *Wide Open* (1998), picked up the coveted (and financially rewarding) IMPAC Dublin Literary Award in 2000, seeing off competition from Philip Roth and Toni Morrison in the process. In 2003 she was chosen by *Granta* magazine as one of the twenty Best of Young British Novelists.

Barker's first novel, which showed the influence not only of Amis but of feminist fabulists such as Angela Carter, was *Reversed Forecast* (1994). Set amidst a series of grimy London locations – Soho pubs, Hackney Dog Track, the least salubrious areas of Kentish Town – it is the story of the ambiguous relationship between Ruby, a part-time photographer and betting-shop worker, and Vincent, whom she first meets when he turns up at the bookies and, in a fit of rage, head-butts one of the glass counters. Vincent moves into Ruby's flat and persuades her to join him in a scheme to rip off the betting shop. Meanwhile Steven John, a band manager, has signed up a strange mother-and-daughter singing duo and the two sets of characters come together when he hires Ruby to photograph his new act. Barker self-consciously peoples the novel with bizarre misfits and weird losers but she invests them with a warmth and a vulnerability that push them out of the straitjacket of caricature and grotesquerie in which, initially, they seem trapped.

Barker followed *Reversed Forecast* with *Small Holdings* (1995), a slim, surreal comic fable set in a park in Palmers Green. The park's gardening tender is up for renewal and the park employees have their own conflicting plans for saving their jobs. These employees, like nearly all of Barker's characters, are several geraniums short of a herbaceous border. The boss, Doug, has just left his wife and is obsessed by circles and the notion that London's troubles are the result of gaps in the postcodes. The absence of South and North-east prevents the city from forming a circle. Phil, the chronically shy gardener, is subject to regular attacks from a martial-arts expert who practises t'ai chi in the park and Nancy, the truck driver, has gone blind in one eye and keeps crashing into things. Saleem has lost a leg while undertaking an arson attack on the park's museum. As the novella unfolds and Doug, Nancy and Phil all become victims of Saleem's malevolence, motifs of the rhythms of the season and natural cycles mingle with bizarre, random acts of violence and odd behaviour.

After another prize-winning collection of short stories, Barker then published what is both her strangest and finest novel to date, *Wide Open* (1998). Its cast includes Ronny, a homeless man the reader first meets waving at passing cars from a bridge. One of the cars stops and a man approaches Ronny. In what is only the first in a cumulating sequence of confusing coincidences and synchronicities, he too is called Ronny. Except that homeless Ronny's name, it turns out, is not Ronny at all, but James, a name he subsequently bestows on the real Ronny, who is thereafter called Jim. (Readers of *Wide Open* are not allowed to maintain their bearings and their sense of the stability of character and behaviour for very long.) The real Ronny, a.k.a. Jim, has a brother, Nathan, who works in the Lost Property Department of the London Underground. Other characters who emerge from Barker's 'determinedly perverse and ungovernable imagination' are Sara, proprietor of a boar farm on the Isle of Sheppey; her daughter, Lily, an angry, dirty seventeen-year-old who worships a boar birth defect she calls the Head; Luke, a fat, handsome pornographer who smells like fish; and Constance, an elfin optician in search of her father's past. In the background, haunting the present, is the ghost of Big Ronny, Nathan and Ronny/Jim's father, who liked little boys. As the two Ronnies (the reference to the British comedy duo is inescapable and made by one of them) become linked, after their chance meeting, in a bizarre, symbiotic relationship, Barker's plot drives her characters towards unwanted revelations, sexual obsessions and (in one case) suicide. Winner of the 2000 International IMPAC Dublin Literary Award, and preferred by the judges of that award to novels by such major American writers as Philip Roth and Cormac McCarthy, *Wide*

Open revels in its black comedy and its grotesquerie yet Barker succeeds in drawing us into the self-contained world she has created and engaging our sympathies for the roll-call of misfits and walking wounded who inhabit it. The sharpness of her wit and the careful structuring of her comic prose, evident in all her fiction, are seen at their best in this strange marriage between magic realism and the English provincial novel.

Since her prize-winning triumph with *Wide Open*, Barker has published three further novels. All have much to admire in them but none succeeds so well as the earlier novel in epitomising the individual strengths of Barker's writing. *Five Miles from Outer Hope* (2000) is her characteristically offbeat take on the coming-of-age story. The year is 1981 and the heroine of Barker's story, sixteen-year-old Medve, is staying for the summer holidays with her father and assorted siblings on an island off the Devon coast. (A thesis could be written on Barker's fascination with islands, near-islands and isolated enclaves as the settings for her fiction. The inner isolation experienced by so many of her characters, their peripheral attachment to the conventional world, is reflected in the settings of the books.) Medve suffers not only the usual pangs of adolescence but also, since she stands more than six feet in height, those extra ones reserved for the physically ungainly. Into her life comes another young misfit, La Roux, a ginger-haired South African refugee from army life, complete with his own set of tics and obsessions, and the novel chronicles the strange, ambiguous relationship that develops between them. *Five Miles from Outer Hope* is brilliantly precise in its evocation of the summer in which it is set and it has all Barker's usual inventiveness and unpredictability. Where it falls down, in contrast to *Wide Open*, is in its failure to marry self-conscious verbal gymnastics and oddball characterisation to an engaging narrative. Too often, instead of combining naturally with the emerging story, the eccentricities appear forced additions to it, as if Barker was wilfully determined to provide each of her characters with a checklist of weirdnesses for the reader to tick off as they progress through the book.

Behindlings (2002) is a return to the mood and locale of *Wide Open*. Set in the freezing mists of Canvey Island, over a period of thirty-six hours, this 500-plus page book charts the trials and torments of another disturbed collection of individuals. The Behindlings of the title are the assorted misfits who trail in the wake of Wesley, the novel's enigmatic central character. Wesley, who first appeared in stories in *Heading Inland*, is here transformed into a charismatic trickster, shaping the lives of his followers through a bizarre kind of treasure hunt he is orchestrating. He hands out portentous clues; they track his nomadic wanderings around the country. Leading a group of his Behindlings on an ambivalent pilgrimage, he arrives in Canvey and moves in with Katherine Turpin, another character who, like Wesley, has a secondary reality in the myths and rumours that surround her. For all its length, *Behindlings* has little in the way of a central, unifying plot but is sustained, like its eponymous characters, by its meanderings and digressions.

Behindlings and, particularly, *Wide Open* are Barker's most successful works of fiction so far and those which most emphasise the almost relentless singularity of her characters and calculated quirkiness of her imagination. They embody the undoubted strengths of her writing – the energy and comic inventiveness of her language, the open-ended generosity of her narratives and her unsentimentally humane focus on the dispossessed and the marginalised – but they also highlight its shortcomings. In the absurdist universe that Barker creates there is no room for the ordinary, for the non-surreal. All characters must be quirky, all similes and metaphors *outré*, all actions and events at least slightly out of kilter with the expected. At its less successful Barker's writing can seem hamstrung by its self-conscious striving for effect; at its best it genuinely provides the shock of the new and the original.

Barker's major works

Love Your Enemies, Faber and Faber, 1993 (short stories).
Reversed Forecast, Faber and Faber, 1994.
Small Holdings, Faber and Faber, 1995.
Heading Inland, Faber and Faber, 1996 (short stories).
Wide Open, Faber and Faber, 1998.
Five Miles from Outer Hope, Faber and Faber, 2000.
Behindlings, Flamingo, 2002.
Clear: A Transparent Novel, Fourth Estate, 2004.

PAT BARKER (born 1943)

In terms of levels of critical acclaim and of book sales, Pat Barker's career has been divided rather sharply in two. Her early novels, published in the 1980s, drew on her knowledge of the past and present of her native Teesside to present portraits of lives bravely created out of unpromising circumstances of poverty and deprivation. Because they centred on stories of working-class women in a very specifically realised part of the country (and a deeply unfashionable one at that), it was easy enough for metropolitan critics either to ignore her work or to dismiss it as 'regional' fiction. As Barker once said herself, 'If you're writing about people who left school at fifteen and haven't got much money, well, this surely isn't a worthy subject for literature'. All this changed with the publication in 1991 of *Regeneration*, the first part of a First World War trilogy that was completed by *The Eye in the Door* (1993) and *The Ghost Road* (1995). Tapping into that deep-rooted and continuing English fascination with the Great War that was also one of the reasons behind the success of Sebastian Faulks's *Birdsong*, published around the same time, the *Regeneration* trilogy substantially raised Pat Barker's profile both with critics and with the general reading public. In her more recent novels she has returned to something like the geographical location and the emotional climate of her earlier books but has added elements to her plotting which occasionally seem to have been borrowed from a psychological thriller.

Pat Barker was born in the small industrial town of Thornaby-on-Tees in 1943. She studied international history at the London School of Economics and went on to teach in further education colleges, while trying to juggle the demands of a young family and her own writing. It was not until she was in her late thirties that her first novel, *Union Street* (1982), was published by Virago. Several further novels followed and the first of the career-changing First World War trilogy appeared in 1991.

All Pat Barker's early novels are distinguished by the unsentimental scrupulousness with which she focuses on working-class life, particularly the life led by working-class women. These are often bleak portraits of confined existences, overshadowed both by social conditions and by the sexual predatoriness of men, but they are suffused with a tender appreciation of the difficulties her characters face and an acknowledgement of the power of female solidarity. Her second novel, *Blow Your House Down* (1984), is probably the strongest of these early books – the story of a Northern city in which a series of killings of prostitutes creates an overwhelming atmosphere of tension and fear. (The book was written at the time of the Yorkshire Ripper murders.) It is also, and much more significantly, a story of female co-operation in the face of male violence. Other novels Barker published in the 1980s include *The Man Who Wasn't There* (1989), in which a young boy, starved of real information about his missing father, creates his own fantasy image of him, and *The Century's Daughter* (1986) (also published under the title *Liza's England*), which through telling the story of one woman's life also tells something of the wider story of women's lives in the twentieth century.

In interviews Barker has said that she was drawn to the subject of the Great War through her memories of her own grandfather's inability to escape the legacy of his experiences in the conflict. The *Regeneration* trilogy is the story of a working-class, bisexual soldier, Billy Prior, and his experiences in the trenches, in wartime London and at the Craiglockhart War Hospital, which, under its chief psychotherapist, William Rivers, specialises in the treatment of the newly categorised mental illness of 'shell-shock'. Throughout the trilogy Barker mixes both fictional characters and her fictionalised versions of real people (Rivers himself, Siegfried Sassoon, Wilfred Owen) in a way that, in the hands of a less skilled novelist, might have seemed forced but, in the trilogy, appears natural and almost entirely convincing. The first book, *Regeneration* (1991), the most powerful and focused of the three, is set at Craiglockhart in 1917. Sassoon, a war hero, has made a public statement condemning the unnecessary prolongation of the war and, rather than face the embarrassment of court-martialling a decorated and well-known officer, the military has packed him off to the hospital for treatment. Much of the book focuses on the interplay between Sassoon and Rivers, the 'disturbed' soldier who appears only too clear-sightedly sane and the therapist whose role is, ultimately, to ready him for a return to the insanity of the front line. Billy Prior remains a slightly peripheral character in the novel.

In the second book, *The Eye in the Door* (1993), he moves centre-stage. Although he is always convincing as an individual and rarely seems only a fictional peg on which to hang the author's arguments, Prior embodies many of the contradictions and ironies that Barker is intent on exploring. He is a decorated soldier who has returned time and again to duties at the front yet he is deeply sympathetic to the pacifism expressed by several of his friends. He is from a working-class background and the war has been the means by which he has, notionally at least, improved his class status in joining the officer corps. He is unashamedly bisexual in his desires at a time when sexual relationships between men – often movingly described by Barker as tender moments of contact amid the brutality and madness of the war – are stigmatised, vilified and illegal. Most confusingly of all for his personal grip on reality, like Sassoon in the first book he is deemed 'sane' when he is able to return to the killing fields of Flanders and 'mad' when he is unable to continue fighting.

The third book in the trilogy, *The Ghost Road* (1995), won the Booker Prize, although, ironically, it is the least successful and most flawed of the three. The narrative moves back and forth between Billy

Prior returning to the front line and William Rivers returning in his mind to an anthropological field trip he made, years before the war, to Melanesia. Billy Prior, entirely invented, and William Rivers, a fictionalised version of a real individual, are both remarkable creations. Prior, the inhabitant of a social and sexual no-man's land that was described more fully in the previous book in the trilogy, is a memorably vivid character. Rivers, haunted and tormented by his past and by his ambivalent role in the 'war effort', fearing that, in his nightmares, the stories he has heard 'would become one story, the voices blend into a single cry of pain', is equally convincing.

However, the ironies of the anthropologists condemning the Melanesian tribesmen as 'savages' for their headhunting practices when the Western society whose intellectual elite they represent is soon to embark on mechanised butchery in the trenches seem too obvious to be as resonant as Barker seems to expect. As readers, we feel nudged too knowingly into making the obvious parallels and contrasts. Yet, despite this criticism, *The Ghost Road* brings to a rounded conclusion one of the best fictional works of the 1990s. The trilogy is often praised as an 'anti-war' masterpiece. It is of course that, but that is not its greatest strength. (After all, being 'anti-war' does not demand enormous imaginative power.) It is remarkable much more for its portrayal of individuals caught up in a historical catastrophe and struggling to retain some sense of themselves and of their own humanity. To do that well *does* demand imaginative power and Barker rises admirably to the challenge.

Barker's first novel after completing the *Regeneration* trilogy, *Another World* (1998), is not a historical novel but the First World War lives on in one of its characters. For the dying Geordie, an elderly man who fought in the war, memories of the death of his brother in the trenches haunt him even on his own deathbed. Geordie's story is interwoven with two others – the familial difficulties of his grandson Nick and the increasingly disturbed behaviour of his stepson, and the secret history of another family, hidden in the past, who used to live in the house that Nick has just moved into. The book is set in the contemporary world but Barker's subject is the power of the past to haunt us (literally, in some scenes) and the wounds that memory can continue to inflict.

Both Pat Barker's most recent novels explore, with unflinching honesty and clear-sightedness, the disturbing power of violence and its ability to reassert itself in both reality and the imagination. *Border Crossing* (2001) is an unsettling book which uses a narrative often reminiscent of, say, the best of Barbara Vine's psychological crime fiction to explore difficult questions about the nature of evil, guilt and responsibility. At the beginning of the book, child psychiatrist Tom Seymour rescues a young man from an apparent suicide attempt by diving into a river and pulling him to safety. By an improbable coincidence, which turns out to be anything but, the man is Danny Miller, whom Seymour had assessed years before when Miller, then a child, committed a murder. It was on the strength of Seymour's testimony that Miller was sent to the institution from which he has only recently been released. Miller wants to talk about the past. Seymour, beset by marital problems and still troubled by an uneasy sense of responsibility for the young man's past and future, believes, as his profession demands, in the healing power of confronting the demons within. He agrees. As the novel progresses Barker skilfully unfolds the secrets of the past which continue to shape both Seymour and Miller. In *Double Vision* (2003) a war correspondent is assailed by his memories of his time in Sarajevo as he struggles to make sense of both his professional experiences and the difficulties of his emotional life. Both novels reveal Barker's ability slowly to open up the interior life of her characters and reveal the demons that drive them, an ability which marked both her earliest fiction and her much-acclaimed war trilogy.

Barker's major works

Union Street, Virago, 1982.
Blow Your House Down, Virago, 1984.
The Century's Daughter (republished as *Liza's England*, 1996), Virago, 1986.
The Man Who Wasn't There, Virago, 1989.
Regeneration, Viking, 1991.
The Eye in the Door, Viking, 1993.
The Ghost Road, Viking, 1995.
Another World, Viking, 1998.
Border Crossing, Viking, 2001.
Double Vision, Hamish Hamilton, 2003.

JULIAN BARNES (born 1946)

It could be argued that Julian Barnes's best two books are not really novels at all. *Flaubert's Parrot* and *A History of the World in 10½ Chapters* playfully appropriate elements from other literary forms – biography, history, the essay – and mingle them with a more conventional fictional narrative to produce an amalgam that is common enough in European writing (which may help to explain Barnes's reputation on the Continent) but relatively rare in Britain.

Barnes was born in Leicester in 1946 and educated at the City of London School and Magdalen College, Oxford, where he studied modern languages. After working as a lexicographer on the *Oxford English Dictionary*, he moved into journalism – as a reviewer, literary editor and TV critic. He published his first novel, *Metroland*, in 1980. This could have been a conventional first novel about clever adolescents making their first onslaughts on the adult world (similar, perhaps, to Martin Amis's *The Rachel Papers*), but it is something more. This may be a reflection of the fact that Amis published his first novel when he was in his mid-twenties. Barnes published *Metroland* when he was in his mid-thirties. The two teenage protagonists, Chris and Toni, spend the early part of the novel as scornful voyeurs of the pretensions and limitations of the suburbia in which they have grown up. They dream of a wider world. As they grow up and apart, Toni clings (half-admirably, half-foolishly) to the ideals of his adolescence, while Chris, by the end of the book, is back in the suburbia he once despised so heartily. 'It's certainly ironic', he comments, 'to be back in Metroland. As a boy, what would I have called it: *le syphilis de l'âme*, or something like that, I dare say. But isn't part of growing up being able to ride irony without being thrown?' Toni can't manage the ride. Barnes followed this novel with *Before She Met Me*, the story of a man's developing obsession with his wife's erotic career before they were married, an obsession that leads to near-mania. It was, like *Metroland*, a sophisticated and witty piece of fiction but neither of Barnes's first two novels really signalled the direction his work was to take.

Flaubert's Parrot and *A History of the World in 10½ Chapters*, which established his reputation, both defy categorisation. Is *Flaubert's Parrot* an eccentric, offbeat exercise in literary biography, a consideration of the ways in which language both reflects and fails to reflect the realities of the world or an essay on the nature of fiction? Do the 10½ Chapters constitute fiction, philosophy, history or a unique amalgam of all three?

In *Flaubert's Parrot*, the narrator is a doctor, Geoffrey Braithwaite, who is obsessively interested in the nineteenth-century French author of *Madame Bovary*. Fascinated not just by the novels but by the minutiae of Flaubert's life and the interaction between the biographical and the fictional, Braithwaite tries to establish the truth about one minor, peripheral detail of his hero's writing life. The central character in Flaubert's novella *Un Coeur simple* possesses a parrot, Loulou. During the writing of the story, a stuffed parrot, borrowed from the museum at Rouen, sat on Flaubert's writing table and provided a 'model' for the fictional Loulou. Braithwaite wants to track down the original bird. Together with the story of Braithwaite's obsession,

Barnes provides the reader with a collage of Flaubertiana: quotations from his novels and letters, 'facts' (often contradictory) about his life, literary criticism, the story of Flaubert's love affair with Louise Colet told from her perspective. A crude description of the book might make it sound dry and uninteresting to all except scholars of nineteenth-century French literature. In fact *Flaubert's Parrot*, as we learn more about Braithwaite as well as his hero, becomes a witty and sophisticated examination of what we make of the past and how fiction, biography and history interpret it.

A History of the World in 10½ Chapters is a sequence of prose pieces rather than a single narrative. Some – the account of the hijacking of a cruise ship by terrorists, for example – could be called short stories. Others – the most successful of the pieces – are closer to philosophical meditations or essays than fiction. The first piece is a retelling of the Noah's Ark story from the perspective of a stowaway woodworm. The last is the description of an imagined heaven where all desires are fulfilled to such an extent that its inhabitants grow sated and long to die. Each of the chapters in between these two points plays subtle and ironic games with the reader, circling around recurrent themes of love, death, art and the value of life without ever seeming pompous or pretentious. Perhaps the most successful is 'Shipwreck', which combines a telling of the real-life disaster of the French ship *Medusa*, wrecked in 1816, and the sufferings of those who survived the wreck, with an analysis of Gericault's painting of *The Raft of the Medusa*. 'How do you turn catastrophe into art?', Barnes asks and, in this chapter of his most striking and original book, he tries both to show how Gericault answered the question and to produce art from catastrophe himself.

Sandwiched between *Flaubert's Parrot* and *A History of the World in 10 Chapters* chronologically is *Staring at the Sun*, the story of one woman's life from childhood in the 1930s through to an advanced old age in 2021 and her attempts to find meaning in life, finally encapsulated by the 'ordinary miracle' reported to her by a pilot in the Second World War who seemed to see the sun rise twice.

Since the publication of *A History of the World in 10½ Chapters*, Barnes has been a versatile expropriator of several literary forms. He has written a novel about middle-class marital breakdown, *Talking It Over*, and, some years later, revisited the same characters in *Love, Etc.* He has produced his own take on the upheaval in Eastern Europe in *The Porcupine*. All his books show Barnes's sophisticated intelligence and wit at work. None of them has been quite as inventive and original as his earlier work.

Talking It Over is the story of Stuart and Oliver, friends since childhood, and of Gillian, who marries Stuart and then rapidly becomes Oliver's lover. Stuart is an unexciting, conventional man with a gift for making money. Oliver is witty, charming and *louche*, with a gift for losing it. Gillian is torn between the two men but eventually decides to divorce Stuart and marry Oliver. Each of the three participants in the triangle tells the story of events directly from his or her perspective. Even this brief précis suggests the problem with the novel. It is too overtly schematic and the format stands in the way of the characters carrying conviction. Would two such disparate individuals as Stuart and Oliver ever have been such close friends? Would Gillian ever have chosen Stuart to marry in the first place? To ask such questions is unavoidable while reading the book but asking them undermines the foundations on which Barnes has built his fiction. The same is true of the sequel, *Love Etc.*, set ten years later. Stuart has spent the intervening years in America, where he has been successful in business. Oliver has pursued a less than successful career as a screenwriter and the years are beginning to compromise his charm. There is a logic to the sequel. As Stuart says in the second book, 'You didn't think that was the end of the story? Maybe I wish it had been. But life never lets you go, does it? You can't put down life the way you put down a novel'. Yet once again the characters fail to escape the limits of the form Barnes has imposed on the book.

The Porcupine is set in an unnamed Eastern European country in the aftermath of the collapse of Communism. Stoyo Petkanov has ruled the country for more than thirty years but has been deposed and put on trial. Petkanov, however, refuses to take his loss of power lying down. At his trial he turns the tables on his prosecutor and accuses the new regime of being little different from his own – built on its own lies, compromises and hypocrisies. Petkanov is an intriguing creation and the battle of wits between him and the prosecutor is engaging, but one always has the feeling that Barnes, not a markedly political writer in his other works, is not entirely comfortable with his chosen material.

Barnes's most original book in recent years has been *England, England*, a satire on ideas of Englishness that, by his own standards of fastidious irony, occasionally seems closer to Tom Sharpe than the Julian Barnes of earlier novels. In a way, that's its strength. That everything of value in English history and tradition is today repackaged to suit a tourist industry that has its own view of what constitutes the country's heritage is a commonplace idea. In *England, England* Barnes uses this commonplace notion as the starting point for a satirical fantasy in which the Isle of Wight is bought by a tycoon and transformed into a theme park dedicated to all the most clichéd images of 'Englishness'. It becomes 'everything you imagined England to be, but more convenient, cleaner, friendlier and more efficient'. Eventually the fake England, with its ersatz versions of Stonehenge and Big Ben, its extras dressed as cheery local bobies and Robin Hood and his Merry Men, and with its own royal family, overtakes the 'real' England, which reverts to an almost pre-industrial state. *England, England* was not received with uniform enthusiasm by the reviewers, but with its energetic pursuit of a central satirical conceit to its logical limits (and beyond) it showed that Barnes is still capable of writing fiction that stretches the boundaries of what a novel might be.

Barnes's major works

Metroland, Cape, 1980.
Before She Met Me, Cape, 1982.
Flaubert's Parrot, Cape, 1984.
Staring at the Sun, Cape, 1986.
A History of the World in 10½ Chapters, Cape, 1989.
Talking It Over, Cape, 1991.
The Porcupine, Cape, 1992.
Letters from London 1990–95, Picador, 1995 (essays).
Cross Channel, Cape, 1996 (short stories).
England, England, Cape, 1998.
Love, Etc., Cape, 2000.
Something to Declare, Picador, 2002 (essays).

WILLIAM BOYD (born 1952)

Boyd's first novel seemed to suggest that he would be a writer to follow in the footsteps of Evelyn Waugh and Kingsley Amis. The anti-hero of *A Good Man in Africa* (1981), Morgan Leafy, is the first secretary of the British Deputy Commission in the imaginary West African country of Kinjanja. Slobbish, resentful and frustrated in his career and in his pursuit of his boss's daughter, Morgan is a man profoundly disillusioned with life and most of what it has to offer. Only beer and sex provide any comfort. 'They were the only things in his life that didn't consistently let him down. They sometimes did, but not in the randomly cruel and arbitrary way that the other features of the world conspired to confuse and frustrate him.' As Morgan battles with local politics and politicians, his own desires and the humiliations fate throws at him, he becomes, like other anti-heroes of British comic fiction, a curiously likeable character. With its echoes of Waugh, Amis and even, at times, Graham Greene, *A Good Man in Africa* is not a strikingly original novel but it is very funny and Boyd showed, for a first novelist, a sure grasp of the material he had chosen.

His third novel was also a variation on a theme visited and revisited by British comic writers. In *Stars and Bars* (1984), Henderson Dores, the conventional Englishman at large in the USA, is close kin to other buttoned-up Brits in fiction faced with the vastness, brashness and self-confidence of America. Henderson works for an auction house and is sent to the States to look into the art collection owned by a Southern millionaire, Loomis Gage. From New York he travels to Luxora Beach, Georgia, where Gage has his family mansion. There the hapless Henderson is propelled into a sequence of increasingly unnerving situations in which his well-bred English politeness and reserve are no use whatsoever. Farcical adventure is piled upon farcical adventure, all with a kind of surreal logic, until Henderson finds himself back in New York, staggering up Park Avenue dressed only in a cardboard box, an object of derision to the passing New Yorkers. It seems the ultimate humiliation, yet it is also a moment of insight: 'Of course, Henderson suddenly realised with tender elation, they think I'm mad . . . It was a moment of true liberation. A revelation. He felt all the restraints of his culture and upbringing fall from him like a cloak slid from his shoulders'.

As these two novels showed, Boyd is a brilliant comic writer with an ability to employ every device from broad pratfall comedy to dry irony. Yet he clearly felt, from the beginning of his career, that the tag 'comic writer' would have imposed unacceptable restrictions on him. His second novel, *An Ice-Cream War* (1982), was set, like his first, in Africa. The two novels couldn't, however, be more different. In *A Good Man in Africa* nearly everything is seen from the perspective of the outraged and outrageous Morgan Leafy. In *An Ice-Cream War* the narrative shifts its focus from one character to another and several different strands run in parallel. *A Good Man in Africa* is the blackly comic saga of one rake's progress. *An Ice-Cream War* is the larger story of many individuals caught up in the coils of history. Set in the years of the First World War, it follows the twists and turns of the campaigns fought between armies from the British and German colonies in East Africa. The central characters – the brothers Felix and Gabriel Cobb, Gabriel's wife Charis, the plantation owner Walter Smith, the German colonist turned soldier Colonel von Bishop – all find their lives upturned and uprooted by historical circumstance. *An Ice-Cream War* has many moments of largely black humour but, as a novel which aims to show the power of history over its characters and the futility of war, it was a clear indication that Boyd had no intention of being pigeonholed as a 'comic novelist'.

William Boyd was born in Ghana, where his father was a doctor, and spent his early childhood there and in Nigeria. Educated at the universities of Nice and Glasgow, he then went to Oxford to do a D. Phil on Shelley. While working on his D. Phil he also began to write and publish short stories. Commissioned to produce a collection of short stories (*On the yankee Station*) and the novel which eventually became *A Good Man In Africa*, Boyd gave up his D. Phil and his part-time teaching jobs in Oxford to concentrate on his writing. As well as his novels he has written literary journalism, film criticism, TV and film screenplays and the fictional memoir of an invented artist, *Nat Tate – An American Artist 1928-1960*, which briefly spoofed many in the art world into thinking that an unknown genius had been rediscovered.

Nat Tate may have been no more than a *jeu d'esprit* but it showed Boyd's interest in weaving his fiction into the real fabric of history. Two of his novels have followed the lives of imaginary artists who meet and interact with the giants of twentieth-century culture. Boyd's most recent novel – *Any Human Heart* (2002) – takes the form of the journals, complete with explanatory annotations, of a writer, Logan Mountstuart. Mountstuart, born in 1906, lives through most of the decades of the twentieth century and through his eyes we see many of the writers and public figures of his times, from Ernest Hemingway and Martha Gellhorn to the Duke and Duchess of Windsor. The danger with the format is that the 'real' characters will seem significantly more interesting than the imagined ones, but the energy and invention of Boyd's prose make Mountstuart a wholly convincing creation. The book is not only a fascinating gallop through twentieth-century cultural history, seen from the perspective of Boyd's imaginary diarist, but a narrative that cleverly and originally expands on the epigraph from which the title is taken – Henry James's remark that you can 'never say you know the last word about any human heart'.

In a sense, Boyd had been there before, though. In *The New Confessions* (1987) John James Todd, born in Edinburgh in 1899, tells his life story. Todd fights in the First World War, becomes a movie director in London and Berlin and travels to Hollywood, where he eventually falls victim to the McCarthy-era blacklist. He describes his adventures from the perspective of old age. Like some British version of Orson Welles, Todd is a genius (certainly in his own eyes), thwarted by philistines and bad luck. Again like Welles, he has spent much of his working life on abortive projects, in Todd's case a never-to-be-completed film version of Rousseau's *Confessions*. In Boyd's ambitious novel Rousseau and his autobiographical work are a constant presence, from the very first lines ('My first act on entering this world was to kill my mother.... The date of my birth was the date of her death, and thus began all my misfortunes') with their very deliberate echo of Rousseau. The difficulty with *The New Confessions* is that the reader is never sure how far Boyd wishes us to believe in Todd's alleged genius. The book shows all the talent for panoramic narrative that was so evident in *An Ice-Cream War* but what are we to make of a narrator whose final thoughts on life are some rather banal reflections on his insignificant place in the universe:

> The world and its people spin along with me, an infinite aggregate of atoms, all obeying Werner Heisenberg's Uncertainty Principle. I look back at my life in this gravid tensed moment and I see it clearly now.... It has been deeply paradoxical and fundamentally uncertain.

Aren't we entitled to expect more from genius than this?

Boyd, like other novelists of his generation (Martin Amis, for instance), is clearly fascinated by the speculations and theories of modern physicists and mathematicians. The problem is that he hasn't found a satisfactory way of incorporating that fascination in his fiction. *Brazzaville Beach* (1990) is, in many ways, the richest of all his novels but the snippets of popular science knowledge about chaos theory and game theory that pepper the book seem poorly integrated into the overall narrative. The focus of that narrative is a young female scientist, Hope Clearwater, who arrives in Africa in flight from the traumas of a relationship with a brilliant but emotionally insensitive mathematician. She takes refuge in the Grosso Arvore Research Centre, where a legendary primatologist called Eugene Mallabar has conducted a long-term study of the behaviour of chimpanzees. When Hope's own observations lead her to contradict the conclusions of Mallabar she becomes a threat to the future of the research centre. The parallels Boyd wants us to draw between the behaviours of the two primate species – chimp and *Homo sapiens* – are clear enough (indeed, over-signposted at times) but the strength of the story lies in the character of Hope and her determination to examine the reality and implications of her experiences.

Even in his weakest novels – *Armadillo* (1998), in which he seems curiously ill at ease with a story set in contemporary London, and *The*

Blue Afternoon (1993), in which all the historical research never seems to ignite much excitement in the plot – Boyd is always an interesting writer. In his best books – *An Ice-Cream War, Any Human Heart* and *Brazzaville Beach* – he has shown himself to be one of the most versatile and engaging novelists of his generation, one who combines consistent readability with intelligence, imagination and a willingness to take risks.

Boyd's major works

A Good Man in Africa, Hamish Hamilton, 1981.
On the Yankee Station and Other Stories, Hamish Hamilton, 1981 (short stories).
An Ice-Cream War, Hamish Hamilton, 1982.
Stars and Bars, Hamish Hamilton, 1984.
The New Confessions, Hamish Hamilton, 1987.
Brazzaville Beach, Sinclair-Stevenson, 1990.
The Blue Afternoon, Sinclair-Stevenson, 1993.
The Destiny of Natalie 'X' and Other Stories, Sinclair-Stevenson, 1995 (short stories).
Armadillo, Hamish Hamilton, 1998.
Nat Tate – An American Artist 1928-1960, 21 Publishing, 1998.
Any Human Heart, Hamish Hamilton, 2002.

A. S. BYATT (born 1936)

Although she is approaching her seventies and has been publishing fiction since the 1960s, Antonia Byatt has only reached the wider audience she always deserved in the past fifteen years and her best works belong to the 1990s. Her erudite novels, fully informed by her own expressed desire to write 'about the life of the mind as well as of society and the relations between people', are large canvasses on which broader cultural movements as well as the fortunes of individuals are painted. Few contemporary British novelists are so skilled at creating characters whose intellectual lives are so convincing yet whose awareness of the limitations of reason in the face of emotion and passion is so acute.

A(ntonia). S(usan). Byatt was born in Yorkshire in 1936 and went to school in York before reading English at Cambridge. After postgraduate work at Bryn Mawr College in Pennsylvania and at Oxford, she embarked on the career as an academic which she pursued until 1983 when she left her position at the University of London to concentrate on her own writing. She published two novels (*Shadow of a Sun* and *The Game*) in the 1960s, but her fiction, although well reviewed, had little of the success enjoyed by that of her half-sister, Margaret Drabble, until the appearance in 1978 of *The Virgin in the Garden*, the first book in what has become a quartet reflecting personal and political changes across the decades. Even this novel was more a *succès d'estime* than a book that stormed the bestseller lists. It was only with the publication of *Possession* (1990), her ambitious exploration of passion and obsession in life and literature, that she managed to combine the critical acclaim her work had always attracted with large sales and a wide audience. The book won the 1990 Booker Prize and continues to be her best-known work. The 1990s proved to be A. S. Byatt's most creative decade and, since the publication of *Possession*, she has produced three more major novels and several volumes of shorter fiction. A distinguished critic and essayist, Byatt has become one of contemporary literature's great and good, serving as judge on a number of literary prizes and sitting for most of the 1990s on the Literature Advisory Panel of the British Council.

Byatt's two earlier novels have as their central characters women who feel in the shadow of others. In her first novel, *Shadow of a Sun* (published in 1964 but, according to Byatt's introduction to a more recent edition, begun ten years earlier), the eclipsing and dominating person is a father. Anna Severell is the daughter of a famous novelist from whose influence she struggles to free herself as she embarks on adult relationships. In *The Game* (1967) the rivalry is sibling rivalry. In the novel two sisters, Cassandra, an Oxford don, and Julia, a writer with a growing reputation, return to their childhood home as their father lies dying. As children the two sisters, like the Brontës, created an elaborate parallel world in their imaginations, modelled on the landscapes of Arthurian romance. In the present the game re-enters their lives in a new form, as does the sinister Simon, a man who has meant much to both sisters in the past. The novel is filled with a melancholic acknowledgement of the gap between adult reality and youthful imagination ('Aren't you appalled that nothing we can do now can possibly measure up to the – the sheer urgency, and beauty and importance of all – all we imagined?', Julia asks her sister at one point) and rehearses many of the themes and preoccupations that were to emerge in Byatt's later fiction.

After *The Game* Byatt published no more full-length fiction for more than a decade, concentrating instead on her career as an academic and on her family. When she did publish a novel again it was *The Virgin in the Garden*, the first instalment in what became an extended work that engaged her for more than twenty years. Byatt has written critical works on the fiction of Iris Murdoch, and Murdoch, with her expansiveness and her fascination with the interplay between the passions and the intellect, is a clear influence on the quartet of novels (*The Virgin in the Garden, Still Life, Babel Tower* and *A Whistling Woman*) which follows Frederica Potter from school and the first awakenings of intellectual and physical passions in the early 1950s to the social and personal upheavals of the 1960s and beyond.

'Temperamentally, and morally', Byatt has said, 'I like novels with large numbers of people and centres of consciousness, not novels that adopt a narrow single point of view, author's or character's'. It is in the Frederica Potter tetralogy that this dictum is most closely followed. Frederica may be at the heart of the books but the cycle of novels, more than a thousand pages long in total, has a huge cast of characters, from charismatic cult leaders and TV journalists to dedicated scientists and student poets, which Byatt marshals into a multifariously unfolding narrative. The sequence opens with *The Virgin in the Garden* (1978), largely set in Yorkshire in 1953, the year of Elizabeth II's coronation. Frederica Potter is seventeen years old and the book chronicles her own intellectual, emotional and sexual awakening amid her gifted and difficult family. Surrounded by a forcefully intolerant father, an older sister who appears to sacrifice a promising academic career in order to marry a curate and a younger brother caught somewhere between visionary experience and mental illness, Frederica struggles to find and assert her own distinctive personality. In *Still Life* (1985) Frederica moves on to Cambridge, where she discovers new opportunities for emotional and sexual relationships (with the poet Raphael Faber, for example, and Nigel Reiver, later to be her husband) while still feeling the pull of her family and her past. Her sister, Stephanie, whose accidental death towards the end of the book is its most brutal and dislocating episode, has children and strives to reconcile herself to domesticity; her brother Marcus continues to be troubled by his own sensitivity and mental distress.

More than a decade passed between the publication of the second part of the quartet and *Babel Tower*. In those years Byatt not only published the Booker Prize-winner *Possession*, but other books (*Angels & Insects* (1992), *The Matisse Stories* (1993), *The Djinn in the Nightingale's Eye* (1994)) in which she deviated from the straight roads of traditional linear narrative, and it was inevitable that this work would influence the Frederica Potter books. The second two of the four are very different to *The Virgin in the Garden* and *Still Life*. (Although *Still Life* includes some rather stilted passages in which the author addresses the reader directly and speculates on the directions the story will take, the first two books are largely conventional in their structure.) In *Babel Tower* (1996) and *A Whistling Woman* (2002) the kind of textual collage that Byatt used in *Possession* creates an overlapping pattern of themes and motifs. The story of Frederica's escape from the confines of her marriage to Nigel Reiver and the child custody case that follows is set against excerpts from a fantasy novel, *Babbletower*, written by a 1960s visionary she comes to know called Jude Mason. The personal and political questions that trouble Frederica and her contemporaries are reflected and refracted in Mason's writings and in other texts, from children's stories to legal rulings, that are shoehorned into Byatt's narrative.

A Whistling Woman, the book which brings Byatt's epic work of fictional historiography to a conclusion, is set as the 1960s begin to founder and many of its characters are those of dreamers and radicals caught in the shipwreck of its hopes and ideals. Frederica is now working in TV (on an improbably highbrow discussion programme) and returns to the Yorkshire of her adolescence. There a religious community has been taken over by a charismatic visionary-cum-madman called Joshua Ramsden (some scenes are narrated from his viewpoint) and the iconoclasts of the counter-culture have gathered in an 'anti-university' that stands in opposition to the learning of a more conventional institution. As the metaphorical storm clouds gather over the moors and Frederica struggles with her own sense of self and purpose, the opposing forces of both book and sequence – mind and passion, reason and unreason, knowledge and faith – clash again.

Possession was Byatt's 'breakthrough' novel and, like so much of her work, explores the minds and hearts of characters for whom literature and intellectual pursuits are central to the shape and meaning of their lives. Two contemporary literary scholars, Roland Mitchell and Maud Bailey, are researching the lives and works of two Victorian poets, Randolph Henry Ash and Christabel LaMotte. Literary historians have assumed that Ash was a doting and faithful husband and that LaMotte's emotional commitment was to her own sex, but as Mitchell and Bailey's researches progress they begin to unravel the hidden story of an illicit but all-consuming affair between the two nineteenth-century writers. As they do so their own rather arid emotional lives are affected. The more they pursue the ghosts of Ash and LaMotte's passion, the more they stretch the limitations they have both placed on themselves.

The book is daring in the material it uses to tell its story. It includes lengthy examples of Ash's and LaMotte's poetry (based on the work of Browning and Christina Rossetti, they demonstrate Byatt's remarkable gifts as a literary ventriloquist), as well as letters and other documents that the two contemporary researchers investigate. It is through the hints and clues contained in these texts that the narrative – a compelling hybrid of detective story, romance and historical novel – largely emerges.

The Biographer's Tale (2000) revisits some of the same territory inhabited by (and uses many of the same techniques as) *Possession*. Its central character is a scholar, Phineas Nanson, who tires of the rarefied atmosphere of literary theory and wishes to engage more directly with the 'real' world of things and facts. A colleague introduces him to a massive biography of a nineteenth-century polymath and adventurer, Sir Elmer Bole (an invented character who owes a good deal to the real Sir Richard Burton, explorer and translator), written by an enigmatic author called Scholes Destry-Scholes. Nanson decides to track down what he can about Scholes but, in doing so, discovers the extent to which facts and things are as slippery and as hard to pin down as the theory he is escaping. How can one ever know others or even oneself when the materials available for study are open to constant interpretation and reinterpretation? Where the earlier novel found space for long excerpts from works by the two nineteenth-century poets its central characters are studying, the narrative of *The Biographer's Tale* is interrupted by the documents – lecture notes, letters, short biographical sketches – which Nanson uses in his attempts to reconstruct Scholes's life.

Over the decades in which she has been publishing, Byatt's fiction has changed and developed but many of her themes have remained consistent and are present as much in her earlier novels of the 1960s and 1970s as in works such as *The Biographer's Tale*. The tangled relationships between art and life, between the body and the mind, between individuals and society have always fascinated her, and her novels, intellectually demanding yet emotionally rewarding, are the means she continues to use to embody that fascination.

Byatt's major works

Shadow of a Sun, Chatto & Windus, 1964 (Vintage edition entitled *The Shadow of the Sun*, 1991).
The Game, Chatto & Windus, 1967.
The Virgin in the Garden, Chatto & Windus, 1978.
Still Life, Chatto & Windus, 1985.
Sugar and Other Stories, Chatto & Windus, 1987 (short stories).
Possession: A Romance, Chatto & Windus, 1990.
Passions of the Mind: Selected Writings, Chatto & Windus, 1991.
Angels & Insects, Chatto & Windus, 1992 (short stories).
The Matisse Stories, Chatto & Windus, 1993 (short stories).

The Djinn in the Nightingale's Eye, Chatto & Windus, 1994 (short stories).
Babel Tower, Chatto & Windus, 1996.
Elementals: Stories of Ice and Fire, Chatto & Windus, 1998 (short stories).
The Biographer's Tale, Chatto & Windus, 2000.
On Histories and Stories: Selected Essays, Chatto & Windus, 2000 (essays).
Portraits in Fiction, Chatto & Windus, 2001 (essays).
A Whistling Woman, Chatto & Windus, 2002.
The Little Black Book of Stories, Chatto & Windus, 2003 (short stories).

JONATHAN COE (born 1961)

Jonathan Coe's career can be divided into two – pre-*What a Carve Up!* and post-*What a Carve Up!*. Before his breakthrough with that 1994 novel, Coe had been just one of the many young novelists whose books had garnered occasional critical praise but had made little impact on the reading public. After the critical and commercial success of *What a Carve Up!* (1994) he has been rightly acclaimed as one of the funniest and cleverest novelists of his generation and has published two more novels which combine intricate plotting with a humour that can range from scathing social satire to downright slapstick. All of his last three novels are lengthy and complex and demand attentive reading. Narratives loop back and forth in time and space. There are stories within stories and a multitude of perspectives. Coe weaves the many threads into sophisticated fictional tapestries with great skill and finesse and an eye for exploring the possibilities of the novel as a literary form. It is no surprise that he has been working over the last few years on a biography of the restlessly experimental novelist of the 1960s B. S. Johnson.

Jonathan Coe was born in Birmingham in 1961. He grew up in the Midlands and took degrees from Cambridge and Warwick universities. He spent some time as the film critic for the *New Statesman* and has written biographies of both James Stewart and Humphrey Bogart. His continuing interest in film is evident in all his novels, most especially in *What a Carve Up!*, whose title is borrowed from that of an archetypally English comedy of the 1960s, the story of which also reflects the twists and turns of the movie's plot. Coe published his first novel, *The Accidental Woman*, in 1987. The book follows its central character, Maria, over more than a decade as she drifts from school to Oxford and then into a moderately successful career. It is a book in which, with the knowledge of Coe's later novels, one can see the seeds of his stylistic development, but the cleverness, elegant prose and distinctive narrative voice are not sufficient compensations for a plot which seems sometimes wilfully to eschew incident and drama.

The Accidental Woman was followed two years later by *A Touch of Love* (1989), an artful exercise in narrative construction which centres on perennial student Robin Grant, who is struggling to get his thesis finished. The book is divided into four parts (and a postscript), each of which includes a story written by Robin. These are read by the other characters in the book – a friend from university, his lawyer in a court case, a foreign student – in the hope that by reading them they will find new insight into Robin's personality. The device of the stories within the story, which could have been archly and self-consciously post-modern, works surprisingly well and the book as a whole is a touching portrait of a group of people searching for love and meaning in their lives and somehow always missing the opportunities to find them.

The Dwarves of Death was published in 1990. 'I find it hard to describe what happened', its narrator William states on the very first page, and this is unsurprising since the book is the first of Coe's entertaining exercises in the bizarre and the offbeat. Twenty-three-year-old William wants to join a new band but his plans are scuppered by the murder of the bass player by two dwarves, a murder to which he is a startled witness. William is left to vent his spleen on his favourite hate object, Andrew Lloyd Webber, sadly the idol of the woman he worships from afar. The plot carries William through the unsettling musical world and his continued pursuit of the Lloyd Webber-loving Madeline until he hears of a punk band whose members include two criminally violent dwarves. As in all of his fiction, Coe plays games with readers' expectations. Is this an experimental novel – its structure ('Intro', 'Theme One', 'Key Change', etc.) echoes the structure of a popular song – or is it a psychological thriller? Is it a black farce – it's certainly filled with some very funny comic set-pieces – or is it a knowing variant of the old-fashioned murder mystery?

Coe waited four years before publishing his next novel, the breakthrough *What a Carve Up!* (1994). Still his best work, the one which best demonstrates his ability to combine formal daring with the tradition of English comic fiction which goes back through Kingsley Amis to Evelyn Waugh, *What a Carve Up!* is a blistering social satire on the rampant materialism of 1980s Britain. The Winshaws, the staunchly Thatcherite right-wing family at the centre of the novel, are ruthless, arrogant, wealthy and powerful. Different members of the clan – an arms dealer selling arms to Saddam Hussein, a banker with a finger in every financially fishy pie, a journalist with no moral scruples whatsoever – represent, individually and collectively, all that was wrong about the country in that low, dishonest decade. Reclusive novelist Michael Owen has been commissioned to write a family biography. His obsession with the 1962 horror/comedy movie *What a Carve Up!* (starring Sid James, Dennis Price, Kenneth Connor, Donald Pleasance and Shirley Eaton, an actress idolised by Owen) and his conviction that the Winshaws have ruined his life convince him to take his revenge upon them by acting out the film, murdering each member of the family in a way that makes the punishment fit the crime. Along the way, each of the Winshaw family's sordid stories is laid bare and Michael Owen's own story is told in sober contrast to their over-the-top shenanigans. *What a Carve Up!*, in contrast to the tightly controlled precision of his first three novels, is a generous, sprawling, flamboyantly enjoyable novel – reviewers regularly reached for the word 'Dickensian' in describing it.

The House of Sleep (1997) is, by some way, Coe's most complicatedly plotted novel to date, so much so that the reader can be forgiven for occasionally losing track, as do several of the characters, between what has and has not 'really' happened. The narrative moves back and forth between two time periods but both halves of it are set in the same place. In the 1980s Ashdown is a university hall of residence. Narcoleptic Sarah is about to break up with Gregory, fed up with being treated like his research subject rather than his lover. Amongst the other residents, Robert, hopelessly in love with Sarah, looks on in mute despair as she becomes drawn into a relationship with a woman, whilst Terry is obsessed with cinema and his spectacular, fourteen-hour Technicolor dreams. Twelve years later Terry, now a film critic but chronically insomniac, hears that Ashdown has become a sleep-disorder clinic. He books himself in and finds that Gregory is now Dr Dudden, the head of the clinic. Another member of the clinic's staff, Dr Cleo Madison, also seems strangely familiar. Many of the best moments in the novel hinge upon the misunderstandings, sometimes comic, sometimes devastating, which result from Sarah's inability to distinguish her extraordinarily vivid narcoleptic dreams from reality. Terry's fledgling career as a film critic takes a dive when Sarah proofreads an article for him. She has a narcoleptic episode halfway through and dreams that she has deleted a crucial footnote as requested by Terry. She has not. The consequences for the reader are very funny but ruinous for Terry. *The House of Sleep* is a richly intricate web of dreams and reality, past and present that confirmed Coe's ability to juggle dozens of narrative strands successfully.

The Rotters' Club (2001) follows a group of Birmingham schoolboys from 1973 to the day in 1979 when the 1980s were kickstarted by the election of Margaret Thatcher. Their growing pains are played out against the backdrop of the social and political events of those years from the bitter strike at the Grunwick film-processing factory to the death of Blair Peach while protesting against the extreme right-wing National Front's provocative march in Southall, London. There are four main players. Doug Anderton has inherited the mantle of radicalism from his shop steward father; Phillip Chase's dreams of forming the definitive progressive rock band are overturned by the advent of punk; Benjamin Trotter, a dreamer torn between becoming a novelist or a composer, is sure of only one thing – his love for the divine Cicely; and Sean Harding is an anarchic prankster with a sense of humour that often proves unsettling. Even more so than in his other novels, Coe takes advantage of every means he can to move his story forward. The duties of narrator swap from character to character, articles from the school newspaper and diary entries are placed in the text, a huge single-sentence monologue (running to over thirty pages) forms one of the book's sections. The book is exceptionally funny, achingly exact in its period detail, and, beneath all the comedy, there is an ever-present awareness that the 1970s wasn't all velvet flares and glitter; the Trotters' lives, for instance, are overshadowed by an IRA pub bombing which leaves Benjamin's sister Lois appallingly injured and her boyfriend dead.

The Rotters' Club and its recently published sequel The Closed Circle (2004) (Coe always planned the books as two parts of one long novel) provide, together with What a Carve Up!, one of the best and most rewarding fictional portraits of life in Britain over the last few decades. Technically adventurous, the three novels nonetheless never lose their readability. They provide a serious critique of the dramatic changes in British society since 1970 without ever sounding pompous or tendentious. They reveal Coe as a novelist who has refused to rest on his laurels and one who continues to search for new ways to expand the possibilities of comic fiction.

Coe's major works

The Accidental Woman, Duckworth, 1987.
A Touch of Love, Duckworth, 1989.
The Dwarves of Death, Fourth Estate, 1990.
What a Carve Up!, Viking, 1994.
The House of Sleep, Viking, 1997.
The Rotters' Club, Viking, 2001.
The Closed Circle, Viking, 2004.

JIM CRACE (born 1946)

Jim Crace has been an unclassifiable but powerful presence in contemporary fiction since the publication of his first book in 1986. He creates strange and original fictional worlds which are uniquely his own, and then imbues them with a conviction that makes them seem as concrete in their detail as the real world which they reflect so elliptically. Whether imagining life in a Stone Age village (*The Gift of Stones*) or recasting the story of Christ's sojourn in the wilderness into a new narrative (*Quarantine*), Crace retains an ability to surprise his readers and he possesses one of the most distinctive and carefully crafted prose styles of any novelist of the last twenty years.

Crace was born in 1946 and brought up in Enfield but he has spent much of his adult life in Birmingham, where he first went as a student in 1965. After graduating he spent two years in Africa with Voluntary Services Overseas before returning to Britain and to Birmingham, working as a freelance journalist. Although his first book did not appear until 1986, Crace began writing fiction in the mid-1970s and several of his short stories and radio plays won awards and critical attention in the years before his work appeared between hard covers. Since 1986 he has published seven further novels and his reputation and readership have grown with each one. He has twice won Whitbread Awards and been shortlisted for the Booker Prize for *Quarantine* and *Being Dead*.

That first book of 1986 was *Continent*, a sequence of seven linked stories set in an entirely invented seventh continent. *Continent* immediately announced the arrival of a unique talent, demonstrating Crace's ability to conjure up imaginary landscapes that are just as vividly present for the reader as the 'real' ones of other writers. Crace's new continent is perhaps not so dissimilar to ones that really exist – he uses most of the stories to chart, in an oblique way, relationships of exploitation and interdependence between the developed world and the Third World – but the book represents a striking achievement in the creation of a self-contained fictional space, remarkable for any writer, never mind one producing his first book. *Continent* was followed two years later by *The Gift of Stones* (1988), a novel that is both an engrossing story set in its own self-contained world and a parable of the clash between two worlds and two technologies. In a Stone Age village the world of its inhabitants is defined and shaped by the stone tools they make, but the advent of new tools and new materials is about to alter that world. The story, cleverly told from two perspectives, has at its centre a boy who loses an arm as the result of an attack on the village. Unable to participate in tool-making, he becomes a wanderer and a storyteller, bringing back news (and people) of a new and encroaching world to the self-enclosed community.

Arcadia (1992), like *Continent*, presents readers with an imagined world (an unnamed city) which both echoes our own and yet is its own self-contained space. Like a novelist, the central character Victor is set on remaking the world on his own terms. Eighty years old and a vastly wealthy tycoon, he is intent on tearing down the old 'Soap Market', site of the city's traditional fruit and vegetable trading, and building a huge, post-modern mall, to be called 'Arcadia', in its place. Victor, as we learn in the course of the novel, grew up in poverty in the old 'Soap Market'. So too did the man who leads the opposition to 'Arcadia', his former henchman, Rook. Crace uses his novel to play with conflicting ideas of what a city and its relationship to the countryside that surrounds it should be. *Arcadia* is both a richly imagined and detailed fantasy and an exploration of the interconnected lives that make up a modern city.

It was followed by *Signals of Distress* (1994) – Crace's most conventional work and a novel that can be placed, unlike his others, within a familiar genre. It is a historical novel, set in an English coastal town in the 1830s. Its central character is Aymer Smith, a shy, repressed, rather pompous bachelor, who arrives in Wherrytown to bring difficult news that his family soap-making firm, thanks to technological change, will no longer be trading with the kelp-gatherers in the town. Coincident with Aymer's arrival in Wherrytown, an American sailing ship, with its crew and passengers, has also made an unscheduled stop there. Aymer is attracted to one of the passengers, a newly married woman awaiting passage to Canada, and dreams of romance while clashing with the Wherrytowners, over his clumsy attempts to ease the blow of the news he brings, and with the ship's captain, over a black slave he helps to escape. As in so much of Crace's fiction, different worlds collide and the 'signals' sent between them are lost in the sending.

Crace's two most powerful novels so far are *Quarantine* (1997) and *Being Dead* (1999). *Quarantine* is his retelling of the New Testament story of the forty days Jesus spent in the wilderness, but it is a retelling that only Crace could create, filled with narrative surprises and a prose that combines both precision and poetry. In some senses, Jesus is not even the central character of the book. He shares the pages, and the wilderness, with other characters who undergo testing times in the desert, most significantly a brutal merchant called Musa. Left behind by a trading caravan because he is ill, Musa is close to death, attended only by his wife. In an apparent 'miracle' Jesus returns Musa to health, but the merchant remains unredeemed and unrepentant. *Quarantine* abounds in ironies – from the large scale (the man brought back to life and turned into an ambivalent evangelist for Jesus is a cruel and abusive rapist) to the small scale, even farcical (Jesus, seeking the word of God, is nearly stunned by a dead donkey hurled from a cliff). The landscape of the desert, the all-too-human failings of its visitors and the spiritual and physical travails of Jesus are brought vividly to life in a novel that reworks the biblical story into a unique piece of fiction.

In *Being Dead* a couple, Joseph and Celice, return to the remote beach where, as graduate students thirty years before, they first made love. Seduced by the nostalgia of the return and by the apparent absence of all but themselves, they begin once again to do so. Suddenly, irrationally, a mentally disturbed killer arrives on the scene and bludgeons both of them to death. The killer is not so much a character in the book as a kind of representative of the unpredictable incursions of death into life and serves also as the means by which Crace's story can be launched. Crace is not interested in why these deaths occurred. Death is not explicable in narrative terms. It just happens. From the moment of these two deaths Crace moves his book both backward and forward. Moving backward, he traces the path of Joseph and Celice from their first encounter through their awkward courtship and marriage to the ordinary events of the day which abruptly closed on them. Moving forward, he charts, in dispassionate and unsqueamish detail, the processes through which their undiscovered bodies decompose and begin to return to the earth:

> Again the crabs and rodents went to work, while there was light, flippantly browsing Joseph and Celice, frisking them for moisture and for food, delving in their pits and caverns for their treats, and paying them as scant regard as cows might pay a turnip head.

In the hands of a writer less sensitive than Crace or one with a less carefully nuanced prose style, the results of this literary post-mortem might seem voyeuristic, but *Being Dead*, although sometimes chilling in its determined detachment, ends by being a poignant meditation on human transience.

In an interview Crace has described *The Devil's Larder* (2001) in the following terms: 'I came to like the idea of writing a sort of cumulative novel, a patchwork of stories that shared all the unities except one: unity of place, time, subject, style, voice – but no unity of character'. The book is a sequence (or patchwork) of sixty-four stories (five of which had appeared in 1995 in a small Penguin volume called *The Slow Digestions of the Night*) which explore our relationship with food. Crace's interest in food is not that of the gourmet or epicure but that of cultural observer, social historian almost. The variety and scope of the vignettes and pieces in *The Devil's Larder* are remarkable. All are short; some are no more than a few lines; the last consists of two words – 'Oh honey'. They range from the comic and farcical to the macabre and unsettling. Visitors to a chic restaurant get to eat no food but pay for the privilege of being seen at its tables. A dinner party is ambiguously enlivened by a game of strip fondue. A professor, intent on the reconstruction of experience during a siege, arranges for a soup to be made from old boots. A woman seasons her food with the ashes of her cremated husband and hears a singing in her stomach. Crace's brief fables show once again his ability to subvert preconceptions and to alert us to the ambiguities that lurk beneath even such a basic act as eating.

Crace, despite the acclaim and success his books have had, has often remained ambivalent about the value of his writing. He has maintained in interviews that good journalism has more impact on the world than good fiction and he has been unpretentiously honest (or, possibly, disingenuous) about the centrality of writing to his life: 'If you were to say to me, "You're not going to write more novels or you're not going to take any more country hikes", I think I'd keep the country hikes'. He has even hinted that he has specific plans for retiring from fiction writing. For those who admire his writing, however, there is no need yet to be concerned. *Six*, an elegantly structured story of the life and relationships of an actor, set in another of Crace's imaginary urban landscapes, was published in 2003. In addition Crace has, for several years, been reported as working on a novel set in America two hundred years in the future. His fictional world is a unique one and readers can assume that it is one which he will continue to extend and enlarge.

Crace's major works

Continent, Heinemann, 1986.
The Gift of Stones, Secker & Warburg, 1988.
Arcadia, Cape, 1992.
Signals of Distress, Viking, 1994.
Quarantine, Viking, 1997.

Being Dead, Viking, 1999.
The Devil's Larder, Viking, 2001.
Six, Viking, 2003.

LOUIS DE BERNIÈRES (born 1954)

Louis de Bernières began his career as a novelist with three books set in South America. All three were entertaining and imaginative, if obviously derivative of Màrquezian magic realism, and he gained a small but enthusiastic readership. De Bernières then wrote one of the defining novels of the 1990s and swept suddenly from the position of cult novelist admired by a small coterie to the writer everybody was reading.

De Bernières was born in London in 1954 and, after studying at Manchester University, was briefly (and, he claims, disastrously) in the British army. After leaving the army he worked as a teacher in South America for some years. With his first novel, *The War of Don Emmanuel's Nether Parts* (1990), he won the Commonwealth Writers' Prize, an achievement he was to repeat with *Captain Corelli's Mandolin*. De Bernières's other two South American novels were published in swift succession in 1991 and 1992.

The War of Don Emmanuel's Nether Parts, *Señor Vivo and the Coca Lord* and *The Troublesome Offspring of Cardinal Guzman* make up a loosely connected trilogy of books set in an imaginary South American republic. All three are narratives in which, beneath a glittering surface of incident and action, farce and tragedy, there is a basic confrontation between the forces of goodness and light and the forces of evil and darkness, between those who favour life, love and magic and those who don't. In *The War of Don Emmanuel's Nether Parts* the battle between the villagers and the rich Dona Costanza, who wants to divert their water supply to fill her swimming pool, is part of the larger confrontation between a vicious military government and the people it is oppressing. The philosophy professor Dionisio Vivo, in *Señor Vivo and the Coca Lord*, is fighting against the drug barons; and *The Troublesome Offspring of Cardinal Guzman* shows the irreconcilable conflict between the anarchic villagers of Cochadebajo and the demon-haunted Cardinal Guzman, who sees hell and damnation lurking in a thousand forms in human pleasures.

The Manichean struggles at the heart of the three books are overlaid with a phantasmagoria of special effects, magical transformations and over-the-top comic invention. De Bernières's republic is one where normal rules are missing. As one character in the first book says, 'In this country reason does not apply to anything'. Resuscitated conquistadors walk again. Dionisio Vivo communicates telepathically with animals and is accompanied in his walks round town by two black jaguars. An Amerindian girl is reborn as a cat and a cardinal's son as a hummingbird. Villagers hang pineapples on lemon trees to confuse visitors. A cowboy is so macho that he smokes even in his sleep. Shape-shifting shamans visit New York in hallucinogenic dreams.

> Ever since his wife had given birth to a cat as an unexpected consequence of his experiments in sexual alchemy, and ever since his accidental invention of a novel explosive that confounded Newtonian physics by losing its force at the precise distance of two metres from the source of its blast, President Veracruz had thought of himself not only as an adept but also as an intellectual.

This quote – taken from the opening paragraph of the second book but representative of many other passages in all three of the novels – gives a good indication both of de Bernières's indebtedness to the magic realism of native South American writers like Gabriel Garcìa Màrquez and Isabel Allende and of the charm and humour with which he can carry off his imitations/parodies.

De Bernières, on the strength of the three South American novels, was chosen as one of the twenty *Granta* Young British Novelists in 1993 – others on the list included Lawrence Norfolk, Tibor Fischer and Jeanette Winterson – but he was about to embark on a change of stylistic direction that was to produce his breakthrough novel. He moved the setting of his fiction from South America to Europe. By and large, he eschewed those fantasy elements of magic realism that had marked his early fiction. (In interviews he later said that he was beginning to find its conventions more limiting than liberating – 'magic realism can make the narrative too easy', he told one journalist, 'it can make you lazy'.) His next novel was planned as one to make use of very traditional storytelling virtues – strong characters, a plot built around basic and powerful emotions of love and loss and fear and courage, a setting in which the dramas of the individual are swallowed by the larger forces of history. The result was *Captain Corelli's Mandolin* (1994).

The book is set on the Greek island of Cephalonia, largely during the Second World War, and traces the story of Dr Iannis and his daughter Pelagia from a pre-war idyll of love and sunshine, through the occupation by Italian troops and on into the bitter, internecine hatreds of the last years of the war and beyond. At the beginning of the book Pelagia falls in love with the fisherman Mandras and they are engaged, but the war soon catches up with their lives and Mandras goes off to fight. Cephalonia is occupied by Mussolini's soldiers and Captain Antonio Corelli arrives in Pelagia's life. Corelli is a gentlemanly invader, a charming and civilised man far more interested in music and his mandolin than he is in the military virtues. His response to a barked 'Heil Hitler' is the far more agreeable 'Heil Puccini'. He and Pelagia embark on an affair that is ultimately threatened by the shifting allegiances and realities of the war and hatred that surrounds them. Mandras returns, transformed by his experiences into a bitter and ruthless guerrilla fighter. The civilization represented by Dr Iannis and by Corelli is swamped by barbarism as the Germans and their erstwhile allies, the Italians, fight one another, and resistance fighters with very different futures planned for their country drive Greece into civil war.

One of the most lovable characters in *Captain Corelli's Mandolin*, the gay Carlo, who also loves Corelli, claims that history is 'the propaganda of the victors' when what it should ideally be is 'the anecdotes of the little people caught up in it'. De Bernières's achievement in his novel is that he honours the anecdotes of the little people he creates and makes so memorable yet he also succeeds in implanting their stories in the brutal context of larger events.

Captain Corelli's Mandolin has been a startling success – it has had millions of readers and John Madden's film version in 2001, starring Nicolas Cage, brought it to the attention of millions more people. It also attracted some fairly abrasive criticism from those who claimed that the novel played fast and loose with the realities of the conflicts it portrayed and who accused de Bernières of historical revisionism. For some years both success and criticism seemed to have paralysed de Bernières as a writer. He published very little. His only substantial work of fiction – and it isn't particularly substantial – was *Red Dog* (2001), the story of an Australian sheep dog that becomes a legend in its own short lifetime. Based on a true story that de Bernières came across when he was touring in Australia and aimed, according to author and publisher, at younger readers, *Red Dog* has its own charm and idiosyncrasy, but it was not the major follow-up to Captain Corelli that the many admirers of that book were awaiting. This came in 2004 in the shape of *Birds Without Wings*, another historical novel set in the eastern Mediterranean. Using as its backdrop the massive enforced movements of people between Turkey and Greece in the 1920s, *Birds Without Wings* shows that de Bernières has lost none of the ability to integrate emotionally compelling stories of the lives of individuals into a sweeping picture of the larger, impersonal forces of history.

de Bernières's major works

The War of Don Emmanuel's Nether Parts, Secker & Warburg, 1990.
Señor Vivo and the Coca Lord, Secker & Warburg, 1991.
The Troublesome Offspring of Cardinal Guzman, Secker & Warburg, 1992.
Captain Corelli's Mandolin, Secker & Warburg, 1994.
Red Dog, Secker & Warburg, 2001.
Birds Without Wings, Secker & Warburg, 2004.

JENNY DISKI (born 1947)

Diski is a writer and critic whose fiction has never attracted the kind of attention and wide readership that its wit and inventiveness deserve. Since the late 1980s she has published nine novels with subject matter that ranges from S & M (*Nothing Natural*) to evolution and Marxism (*Monkey's Uncle*), from a petulant God desperate for love (*Only Human*) to the clash between a need for order and an overpowering sexual desire (*Rainforest*). Perhaps the lack of mass-market popularity is a reflection of the fact that much of her fiction is uncompromising in the way in which it confronts difficult issues – mental health, depression and difficult relationships between mothers and daughters. These are subjects of which Diski, as she has revealed in non-fiction works like *Skating to Antarctica* (1997) and *Stranger on a Train* (2002), has her own troubling experiences on which to draw.

Jenny Diski was born in London in 1947. She has suffered from periodic depression since she was fourteen, when she made her first suicide attempt and was hospitalised. She had been sent to boarding school by social workers after both parents proved unable to look after her. After her release from hospital she was taken in by Doris Lessing, whose son also attended Diski's boarding school, with whom she lived for almost four years. After studying at University College, London, she worked during the 1970s and 1980s as a teacher, and her first novel, *Nothing Natural*, was published in 1986. In addition to her work as a novelist, she has proved an acerbic and insightful critic, particularly in her long essays for the *London Review of Books*. (A selection of her reviews and essays has been published under the title *Don't* (1998).)

Her first two novels, *Nothing Natural* and *Rainforest* (1987), were, in their different ways, studies of sexual obsessions released when individuals move out of the comforting confines of their everyday lives. In *Nothing Natural* Rachel, a self-sufficient single parent, becomes caught up in an S & M relationship with the sinister but compelling Joshua and, in the process, discovers disturbing facets of her own nature. *Rainforest* tells the story of Mo, a female anthropologist, who leaves her safe London life to carry out a field study in Borneo. There she finds her cool, scientific approach to the world is inadequate in the face of the pullulating life and vitality of the rainforest. She is overwhelmed by a powerful sexual need and desire for her colleague Joe. In her ordered and strictly controlled life in London this has been suppressed, ignored, not even consciously noticed, but his sudden appearance in Borneo and questioning of her work overpowers and almost destroys her.

Further fiction revealed Diski's versatility and virtuosity as a teller of strange and disturbing stories. *Like Mother* (1989) is the story of Frances, another of the troubled and alienated female characters who regularly appear in Diski's books. Unsettlingly the book is narrated in the voice of her child Nonentity, a baby born with only enough brain matter to survive in the most basic manner, in conversation with a nameless listener. *Then Again* (1990) is a powerful and complex narrative that mingles the parallel stories of two fourteen-year-old girls, one in the present day and one in fourteenth-century Poland. In the historical story Esther has been raised as a Christian but comes to learn the truth about her Jewishness and the fate of her real family and community, a truth which destroys her. In the parallel story Katya, suffering from despair and doubt about her position in the world, is incarcerated in a mental hospital. *Happily Ever After* (1991) – such a title is necessarily ironic when attached to one of Diski's stories – is a more deliberately comic novel than any of her others. Following the relationship between an eccentric old woman and her middle-aged, alcoholic landlord, it is often very funny but aims for a kind of droll irony about everyday life that seems at odds with Diski's real talent as a writer. *The Dream Mistress* (1996) is a much more satisfying book, one of Diski's characteristic fictional prowlings along the boundaries between reality and fantasy, madness and sanity. Mimi, a woman who suffers from a kind of narcolepsy, an inability to stay in waking contact with the world, discovers a bag lady unconscious behind a London cinema and calls an ambulance. Both Mimi, taking to her bed, and the bag lady, dead to the world in the hospital, search for clues to their identities and, in doing so, unfold Diski's complicated narrative of missed connections between mother and daughter and between men and women.

In Diski's most interesting and original novels she has abandoned any pretence at realism and embraced the possibilities inherent in fantasy and the imagination. In *Monkey's Uncle* (1994) fifty-year-old Charlotte Fitzroy, after the death of her daughter, descends into a depression and is admitted to a mental hospital. There she finds herself in an Alice in Wonderland fantasy revolving around tea parties attended by Darwin, Freud, Marx and Jenny, an orangutan with firmly held opinions. The three theorists with the most influence on the twentieth century's view of human nature become participants in a clever and witty fictional debate that reveals the strengths and failings of their views. In the more recent *Only Human* (2000), written with Diski's characteristically playful wit and subversion of received wisdom, the reader gets a startling retelling of the biblical story of Abraham and Sarah as a kind of love triangle in which God makes up the third party. Diski's God, who narrates part of the book, is no distant creator, aloof from human concerns and untroubled by human emotion. Testy, jealous of the love between his creations, he sometimes seems more human than the human characters. Sarah stoically endures her many trials — exile, desert wanderings and the barrenness which Abraham endlessly laments. In the battle between Sarah and God for Abraham's love, the novel becomes an ironic exploration of what it means to be 'only human'. Diski's most recent novel, *After These Things* (2004), is a kind of sequel to the earlier novel, in which she returns to the Old Testament to give her own idiosyncratic version of the stories of Isaac and Jacob. Once again the Bible narrative is upturned and subverted.

Jenny Diski once described her novels, self-deprecatingly, as 'long things I make up'. They are, of course, much more. The long things she has made up over the last fifteen years have been amongst the most unusual novels of the last twenty years. Her voice — drily ironic and funny even when confronting the most harrowing of material — is unique. From her early novels exploring the emotions and passions aroused when people are removed from the context which defines them, to her more recent exercises in fantasy and darkly playful fiction of ideas, she has created her own immediately recognisable world.

Diski's major works

Nothing Natural, Methuen, 1986.
Rainforest, Methuen, 1987.
Like Mother, Bloomsbury, 1989.

Then Again, Bloomsbury, 1990.
Happily Ever After, Hamish Hamilton, 1991.
Monkey's Uncle, Weidenfeld & Nicolson, 1994.
The Vanishing Princess, Weidenfeld & Nicolson, 1995.
The Dream Mistress, Weidenfeld & Nicolson, 1996.
Skating to Antarctica, Granta, 1997 (travel/memoir).
Don't, Granta, 1998 (essays).
Only Human: A Comedy, Virago, 2000.
Stranger on a Train, Virago, 2002 (travel/memoir).
A View from the Bed, Virago, 2003 (essays).
After These Things, Little, Brown, 2004.

HELEN DUNMORE (born 1952)

Helen Dunmore began her writing career as a poet – she has continued to publish poetry in tandem with her fiction – and her novels have all shown a poet's gift for language that combines vibrant imagery with precision of meaning and that can be either spare or richly sensuous as the occasion demands. Yet her books are in no way abstruse. Most deal with the tensions of sexual and familial relationships, subtly exploring the pleasures, pains and betrayals inherent in them and often doing so through the use of elements of the suspense novel or psychological thriller.

Helen Dunmore was born in Beverley, Yorkshire, in 1952. After studying English at York University, she spent two years teaching in Finland. She began publishing her poetry when she was in her early twenties and has produced several collections, including *Out of the Blue* (2001), a volume which includes poems from 1975 to 2001. She has also written children's books and is a skilled short-story writer, capable of condensing the themes and interests of her full-length fiction into a more concentrated form. *Ice Cream*, published in 2000, is a collection of eighteen of her stories.

Her first published novel was *Zennor in Darkness* (1993), a story set in Cornwall during the First World War where the novelist D. H. Lawrence and his German wife are living, provoking local suspicions and gossip through their unconventional behaviour and opinions. The novel is narrated by Clare Coyne, a young artist who becomes fascinated by the Lawrences. This was followed by *Burning Bright* (1994), which tells the story of Nadine, a naïve sixteen-year-old runaway whose Finnish lover sets her up in a rundown house. Nadine becomes friendly with Enid, the ageing sitting tenant. Enid is deeply sceptical of the lover's motives in making these arrangements for Nadine – rightly so, since it emerges he plans to rent her out to a government minister with a taste for perversity. Working both as a taut thriller, in which the lover Kai's plans are slowly unravelled, and as a study of female friendship between the generations, *Burning Bright* was an indication of Dunmore's willingness to use some of the conventions of genre fiction to explore issues outside the range of most genre writers.

A Spell of Winter (1995) won the Orange Prize in 1996, the first year the prize was awarded. Echoing the traditions of English Gothic fiction dating back through *Wuthering Heights* and *Jane Eyre* to the eighteenth century and women novelists such as Mrs Radcliffe, it is set on a bleak country estate in the early part of the twentieth century. The book tells of the intensifying intimacy between a brother and sister (Rob and Catherine) left to their own devices when their mother deserts them and their father descends into madness. The relationship becomes sexual. Catherine becomes pregnant and endures a gruesomely described abortion. The terrible tensions of the household, brilliantly evoked by Dunmore, build and build until events outside the claustrophobic clutch of the family break in. The outbreak of the First World War frees first Rob and then Catherine. Dunmore's visceral and unsqueamish language is used to great effect in her descriptions of a household riddled with secrets and undercurrents of violence, and the elements of the ridiculous and the unconvincing that always lurk at the edges of Gothic fiction of whatever era are kept firmly at bay.

A Spell Of Winter was followed by what is probably Dunmore's most powerful and well-worked novel so far. *Talking to the Dead* (1996) is both a mystery that unfolds with the dexterous plotting of the best crime novel (clues planted for the reader at strategic moments in the story) and a highly intelligent study of the complexities of family life and the secrets which may lie hidden for years but which can both shape and destroy lives. The story is narrated by Nina, a woman working as a freelance photographer in London. Her sister Isabel, living in the countryside, has just given birth to her first child. Nina visits her sister and finds her weak from the birth, caught up in a fearful love for her new son and in retreat from the rest of the world. As Isabel becomes more and more withdrawn, Nina is drawn into a sexually obsessive affair with her sister's husband Richard. The heat of the summer intensifies and so too do relationships within the household. Nina begins to remember scenes from her childhood with Isabel, in particular disturbing memories of their brother Colin, who died at three months, supposedly of cot death. The pace of the narrative quickens as it works towards its climax, when Isabel goes missing.

Talking to the Dead uses language of compelling sensuousness (sex, food and the details of the natural world are lovingly described) to tell another dark, almost Gothic story of family dysfunction, sibling rivalry and transgressive relationships.

Two more novels explore that territory where the genres of domestic drama and thriller interestingly collide. In *Your Blue-Eyed Boy* (1998) Simone, a newly appointed district judge, receives a letter from an old lover, threatening her with blackmail. With two young sons, a bankrupt and disturbed husband and the pressures of a new job, Simone has enough problems already in her life but is forced to confront one more. Skilfully moving the narrative back and forth between past and present, Dunmore produces a novel that has all the tension of a thriller but is also a subtle revelation of how impossible it is to escape one's past and the memories it has created. *With Your Crooked Heart* (1999) is the story of a fraught triangular relationship, of three people caught up in a web of guilt, sexual desire and mutual interdependence. Paul marries Louise but his protective bond with his younger brother Johnnie runs so deep that she finds herself the third party in their relationship. Paul is wealthy, a man who has made money from property development; Johnnie, much younger and irresponsible, flirts with drugs and criminality. When Anna is born, the daughter of Johnnie rather than Paul, Louise drowns her guilt in alcohol, dragging Paul and Anna down into her misery until she seizes a final chance to save Johnnie from the consequences of his irresponsibility. In *With Your Crooked Heart* Dunmore succeeds again in marrying a suspenseful plot, poetically evocative language and an exploration of the intimate intensity of a series of troubled relationships.

At first sight, Dunmore's next novel is something of a departure in that it is set in Leningrad during the Second World War and deliberately looks to explore broader themes of history and politics than the domestic tragedies and mysteries of the earlier novels. On closer inspection, however, *The Siege* (2001) appears less of a dramatic and sudden change in direction in her fiction. The backdrop may be world-changing events, but Dunmore's focus, as always, is on the individual and how she or he is shaped by past and present. The reader is always aware of the terrible events of the siege, of the large-scale forces of history rolling, juggernaut-like, over individual lives, but it is the particulars of some of those individual lives that carry the novel. The central characters are Anna Levin, a young woman who has struggled to raise her five-year-old brother Kolya since her mother died; her father, a blacklisted writer; Marina, a blacklisted actress who was once the father's lover; and Andrei, a medical student with whom Anna falls in love. Anna and her father are determined that five-year-old Kolya Levin will survive. Through the household's day-to-day struggles and Anna's deepening feelings for Andrei, Dunmore explores the ways in which resilience, determination and love can survive in the face of extreme suffering. The book constantly juxtaposes the abstractions of politics and large-scale, world-shattering events with the concrete details of life as it is lived – and endured – by the individual. Dunmore and her characters are on the side of the practical and the empirical:

> [Andrei] believes in what he can see and touch and smell, what he has held in his hands ... [he] did not see 'desperate counter-attacks' or 'valiant resistance'.... What he saw was men without weapons, fighting with their bare hands, snatching up spades, pitchforks and the rifles of the dead.

In *The Siege* Dunmore broadened the canvas on which she works but she retained her ability to use her flexible and sensuous prose to pin down the particularities of individual lives. Her most recent novel, *Mourning Ruby* (2003), returns to the fraught emotional lives of the English middle classes that she explored in, for instance, *Your Blue-Eyed Boy*, but the new novel opens out into an interlocking network of stories, including a novel within a novel, that range back and forth in time and space. The book is centred, like Ian McEwan's *The Child in Time*, on a moment of terrible loss – the death of a child in a road accident. The child's parents, Rebecca and Adam, are driven apart by the tragedy. Rebecca's despair can only finally be assuaged through the healing power of the imagination. *Mourning Ruby* is a novel that echoes some of Dunmore's earliest fiction but one that could not have been written in the form it takes without the ambitious experiment of *The Siege*. It demonstrates how powerfully and adventurously Helen Dunmore can now combine formal inventiveness with the kind of resonant and poetic prose that has always been one of her hallmarks as a novelist.

Dunmore's major works

Zennor in Darkness, Viking, 1993.
Burning Bright, Viking, 1994.
A Spell of Winter, Viking, 1995.
Talking to the Dead, Viking, 1996.

Love of Fat Men, Viking, 1997 (short stories).
Your Blue-Eyed Boy, Viking, 1998.
With Your Crooked Heart, Viking, 1999.
Ice Cream, Viking, 2000 (short stories).
The Siege, Viking, 2001.
Mourning Ruby, Viking, 2003.

ROBERT EDRIC (born 1956)

Robert Edric is not a name known to as many readers as it should be, but there is a case to be made that he is the finest and most adventurous writer of historical fiction of his generation. Certainly he is one of the most wide-ranging in his subject material. (Maybe one of the reasons for his comparative neglect is that he refuses to be easily pigeonholed.) He has written superb, intelligent novels set in (amongst other places and times) the Belgian Congo at the height of exploitative imperialism, the Arctic wastes in the era of heroic European exploration and P. T. Barnum's American Museum at the time of the American Civil War.

Robert Edric is the pseudonym of Gary Edric Armitage. Born in Sheffield, Armitage read geography at Hull University before embarking on a doctoral dissertation on landscape and the Victorian novel. He moved to Hornsea in East Yorkshire in the early 1980s, when his wife took a teaching job in the town, and he has lived there ever since, remaining creatively aloof from the hothouse atmosphere of literary London. His first novel, *Winter Garden*, was published in 1985 under a pseudonym which made use of his own unusual Anglo-Saxon-sounding middle name. The story of faded seaside entertainers inhabiting a dingy boarding house in a resort town, *Winter Garden* won the James Tait Black Prize, a long-established literary award more recently won by writers as diverse as Zadie Smith and Beryl Bainbridge. Its louche milieu of seedy small-town theatres and its background of murder and hidden truths exerting their baleful influence were revisited and echoed more than a decade later in *The Sword Cabinet* (1999). In the later novel the protagonist, Mitchell, tries to keep his balance as he negotiates a kaleidoscope of interlocking stories in search of the truth about his mother's life and death, a truth that's inextricably linked with the history of a dynasty of circus performers and escape artistes and with a series of killings in the 1950s. *Winter Garden* was followed by two novels, *A New Ice Age* (1986) and *A Lunar Eclipse* (1989), a concisely moving study of death and bereavement in which its central character struggles to cope with the loss of her husband and the persistence of past experience.

Edric's developing mastery of the historical novel and his ability to place his characters convincingly in varying historical eras and geographical locations were seen in three novels published in the early 1990s. *In the Days of the American Museum* (1990) examined, in Edric's characteristically cool and measured prose, the bizarre lives of the 'freaks' on show in the New York exhibition of P. T. Barnum. In the larger world beyond the museum the Civil War is tearing the nation apart, but Edric focuses on the interactions of Barnum's human exhibits. *The Earth Made of Glass* (1994) also looks at a group of people turned in on themselves. Set in a Lancashire village in the late seventeenth century, it recreates the circumstances surrounding a woman's death. Into the xenophobic isolation of the small community comes an outsider, a church dignitary, who is drawn into investigating events thirty years previously. Despite their very different settings the books shared an interest in the ways in which groups of people who define themselves in opposition to others react to the impingement of external events.

Sandwiched between these two was another story of people in isolation, *The Broken Lands* (1992), based on the true story of the Franklin expedition of the 1840s. In his journey into the Arctic in search of the fabled Northwest Passage and in his mysterious disappearance, together with his men, Sir John Franklin became one of the great tragic heroes of the Victorian era. In his novel Edric, unlike many other modern writers who look back to the nineteenth century, is uninterested in scoring easy points by revealing feet of clay or highlighting hypocrisies with a knowing irony. The heroism of Franklin and his men, although seen from a perspective unavailable to the explorer's contemporaries, is not radically undermined. Instead we see men gradually destroyed by their own necessarily blinkered assumptions about the world and by an unforgiving natural environment in which the moral values of the society from which they come cannot save them. The ice which traps them and the landscape in which they make their harrowing and ultimately futile journey back towards civilisation are brilliantly evoked in a book which follows, with convincing psychological realism, their inexorable decline.

In Desolate Heaven (1997) reflects the continuing fascination many contemporary novelists feel for the physical and emotional devastation wrought by the First World War but, unlike Sebastian Faulks or Pat Barker, Edric makes no attempt to tackle battles and bloodshed directly. His story is set in a Swiss mountain resort in 1919. Elizabeth Mortlake is staying in a hotel in the town, together with her sister-in-law, who has been widowed by the war and is traumatised by grief. The resort is home to many others suffering the long-term effects of the war. There is a hospital for the wounded on the outskirts of the town and Elizabeth regularly sees those whose lives have been altered beyond recognition by the war. She also meets another emotionally scarred veteran, Jameson, employed as a dealer in rare books and manuscripts and haunted by a sense of responsibility for Hunter, a shell-shock victim housed in the hospital and awaiting a possible court martial. As Edric's narrative, centred on the ambiguous relationship between Elizabeth and Jameson, slowly unfolds, the legacy of war and violence hangs over all the book's characters.

Five years later, Edric returned to ideas of the persistence of wartime experience in *Peacetime* (2002), using the same understated, elliptical prose he employed in *In Desolate Heaven* to create a story set in the aftermath of the Second, rather than the First, World War. *Peacetime* reveals, with dispassionate and detached irony, the extent to which its characters still struggle for peace and depicts an enclosed community turning, with venomous hostility, on outsiders. James Mercer is an engineer charged with the responsibility of dismantling gun emplacements on the East Anglian coast. The locals are suspicious of Mercer and become more so because of the relationship he develops with two men working for him. Jacob Haas is a Dutch Jew who has survived the concentration camps and Mathias Weisz is a German prisoner of war. To the Fenland villagers both men, despite the suffering they have experienced, remain irredeemably foreign and outcast. The return to the village of a brutal ex-soldier is the catalyst for violence and a reassertion of tribal insularity.

Several of Edric's novels have dealt, directly or indirectly, with the impact and consequences of colonialism, with sometimes brutal and uncomprehending attempts by Westerners to impose their own beliefs and values on societies alien to them. The Arctic landscape and the Inuit who inhabit it are seen by the explorers in *The Broken Lands*, for instance, as blank sheets waiting for Europeans to inscribe their future on them. The tragedy of Franklin and his men lies partly in their inability to acknowledge the difference and otherness of the world they have entered. The Arctic explorers are uncomprehending of both the landscape and the people, the Inuit, who thrive in it. In *Elysium* (1995) the nineteenth-century Tasmanian colonists who consign the aborigines to oblivion are brutal. Told as a mosaic of concise scenes narrated by different voices and moving backwards and forwards in time, the book focuses on William Lanne, derogatorily nicknamed 'King Billy' by the colonists, who becomes the last full-blooded aboriginal man. Caught between his own culture and a triumphalist imperialism whose victory he recognises as inevitable, Lanne is a sympathetic character. His oppressors, from soldiers indulging in thoughtless violence to the scientist Fairfax, who sees him as an exhibit in some ethnographical museum to be measured and classified, are only consistent in their refusal to grant him full humanity.

The Book of the Heathen (2000) is Edric's most sustained and powerful investigation of the degradation colonialism inflicts on victims and perpetrators alike, a late twentieth-century fictional journey into a Conradian heart of darkness. Set in 1897 (two years before the publication of Conrad's novella), the book is narrated by James Frasier, an ordinary, decent man plunged into circumstances for which nothing in his previous life has prepared him. Significantly, Frasier is a mapmaker, but when he travels to a small British trading concession in the Belgian Congo he finds himself on physical and moral terrain for which no maps have been, or can be, created. As the book opens, Frasier's much-admired friend Nicholas Frere is in prison, charged with the seemingly senseless murder of a native girl. Frere refuses to deny any of the charges and awaits his inevitable conviction. Off the map of 'civilisation', characters like the slaver Hammad and the corrupt, exploitative priest Father Klein are more at home than Frasier can ever be or can ever want to be. As the narrative winds menacingly towards the devastating revelation of what really happened between Frere and the girl, it becomes a microcosm of all the larger-scale failures of the colonial enterprise.

With his most recent novel Edric may have seemed to turn away from many of the settings and motifs which have characterised his previous work. *Cradle Song* (2003), the first in a promised trilogy, is set in the present, partly in the East Yorkshire landscapes he has made his home, and embraces quite overtly the genre of crime fiction – many of whose practitioners, especially American, Edric admires. Private investigator Leo Rivers, at home in the seedier locales of Hull, is hired by the father of a teenager, missing and presumed a victim of a paedophile killer, to reopen the case. An imprisoned child murderer is prepared to bargain for a reduced sentence with information about victims whose bodies have not yet been discovered. Rivers finds himself thrown into a morass of corruption and exploitation, and new murders and renewed violence result. Yet the change of direction is deceptive. Edric's fiction has often circled the subjects with which the novel deals. His work is filled with the lost children, hidden acts of violence and return of the past which animate *Cradle Song*. In that sense the trilogy on which Edric has embarked may provide yet another vehicle through which this most versatile of modern novelists can explore the ideas, characters and kinds of stories that have always fuelled his work.

Edric's major works

Winter Garden, Andre Deutsch, 1985.
A New Ice Age, Andre Deutsch, 1986.
A Lunar Eclipse, Heinemann, 1989.
In the Days of the American Museum, Cape, 1990.
The Broken Lands, Cape, 1992.
The Earth Made of Glass, Picador, 1994.
Elysium, Duckworth, 1995.
In Desolate Heaven, Duckworth, 1997.
The Sword Cabinet, Doubleday, 1999.
The Book of the Heathen, Doubleday, 2000.
Peacetime, Doubleday, 2002.
Cradle Song, Doubleday, 2003.

SEBASTIAN FAULKS (born 1953)

In *Birdsong*, his most successful work so far, both commercially and critically, Sebastian Faulks manages to write a war novel that is not afraid to tackle large themes of sexuality and mortality and does so without sounding overly portentous or melodramatic. Male writers often write well about warfare and the comradeship of men in battle. The same writers do not usually handle the subtle and nuanced ebb and flow of human relationships with equal success; nor are they usually as skilled at evoking place. In *Birdsong* love, war and landscape all have central roles to play in the unfolding of the narrative and Faulks seems equally at ease in writing about all three.

Sebastian Faulks was born in Newbury in 1953 and educated at Cambridge. After graduating he worked briefly as a teacher and then became a journalist. He joined the *Independent* at its foundation in 1986 – as literary editor – and was assistant editor of the *Sunday Independent*. In 1991 he gave up journalism to concentrate on fiction. His first novel, *A Trick of the Light* (1984), was followed by *The Girl at the Lion d'Or* (1989), the first book in which Faulks showed his twin interests in French society and in the ongoing effects of the First World War. Set in a provincial town in the 1930s, its central character is a hotel waitress, Anne Louvet, who is drawn to an unhappily married lawyer, Charles Hartmann. Anne carries with her memories and secrets of a childhood blighted by the war. Hartmann is himself a veteran of the war. The love between them is constantly threatened, in different ways, by both their pasts. What could easily have been a rather unadventurous story of an affair destroyed by social conventions is redeemed by the subtlety of Faulks's prose and his sophisticated awareness of historical realities and the interplay between the individual and the larger society.

Birdsong (1993) opens in 1910 as a young Englishman, Stephen Wraysford, arrives in Amiens to stay with the Azaire family and to learn about the textile business. M. Azaire is a self-satisfied, self-absorbed *petit bourgeois*, largely indifferent to the needs of his younger wife. From the very first pages of the novel Faulks hints that an affair between Wraysford and Mme. Azaire is an inevitability and it would be an obtuse reader indeed who did not pick up signs of the author nudging his narrative in that direction. Even the characters themselves seem aware of it. 'I am driven by a greater force than I can resist', Stephen writes in an unsent letter; 'I believe that force has its own reason and its own morality even if they may never be clear to me while I am alive'.

Stephen and Isabelle Azaire leave Amiens to live with one another but the affair does not last. Emotionally destroyed by Isabelle's decision to leave him, Stephen is soon to be driven by another greater force than he can resist, the force of history. By 1916, the year in which the second part of the novel is set, he is an experience-hardened officer in the trenches of the Western Front. The stalemate alternating with slaughter of the First World War battlefields is so deeply embedded in the collective imagination, through poetry, memoirs, history, film and popular culture, that it is exceptionally challenging for any writer now to avoid the pitfalls of cliché and stereotype. Faulks rises to the challenge. His prose is precise and visceral, allowing the horror of what he describes to emerge unmelodramatically from the language. Here, for example, is his description of a soldier suffering from shell-shock:

> Tipper's face appeared to have lost all its circulation. The whites of his eyes, only a few inches from Stephen's face, bore no red tracery of blood vessels; there was only a brown circle with a dilated pupil floating in an area of white which was enlarged by the spasmodic opening of the eye.

As the novel progresses and Stephen sees men die all around him, he discovers in himself a surprising determination to survive. No précis can do justice to Faulks's evocation of the damaged landscape and the men trapped in it. The claustrophobic power of his descriptions is such that the chapters where the narrative moves forwards to the 1970s and the story of a woman searching for information about her grandfather who fought in the war give the reader the feeling of emerging from one of the underground tunnels that Stephen's men dig into the light.

In most ways Faulks is a very traditional novelist and storyteller. *A Fool's Alphabet* (1992), his second novel, is the nearest he has come to an experimental fiction. It tells the story of photographer Pietro Russell, the son of an English father and an Italian mother, from the time of his parents' meeting in the Second World War to the 1980s. It does so in twenty-six chapters, one for each of the letters of the alphabet. Each letter is the first letter of a place associated with Russell's life. Faulks doesn't always seem entirely comfortable with the form he has chosen for his novel, which moves restlessly back and forth in time and across countries, but his prose is as elegant as it always is and his central character slowly and convincingly emerges as the chapters unfold.

Since *Birdsong* Faulks has published *Charlotte Gray* (1998) and *On Green Dolphin Street* (2001). In *Charlotte Gray* he is (perhaps too clearly) trying to use a narrative set in the Second World War to investigate the same kind of relationship between the small-scale drama of the love affair and the vast drama of war that his First World War narrative does in *Birdsong*. 'I wanted to look at the insidious way that war affects individual lives', he once said in an interview, and it would be difficult to guess which of the two novels he meant. (He was actually referring to *Charlotte Gray*.) Charlotte Gray is a young Scottish woman who falls in love with a Royal Air Force pilot, Peter Gregory. When Gregory fails to return from a mission, Charlotte chooses to volunteer for work with the Resistance in France. She speaks fluent French and, armed with a new identity, she finds herself in a small town called Lavaurette. There she is soon involved in attempts by some of the inhabitants to protect two children whose parents have been arrested and sent to a concentration camp.

If *Charlotte Gray* is not as successful a novel as *Birdsong* (and it isn't), it may well be because Faulks seems unsure, in a way never apparent in *Birdsong*, of the tone and style he wants to use. The love affair between Charlotte and Peter Gregory is often perilously close to the clichés of romantic fiction in a way in which the relationship between Wraysford and Mme. Azaire in the earlier novel never is. When talking about her love (which she does rather a lot), Charlotte can sound pompous and unconvincing:

> I believe in the purity of the feeling that I have for him and that he has for me. I think its force is superior to that of any other guiding force and I can't organise my life until I know whether he's alive.

All this sits rather uneasily with the moral complexities that Faulks, much more successfully, explores when Charlotte is with the Resistance.

On Green Dolphin Street is set mostly in America at the end of the 1950s. A bald outline of the plot might once again suggest the clichés of romantic fiction. Mary van der Linden is married to a British embassy employee in Washington. She embarks on a love affair with an American journalist, travelling to New York to be with him. Torn between the two, she eventually decides to 'do the right thing' and return to her needy husband, who has cracked up in her absence. What rescues the book from cliché is the power of Faulks's historical imagination and his ability to situate the dramas of his characters' lives in historical context – in this case an America about to launch itself into the 1960s and engrossed in the presidential contest between Nixon and the youthful Jack Kennedy.

Faulks's great success as a novelist is based on his ability to filter into the 'literary' novel some of the devices and the raw emotions to be found in less sophisticated novels. He is unafraid to borrow from romantic fiction the idea that major parts of the plot will be driven by an overwhelming sexual passion. From war fiction he takes concepts of comradeship and male bonding that could appear old-fashioned or even risible. He then blends these with his own fluent powers of narrative, his rich, descriptive prose and his ironic knowledge of the costs not only of war but of love to create works that straddle the divide between popular fiction and 'literary' fiction. In some of his fiction (parts of *Charlotte Gray* and *On Green Dolphin Street* for example) the blend seems contrived and melodramatic. When the blend works, it produces a novel as rich and as moving as *Birdsong*.

Faulks's major works

A Trick of the Light, Bodley Head, 1984.
The Girl at the Lion d'Or, Hutchinson, 1989.
A Fool's Alphabet, Hutchinson, 1992.

Birdsong, Hutchinson, 1993.
The Fatal Englishman: Three Short Lives, Hutchinson, 1996 (biography).
Charlotte Gray, Hutchinson, 1998.
On Green Dolphin Street, Hutchinson, 2001.

TIBOR FISCHER (born 1959)

Tibor Fischer's first novel, *Under the Frog* (1992), takes its title from a Hungarian saying. To be 'under the frog's arse down a coal mine' means, as one might guess, to be at a low point in one's life. It is a picaresque story of the adventures of two Hungarians, Pataki and Gyuri, as they tour their country with a national basketball team in the years between the end of the Second World War and the Hungarian uprising in 1956. Trapped in the everyday lunacies of totalitarianism, the two young men and their team-mates are interested primarily in sex, drink, food and maintaining their place in the squad. Outside the cocoon of the team and the special train on which it travels swirls the madness of the Communist regime. *Under the Frog* provides plenty of examples of the kind of linguistic exuberance that is one of the distinguishing features of Fischer's work.

Both Tibor Fischer's parents were basketball players for the Hungarian national team and they took refuge in Britain after the failed Hungarian uprising of 1956. Fischer was born three years later. He studied modern languages at Cambridge and then worked as a journalist, spending a brief period as a correspondent back in his parents' native Hungary. His first novel, published by a relatively small Scottish publisher, gained admiring reviews and won him a Betty Trask Award. He was chosen as one of the Best of Young British Novelists in a list sponsored in 1993 by *Granta* and by Waterstone's. Since then he has published three further novels, *The Thought Gang* (1994), *The Collector Collector* (1997) and *Voyage to the End of the Room* (2003), and a volume of short stories, *Don't Read This Book If You're Stupid* (2000).

On first publication *The Thought Gang* was described by one reviewer, in something of an understatement, as 'unlike any other cops and robbers story ever written'. The narrator of the book is a middle-aged philosophy professor, Eddie Coffin. Monumentally lazy, hedonistic and devoted to the consumption of prodigious quantities of fine wine, Coffin is also cheerfully amoral and selfish. And, thanks to his wit and philosophical training, he has no difficulties in providing intellectual justification for his amorality. When his fraudulent scheme to divert the proceeds of a research foundation into his own pocket is discovered, Coffin takes off for France. There he meets Hubert, an incompetent one-armed robber. Eddie needs little persuading that bank robbery is an ideal career choice:

> as lawbreaking activities with long jail sentences go, bank robbery seems fairly blameless. Banks seem to have more money than they need – it's just lying about all over the place. And everyone hates a) banks and b) bankers.

The mismatched pair embarks on a cross-country bank-robbing spree. Each robbery is devised by Eddie to reflect, in some way, the ideas of a school of ancient philosophy. Soon Eddie and Hubert gain notoriety as the Thought Gang and the plot sends them zigzagging towards their most ambitious heist.

Fischer's style is clear from the novel's first paragraph, one of the more memorable first paragraphs in recent fiction:

> The only advice I can offer, should you wake up vertiginously in a strange flat, with a thoroughly installed hangover, without any of your clothing, without any recollection of how you got there, with the police sledgehammering down the door to the accompaniment of excited dogs, while you are surrounded by bales of lavishly produced magazines featuring children in adult acts, the only advice I can offer is to try to be good-humoured and polite.

It is not a style that is entirely original – like many male novelists of his generation, he was clearly bowled over by Martin Amis's fiction at some point in his life – but Fischer has more than enough verbal ingenuity to create a voice for Eddie that is convincing and very funny. Puns, epigrams and neologisms fizz off the page. Clichés are subverted and turned to new purposes. Quotations are reworked. ('You've got to try everything once, except those things you don't like, or that involve a lot of effort and getting up early.') The energy, ironically, of Coffin's narration is startling. There are affectations and misjudgements in the book – the regular use of extraordinarily obscure words simply because they happen to begin with the letter 'Z' is not quite as hilarious as Fischer seems to think – but *The Thought Gang* is a remarkable achievement.

The wit and wordplay that are central to *The Thought Gang* are equally in evidence in Fischer's third novel, *The Collector Collector*, although the overall tone of the book is much darker and more misanthropic. Fischer seems unprepared to allow his human characters any redeeming values. All are motivated by lust, selfishness, greed and hypocrisy. The Seven Deadly Sins, and several more, are on permanent display in the *mélange* of stories, ancient and modern, that the form of his book enables him to tell. The narrator of *The Collector Collector* is, unusually, an ancient Sumerian bowl, a piece of pottery that has somehow been made sentient and observes millennia of human folly and vice parade before it. As Fischer wryly observed in an interview, 'The one drawback to having a bowl as your central character is that it's rather immobile and can get quite dull just sitting on a shelf'. His answer to the challenge is to provide the bowl with further powers beyond mere sentience. It can read the memories of those who touch it and can communicate its own memories of what has happened to it. The novel switches between the dozens of mini-narratives the bowl recalls from the past (all unflattering to human vanity and ideas of dignity) and the story of the modern art expert, Rosa, who has current possession of it. Into Rosa's household comes Nikki, a klepto-nymphomaniac, and a new drama of sexual and financial treachery begins to unfold in front of the bowl, which has, of course, seen it all before. As in *The Thought Gang*, style is as important as substance and Fischer's verbal gymnastics are on full display. As in *The Thought Gang*, there are recurring jokes that don't work – the bowl's habit of placing things and people in ranked lists, like a ceramic version of a Nick Hornby character, becomes irritating rather than amusing – but *The Collector Collector* is an original and darkly entertaining novel.

Fischer's most recent books are a volume of short stories, provocatively titled *Don't Read This Book If You're Stupid* (2000) (the name was actually changed for the American edition, perhaps in the belief that American readers are more easily provoked by a book title than British ones), and a fourth novel, *Voyage to the End of the Room* (2003). His wisecracking and profound pessimism, his verbal dancing on an existential abyss are once more in evidence in the short stories, which range from a fantasy about a man who aims to read all the books written in English to an account of an empty, egotistical comedienne and her failed attempts to give her life some meaning. If anything, the cynicism and misanthropy are even darker than in *The Collector Collector*. His comic invention rarely flags but his vision of the world is irredeemably bleak. *Voyage to the End of the Room* explores the nature of the connections between people in a world of cyberspace and the internet through the story of Oceane, a graphic designer who has retreated to the confines of her flat and communicates almost exclusively via her computer. Through Oceane's worldwide links on the internet, through her vicarious travels with the debt collector she employs and through her own recollections of her earlier life in a sex club, Fischer opens out his narrative in a work that, despite its title, is as wide-ranging as his other works. Both short stories and novel confirm Fischer's position as the most gifted and original misanthrope in modern fiction.

Fischer's major works

Under the Frog, Polygon, 1992.
The Thought Gang, Polygon, 1994.
The Collector Collector, Secker & Warburg, 1997.
Don't Read This Book If You're Stupid, Secker & Warburg, 2000.
Voyage to the End of the Room, Chatto & Windus, 2003.

MARGARET FORSTER (born 1938)

A prolific biographer and memoirist as well as novelist, Margaret Forster had the first big success of her literary career in 1965 with the publication of *Georgy Girl*, later made into a defining film of the 1960s, but much of her best and most characteristic work, in both fiction and non-fiction, belongs to the last twenty years. Most of Forster's fiction deals with the domestic lives of women and their place in family relationships as wives, mothers and daughters and is informed by a strong awareness of the social issues which can affect them (adoption in *The Battle for Christabel* and *Shadow Baby*, adolescent violence in *Mother's Boys*, old age and Alzheimer's in *Mother Can You Hear Me?*). Her books often explore the contradictions between the expectations of women in the modern world and the traditional demands of female familial duty (still very much alive) and show her characters as they battle to assert their own individuality in the face of other characters and social forces which seek to quash it. Unsentimental and filled with both humour and the results of a marvellous eye for the domestic detail in women's lives, Forster's fiction is a celebration of the endurance and resilience of her characters.

Margaret Forster was born in Carlisle in 1938 and educated there and at Somerville College, Oxford, where she read history. After a brief period working as a teacher in north London, the success of *Georgy Girl* enabled her to become a full-time writer. In addition to her fiction, she has published biographies (*Elizabeth Barrett Browning* won the Royal Society of Literature's Award in 1988 and *Daphne du Maurier* was awarded the 1994 Fawcett Book Prize), and two best-selling reconstructions (*Hidden Lives* and *Precious Lives*) of her own family's history. Margaret Forster is married to the writer Hunter Davies and divides her time between London and the Lake District.

Georgy Girl (1965), the story of a gauche, funny and energetic young woman caught up in the sexual and social upheavals of the 1960s, captured both the new freedoms that the era offered and the confusing new choices that that freedom involved. The heroine's attempts to balance all the elements in her life – the temptations of potential love affairs, the responsibility she feels for the unwanted baby of her beautiful but frivolous flatmate – were neatly chronicled in a novel that managed to walk the tightrope between comedy and pathos. Catching the mood of the moment, the book was a bestseller and was made into a film in 1966 starring Lynne Redgrave, Charlotte Rampling, Alan Bates and James Mason. It has proved more than just a novel for its own fleeting moment, however. It is still in print and remains vivid not only as a brilliant evocation of mid-1960s London but as a lively portrait of a young woman learning that love, relationships and responsibilities are more complicated and demanding than her upbringing has taught her. The rest of Forster's early fiction has been overshadowed by *Georgy Girl*. Other novels – *The Travels of Maudie Tipstaff* (1967), *Miss Owen-Owen Is at Home* (1969) and several more – followed but none has its freshness and vitality.

Mother Can You Hear Me? (1979) marks a turning point in Forster's fiction, the moment when it succeeded decisively in escaping the shadow cast by *Georgy Girl* and took a new path. The focus moves from the individual trying to find her place in life to the relationships between generations, particularly the often fraught relationships between mothers and daughters. In *Mother Can You Hear Me?* the central character, Angela Bradbury, feels trapped in the suffocating web of family life. Her mother, a doleful self-sacrifice on the altar of the 'family', has spent a lifetime perfecting techniques of emotional blackmail which alternately enrage Angela and send her into paroxysms of guilt. Alarmingly she can now see similar patterns emerging in her relationship with her own adolescent daughter, the sulky and resentful Sadie. The novel follows Angela's attempts to escape the apparently inevitable chains of family life.

The Bride of Lowther Fell (1980) and *Marital Rites* (1981) were followed by *Private Papers* (1986). This is a cleverly constructed exploration of the varying interpretations that different individuals can place on the events of family history. Penny, matriarch of the Butler family, decides to write its history as it unfolds. To Penny the family is everything, but for her four daughters the idea that the summit of ambition and achievement lies within the family has proved more of a destructive inheritance than a creative one. One of the daughters, Rosemary, finding her mother's 'private papers' and being outraged by what she sees as wilful distortions of the truth, decides to write her own version. Set against the far-reaching social changes of the Second World War and the post-war years, the novel is a witty and unflinching dissection of the internecine struggles that can take place within the confines of one family.

Forster's next novel, *Have the Men Had Enough?* (1989), entered even more uncomfortable territory in its story of the effects on family relationships of caring for an ageing and senile relative and of the ways in which caring for the elderly almost always falls to women. As the double-edged title suggests, men will be there when the care and attention are directed towards them but have had enough when the tables are turned. Although the indomitable Grandma has devoted her life to men it's left to the women of the family, in particular her daughter Bridget, with whom she lives, to care for her as she descends into dementia. Told through the voices of three women in the family, *Have the Men Had Enough ?* uses a mixture of black humour, pathos and unsentimentally precise observation to examine the ties that bind and the ways in which circumstance and illness threaten them.

In the late 1980s Forster published a prize-winning biography of the Victorian poet Elizabeth Barrett Browning. An unexpected but welcome consequence of her research for the biography was the long historical novel *Lady's Maid* (1990). Twelve years earlier Forster had created a fictionalised memoir of Thackeray, told, with mixed success, in his own voice. In retelling the well-known story of Robert and Elizabeth Browning from the point of view of Elizabeth's maid, Elizabeth Wilson, however, Forster's control of her material never wavers. Few facts are known for certain about Wilson, which allows Forster a freedom to invent a voice for her, largely by means of letters she writes to her family and friends, that is almost entirely convincing. The relationship between mistress and maid – they are mutually dependent and intimate yet also forever separated by the enormous gulf of class distinction – is skilfully delineated, and Wilson's own story of the loves and losses of an ordinary life are neatly (and ironically) counterpointed with the more grandiose dramas of what is one of the best-known love stories in English history.

The Battle for Christabel (1991) and *Mothers' Boys* (1994) returned Forster to the present. Both are books which, superficially, appear to deal with single social issues. *The Battle for Christabel* is 'about' fostering; *Mothers' Boys* is 'about' teenage violence. Yet Forster is far too subtle and intelligent a novelist to produce simple solutions to the problems on which she focuses. In *The Battle for Christabel*, the five-year-old Christabel is caught, uncomprehendingly, in the middle of a struggle between her maternal grandmother and her foster mother in the months after her own mother is killed in a climbing accident. With great sensitivity and a scrupulous detachment from easy moral judgements, Forster explores a conflict in which everyone (with the exception of blinkered officialdom) wants the best for the child but falls short of achieving it. *Mothers' Boys* examines a random act of teenage violence and its effects on family life from the point of view of the mother of the victim and the grandmother of the perpetrator. Joe is the fifteen-year-old victim and Leo the previously well-behaved assailant, but Forster's focus is on Harriet, Joe's mother, and Sheila, Leo's grandmother, who raised him, as they battle with conflicting emotions of love, guilt and forgiveness in their attempt to understand what happened and why.

In the late 1990s Forster's fiction and non-fiction writing followed parallel paths. In *Hidden Lives* (1995) she wrote a prize-winning account of her own family history, particularly that of the women in it, delving into the secrets of memory and the imprisoning power of social circumstance. Her fiction in the last six years has reflected similar themes of memory, motherhood and the search for the truth amidst family inventions and evasions. *Shadow Baby* (1996) tells the stories of Evie, born in Carlisle in 1887, and Shona, born almost seventy years later. They come from very different backgrounds but they share the common ground of abandonment by their mothers at birth. Both become obsessed by their mothers' identities, while both mothers dread being unmasked. Moving between social eras and between the perspectives of mothers and daughters, *Shadow Baby* explores the effects of abandonment and guilt with subtlety and an emotional power that stems from Forster's sympathy with the choices all her characters make and the consequences they face. In *The Memory Box* (1999) the central character is Catherine, whose mother died when she was still a baby. The mother, Susannah, has left behind memories enshrined both in the stories Catherine hears of her as she is growing up and in the 'memory box' of objects she bequeathed her. As a woman, and after the deaths of her father and stepmother, Catherine opens the memory box and strives to reconcile the two versions (or more) of her mother that she now possesses.

Margaret Forster is an unshowy, unflamboyant but very skilful novelist who has, for nearly forty years, chronicled the lives of women in changing social circumstances. In many ways her reclaiming of her own family's history through her memoirs has been a means of revitalising her fiction and re-emphasising the themes that have always been present in her novels. Her most recent work of fiction, *Diary of an Ordinary Woman* (2003), shows that clearly. The fictionalised diary of Millicent King, an 'ordinary' woman who lived from 1901 to 1995, allows Forster again to explore the changes in women's lives through the twentieth century and demonstrate, as so much of her work has done, the strength and courage embodied in seemingly mundane lives.

Forster's major works

Georgy Girl, Secker & Warburg, 1965.
The Travels of Maudie Tipstaff, Secker & Warburg, 1967.
Miss Owen-Owen Is at Home, Secker & Warburg, 1969.
The Seduction of Mrs Pendlebury, Secker & Warburg, 1974.
Memoirs of a Victorian Gentleman: William Makepeace Thackeray, Secker & Warburg, 1978.
Mother Can You Hear Me?, Secker & Warburg, 1979.
The Bride of Lowther Fell: A Romance, Secker & Warburg, 1980.
Marital Rites, Secker & Warburg, 1981.
Significant Sisters: The Grassroots of Active Feminism 1839–1939, Secker & Warburg, 1984 (history).
Private Papers, Chatto & Windus, 1986.
Elizabeth Barrett Browning: A Biography, Chatto & Windus, 1988 (biography).
Have the Men Had Enough?, Chatto & Windus, 1989.
Lady's Maid, Chatto & Windus, 1990.
The Battle for Christabel, Chatto & Windus, 1991.
Daphne du Maurier, Chatto & Windus, 1993 (biography).
Mothers' Boys, Chatto & Windus, 1994.
Hidden Lives: A Family Memoir, Viking, 1995 (memoir).
Shadow Baby, Chatto & Windus, 1996.
Precious Lives, Chatto & Windus, 1998 (memoir).
The Memory Box, Chatto & Windus, 1999.
Diary of an Ordinary Woman: A Novel, Chatto & Windus, 2003.

ALASDAIR GRAY (born 1934)

There has been a renaissance in Scottish fiction in the last twenty years and its universally acknowledged founding father is Alasdair Gray. In 1981 he published what the writer and critic Magnus Linklater has described as 'the landmark post-war Scottish novel', which fused 'science fiction, quasi-autobiography and an apocalyptic vision into one of the wittiest, darkest, most readable books of the last fifty years'.

Gray was born in Glasgow in 1934 and attended Glasgow Art School in the mid-1950s. Before he gained fame as the author of *Lanark*, Gray had worked as a painter, art teacher and set designer for the theatre. During the 1960s and 1970s he wrote for stage, radio and television and had more than twenty plays performed in these media. In the late 1970s he was writer in residence at Glasgow University and, more recently, he has been Professor of Creative Writing at the same university. *Lanark* was published in 1981 and was immediately recognised as a landmark work of fiction, winning the Scottish Book of the Year Award and other literary prizes both inside and outside Scotland. In the twenty years since then, Gray has published nearly twenty other books. He has always stuck with his own laconic description of himself as a 'self-employed verbal and pictorial artist' and, in tandem with his literary career, he has continued to work as a painter.

'Where other novelists write fiction', the critic John Sutherland has written, 'Gray creates books', and it is true that the Scottish author shows a fascination with the whole craft of book-making. He involves himself in the design and appearance of his works to an unusual extent and most of his books are enriched by his own, stylishly idiosyncratic illustrations scattered through the text. Books like *The Book of Prefaces* (2000), Gray's long-gestated anthology of other people's texts, are integrated works of art, designed by Gray to combine the visual and verbal. Even errata slips, usually unconsidered and ephemeral, do not evade Gray's attention and become the targets of his puckish wit. 'This erratum slip has been placed in this book in error', reads one placed between the pages of the first edition of *Unlikely Stories, Mostly* (1983). 'I don't read books', one of Gray's characters admits. 'I'm glad to hear it', he's told; 'They can be terribly misleading'. Gray may love books and the process of creating them but he sees no reason why his own should necessarily conform to the conventions usually applied to others or do anything other than revel in their power to mislead. *Lanark* begins with 'Book 3', includes a 'Prologue' after a hundred pages and then moves on, unapologetically, to 'Book 1'.

Lanark was a long time in the making. One of its chapters began life as a short story that was runner-up in a competition organised by the *Observer* in 1958. When, more than two decades later, the book was finally published, it was a baggy monster that showed the marks of the time and creative energy Gray had lavished upon it. Great novels defy précis and, by that criterion if no other, *Lanark* is a great novel. Like few other novels of the last half-century it embraces both realism and fantasy. Its pages move between the two worlds of 1950s Glasgow, where its central character Duncan Thaw searches for love and meaning in his life, and of the city of Unthank, where the dead Thaw is reincarnated as a young man who, rather arbitrarily, has chosen the name Lanark. Yet because of its disrupted structure (Book 1, remember, follows rather than precedes Book 3) readers are not immediately aware of the connections between the two worlds and have to work them out as they progress through Gray's text. As the novel opens – in Book 3 – the self-named Lanark arrives by train in a strange and bleak city where the sun never properly shines and where the aimless, disoriented people suffer from odd diseases. Lanark himself suffers from 'dragonhide', which covers his flesh in scaly armour. Others have developed gaping mouths on hands and body. Spirited away to a sinister 'Institute' which cures his disease but holds gruesome secrets, Lanark is eventually able to consult an oracle, which tells him of the life he led before Unthank. The novel segues into Books 1 and 2, the oppressive *Bildungsroman* of Glaswegian artist Duncan Thaw. From allegory readers are led into naturalism – the story of the crushing of Thaw's spirit – before the text moves back, in Book 4, to an altered Unthank.

Lanark has been compared often enough to *Ulysses* and, just as *Ulysses* overshadows the rest of Joyce's fiction, *Lanark* sometimes stands in the way of a true appreciation of the diversity and quality of Gray's other work. Throughout his career he has been an adept, often inspired writer of short fiction, from the motley narratives collected in *Unlikely Stories, Mostly* to his most recently published stories, *The Ends of Our Tethers* (2003). Most notably he has published at least four other novels which, even had he not written *Lanark*, would guarantee him a major significance in modern Scottish literature.

Just as social realism and fantasy rub shoulders in *Lanark*, they jostle for position in Gray's other novels. In *1982 Janine* (1984) much of the verbal energy goes into the creation of the sexual fantasies which assail the central character, Jock McLeish. For most of his books, Gray writes his own tongue-in-cheek cover blurb. That for *1982 Janine* is to the point:

> This already dated novel is set inside the head of an ageing, divorced, alcoholic, insomniac supervisor of security installations who is tippling in the bedroom of a small Scottish hotel. Though full of depressing memories and propaganda

for the Conservative party it is mainly a sadomasochistic fetishistic fantasy.

Gray is, of course, poking his own particular form of fun at the more po-faced conventions of blurb-writing but his words provide an undeniably accurate précis of the book. Through the continually abridged fantasies that overwhelm Jock McLeish and the personal failures and frustrations that, the reader assumes, fuel them, Gray explores ideas of power and powerlessness and the insidious corruptions of pornography with remarkable honesty and imagination. *1982 Janine* was followed by *The Fall of Kelvin Walker* (1985), subtitled *A Fable of the Sixties*, which chronicled its ingenuous hero's pilgrimage through the media world and political arena of that decade. Travelling down to London, like so many ambitious Scots before him, Kelvin Walker pretends to be a success before he is and this pretence propels him into a fame that corrupts him. Mouthing platitudes and catchphrases, he rises higher only for his fall to be the more precipitous. Working more as comic fantasy than mordant satire, *The Fall of Kelvin Walker* is one of Gray's least complicated and most accessible fictions.

The early 1990s were a productive period for Gray. *Something Leather* (1990), which mixes Gray's idiosyncratic take on pornographic narratives with an account of the lives of several Glaswegian women over the decades, and *McGrotty and Ludmilla* (1990), another comic fantasy in which Mungo McGrotty rises inexorably to political power through possession of the mysterious Harbinger Report, inaccessible to anyone else, are not among Gray's most successful works, but the two major triumphs of these years were *Poor Things* (1992) and *A History Maker* (1994). *Poor Things* takes the form of a spoof memoir complete with scholarly annotations by its supposed editor, Alasdair Gray himself. The memoir is that of a nineteenth-century Scottish doctor, Archibald McCandless, who describes the achievement of his brilliant colleague Godwin Bysshe Baxter in creating life – resuscitating a lifeless body, he has produced Bella, a woman with the mind of a child. *Poor Things* mingles pastiche of Victorian popular fiction – there are echoes of other writers beyond the obvious parallels with Mary Shelley and Robert Louis Stevenson and McCandless admits to having 'raved in the language of novels I knew to be trash, and only read to relax before sleeping' – with twentieth-century satire. In *A History Maker* Gray once again showed his blithe disregard for the genre constraints which fence in other writers. The book is a futuristic fable set in the twenty-third century yet it also borrows elements from Scottish historical fiction. Talk of space travel and immortality shares the page with claymores and kilts. *A History Maker* is again in the form of a memoir – that of Wat Dryhope, a sensitive warrior in the staged battles that have become a TV spectator sport in the matriarchy of the future.

Since *A History Maker*, Gray has produced no major novel. *Mavis Belfrage* (1996), six progressively shorter tales which range from a title novella of seventy pages to the three-page *jeu d'esprit* named 'The Shortest Tale', is his most substantial book of the past decade. Yet, as he approaches his seventies, Gray continues to publish fiction that demonstrates the quirky energy, black humour and rich imagination that have always characterised his writing. His collection of short stories *The Ends of Our Tethers* may not be an extensive one, but a story such as 'Job's Skin Game', in which the sufferings of a father who has lost his sons in the September 11th attacks become written on his body, shows Gray continuing to respond to the world with his unique combination of fantasy, wit and hard-edged realism.

Gray's major works

Lanark, Canongate, 1981 (reissued 2002).
Unlikely Stories, Mostly, Canongate, 1983 (short stories).
1982 Janine, Cape, 1984.
The Fall of Kelvin Walker: A Fable of the Sixties, Canongate, 1985.
McGrotty and Ludmilla, Dog and Bone, 1990.
Something Leather, Cape, 1990.
Poor Things, Bloomsbury, 1992.
Ten Tales Tall and True, Bloomsbury, 1993 (short stories).
A History Maker, Canongate, 1994.
Mavis Belfrage, Bloomsbury, 1996.
The Book of Prefaces (editor), Bloomsbury, 2000 (anthology).
The Ends of Our Tethers, Canongate, 2003 (short stories).

PHILIP HENSHER (born 1965)

In the 1990s Philip Hensher published three novels and a collection of short stories which established him as a young writer to watch, a waspishly witty – even cynical – observer of the contemporary scene and of urban manners. All of these books were noted for their ironic, knowing distance from their characters and their icily precise skewerings of pretension and hypocrisy. In his fourth novel, *The Mulberry Empire*, published in 2002, Hensher reinvented himself as a historical novelist, creating a large canvas of nineteenth-century imperialism, albeit one refracted through a prism of irony and pastiche.

Hensher was born in London in 1965 and took his first degree at Oxford. He went on to do postgraduate work at Cambridge on eighteenth-century painting before moving back to London to take a job as a clerk in the House of Commons. (This experience was to provide him with ideas and material for his second novel, *Kitchen Venom*.) Sacked from his job at the Commons after a characteristically outspoken interview he gave to a gay magazine, Hensher has become a well-known, often acerbic critic and journalist. As well as his novels, he has written short stories – a collection, *The Bedroom of the Mister's Wife*, was published in 1999 and he was the only writer of his generation to have a story chosen for A. S. Byatt's 1998 anthology *The Oxford Book of English Short Stories*. He also wrote the libretto for Thomas Ades's opera *Powder Her Face*, which was based on the life and (many) loves of the 1950s scandal-maker the Duchess of Argyll. In 2003 Hensher was chosen as one of Granta's twenty Best of Young British Novelists.

Hensher's first novel was *Other Lulus* (1994). Juxtaposing the life of Alban Berg and the gestation of his opera *Lulu* with a story of a singer in contemporary Austria and her English musicologist husband, the novel finds parallels between past and present as well as between the themes of Berg's work and the unravelling of the marriage. It was followed by *Kitchen Venom* (1996), winner of the Somerset Maugham Award, which drew on Hensher's years of working at the House of Commons to create a story in which much was made of the ironic potential inherent in the contrast between an ancient institution, rich in arcane ritual and tradition, and individual dramas of sexual and social intrigue played out against its backdrop. The book's chief characters work as clerks in the Journal Office of the Commons, their lives absurdly regulated by their seemingly pointless work: 'What their job was no Member knew; what their purpose was, not even they quite understood. From day to day, they performed small rituals, and they recorded, and they checked what they had recorded'. Beneath the surface of ordered absurdity, however, unruly desires and passions lurk, and the blackly farcical plot, involving rent boys, bought sex in the afternoons and murder, chronicles the moments when they surface.

With *Pleasured* (1998), set in Berlin just before the fall of the Wall, Hensher engages with the Europe of shifting boundaries and falling barriers that the city represented in one of the milestone years of post-war history. The central character, Friedrich Kaiser, leads the slacker lifestyle in Kreuzberg, a district of West Berlin in which squats and ramshackle alternatives to consumerism proliferate. The book follows the unlikely friendship that develops between the straight Kaiser and a gay English businessman, Peter Picker, whom he meets when he hitches a lift with him. As the year before the breach of the Wall passes, Kaiser and Picker warily assess one another, revealing more to the reader of their past histories and their contrasting responses to the social and political changes surrounding them. The reader also meets middle-class student Daphne, in revolt from her comfortable background, and her boyfriend Mario, a refugee from the East who regularly cycles the circumference of the Wall that defines both his old and his new life. Events in the book are minimal, even unconvincing – at one point, for example, Kaiser, Picker and Daphne engage in an unlikely scheme to despatch thousands of free Ecstasy pills to the East – but Hensher's interest is in what the lives of these disparate characters reveal about the unfolding process of political change and its impact on individuals.

In the stories collected in *The Bedroom of the Mister's Wife* (1999) the often cruel wit and cool observation of contemporary mores shown in the first three novels were further on display. A bereaved husband believes himself haunted through the internet by his dead wife; a middle-aged gay man finds his equanimity disrupted by his desire for a young rent boy. There was no indication of the change of direction about to take place in his fourth novel, *The Mulberry Empire* (2002). This is, by a long way, Hensher's most ambitious novel to date, an expansive attempt to write a book that can be read both as an epic historical narrative and a knowing, post-modern subversion of all such narratives. Set in the 1830s and 1840s, the book deals with imperial Britain's fated and tragic attempts to extend its sphere of influence into the remote realm of Afghanistan. Drawing on, and pastiching, early-Victorian novelists like Dickens and Thackeray, later chroniclers of imperial expansion such as Kipling and Rider Haggard and analysts of empire's hearts of darkness like Conrad, Hensher creates a multilayered narrative which refuses the comforting closures offered by the Victorian and Edwardian novel, choosing instead to emphasise open-endedness and the unpredictable contingency of events.

The book's subject matter is drawn from the real history of one of the lesser-known and least successful episodes of imperial history. It begins in Kabul with the arrival of Alexander Burnes, an ambitious young Scot, who is half self-seeking adventurer and half a man genuinely enthralled by what is, to him, the exotic and the alien. News of his arrival soon reaches the country's ruler, the amir, Dost Mohammed Khan, for whom

> the arrival of the new European in town was like the dropping of a rock into the opaque pool of water which was the city, ruffling the surface immediately in ordinary and predictable ways, but disturbing the substance and mass beneath in a manner which could not be seen, or predicted.

Certainly, the ripples from this particular rock prove far-reaching and unpredictable. Burnes returns to London, writes a book on his Eastern adventures and becomes the latest sensation of the season. Their interest aroused and their paranoia about possible Russian plans to make new moves in the Great Game excited, the British turn their attention to the hitherto independent Afghanistan. They march into Kabul, unseat the amir and put in his place a ruler they imagine will be more responsive to British interests. However, Afghanistan and the Afghans remain resistant to imperial presumption and a few years after the triumphal entry into Kabul the occupying forces are obliged to make a retreat which becomes a rout.

This is the historical narrative which *The Mulberry Empire* follows, but Hensher does this at the kind of leisurely and digressive pace typical of the nineteenth-century novels he so frequently echoes. The characters – more than a hundred – are carefully listed in a *dramatis personae* and Hensher moves back and forth between them, often leaving stories unresolved in narrative limbo, suggesting a future return which doesn't always materialise. (Hensher's intention here is clear enough – he wants to emphasise his novel's difference from those Victorian narratives where all loose ends are, over-conveniently, tied up – but the effect can be irritating for the reader.) As well as Burnes, the amir and the representatives of British imperialism, the book follows the fortunes of Bella Garraway, launched into the London season and an affair with Burnes; Charles Masson, a deserter from the Indian army who takes up residence in Kabul; and a group of bickering, bantering, unsuccessful London literati who could have escaped from the pages of Gissing's *New Grub Street*. At one point the narrative perspective changes from the British to the Russian side and Hensher introduces us to Vitkevich, a dandified Russian aristocrat with radical ideas about his own society, who is sent on a mission to Kabul, where he meets and finds common ground with Burnes.

From its very opening, with its echoes of the rhythm and language of folk tales ('The Amir Dost Mohammed Khan had fifty four sons. And his favourite among these sons was Akbar. One day Dost Mohammed feared that he was ill, and close to dying, and he called his fifty-four sons to him'), *The Mulberry Empire* plays games with all kinds of narrative forms. Its playfulness and knowing irony are familiar from Hensher's early fiction, where they are directed towards the inanities and self-obsessions of contemporary mores. By creating a complex, multilayered saga of imperial expansion which also makes use of them, Hensher has written a book that takes the Victorian novel, with all its strengths and faults, and turns it on its head.

Hensher's major works

Other Lulus, Hamish Hamilton, 1994.
Kitchen Venom, Hamish Hamilton, 1996.
Pleasured, Chatto & Windus, 1998.
The Bedroom of the Mister's Wife, Chatto & Windus, 1999 (short stories).
The Mulberry Empire, Flamingo, 2002.

ALAN HOLLINGHURST (born 1954)

Alan Hollinghurst's first novel, *The Swimming-Pool Library*, was greeted with almost universal acclaim when it was published in 1988 and described by Edmund White as 'the best book on gay life yet written by an English author'. Hollinghurst's mandarin, often self-consciously old-fashioned prose was used to tell an elegiac story of promiscuous gay sex in the pre-AIDS era in a way that startlingly combined graphic description with stylistic restraint and irony. It was as if an up-front and out-of-the-closet E. M. Forster had chosen to turn a cool, analytic eye on the couplings and uncouplings of gay sexual relations and the book was markedly unlike almost all other 'gay' fiction then published. In the fifteen years since *The Swimming-Pool Library* Hollinghurst has published only two further novels but each, in its very different way, has shown him to be one of the most original fiction writers of his generation.

Hollinghurst was born in Gloucestershire in 1954 and educated at Magdalen College, Oxford. He was on the staff of the *Times Literary Supplement* from 1982 to 1995 and has edited volumes of new writing and works by writers such as Ronald Firbank and A. E. Housman. On the strength of *The Swimming-Pool Library*, he was included on Granta's list of twenty Best Young British Novelists in 1993.

Set in the world of early-1980s, pre-AIDS gay London, *The Swimming-Pool Library* tells the story of William Beckwith – young, rich, unemployed, self-absorbed and promiscuous – who saves the elderly Lord Nantwich from an ignominious death in a public toilet. The two become friends and Beckwith is asked to write Lord Nantwich's biography. He agrees, although his careless promiscuity proves a distraction. Nantwich's story is that of his life in the early twentieth century, first at Oxford and then in colonial Africa, a very different time for gay men to the one in which William is living. *The Swimming-Pool Library* uses the relationship between the doddery, ever so slightly senile Nantwich and the charming, irresponsible Beckwith as the means of creating a witty and convincing portrait of gay subculture in Britain from the time of the First World War to the period just before the advent of AIDS. (AIDS is an offstage presence in the book, casting a retrospective shadow over events for readers if not for characters.) Neatly revealing, among many other things, how the English class system and relationships of power operate in their own way within the subculture, Hollinghurst carries his narrative towards a surprising conclusion in which the conflicts between social position and sexuality are revealed.

Hollinghurst waited six years before publishing his next novel. Shortlisted for the 1994 Booker Prize, *The Folding Star* (1994) is about loss and sexual obsession. Newly arrived in Belgium and in search of a new life, the narrator, thirty-three-year-old Edward Manners, teaches two young men English. He becomes erotically fixated on one of them, seventeen-year-old Luc, with whom he falls in love at first sight. His love remains undeclared, but he indulges in endless, graphically described fantasies, including one of Luc urinating on him, and steals Luc's soiled underwear and socks to wear. His desires frustrated, Manners begins affairs with two other men. When working on a catalogue for the local museum he finds parallels between his own obsession and that of the Symbolist painter Edgard Orst. After falling in love with a famous actress who drowned off Ostend at the turn of the century, Orst made her the subject of all of his paintings for the remainder of his life. Manners moves between his own obsession and his attempts to understand both Orst's emotional relationship with his drowned muse and the ambiguous circumstances in which he died during the Nazi occupation. Infused with Hollinghurst's characteristic brand of sensuality and melancholy irony, *The Folding Star* is like an updated version of *Death in Venice*, set in the colder and bleaker atmosphere of his unnamed Flemish city. Moving from uninhibited description of gay sexuality to erudite discourse on Symbolist aesthetics, from the past to the present, Hollinghurst unfolds his narrative with same confidence in his own ability to do so that was apparent in his debut novel.

Hollinghurst's third novel, *The Spell* (1999), is noticeably different in tone to his first two. The wit and the elegant prose are still much in evidence but they are turned on a story of the convoluted affairs of four men. Robin Woodfield, tiring of the frenetic gay scene of the capital, sets up what he hopes will be a country idyll in Dorset together with his young lover, Justin. Justin, however, is reluctant to give up the bright lights, and Robin's son, Danny, also gay, is firmly entrenched in the club scene. On the edge of all this is Alex, a quiet and shy civil servant and one-time lover of Justin, down in Dorset on a weekend visit from London. When Alex falls for twenty-two-year-old Danny he finds himself drawn into the sort of delights that Justin is finding hard to quit. Hollinghurst skilfully juggles the contrasting elements of his story – the drug-fuelled excitement of the city against the quieter pleasures of the country, the search for sex and the search for love – and the camp bitchiness of Justin is often very funny. As a gay comedy of manners the book works well enough, but it lacks the originality of his first two novels and, five years after *The Folding Star*, seemed something of a disappointment.

In 2004 Hollinghurst returned to the elegant memorialising of gay life in modern Britain that he had begun with *The Swimming-Pool Library*. *The Line of Beauty*, his fourth novel, opens in 1983 and charts the progress of the young Nick Guest through a Thatcherite London, obsessed by money and the pursuit of power. The kind of carnal and political innocence evident in the earlier novel is no longer possible and *The Line of Beauty* is a darker book than its predecessor but it shares the qualities that have distinguished all of Hollinghurst's fiction. Few contemporary novelists have charted the intertwining passions of art and sex with such erudite panache as he has done.

Hollinghurst's major works

The Swimming-Pool Library, Chatto & Windus, 1988.
The Folding Star, Chatto & Windus, 1994.
The Spell, Chatto & Windus, 1998.
The Line of Beauty, Picador, 2004.

NICK HORNBY (born 1957)

No writer in the 1990s was as adept and as funny as Nick Hornby in portraying the emotional confusions and immaturities of white, middle-class urban man. He staked out his territory in his first (non-fiction) book and in the two novels that followed it he played fictional variations on the themes he had established. All three books met with great critical and commercial success, although some critics soon began to argue that he was restricting himself to a narrow field and that he had rapidly exhausted its potential. Hornby himself was well aware of the dangers of endlessly retreading the same ground and his third, and most recent, novel is a clear attempt to show that he can write about something other than middle-class men and their emotional incompetence.

Nick Hornby was born in 1957 into a family several rungs further up the subtly graded ladder of the English class system than one might suspect from a casual reading of his books. He read English at Cambridge and then worked as a teacher and journalist before the spectacular success of his first book allowed him to write full time.

This first book (other than a short critical work on contemporary American fiction) was *Fever Pitch* (1992), an autobiographical account of his obsession with football in general, and Arsenal FC in particular. Football writing before *Fever Pitch* had been largely confined to ghosted autobiographies of players and blandly written histories of the game. Unlike cricket or boxing, say, it was not a literary sport. It did not attract writers accustomed to see their work in hard covers rather than on the back pages of the papers. Hornby was one of the first middle-class fans to own up to his love of football. 'It's in there all the time', he wrote in the book, referring to this love, 'looking for a way out'. In *Fever Pitch* it found its way out and the result was a funny and touching memoir of a man who had invested too much of his emotional energy in 'the beautiful game'. That he was not alone was apparent from the book's success. A whole generation of white-collar fans emerged from their hiding places and proclaimed their allegiance from the rooftops.

Hornby could, no doubt, have continued to produce memoirs rather than fiction but it did seem inevitable that he would turn to the novel. *High Fidelity* was published in 1995. In the novel, music plays for the central character Rob the role that football does for the Hornby persona in *Fever Pitch*. Rob owns a small record shop, a vinyl museum of old singles and LPs. Pop music is as important to him as it is to his customers – 'young men, always young men, with John Lennon specs and leather jackets and armfuls of square plastic bags, who seem to spend a disproportionate amount of their time looking for deleted Smiths singles and ORIGINAL NOT RERELEASED Frank Zappa albums'. It is the hook on which Rob can hang his love of facts and list-making, the means by which he keeps the disorderly chaos of life at bay, and the barrier he places between himself and real emotional connection. The book opens with Rob in the messy aftermath of another failed relationship. His way of coping is to record his emotional life as if it was a succession of pop singles striving for a place in the charts:

> My desert-island, all-time, top five most memorable split-ups, in chronological order:
>
> 1. Alison Ashworth.
> 2. Penny Hardwick.
> 3. Jackie Allen.
> 4. Charlie Nicholson.
> 5. Sarah Kendrew.
>
> These were the ones that really hurt. Can you see your name in that lot, Laura? I reckon you'd sneak into the top ten, but there's no place for you in the top five.

High Fidelity is very funny, filled with both comic set-pieces and almost aphoristic one-liners ('My friends don't seem to be friends at all but people whose phone numbers I haven't lost') and chronicles Rob's slow, backsliding journey towards a distant, beckoning maturity that is constantly disappearing over the horizon. The crucial moment occurs when he is reconciled with Laura and realises definitively that the lyrics of his life, taken from all the records he has played, are nothing but fantasies and half-truths. The look of love, as celebrated in song by Dusty Springfield, may still provide Rob with the soundtrack to the reconciliation but he now appreciates that

> the look of love isn't what I expected it to be. It's not huge eyes almost bursting with longing situated somewhere in the middle of a double bed with the covers turned down invitingly; it's just as likely to be the look of benevolent indulgence a mother gives a toddler, or a look of amused exasperation, even a look of pained concern.

Fatherhood is the great challenge to male fecklessness and fatherhood is at the heart of Hornby's second novel *About a Boy* (1998). The central character, Will Freeman (an over-archly ironic surname), is clinging to cool in North London as he reaches his mid-thirties and living off royalties from a jingle his father wrote decades earlier. His father is gone but still controls Will insofar as the money from his work means that Will has no need to strive for independence. Pretending to single fatherhood as a means of ingratiating himself with desirable single mothers, Will meets Fiona and, more importantly, her twelve-year old son Marcus. Marcus, so unhip that he likes Joni Mitchell and mistakes Kurt Cobain for a Manchester United footballer, latches on to Will, who finds himself, at first very unwillingly, cast in the role of the father figure that he has previously been merely playacting for selfish purposes.

The commonest criticism levelled at Hornby is that he writes bland, safe fiction. This is often a reflection of the fact that, unlike so many male writers, he is quite happy to write 'domestic' fiction. In an interview he has said:

> I read a lot of books by women and identified with them much more because I lived a domestic life – and most of us do – and that really wasn't reflected in any of the books written by men. It seemed odd to me that most of us bring up families and go to work and yet the books our male representatives are writing are about huge things in history and people on the edge. Of course we have a need of those books but there did seem to be a bit of a hole where no one was writing about what actually happened.

To claim Hornby is bland because he writes about 'what actually happened' is unfair and yet there is a sense throughout *About a Boy* that he is treading ground he has covered before – and better.

Hornby himself must have been aware of the criticism because in his third novel, *How to Be Good* (2001), he made a bold narrative decision. The physical geography of the book is the same as in his two earlier novels – North London – but the mental and emotional geography is necessarily different. Hornby decided to make his narrator a woman. In interviews he has downplayed the importance of this ('I've come to the conclusion that it's a myth that there's this huge divide between men and women') but, particularly for a writer so associated with a certain type of masculine sensibility, it was a risky option rather than a 'bland' or 'safe' one.

The central character in the book is Katie Carr, a forty-something GP whose marriage, to David, a bilious and cynical journalist, is under pressure. A middle-class marriage on the rocks provides exactly the kind of domestic, mundane troubles that Hornby has said he wants to illuminate in his fiction. Katie remarks, 'It seems to me now that the plain state of being human is dramatic enough for anyone; you don't need to be a heroin addict or a performance poet to experience extremity. You just have to love someone'. This could almost be Hornby's own credo for the novels he writes. Yet, in an unpretentious way, *How to Be Good* soon begins to touch on some of the most fundamental questions about what it is to be human and to relate to others. David undergoes a 'Road to Damascus' conversion from cynicism and bitterness to 'goodness'. Under the influence of a New Age guru, a man he would previously have dismissed as a charlatan, he wants to invite the homeless to share their meals. He gives away the contents of his wallet to a beggar, donates one of the family's computers to a battered women's shelter and badgers their children into giving up their favourite toys for charity. The self-styled 'angriest man in Holloway' is transformed into a zealous do-gooder. Kate, the caring GP who has previously had little difficulty thinking of herself as a 'good' person, is now the 'bad' person in the relationship, guiltily involved in an extramarital affair and resisting David's new-found moral mission to the socially deprived of North London. Like all of Hornby's writing, *How to Be Good* is funny, rooted in topicality and the particular, yet it does show the ways in which big ideas have a part to play in small lives. It shows that Hornby's preferred 'domestic' fiction need not be incapable of accommodating major themes. The book is a clear demonstration that Hornby has never been quite the bland and safe writer that his critics have claimed and indicates that, in future novels, he may well have more surprises up his sleeves.

Hornby's major works

Fever Pitch, Gollancz, 1992 (memoir).
High Fidelity, Gollancz, 1995.
About a Boy, Gollancz, 1998.
How to Be Good, Viking, 2001.
31 Songs, Viking, 2003 (memoir/music criticism).

KAZUO ISHIGURO (born 1954)

Born in Japan but brought up and educated in England, Ishiguro has made of his fiction a mirror to reflect obliquely the characteristics of his two nationalities. His first two books, *A Pale View of Hills* (1982) and *An Artist of the Floating World* (1986), were enigmatic, poetic studies of individual Japanese trying to come to terms with the realities of the nation's recent past. Two of his other novels, *The Remains of the Day* (1989) and *When We Were Orphans* (2000), have been subtle examinations of, among other things, the emotional reticence that can blight and misshape English lives.

In *A Pale View of Hills* the narrator is Etsuko, a middle-aged Japanese woman living in England who finds that the suicide of her daughter recalls troubling thoughts and emotions from her past amid the post-war traumas of Nagasaki. In particular her mind returns to another woman whose life seems to parallel and foreshadow her own rejection of the role traditional Japanese culture had mapped out for her. Like Etsuko's own choices about her life, those of Sachiko, a war widow who took an American lover, had disturbing consequences for her daughter. In his first novel, Ishiguro's prose already shows all the characteristics that have marked it in his later career. Allusive and suggestive rather than baldly declarative, his language maps out delicate connections between the two women and their life histories. *A Pale View of Hills* has been well described as 'a memorable and moving work, its elements of past and present, of Japan and England held together by a shimmering, all but invisible net of images linked to each other by filaments at once tenuous and immensely strong'.

An Artist of the Floating World is the story of Masuji Ono, an ageing artist in a Japanese city still suffering from the after-effects of wartime devastation. The 'floating world' of the title is the bohemian milieu of his youth – 'the night-time world of pleasure, entertainment and drink which formed the backdrop of all our paintings', as he nostalgically recalls it. Yet, as so often in Ishiguro's work, memory is deeply ambivalent. Ono's past is not just one of idle bohemianism and sensitive aestheticism but, as is subtly revealed in the course of the book, one of complicity in the expansionist imperialism that brought such suffering to his country and, the reader learns in hints and oblique suggestions, to Ono himself. In the new world of post-war Japan, Ono is not only an anachronism whose values have been rejected by a younger generation but a potential embarrassment to his daughters.

His younger daughter is engaged and her sister worries that their father's past may compromise their present and future.

The Remains of the Day, Ishiguro's Booker Prize-winning third novel, continues to be his best-known work and its fame was only enhanced by the 1993 Merchant-Ivory film version starring Anthony Hopkins and Emma Thompson. In a way, the book is almost like a reprise of its predecessor, a translation into an English setting of *An Artist of the Floating World*'s story of a man looking back on his life, unable to acknowledge, save in hints and suggestions, the failings it has embodied. In place of the artist Ono, *The Remains of the Day* has the ageing butler, Stevens, who embarks on a physical journey (through the West Country on a motoring holiday) that also becomes a journey, in his memory, through his own past. The year is 1956 and Stevens's employer for more than thirty years, Lord Darlington, has just died. The new owner of Darlington Hall, an American, allows Stevens to travel to Cornwall, ostensibly to look into the possibility of rehiring a former housekeeper who now lives there. The book takes the shape of Stevens's journal of his trip.

Stevens is another of Ishiguro's self-deceiving narrators, telling a story which reveals far more to the readers than he thinks. Stevens has prided himself on his 'professionalism' as a butler and on the fact that he has served a 'great' man in Lord Darlington. His own life is vindicated by its connection with that of a man who has made a genuine impact on history. This is what Stevens continues to tell himself, but what are increasingly revealed beneath the surface of his account are the twofold realities that he is unable to face. One is that Lord Darlington was far from being a great man whom history will fondly memorialise but a rather shoddy appeaser in the 1930s whose political actions were, at best, misguided. More personally, and more poignantly, Stevens missed his opportunity for love through his inability to deal with his attraction to Miss Kenton, the housekeeper. Beneath the repressed formality of Stevens's prose lurks his own, unacknowledgeable half-awareness that he has wasted the best opportunities that life has offered him.

In an interview, Ishiguro once said:

> I'm interested in memory because it's a filter through which we see our lives, and because it's foggy and obscure, the opportunities for self-deception are there. In the end, as a writer, I'm more interested in what people tell themselves happened than in what actually happened.

He could have been talking about almost any of his novels but he was referring specifically to *When We Were Orphans*. *When We Were Orphans* is the story of Christopher Banks, another of those Ishiguro protagonists who are caught between two worlds, uncertain of which has the most claim on him. He is also, like Stevens in *The Remains of the Day* or Masuji Ono in *An Artist of the Floating World*, a narrator whose language serves to disguise the reality of his life. Banks is a detective in 1930s England but his roots lie in Shanghai, where he was brought up, the son of parents who were involved, in different ways, in the illicit opium trade. His parents disappeared when he was a boy, presumed victims of a Chinese warlord. Banks travels back to Shanghai to put his skills as a detective to work on the great mystery of his own life – what exactly happened to his parents. Like Stevens in *The Remains of the Day*, Banks is a man who has repressed his emotions until he is incapable of recognising them, and this is reflected in the prose he writes (as narrator). Formal, cautious and stilted, his language is attempting to exercise a tight control over the world it is describing. But the world it is describing – or trying to describe – is one that is far too chaotic, violent and out of control to be amenable to the restrictions Banks wants to impose upon it. He arrives back in China in the midst of the bloody brutality of the war between China and Japan and Shanghai itself is a city of ruins and desolation. *When We Were Orphans* is a curious amalgam as a novel. It is a parody of old-fashioned detective and adventure stories mixed with Ishiguro's characteristic interest in the language of self-repression and a character's journey towards some moment of half-recognised self-knowledge. The danger is that the parody can become self-parody. One reviewer, unkindly but with an element of truth, remarked that 'the emotionally-strangulated butler-speak' that Banks shares with Stevens 'sounds increasingly and disconcertingly like John Major'. The reader often has the feeling that it is not only Banks's language but Ishiguro's that is inadequate to the task of describing the events of the novel.

The odd man out in Ishiguro's fiction – indeed, it is, one could argue, one of the oddest novels published by a major writer in the last decade – is *The Unconsoled* (1995). This massive novel begins as the story of a celebrated pianist arriving in an unnamed European city to give a concert. From there the book becomes a sequence of surreal encounters between the pianist, Ryder, and a host of characters who may or may not be people from his past. As in a dream, space and time are flexible dimensions. A broom closet opens into a cocktail party, his hotel room seems uncannily like the bedroom in which he slept as a child, cities and forests seem to co-exist side by side. Ryder suffers the indignities we can suffer in nightmares. In one scene he is attending a formal banquet when he discovers that he is dressed only in his bathrobe. The book can be as bewildering for the reader as the events in it are for Ryder but Ishiguro marshals his clashing dreamlike narratives with exceptional skill. At first thought, he might seem an unlikely writer to attempt surreality but, in fact, his careful, precise prose (as evident here as in his other books) works to his advantage. His elegant control of the language imposes an order and a temporary sense on even the most bizarre of happenings.

The Unconsoled, at the time of publication, seemed to mark a move in Ishiguro's work away from the miniaturist exactitude of his first three novels. *When We Were Orphans*, although it saw a return to the ironic use of a self-deluding narrator, also demonstrated an ambition to incorporate more into his fictional world. In all his novels, Ishiguro has been an adept and perceptive investigator of the power of memory, loss and emotional reticence to shape and distort his characters' lives.

Ishiguro's major works

A Pale View of Hills, Faber and Faber, 1982.
An Artist of the Floating World, Faber and Faber, 1986.
The Remains of the Day, Faber and Faber, 1989.
The Unconsoled, Faber and Faber, 1995.
When We Were Orphans, Faber and Faber, 2000.

HOWARD JACOBSON (born 1942)

In the early 1980s the English campus novel, a seemingly moribund form, was given new life by two writers. One was David Lodge, whose novels of transatlantic academics, enmeshed in misunderstandings and misalliances, reworked themes aired in earlier books by himself, Malcolm Bradbury and others. The other was Howard Jacobson, whose first novel, *Coming from Behind* (1983), was a riotously comic version of campus fiction with its own, idiosyncratic bite.

Howard Jacobson was born in Manchester in 1942 and read English at Cambridge before beginning a career as an academic. He was a lecturer at universities and polytechnics in both Britain and Australia and his first publication was a work of literary criticism. Unlike most of the novelists in this book, Jacobson was in his forties before he published his first novel. After his debut he was able to leave academic life and work full time as a writer, critic and broadcaster. In the later

1980s and 1990s Jacobson became a familiar figure not only in the literary world but also on TV, presenting documentary series on his own sense of Jewish roots (*Roots Schmoots*) and on the notoriously difficult subject of the meaning and value of comedy (*Seriously Funny*), as well as appearing as a notably grumpy commentator on cultural events. At one time it seemed impossible for the Booker Prize to be televised without Jacobson on the panel of experts explaining just why he didn't like any of the books on the shortlist.

The anti-hero of *Coming from Behind* (1983) is in a fictional tradition established at least as early as 1954 and Kingsley Amis's Jim Dixon. Stranded as an unwilling teacher of English literature in a dismal polytechnic college in the Midlands yet dreaming of Oxbridge glory, morbidly obsessed by failure and affronted by success, Sefton Goldberg is, in essence, a character exhibiting a mixture of wit and disillusionment familiar in English comic fiction. The difference is that he is Jewish, which adds a new potential for both alienation and comedy. Not only is Goldberg temperamentally uninterested in much that obsesses his peers (sports, the natural world, beer), a 'failing' which Jacobson ascribes to his Jewishness. He is also viewed warily, even by fellow misanthropes, because of his Jewishness. Jacobson has much fun with stereotype. Goldberg's friendship with Peter Potter is shaped by Sefton's awareness that he is 'the first Jew Peter had ever struck up friendship with' – 'he wanted to make the experience easy for him. As long as he remained hunched and dejected he was fairly sure that Peter could cope'. Goldberg's Jewishness becomes central to the humour of *Coming from Behind* and it gives it a mordant, discomfiting edge that goes beyond other novels in the tradition in which Jacobson is working.

Jacobson followed *Coming from Behind* with two other novels which similarly mixed erudite farce and erotic mishap, *Peeping Tom* (1984) and *Redback* (1986). The central character of *Peeping Tom* is Barney Flugelman, a Jewish writer with a love for literature but a peculiar hatred for Thomas Hardy and all that he represents in English fiction. To Flugelman, Hardy, memorably, is 'a morbid, superstitious little rustic who confused high peevishness with tragedy, niggardliness with humour (and) mean naturedness with melancholy'. Yet in the course of the novel it is Hardy's sexual obsessions that become Flugelman's. Indeed Flugelman comes to fear that he has become Hardy reincarnated as he exchanges urban (or at least suburban) civilisation for the discomforts of rural living and disorienting sexual encounters with the haughty Camilla. *Redback*, published two years later, provides an inventive take on the well-worn theme of the Englishman out of his depth in foreign climes. In Jacobson's novel the threatening otherness, malignantly intent on destroying or, at the very least, humiliating his Jewish protagonist Leon Forelock, is represented by Australia. Everything and everyone in the country – from its wide, open spaces and malicious wildlife to its radical feminists and academics – seems designed to assault Forelock's sense of self. Consciously over the top in its comedy, *Redback* is satire that finds its targets lurking everywhere.

Redback brought the first phase of Jacobson's career as a novelist to an end. Six years passed before the publication of *The Very Model of a Man* (1992), an attempt to write fiction very different from the kind with which, by the early 1990s, Jacobson's name was associated. This is a book that owes more to Joseph Heller and the acerbic biblical pastiche of *God Knows* than it does to the sometimes cosy conventions of English comic fiction. Through a retelling, informed by a modern sensibility, of the story of Cain and Abel, Jacobson creates a bleakly imaginative version of biblical myth. The book is narrated by Cain himself, as he journeys from first family to Tower of Babel, but this is a Cain weighed down by the anxieties of modern and post-modern man. God is a malevolent, resented presence; Cain a mordantly witty rebel against his Creator and against nature, weighed down by the burden of self-knowledge and self-consciousness. The novel is often very funny – no novel by Jacobson could fail to be – but it is also very unlike his other fiction. *The Very Model of a Man* was not a great commercial and critical success and it represents an experiment Jacobson has not repeated, but it has a disturbing power unmatched in anything else he has written.

Whether or not Jacobson was perturbed by the reception given to *The Very Model of a Man* (it was praised by many but some reviewers seemed personally affronted by its lack of similarity to the earlier books), he published no more fiction for six years. Yet the next four years saw the publication of three novels. One was a coming-of-age story set in the world of Jacobson's own past. In *The Mighty Walzer* (1999), drawing on his own memories, he recreates Jewish life in 1950s Manchester with an autobiographical intensity that is always present, lurking beneath the surface comedy. The book simultaneously celebrates and sends up the idiosyncrasies of the Jewish community. The protagonist is Oliver Walzer, entering adolescence, with all its potential for embarrassment and humiliation, armed only with a champion's skill at table tennis. Oliver combines teenage shyness with the confidence of a prodigy:

> I blushed with such violence in these years that I must have
> been in danger of combusting... as soon as I played against

another person the ovens came on. It wasn't fear of losing – I knew I couldn't lose. It was the exposure. Call it compound contradictory existential bashfulness. 1) I was ashamed of existing, and 2) I was ashamed of existing so successfully.

The other two novels were despatches from the front line of the battle between the sexes, Jacobson's defiantly rebarbative accounts of men clinging to their ageing libidos. Jacobson has little time for the overly sanitised ideas of masculinity and of the relationship between the sexes that inform a lot of modern fiction. To his detractors this makes his writing insensitive, even misogynist; to admirers it reflects an honesty and an acknowledgement of the messy complexity of life that eludes advocates of 'political correctness'. *No More Mr Nice Guy* (1998) follows Frank Ritz on the odyssey of sexual excess and comic embarrassments which engulf him when he is rejected by his partner. Tormented as well as defined by his raging libido, Frank becomes its despairing victim in a novel that pulls few punches in its depiction of a man using sex to fight off other fears. The central character of *Who's Sorry Now?* (2002) is Marvin Kreitman, a middle-aged businessman with 'a nostalgic affection for many of the old discredited categories of masculinist swagger', who zigzags between the lives and beds of several women in addition to his wife. Kreitman is best friends with a writer, Charlie Merriweather, whose own uxorious existence seems happily built on a foundation of satisfying, 'nice' sex with his wife. Yet it is Charlie who, in the course of a boozy lunch, suggests an 'exchange' of sex lives, Kreitman to bed Mrs Merriweather and Charlie himself to have his choice from his friend's array of partners. And it is Kreitman who rejects the idea, only to find fate intervening in the shape of a post-lunch accident in the Soho streets that leads unexpectedly to a carousel of sexual adventure and misadventure. *Who's Sorry Now?*, as much tragedy of obsession and existential discontent as it is sexual comedy, is full of wit and laughter but it is laughter in the dark and often as chilling as it is funny.

The fact is that Jacobson's writing has always been both defined and limited by its regular categorisation as 'comic fiction'. His most recent novel, *The Making of Henry* (2004), the story of a man whose life of disappointment and setback finally seems about to change, is another work which revels in the black comedy that can emerge from circumstances that another novelist might treat as serious, even tragic, drama. The idea persists that no writer as funny as Jacobson is – as skilled in laugh-out-loud one-liners as any stand-up, as adept as any stage farceur in establishing comic situations – can be thought of, in the final analysis, as a 'serious' novelist. Echoing the title of one of his non-fiction books, however, his novels, from *Coming from Behind* onwards, have always been seriously funny and any critique of his work needs to take that essential seriousness as its starting point.

Jacobson's major works

Coming from Behind, Chatto & Windus, 1983.
Peeping Tom, Chatto & Windus, 1984.
Redback, Bantam, 1986.
In the Land of Oz, Hamish Hamilton, 1987 (travel).
The Very Model of a Man, Viking, 1992.
Seriously Funny: From the Ridiculous to the Sublime, Viking, 1997.
No More Mister Nice Guy, Cape, 1998.
The Mighty Walzer, Cape, 1999.
Who's Sorry Now?, Cape, 2002.
The Making of Henry, Cape, 2004.

A. L. KENNEDY (born 1965)

The much-touted renaissance in Scottish writing in the 1980s and 1990s often seemed a very masculine affair – dominated by the likes of Alasdair Gray, James Kelman and, later, Irvine Welsh and Alan Warner. Yet one of the most distinctive and wholly original voices in Scottish writing, indeed in British writing, over the last twenty years has been that of A. L. Kennedy. Kennedy's use of a black, biting humour and precisely chosen language to explore themes of isolation, emotional impoverishment, sexual passion and love is extraordinarily powerful and has won her admirers from Salman Rushdie to A. S. Byatt.

Kennedy was born in Dundee in 1965 and graduated from Warwick University in 1986 with a BA in theatre studies and drama. She worked for many years for the arts and special needs charity Project Ability. She began her writing career with short stories. *Night Geometry and the Garscadden Trains*, which won the Saltire and John Llewellyn Rhys Prizes, was published in 1990. Its stories of single women and their discontents with their relationships, of loneliness and isolation, are immediately recognisable as the work of a remarkable and unusual sensibility. Kennedy has since published several other volumes of short stories – *Now That You're Back* (1994), *Original Bliss* (1997) and *Indelible Acts* (2002) – and three novels. She has been a Booker Prize judge, a Guardian First Book judge and an Orange Prize judge (2002) and has held several writer-in-residence posts.

Of her volumes of short stories, the most substantial is *Original Bliss* which includes an eponymous novella of great power. It tells the story of Helen Brindle, a painfully shy woman, the victim of a violent mocking husband, who has lost her 'original bliss', the ability to pray and have faith that her prayers will be answered. Seeing cybernetics professor Edward E. Gluck talking on TV about his theories on self-help, she travels to a Stuttgart conference to meet him and the two become enmeshed in a strange relationship, healing for both but complicated by Gluck's obsession with pornography.

Kennedy's first novel was *Looking for the Possible Dance*, published in 1993. Told with the same quirky sensitivity to language and the nuances of what is said and not said in relationships that characterised her early short stories, it was about Mary Margaret Hamilton, a Scots woman passionately attached to her father and now forced to deal with the intricacies of human relationships, from her difficulties with her lover, Colin, to the broader social relationships of life.

Two years later A. L. Kennedy published *So I Am Glad* (1995), the bizarre and unsettling story, told with wit and poignancy, of Jennifer, a woman who hopes to avoid the complications of love and life. She is a radio announcer and spends much of her time in isolation behind closed studio doors, intent on suppressing the emotions, the 'moles' as she refers to them, lurking within. 'Like manholes and poison bottles I was made to be self-locking', Jennifer says, 'and I could no longer be bothered pretending I might have a key. . . . I stopped trying to be normal and began to enjoy a small, still life that fitted very snugly around nobody but me'. Into this cribbed and confined life comes a strange roommate, an amnesiac called Savinien Cyrano de Bergerac (who may or may not be the ghost of Rostand's hero). Savinien is an ardent advocate of emotional connection and the flamboyant display of feeling. Having deliberately chosen emotional numbness (after a childhood in which her parents refused to wrap the harder truths up for her and even made love in front of her), Jennifer finds the possibilities of connection with another difficult to contemplate but begins to feel something, the 'moles' within stirring, when she surrenders herself, both emotionally and sexually, to Savinien. *So I Am Glad* is a strange fable for adults in which Kennedy tells her idiosyncratic story with an imaginative sympathy and mordant humour that give it complete conviction.

Everything You Need (1999) is both Kennedy's most ambitious book and, in some ways, her most conventional fiction so far. On Foal Island, an island off the Welsh coast, Nathan Staples lives in a close-knit writing community, the members of which seem to feel compelled to subject themselves to extreme hardship. Still in love with his estranged wife, Maura, and ever hopeful of a reunion, Nathan contrives to have his nineteen-year-old daughter, Mary, a fledgling writer, offered a place in the community so that he can tutor her without revealing his identity. Nathan has not seen Mary for fifteen years. She has been told that he is dead and it is not until she has lived on the island for several years that he finally finds the courage to reveal his identity. *Everything You Need* gains much of its power from the strength of its characterisation of Nathan and Mary – the father filled with abrasive misanthropy, the daughter edging towards some kind of self-understanding – and from the ambivalent, sexually fraught relationship that develops between them. Throughout her writing career Kennedy has always been sensitive to the minefields of misunderstanding and self-deception that threaten communication between people. In her short stories and novels she has charted, with a sardonic tenderness, the complex ways in which her characters try to negotiate those minefields.

Kennedy's major works

Night Geometry and the Garscadden Trains, Polygon, 1990 (short stories).
Looking for the Possible Dance, Secker & Warburg, 1993.
Now That You're Back, Cape, 1994.
So I Am Glad, Cape, 1995.
Original Bliss, Cape, 1997 (short stories).
Everything You Need, Cape, 1999.
Indelible Acts, Cape, 2002 (short stories).

HANIF KUREISHI (born 1954)

Kureishi was born in Bromley in 1954, the son of a Pakistani father and an English mother. After schooling in Bromley, he studied philosophy at the University of London and then took on a variety of jobs (including the writing of pornography under the pseudonym Antonia French) while trying to make his mark in the theatre. His first play was staged in 1976 and by the early 1980s Kureishi was recognised as a promising young playwright with an individual take on race, sex and politics. He reached a larger audience in 1985 when his screenplay *My Beautiful Laundrette* was made into a compelling film by director Stephen Frears. Other screenplays followed (*Sammy and Rosie Get Laid*, *London Kills Me*) and Kureishi also turned his attention to prose fiction, publishing his first novel, *The Buddha of Suburbia*, in 1990.

In the 1990s and the first years of the new century, much of Kureishi's creative energy has gone into prose fiction, although he has continued to write for the screen – both cinema and TV. He has proved a particularly effective writer of short stories – collections such as *Love in a Blue Time* (1997) and *The Body and Other Stories* (2002) provide ample proof of this – and he has published three more novels. Yet *The Buddha of Suburbia* remains his best-known and, in many ways, his most successful longer fiction. The TV adaptation of the book, which was first screened in 1993, brought it to a wider audience. It works so well because Kureishi takes traditional forms and themes of English fiction and uses them to examine ideas of race, sex and personal identity that have rarely found a home within the tradition. The conventional *Bildungsroman* encompasses race relations; familiar picaresque meets suburban striving.

> Englishman I am (though not proud of it), from the South London suburbs and going somewhere. Perhaps it is the odd mixture of continents and blood, of here and there, of belonging and not, that makes me restless and easily bored. Or perhaps it was being brought up in the suburbs that did it.

Thus the narrator of *The Buddha of Suburbia*, Karim Amir, introduces himself. Immediately the book is placed in a familiar tradition of English fiction in which the city, representing vitality, energy and sexual freedom, is set against stultifying suburbia. Yet there is much in the book that is less familiar in English fiction, most obviously its hero's ambivalent relationship to his own ethnic background. Karim Amir believes himself shaped, not so much by this, as by the popular culture which has surrounded him, which gives him a shared generational language with others from very different social groups. The novel's action shows how far this is true and how far Karim is deceiving himself. As his father sheds one image – changing from civil servant to self-proclaimed guru – Karim is catapulted into a world of shifting sexual, social and racial identities. His father's affair with Eva, one of the more glamorous of his followers, brings Karim into contact with the fringes of metropolitan bohemia and he seizes the social and sexual opportunities it offers. Eva's would-be rock star godson, Charlie, becomes his lover. Yet Karim's own status in this new world is founded on the caricatures of his own ethnic background, which he is obliged to play as an actor. Only by exoticising and falsifying himself can he enter the promised land dangled before him. *The Buddha of Suburbia* is, however, an ultimately optimistic novel and one unabashed in its celebration of pleasure and opportunity. Karim *is* largely successful in negotiating his path through the conflicting forces which shape him.

The themes of personal and cultural ambiguity are pursued in Kureishi's second novel, *The Black Album* (1995). Just as Karim describes himself as 'an Englishman born and bred, almost', so too Shahid Hasan, protagonist of *The Black Album*, resists exact labelling. When an Asian Muslim embraces him and calls him 'fellow countryman', he replies, 'Well...not quite'. Arriving at a London community college, Shahid finds himself torn between the troublesome glamour of modernity, in the shape of his sexy lecturer Deedee Osgood, and the tempting certainties of conservative Islam as represented by the militant Muslim group led by the charismatic Riaz. *The Black Album* is often as funny as its predecessor and shows again Kureishi's gift, honed by screenwriting, for creating convincing voices for very different characters, but it is sometimes too schematic for its own good. Not only is the diagrammatic opposition between Deedee and Riaz, as they battle for Shahid's body and soul, made too obvious, it's also too obvious which way Shahid will eventually jump.

Kureishi's third novel, *Intimacy*, aroused much controversy and bad feeling when it was published in 1998. (Controversy only increased with the release of Patrice Chereau's 2001 film version.) Was it a searingly honest assessment of a relationship destroyed by egotism and selfishness or was it a spiteful, self-justifying account of the ending of an affair, a piece of vindictive autobiography masquerading as fiction? Much of the criticism levelled at the book at the time of publication, amid a brouhaha fuelled by newspaper pieces by Kureishi's ex-partner and others, seems strangely misplaced now. Many novelists rework autobiographical experience into fiction and Kureishi's work has always drawn quite openly on his own life. In *Intimacy*, a writer called Jay is preparing to leave his partner, and the book, short and condensed, follows his thoughts, dreams and memories during the night before he does so. Kureishi makes little attempt, superficially, to present Jay as a sympathetic character. Self-absorbed and self-pitying, he is a shallow egotist who mistakes evasion of responsibility for commitment to personal freedom. As a friend tells him, 'You remind me of someone who only ever reads the first chapter of a book. You never discover what happens next'. Kureishi seems to thrust the knife quite as ruthlessly into Jay as into the shrewish Susan, the woman Jay is about to desert. Yet reading *Intimacy* it is hard to avoid the conclusion that, beneath the apparent criticism, there does lurk a strong element of subtly disguised special pleading by Kureishi on Jay's behalf. We are invited to see him, not as the Peter Pan of erotic relationships that he so clearly is, but as some kind of daring warrior in the cause of sexual freedom. 'Desire', he proclaims portentously, 'is naughty and doesn't conform to our ideals.... Desire is the original anarchist and undercover agent'. *Intimacy*, in the final analysis, fails as a novel, not because it plunders private experience for its material (plenty of novels do that), but because its central character is compromised by his creator's wish to have his moral cake and eat it.

After the claustrophobic constriction of *Intimacy*, *Gabriel's Gift* (2001) is a return to the more expansive, inclusive narratives of Kureishi's first two novels. The book focuses on the fifteen-year-old Gabriel Bunch, struggling to affirm his own identity amid the chaotic comings and goings of his North London boho family. Gabriel's father is an ageing musician, living on his past glories as guitarist in the band of rock legend Lester Jones. His mother, once a costume designer who worked with Ossie Clark, is now working nights in a pub. Weary of her husband's idealistic fecklessness ('We're not so desperate that we're going to start working for a living', he grandly informs someone offering him employment), she has thrown him out of the family home and he has taken up residence in a markedly squalid bedsit. Gabriel, coming of age in his dysfunctional family, copes by smoking dope, experimenting with his emerging sexual self and cultivating his 'gift' – his talent as an artist. This talent comes to the attention of Bowie-like superstar Lester Jones and the stage is set for Gabriel to effect a surprising reconciliation between his parents.

Gabriel's Gift makes use of an eclectic range of fictional devices – some more successfully than others. Elements of a kind of downbeat, urban magic realism (Gabriel chats with his dead twin brother; the subjects of his drawings come to life in his room) alternate with the humour and sprightly dialogue familiar from Kureishi's screenplays and from *The Buddha of Suburbia*. The result is a novel that escapes from the confining bitterness of *Intimacy* and many of his recent short stories and returns to the comedy of contemporary social manners and clashing generations that Kureishi does best.

Kureishi's major works

My Beautiful Laundrette, Faber and Faber, 1986 (screenplay).
The Buddha of Suburbia, Faber and Faber, 1990.
The Black Album, Faber and Faber, 1995.
Love in a Blue Time, Faber and Faber, 1997 (short stories).
Intimacy, Faber and Faber, 1998.
Midnight All Day, Faber and Faber, 1999 (short stories).

Gabriel's Gift, Faber and Faber, 2001.
The Body and Other Stories, Faber and Faber, 2002 (short stories).
Dreaming and Scheming, Faber and Faber, 2002 (essays).

JOHN LANCHESTER (born 1962)

Although John Lanchester has had a brief career as a novelist, he has already shown a disconcerting versatility and an impressionist's ability to bring to life very different narrative voices. There could hardly be two more contrasting works of fiction than his first two novels, *The Debt to Pleasure* (1996) and *Mr Phillips* (2000). One is a dazzling, self-conscious display of pastiche, irony and verbal pyrotechnics built around a flamboyant central character, the other a deliberately restrained story of a fictional everyman. One novel is surface glitter beneath which serpents lurk, the other a bland pool in which, nonetheless, the occasional exotic fish can be glimpsed.

The Debt to Pleasure begins with the narrator's archly ironic statement: 'This is not a conventional cookbook'. What follows is not a conventional first novel. On first publication the word 'Nabokovian' was used by very nearly every reviewer. It is easy to see why. In everything from its long, carefully constructed sentences, packed with lush vocabulary, to its theme of the frustrated artist manqué, the book is reminiscent of the Nabokov of *Lolita* and other elaborately wrought fictions. Constructed around four seasonal menus, *A Debt to Pleasure* begins as an apparent memoir of its narrator, gourmet and aesthete Tarquin Winot, centred on his love and knowledge of food and cooking. At first Tarquin seems little more than a self-satisfied intellectual and cultural snob, almost absurdly delighted by his own superiority to lesser mortals. His barbed criticisms and aphorisms, directed at just about everybody who has the misfortune not to be Tarquin Winot, are funny and heartless, and begin by seeming no more than verbal exuberance and a form of preening self-congratulation:

> 'Ooh, that looks nice,' she would say. 'Lovely and pink,' she would sometimes add, a weakness for the colour pink being an infallible sign of the defective taste one associates with certain groups and individuals: the British working classes, grand French restaurateurs, Indian street-poster designers and God, whose fatal susceptibility for the colour is so apparent in

the most lavishly cinematic instances of his handiwork (sunsets, flamingos).

As the book progresses, however, it becomes increasingly clear that Winot, one of the most unreliable narrators in recent English fiction, has much to hide beneath the extravagant verbal edifices and conceits he creates. His parents died in a mysterious accident; his brother, a famous sculptor whose work Winot dismisses as tasteless kitsch, is also dead. As he writes his witty and erudite observations on food and taste and art, Winot is journeying towards his home in Provence but, it gradually emerges, he is shadowing a honeymoon couple. The woman in the couple is writing a biography of Tarquin's late brother. By the time readers reach the last section of *The Debt to Pleasure* they are uncomfortably aware that, to Tarquin, his aphorisms and paradoxes ('it is not that the megalomaniac is a failed artist but that the artist is a timid megalomaniac') are not just verbal games but expressions of genuine beliefs. Beliefs on which he has acted already and will act again.

'Modernism was about finding out how much you could get away with leaving out. Postmodernism is about how much you can get away with putting in', says Tarquin in another of his self-conscious epigrams. Lanchester is post-modernist insofar as he crams Winot's 'gastro-historico-autobiographico-anthropico-philiosophic lucubrations' with as much wit, arcane knowledge, linguistic invention and culinary erudition as he can. The result is one of the more exceptional first novels of the past two decades – a glittering exercise in style and a compelling portrait of a brilliant monster, vainly strutting his stuff in front of the reader, unaware that he is simultaneously revealing his utter moral emptiness.

If *The Debt to Pleasure* is Lanchester's post-modernist fiction, then his second novel is his exercise in modernism, a deliberate attempt to see how much of the flamboyance of his first novel he could get away with leaving out. The eponymous protagonist of *Mr Phillips* has none of Tarquin Winot's peacock vanity or verbal panache. Throughout the book he remains the ordinary suburban man his name suggests – he doesn't even merit the distinguishing mark of a Christian name until the last few pages of the novel and then it is the ironically inappropriate Victor. Mr Phillips is not one of the victors in life's battle. He is an accountant, just made redundant, who has not yet had the courage to tell his wife of his dismissal. He continues to go through the motions of leaving home in the morning and catching the tube to

Central London. Instead of working he wanders the city, a voyeuristic witness to mundane happenings. He observes the tics and idiosyncrasies of his fellow commuters. He watches women playing tennis in a park. He visits an art gallery and a porn cinema. He has lunch with his son in Soho. Throughout the day he also muses on large and small questions of life, sex and death, carefully working out statistics and percentages like the accountant he has so long been. (He works out that, on a given day, there is an average probability of 96.7 per cent that he won't have sex.) *Mr Phillips* is emphatically not a plot-driven novel. The one dramatic occurrence in the book – a bank robbery – seems out of place, a scene that has slipped into *Mr Phillips* from another novel. Its effects depend on an extraordinarily skilful evocation of ordinariness. Very occasionally Lanchester's control slips and the narrative voice hints at the verbal gymnastics on display in *The Debt to Pleasure* but for most of the novel it remains resolutely undemonstrative. Lanchester's challenge is to make the reader interested in his character's very ordinariness and the danger is that his deliberate restraint will backfire. Being ordinary will equal being boring. For most of the novel he rises to the challenge and Mr Phillips, himself seeing the world anew in his changed circumstances, acts as a filter through which the reader can reimagine the everyday. The last encounter – between Mr Phillips and the widow of one of his old teachers – and the novel's final line as he turns for home ('He has no idea what will happen next') are moving because of, rather than despite, the consciously low-octane prose.

After two such very different novels, it might have seemed hard to predict what direction Lanchester's fiction would take next but to anyone familiar with the outline of his biography his third novel, *Fragrant Harbour*, would probably have not been too much of a surprise. Lanchester studied English at Oxford, working as a graduate on poets of the 1950s, before earning his living in London as a restaurant critic and literary journalist. However, much of his childhood and adolescence was spent in the Far East, specifically Hong Kong. It is the changing history and fortunes of Hong Kong over the last seven decades that provide the backdrop to the narratives of *Fragrant Harbour*.

Nor is it surprising that Lanchester, who has already amply shown his ability to inhabit very different fictional voices, chooses to tell his Hong Kong stories through several narrators. The first part of the book is told by an ambitious journalist, Dawn Stone, who arrives in Hong Kong in the early 1990s to pursue her career on a glossy magazine. Driven and largely unendearing, Stone tells her story without being aware of its significance. She seems to believe that she is describing a career of upward mobility and material ambition fulfilled. Lurking behind her own version of her 'success' is a far bleaker story of financial temptation and corruption.

Much the largest section of *Fragrant Harbour* is told in the voice of Tom Stewart, a young Englishman travelling to Hong Kong in the 1930s who spends the rest of his long life there. Stewart, like Stone, tells a story whose significance he is unable, or at least unwilling, to acknowledge. The larger world of politics and history has a major impact on his life. He sees the decline of old-fashioned colonialism, the Japanese capture of the city, the imprisonment and torture of many of its inhabitants. Yet his narrative voice – reserved and understated – veers away from direct engagement with what he has witnessed. The same is true of his personal life. On his original voyage out to Hong Kong he meets a young, attractive woman who agrees to teach him Cantonese. He remains in contact with her years afterwards, but she is a nun, committed to the love of God not an individual man. Only in the turmoil of the Japanese invasion does their love have a fleeting, physical expression. Stewart's entire emotional life is quite clearly built around his feelings for Maria but again this emerges indirectly from his narrative. In his own much more sympathetic way, Stewart is as self-deluding as Dawn Stone.

Throughout *Fragrant Harbour* Lanchester mingles personal histories with the life of the city, showing how the past continues to reverberate even in a place as firmly committed to modernity as Hong Kong. The narrator of the book's last section is a young entrepreneur called Matthew Ho. His future is entwined with the future of Hong Kong but, in his recognition that his life has been decisively shaped by the past, Ho seems the most self-aware of Lanchester's narrators. All of the narrative voices in *Fragrant Harbour* demonstrate that skill in creating a particular idiom and tone for his characters that has been Lanchester's defining characteristic as a novelist so far.

Lanchester's major works

The Debt to Pleasure, Picador, 1996.
Mr Phillips, Faber and Faber, 2000.
Fragrant Harbour, Faber and Faber, 2002.

IAN MCEWAN (born 1948)

McEwan was born in Aldershot, the son of a professional soldier, and spent part of his childhood abroad – in Africa and the Far East – before reading English at the University of Sussex. He went on to become one of the first students on Malcolm Bradbury's famous creative writing course at the University of East Anglia and his stories began to appear in magazines in the early 1970s. Soon recognised as a major new talent in English fiction, he published his first book in 1975 and has since published nine novels, as well as collections of short stories and TV and screenplays. His work has won most of the best-known awards for fiction, including the Booker Prize (*Amsterdam*) and the Whitbread Prize for Fiction (*The Child in Time*). His most recent novel, *Atonement*, was awarded a prestigious American prize – the National Book Critics' Circle Award.

McEwan's first two, much-acclaimed, books were collections of short stories. In *First Loves, Last Rites* (1975) and *In Between the Sheets* (1978) he created a reputation for glacially cool prose directed at macabre and bizarre subject matter. These are unsettling stories told with a chilly precision of language. His first two novels followed the short stories in being pared-down, ruthlessly concise narratives in which not a single word was wasted as they moved towards dark revelations. *The Cement Garden* (1978) is as effective as Golding's *Lord of the Flies* in destroying any sentimental notions of the innocence of childhood. Four children, orphaned by the sudden deaths of first father and then mother, conspire together to create their own self-contained reality. In less than 160 pages of tightly controlled prose, McEwan uses the voice of one of the children, the adolescent Jack, to narrate the gradual shedding of adult-imposed morality. Removed from the constraints of convention the children recreate their lives through their own fantasies and hitherto unacknowledged desires. The events of the book are shocking and transgressive yet the language McEwan uses is very deliberately matter of fact and unhysterical, its revelation of 'nature' lurking beneath the artificiality of ordinary life, only waiting for the chance of release, all the more powerful.

In *The Comfort of Strangers* (1981) a couple holidaying in Venice are drawn into a world of sadomasochistic sex and violence through a chance encounter. Subtle hints of menace are present from the beginning – even in the 'methodical chipping of steel tools against the iron barges moored by the hotel café pontoon' which wakes the couple on the first page – but McEwan is superbly skilful at gradually cranking up the tension as the story progresses until it reaches a nightmarish denouement. Both of McEwan's first two novels shared with his short stories an unblinking meticulousness in the description of unsettling events and a remarkable ability to create and control a feeling of mounting unease in the reader.

Six years passed before McEwan published another novel, and *The Child in Time* (1987) marked a distinctive step in the development of his writing. His collections of stories and his first two novels, although they showed precocious technical talent from the beginning, seemed to take place in an enclosed fictional world which referred only incidentally to the world of reality. They were exceptionally ingenious literary exercises in the Gothic. In *The Child in Time* McEwan moved his fiction into a different alignment with the real world and real human emotions. The novel opens with the kidnapping of a child. The father, Stephen Lewis, is paralysed by his loss and as he attempts to reconstruct his life in the wake of his bereavement McEwan plays sophisticated games in his narrative with the notions of time and its passing.

The Innocent (1990) is McEwan's idiosyncratic version of the spy thriller, published in the year that the Berlin Wall came down. As one might expect from McEwan, the emphasis in his novel is far more on the psychological journeys made by his characters than on cloak-and-dagger espionage. The innocent of the title is Leonard Markham, a naïve and virginal Englishman, a Post Office employee who arrives in Berlin in 1955 to work on what he believes to be an innocuous telecommunications project. The book charts Markham's political and erotic education as he realises that there is far more to his work than he thought and as he embarks on an affair with an older German divorcée. It culminates in a terrifyingly intense scene, the aftermath of a murder, in which Markham's loss of innocence is only too apparent. McEwan uses many of the motifs of the genre he has adopted and the book works as a thriller in the most fundamental way – the reader wants to know what happened next – but he is also engaged in exploring character with more subtlety than most thriller writers and in examining the extended meanings of innocence and its loss.

In *Black Dogs* (1992) the narrator writes to unravel the mysteries of the relationship between his wife's estranged parents, Bernard and June Tremaine. Married just after the Second World War, they go on to lead very separate lives while still feeling themselves ultimately linked. Bernard, a communist until the 1956 invasion of Hungary, represents determination to engage with the world and change it through political action; June, living for the most part in isolation in the French countryside, strives to find her own, private, religious meaning in life. The event which sets them on their separate paths is an encounter on their honeymoon in France with the eponymous black dogs. *Black Dogs* runs the risk of appearing too schematic and the characters of Bernard and June wooden representations of abstract ideas. The success of the whole book also depends on the extent to which the reader is prepared to accept the terrible encounter with the black dogs – foreshadowed throughout the text but only described fully as the novel draws to an end – as both real and symbolic of the irruptions of evil into the everyday.

One of McEwan's persistent themes is the intrusion of brutal, inescapable reality into comfortable lives that the black dogs represent. However ordered or rational lives might be, in McEwan's fictional world indifferent chance or the hell that is other people can unsettle them in a moment. Just such a moment is the starting point of *Enduring Love* (1997). The character about to be given a lesson in the fragility of reason and happiness is the narrator Joe Rose, a science writer picnicking with his partner in the countryside. Suddenly a hot-air balloon, out of control and with a man clinging to a rope hanging from its basket, comes into view. Joe and several other picnickers rush to try and help: 'We were running towards a catastrophe, which itself was a kind of furnace in whose heat identities and fates would buckle into new shapes'. The country idyll is destroyed and a man is killed, but that is not what is to tear apart Joe's life. The catalyst for that is the chance encounter with one of the other men who is running towards the scene of the impending tragedy, Jed Parry. Jed becomes Joe's stalker, obsessively convinced that some deep connection – beyond words and reason – has been created between them. Under the pressure of Jed's deranged pursuit, Joe's relationship with Clarissa crumbles and his entire view of the world as explicable and amenable to reason is threatened. *Enduring Love* is one of McEwan's finest novels, a brilliantly gripping account of one man's attempt to retain narrative control of his life as it seems to be slipping into chaos and contingency. Joe eventually finds a scientific explanation for Jed's behaviour that is consonant with his need for such an explanation but much of the strength of the book depends on McEwan's descriptions of the power of irrationality and the essentially inexplicable in all our lives.

McEwan more than deserves to have won the Booker Prize. Whether or not he deserves to have won it for *Amsterdam* (1998) is another question. It is one of his least satisfying books and there is almost a sense that the Booker judges, in awarding it the prize, were tacitly apologising for ignoring the much better *Enduring Love* the previous year. Set amid the great and good of the English class system's upper echelon, *Amsterdam* takes as its starting point the funeral of Molly Lane, a glamorous photographer married to a rich publisher but with a long list of ex-lovers among the powerful and the gifted. The novel follows a twisting and turning plot as two of these ex-lovers, an internationally famous composer and a newspaper editor, attempt to use the dead Molly and her promiscuity as a means of destroying a prominent politician. *Amsterdam* is witty and well written – what else would one expect from so skilled a practitioner as McEwan? – but it lacks the resonance of *Enduring Love* or *Atonement*. McEwan doesn't always seem at home with the characters and the milieu he has created and the satire appears directed at easy targets, set up for the sole purpose of being the victims of his sardonic prose.

Atonement (2001) is McEwan's most expansive and remarkable novel so far, a narrative that succeeds both as an exploration of guilt and reparation over sixty years and as a subtle demonstration of the powers of storytelling to blight the future and redress the past. The book is divided into three parts. The first is set in a Surrey country house in 1935. The central character, Briony Tallis, is thirteen years old, inhabiting 'the ill-defined transitional space between the nursery and adult world'. An aspiring writer, she watches, and half-understands, the sexual attraction between her older sister Cecilia and a Cambridge graduate Robbie Turner, but half-understanding is not enough. Trusted as a go-between by the two would-be lovers, she allows the story she has constructed about what is happening to stand in the way of acknowledging what really is. The result is tragedy not only for Robbie and Cecilia but also eventually for herself, left with a rosary of guilt 'to be fingered for a lifetime'. The second part takes place in May 1940 as Robbie takes part in the retreat to Dunkirk and Briony seeks atonement for the misery she has caused by training as a nurse. Finally, in a coda set in 1999, we learn that Briony has become a distinguished novelist and the earlier narrative of *Atonement* is a confessional text that she has fashioned over the decades. It may or may not represent what 'really' happened.

Atonement reveals Ian McEwan's continued commitment to expanding the range and power of his work. Few writers in the past three decades have been so critically acclaimed as McEwan, who was hailed as a 'great white hope' for British fiction almost as soon as he stepped out as a graduate (one of the first) from the University of East Anglia creative writing school. A less determined writer might have buckled under the weight of expectation or settled into a comfortable groove. McEwan has done neither. From the steely precision of his early short stories to the major novels like *Enduring Love* and *Atonement*, he has shown a willingness to take risks and extend himself as a writer that marks him out as one of the most consistently exciting and original novelists of his generation.

McEwan's major works

First Love, Last Rites, Cape, 1975 (short stories).
In Between the Sheets, Cape, 1978 (short stories).
The Cement Garden, Cape, 1978.
The Comfort of Strangers, Cape, 1981.
The Child in Time, Cape, 1987.
The Innocent, Cape, 1990.
Black Dogs, Cape, 1992.
The Daydreamer, Cape, 1994.
The Short Stories, Cape, 1995 (short stories).
Enduring Love, Cape, 1997.
Amsterdam, Cape, 1998.
Atonement, Cape, 2001.

PATRICK MCGRATH (born 1950)

Patrick McGrath's first novel was called *The Grotesque*, and the title is a good indicator of the Gothic sensibility that informs much of his fiction. All of McGrath's novels to date focus on characters who have disturbed relationships with reality and other people, whose inner world is haunted by fantasy and psychosis. His narrators unfold their skewed vision of events, often proving wholly unreliable in their interpretation of what is happening. His novels begin by appearing deceptively simple accounts of ordinary life but swiftly turn into stories of disturbing darkness hidden not too far beneath the surface of the mundane.

McGrath was born in London in 1950. His father was, for many years, medical superintendent at Broadmoor Hospital, and the young McGrath was brought up in close proximity to the mentally ill, an upbringing that clearly still influences his fiction. After studying English at the University of London, he worked as a teacher before moving to New York in the early 1980s. In interviews McGrath has described this as a turning point in his life, providing him with the freedom and distance from Britain that allowed him to write. He is married to the actress Maria Aitken and divides his time between London and New York.

McGrath's first book was *Blood and Water and Other Tales* (1989), a collection of determinedly strange short stories, echoing, in a clearly modern voice, the work of late-Victorian and Edwardian writers like W. W. Jacobs and M. R. James. Severed hands, dead monkeys, swarming insects, pickled body parts and menacing pigmies proliferate in narratives where ghosts lurk and spiritual and physical decay presides. This was followed by *The Grotesque* (1989), a kind of bizarre country house drama set in the late 1940s. From a wheelchair parked in a corner of his crumbling mansion, the brain-damaged Sir Hugo Coal recounts the events that led to his downfall. It is the arrival of the sinister Fledge as the new butler of Crook Hall that heralds the onset of disaster. Sir Hugo is reconstructing the skeleton of a dinosaur that will crown his paleontological career, but at every turn he is frustrated: by Harriet, his neglected wife; by giggling Cleo, their adored daughter, and her limp fiancé Sidney Giblet; but most of all by the sly usurper Fledge himself, whose insidious plotting brings chaos to the decaying mansion. Knowingly ironic in its use of the motifs and themes of Gothic and horror fiction of the past, and told in a prose that, in its deadpan understatement, is deliberately at odds with its subject matter, *The Grotesque* is a remarkable exercise in the sinister and macabre.

In his second novel McGrath chose to focus, with unnerving intensity, on one deeply damaged individual. *Spider* (1990) is set in 1957 and tells the story of Dennis Clegg, otherwise known as Spider, a lonely figure who returns to the East End of London after twenty years in an asylum. Spider moves into a cheap boarding house and begins to write an account of his childhood, the text that McGrath is inviting us to read. As the narrative moves between the 1950s and the years of Spider's horribly deprived and grey childhood, our confidence in the reliability of the story he is telling is further and further undermined. Not only does McGrath provide a disturbing vision of psychotic illness from inside, but he succeeds in maintaining a dual tension in his narrative. Gradually we approach the truth about what happened to Spider as a child, while we are also being drawn into the tightening circle of fantasies spun by the adult and a voyeuristic curiosity about where they will drive him.

Both of McGrath's next two novels used the neo-Gothic themes that he had made his own in his early works to explore erotic obsession and the imprisoning power of intense love. *Dr Haggard's Disease* (1993) is set in a crumbling mansion on the British coast during the Second World War. Dr Edward Haggard is a sick man. Haunted by an affair long ended, he is being slowly poisoned by loss and regret, twisted by unhappiness. Finding relief only in his quiet life by the sea and the occasional ministrations of the hypodermic, he is revived by the appearance of a new patient, a fighter pilot who is the son of the woman he loved. But with that revival comes renewed pain and, possibly, the ghost of his love, made a strange kind of flesh. Narrated by Haggard and told largely in flashback through his confessional revelations to the young pilot, the book moves towards an extraordinary and grotesque conclusion in which the metaphors of disease and obsessive love that McGrath has deployed reach a startling culmination.

Asylum (1996) is the story of the development of an obsessive and destructive relationship between the inmate of a hospital for the criminally insane and the bored, lonely wife of its medical superintendent. Trapped by her marriage to the uncharismatic Max, Stella Raphael becomes infatuated by Edgar Stark, a sculptor who murdered and mutilated his wife. McGrath's labyrinthine plot unfolds through the careful narration of Peter Cleave, colleague of Max Raphael, and the twists and turns increase as the reader begins to realise that Cleave, like McGrath's other narrators, is not to be trusted. *Asylum* is compelling both as a psychological thriller – we want to know what 'really' happens – and as a study of obsession. It is also a book haunted by our anxieties about psychiatrists, the late twentieth century's equivalent of witchdoctors, insidiously intent (it would seem) on possessing our souls. Cleave, significantly weirder than any of his patients, welcomes Stella's confidences, set as he is upon 'stripping away her defences and opening her up'.

McGrath's historical novel *Martha Peake* (2000) is, in some ways, his most ambitious book to date. Set in the late eighteenth century, it draws not only on the Gothic fiction that fuelled McGrath's earlier books but also on the motifs of historical romance and melodrama, put to ironic uses unimagined by most practitioners of the genre. When the Byronic smuggler Harry Peake is disfigured in a tragic accident, he and his daughter, Martha, are forced to move from Cornwall to the dank streets of London. There Peake makes a precarious living by displaying his deformities as 'the Cripplegate Monster' and reciting his poetry. Peake is maimed mentally as well as physically:

> The world still knew him for a monster. However fresh the springs of the spirit within him, this could not be overcome, for this, his body, in the eyes of the world was his nature; and glimpsing this, in his bitterness and spite, he had jettisoned his humanity and embraced the monster.

Embracing the monster leads him into drink and to an act of drunken sexual violence which drives his daughter away from him, first to the asylum of an English nobleman's family home and then to relatives in America. The colonies are about to break out in revolution and Martha is drawn into the rebellion. She remains, however, unable to escape her past, which returns to haunt the decisions she has to make about her new life. Once again McGrath uses an elaborate narrative structure to tell his tale. Harry and Martha Peake's story emerges through the deathbed confessions of a man relating it fifty years later to his nephew. The nephew, another of McGrath's unreliable narrators, withholds information from the reader until a final revelation of the Peakes' fate. *Martha Peake* is an exceptionally clever piece of storytelling which appropriates clichés of genre fiction and echoes of eighteenth- and nineteenth-century classics and puts them to McGrath's own uses. Employing ironies and knowing anachronisms that mark it as 'post-modern', it also succeeds as an enthralling adventure story and psychological drama.

Patrick McGrath's most recent novel, *Port Mungo* (2004), is a story of sibling obsession and the importunate demands of creativity that stretches across decades and ranges in setting from Glasgow and London to the West Indies and to the swamp-surrounded town in Honduras that gives the book its title. The luxuriant decaying ambience of Port Mungo is an ideal setting for McGrath's imagination, and his story of a painter and his chaotic relationships, told from the perspective of his adoring sister, moves towards a characteristically dark conclusion. In his six novels, different though they are, McGrath has created an instantly recognisable world, peopled by disturbed (and disturbing) characters forever teetering on the edge of breakdown and psychosis. All of his books emphasise their status as works of fiction – they make little pretence at any form of conventional realism – but they all work simply as gripping narratives.

McGrath's major works

Blood and Water and Other Tales, Penguin, 1989 (short stories).
The Grotesque, Viking, 1989.
Spider, Viking, 1990.
Dr Haggard's Disease, Viking, 1993.
Asylum, Viking, 1996.
Martha Peake, Viking, 2000.
Port Mungo, Bloomsbury, 2004.

SHENA MACKAY (born 1944)

Shena Mackay began publishing her fiction in the 1960s – the two novellas *Dust Falls on Eugene Schlumburger* and *Toddler on the Run* were written when she was a teenager and published together in 1964 – but she had a long period (more than a decade) when she was unable to get her work published and it was only in the 1980s and 1990s that she was finally recognised as one of the country's sharpest and funniest comic novelists. She combines a keen social observation of everyday life, most often in suburban London, with an eye for the absurd and an appreciation for the eccentric and those who march to the sound of a different drum. Her characterisation of women struggling to raise families in difficult circumstances, hindered rather than helped by feckless, occasionally threatening men, is particularly sympathetic.

Shena Mackay was born in Edinburgh in 1944 and left school at the age of sixteen, already intent on a career as a writer after winning a poetry competition in the *Daily Mirror*. After the two novellas published in 1964, she wrote three novels which marry kitchen-sink realism, of the kind familiar in fiction of the 1960s, with a less easily classifiable, offbeat quirkiness. *The Music Upstairs* (1965) is set in London's Earl's Court in the early 1960s and explores the friendship between two young women sharing a bedsit. *Old Crow* (1967) takes place in an English village in the late 1950s and is a quietly chilling tale of rural malice and small-mindedness. When the central character has an illegitimate child, a gathering campaign against her begun by a mean-spirited widow in the village escalates into a witch-hunt. Both have much in common with other fiction of the period – with Margaret Forster's early novels, say, or even more overtly 'working-class' narratives like Nell Dunn's *Up the Junction* – but there is also an unapologetic oddity to Mackay's early books, an unwillingness to pander to the expectations of readers which is best seen in *An Advent Calendar* (1971). This is a story with a constant undercurrent of menace and black humour which begins with a fingertip disappearing into a butcher's mincer, to be included in the parcel of meat which the central character takes home to his uncle. As the story progresses, the mundane constantly transmutes into the macabre, apparently ordinary Londoners harbour obsessions and oddities and everyday 'normality' seems a shifting and unreliable façade. In Mackay's early fiction happiness and security are merely provisional and everyone is like the troubled couple John and Marguerite as they come together to celebrate Christmas – 'carousing on a sandbank in time, music and laughter, forks and glasses drowning the sound of tomorrow's tide'.

It would seem that Mackay's fiction was too difficult to classify and too distinctive for the time. For twelve years after the publication of *An Advent Calendar* she was able to publish nothing until a collection of short stories, *Babies in Rhinestones*, appeared in 1983. (Mackay has always been an adept exponent of the art of the short story. Penguin published her *Collected Stories* in 1994 and a more recent collection, *The World's Smallest Unicorn and Other Stories*, appeared in 1999.) A novel, *A Bowl of Cherries*, was published by Harvester Press in 1984, largely on the recommendation of Iris Murdoch, an admirer of Mackay's work. It was followed in 1986 by *Redhill Rococo*. These two novels, together with the short stories collected in *Babies in Rhinestones* (1983) and, later, *Dreams of Dead Women's Handbags* (1987), brought Mackay a renewed reputation as a laconic chronicler of the ups and downs of a certain kind of semi-seedy suburban life, of those caught, like Pearl Slattery in *Redhill Rococo*, 'between respectability and ruin'.

A Bowl of Cherries focuses on twin brothers – Rex, an egotistical writer turning out successful detective stories in partnership with his wife Daphne, and Stanley, a poet whose work is so unsuccessful that he is forced to earn money washing dishes. Rex and Daphne's daughter Daisy, overweight and miserable, has married estate agent Julian, a petty domestic tyrant and pathetically shameless social climber. ('Surely...you must realise that I've moved out of the stew and dumplings bracket', he tells his mother when she has the misfortune to present him with too proletarian a meal.) Rex's illegitimate son, Seamus, accidentally coming to know his half-sister, is the catalyst for the revelation of family secrets that affect all their lives. In *Redhill Rococo* Pearl Slattery is struggling with the cards fate has dealt her – husband in jail, children with no respect for her, a dead-end affair with her boss in her dead-end job – when a lodger moves in to her chaotic household and turns everything on its head by falling in love with her.

Dunedin (1992) takes place largely on Mackay's familiar home territory of modern South London but is also an ambitious attempt to extend the scope and range, geographical and historical, of her fiction. The title refers both to the name of a house and to the town in New Zealand which is the scene of the two framing chapters of the story. These two chapters are set in the Edwardian era and focus on Jack Mackenzie, a tyrannical and unsaintly Presbyterian minister who has been posted, together with his family, to the Antipodes. Mackenzie's sins and selfishness not only affect his own life and those of his family but echo down the decades. The main part of the novel explores the lives of Mackenzie's grandchildren, William and Olive, who still labour under the emotional legacy he has passed on. Brother and sister, both unhappy and guilt-ridden, reluctantly share a house. Another of Mackenzie's grandchildren, descendant of an exploitative extramarital relationship, arrives in Britain in search of answers to his own questions. Told in Mackay's characteristically barbed, often very funny prose, *Dunedin* tells a story of lives in which angst and anger lurk menacingly beneath mundane surfaces.

With *The Orchard on Fire* (1995), which was shortlisted for the Booker Prize, Mackay's fiction seemed at last to have moved into the mainstream and to have gained the kind of widespread recognition it deserves. The novel opens in the present day but soon takes its central character, April Harlency, back into the past. In 1953 eight-year-old April's parents escape from their gloomy Streatham pub to take over the running of the Copper Kettle tea rooms in a small village in Kent. When April meets Ruby they become best friends, forming an exclusive alliance against the rest of the world. They create their own refuge in the orchard of the title; they write letters to one another in invisible ink and call to each other using secret signals. Part of the novel is an almost idyllic and beautifully exact reconstruction of a 1950s childhood but there are plenty of serpents in this particular Eden. Ruby is the victim of physical abuse from her boorish father. One of the villagers, an apparently perfect gentleman called Mr Greenidge, inveigles April into an unhealthy and unwelcome physical relationship, soliciting kisses and embraces from the embarrassed and puzzled child. The adult April, looking back on this year, is still alone and mourning the passing of her friendship with Ruby. Unsentimentally touching in its creation of a child character half-glimpsing or misinterpreting the adult world around her, *The Orchard on Fire* remains one of Mackay's best books.

It was followed by *The Artist's Widow* (1998), in which she turns her beadily satirical gaze on the contemporary London art world. The book opens on a sweltering summer evening in Mayfair where the cognoscenti are gathered for the private view of the 'Last Paintings' of John Crane. Crane's elderly widow Lyris watches the evening unfold with a mildly jaundiced eye. Her great-nephew Nathan, a budding conceptual artist with an eye for the main chance, is at his most boorish and primarily interested in the charms of a statuesque filmmaker called Zoe. Her next-door neighbours are uncomfortable amidst the superficial hypocrisies of the art world. Bookseller Clovis drifts amiably but aimlessly through the party as he does through life. The reader follows the characters introduced in the opening scene at the private view through one summer in the 1990s. Little dramatic occurs in the novel – Nathan attempts to cozen money from his great-aunt, Zoe tries to recruit her for a film about overlooked women artists, Clovis finds his ex-wife a continuing source of tension and Lyris becomes surprisingly close to one of Nathan's former girlfriends – but Mackay's keen ear for the undercurrents of apparently idle conversation and her ability to capture petty foibles in a few taut acerbic phrases are in evidence throughout.

Mackay's next, and most recent, novel, *Heligoland* (2003), carries echoes of *The Artist's Widow* – Lyris Crane and the egregious Nathan make guest appearances as peripheral characters, for example – and also takes a satirical, offbeat look at genteelly cultured, elderly people struggling with the encroachments of an unsympathetic modern world and at those who feel themselves at odds with contemporary London. The central character is fifty-something Rowena Snow, one of life's perpetual orphans, who has never found her place in the world. Searching for a private sanctuary of contentment, 'a hazy, faraway, indefinable place of solace and reunion' – Heligoland, named in the radio broadcasts of her childhood, has come to represent this – she arrives as a housekeeper at the Nautilus, a 1930s artists' colony built in the shape of a spiral shell. Only two of the original artists survive – Celeste, widow of the Nautilus's architect, and Francis, a minor poet clinging querulously to what little reputation he retains – but Rowena finally feels, however tentatively, that she has found a home. As in so many of Mackay's books, the plot is secondary to the pleasures of the prose. Mackay has always shown a striking ability to evoke moments of everyday epiphany, the usually fleeting instants when ordinary people, weighed down by the mundane, are nonetheless surprised by joy, and Rowena's acknowledgement at the end of the novel that, 'for the first time, the tantalising flashes of colour on the edges of her memory...seem within her grasp' is very moving.

Mackay's fiction, ever since her precocious debut in the 1960s, has resisted easy categorisation. From that early beginning she has written in a comic prose that has always been unique, rooted in a gift for the unexpected simile, the offbeat observation and the upsetting of the reader's expectations. In her novels of the last ten years she has allied that comic talent to an unsentimental but touching ability to shine a fictional light on characters who are powerless, marginalised or unhappy and to give their lives a value and significance other novelists bestow on the more overtly 'interesting'. Novels like *The Orchard on Fire* and *Heligoland* are not filled with flamboyant or glamorous people, leading frenetically exciting existences, but Mackay's sympathetic, ironic attention to her characters gives the books a place amongst the most rewarding fiction of the 1990s.

Mackay's major works

Dust Falls on Eugene Schlumburger/Toddler on the Run, Andre Deutsch, 1964.

Music Upstairs, Andre Deutsch, 1965.
Old Crow, Cape, 1967.
An Advent Calendar, Cape, 1971.
Babies in Rhinestones and Other Stories, Heinemann, 1983 (short stories).
A Bowl of Cherries, Harvester, 1984.
Redhill Rococo, Heinemann, 1986.
Dreams of Dead Women's Handbags, Heinemann, 1987 (short stories).
Dunedin, Heinemann, 1992.
The Laughing Academy, Heinemann, 1993 (short stories).
Collected Stories, Penguin, 1994 (short stories).
The Orchard on Fire, Heinemann, 1995.
The Artist's Widow, Cape, 1998.
The World's Smallest Unicorn and Other Stories, Cape, 1999 (short stories).
Heligoland, Cape, 2003.

HILARY MANTEL (born 1952)

Author of both historical and contemporary novels, Hilary Mantel is a writer who eludes pigeonholing or easy definition. She has written books that examine inequalities of class, race and gender in South Africa (*A Change of Climate*) and in Saudi Arabia (*Eight Months on Ghazzah Street*). She has written a sweeping, rather old-fashioned novel about the French Revolution (*A Place of Greater Safety*) and a strange, haunting parable of religion and possible redemption (*Fludd*) that would not look too out of place in the collected works of Muriel Spark. Whatever she writes, Mantel brings to it a unique sensibility, a strange combination of compassion and often blackly detached humour, and a memorably precise prose style.

Hilary Mantel was born in Glossop in 1952 and educated at a convent school in Cheshire before going on to study Law at the London School of Economics and Sheffield University. After university she worked briefly as a social worker in a geriatric hospital, experience which she used in her novels *Every Day Is Mother's Day* and *Vacant Possession*. In 1977 she went to live in Bostwana with her geologist husband, and stayed there five years. In 1982 they moved to Jeddah (the setting for her novel *Eight Months on Ghazzah Street*), where they lived for four years. Mantel returned to the UK in 1986, a year after her first novel was published. She has since become one of the most respected of contemporary novelists, winner of several major prizes and admired for her versatility and acuity.

Mantel's first novel, *Every Day Is Mother's Day* (1985) told of the claustrophobic relationship between an apparently retarded girl, Muriel Axon, and her mother Evelyn, a widowed spiritualist. After a series of bureaucratic failures the Axons are left without a social worker. Muriel becomes pregnant and gives birth without anyone knowing. Colin Sidney, the son of the Axons' next-door neighbour becomes engaged in a sordid affair with Isabel, social worker to his own aged mother and later to the Axons. As a mordant commentary on 1970s England, blackly comic and unforgiving in its portrayal of its characters, *Every Day Is Mother's Day* is a remarkable first novel and announced the arrival of a writer who could skewer human pretensions and failings with a single sentence or phrase. Mantel followed it with a sequel, *Vacant Possession* (1986), which picks up the story ten years later. At the end of *Every Day Is Mother's Day* Muriel Axon is shunted into an institution after her mother's death. In *Vacant Possession* she emerges from the institution and reappears in the lives of the other characters from the first novel, although most do not recognise who she is. As in the first book, dark comedy and ironies abound in the weird merry-go-round that Mantel inflicts on her characters.

Her next novel was a very different one. Drawing on Mantel's own experience of living in Saudi Arabia, *Eight Months on Ghazzah Street* (1988) is her most overtly political novel, filled with a sense of outrage at the Saudi social system and Western willingness, for financial reasons, to turn a blind eye to its human rights abuses. Frances, a cartographer, joins Andrew, her engineer husband, in Jeddah. Bored with the constricted life that is all she can have, Frances begins to speculate on the goings-on in the supposedly vacant flat upstairs. Mantel captures both the claustrophobia of Frances's world, confined almost entirely to the couple's flat, and the draconian restrictions under which Saudi women are forced to live. Slowly, and with great control and skill, she ratchets up the tension and suspense as Frances's boredom turns into the realisation that something more sinister than she first believed is taking place.

In interviews Mantel has acknowledged the influence of Muriel Spark, and *Fludd* (1989) is the novel which most clearly demonstrates it, yet it also has a quirky individuality which is entirely Mantel's own. The novel is set in the grim, claustrophobic mill village of Fetherhoughton in the North of England in 1956. Father Angwin, the village priest, has lost his faith. Hoping to rid himself of Angwin, the bishop has told him that a curate is to be despatched to help put into practice the bishop's modernisation plans. When Fludd (named after the seventeenth-century alchemist Robert Fludd) appears suddenly one evening, he's assumed to be the curate. Fludd proceeds to transform the village, breaking down rivalries and bringing the quarrelling inhabitants of Fetherhoughton to an understanding of their humanity, albeit by unconventional means: flustering the local convent's nuns; arousing the passion of Sister Philomena; and provoking Father Angwin into a fit of self-examination while remaining seemingly unmoved himself.

A Place of Greater Safety (1992) is set during the French Revolution and has the revolutionary leaders Danton, Robespierre and Camille Desmoulins as its central characters. Mantel blends fact with fiction to reconstruct the three lawyers' early lives, following them from the provinces to Paris, through the heady days of the early Revolution, the intricate political manoeuvrings and the Terror to their eventual deaths on the guillotine. *A Place of Greater Safety* is a large-scale (nearly 900 pages) and ambitious novel which doesn't always succeed. There is a danger in trying to fictionalise such very well-known historical events as those of the French Revolution – that the fiction won't always match the historical accounts that already exist and will thus appear slightly superfluous. Mantel doesn't always avoid the danger but, switching the narrative focus rapidly from one character to another, she does succeed in conveying the electric excitement and sense of potential that fuelled the Revolution, and her portrait of the complicated, triangular relationship between her three main figures is entirely convincing.

A Change of Climate (1994) is the story of Ralph and Anna Eldred, a couple who are forced to face up to a long-buried tragedy. The narrative switches back and forth between 1980s East Anglia, where the Eldreds run a charitable trust for young offenders, and 1960s South Africa, where they were activists against apartheid. A thorn in the South African government's side, the Eldreds are sent to Bechuanaland (now Botswana, where Mantel lived for five years) and it is here that tragedy overtakes them – their son is abducted and his body never found. Mantel sharply portrays the injustices, miseries and complexities of the apartheid system but the real strength of the novel lies in its unflinching and unsentimental acknowledgement of the power that memory has to haunt and disfigure the present. The Eldreds are 'good' people and remain incapable of fully confronting the 'evil' that was done to them. The loss of their child is the dark and unmentionable shadow that hangs over the life of the family and it returns to unleash new and cathartic emotions.

Mantel's often bleak awareness of the gap between what might be and what is is also evident in *An Experiment in Love* (1995). The novel is told, in effect, as a sequence of prolonged flashbacks as Carmel McBain returns to her university days in London in the early 1970s with friends Karina and Julianne and to their schooldays in a North of England convent school. The experiment in love of the title consists not so much of the first adventures in sex and relationships that the women essay but of the complicated, interdependent bonds that tie the three of them – all very different characters – together. Unsurprisingly in a novel by Hilary Mantel, the bonds are not able to withstand the onslaught of time and circumstances. The experiment is, finally, a failure and the narrative moves towards a characteristically dark, even shocking conclusion.

With *The Giant, O'Brien* (1998) Mantel returned to the historical novel, although this obliquely told fiction could hardly be more different to the expansive sweep of *A Place of Greater Safety.* Set in Ireland and London in the 1780s, and drawing knowingly on the conventions of Gothic fiction, the book is based on the true story of the eponymous giant Charles O'Brien, rapidly growing out of his own skeleton, who leaves Ireland to make his fortune as a sideshow attraction in London, taking a motley band of followers with him. Alternating with O'Brien's narrative is that of the obsessed Scottish doctor/anatomist Dr Hunter, who is determined to add the giant to his collection of human oddities. The conflict between the scientific rationalism and determination to master the secrets of nature represented by Hunter and the imaginative, romantic interpretation of the world that emerges from O'Brien's storytelling and mythmaking can sometimes be overly schematic, but the prose in which Mantel tells her story – as so often in her books – is memorably distinctive and evocative.

With eight novels to her credit, Mantel has shown herself to be one of the most original novelists of the last twenty years, and her latest book *Giving Up the Ghost* (2003) shows that she has lost none of her commitment to variety and ringing the changes in form and genre. It mingles fiction and non-fiction into an autobiography taking readers from early childhood through to the discoveries of adulthood. A series of short stories about growing up, clearly related to her own upbringing, is followed by more directly autobiographical material which investigates the ghosts that have haunted her and have led to the fiction that attempts to exorcise them.

Mantel's major works

Every Day Is Mother's Day, Chatto & Windus, 1985.
Vacant Possession, Chatto & Windus, 1986.
Eight Months on Ghazzah Street, Viking, 1988.
Fludd, Viking, 1989.

A Place of Greater Safety, Viking, 1992.
A Change of Climate, Viking, 1994.
An Experiment in Love, Viking, 1995.
The Giant, O'Brien, Fourth Estate, 1998.
Giving Up the Ghost: A Memoir, Fourth Estate, 2003.
Learning to Talk: Short Stories, Fourth Estate, 2003 (short stories).

TIMOTHY MO (born 1950)

Timothy Mo was born in Hong Kong in 1950 to an English mother and a Chinese father and his family moved to England when he was ten years old. Mo attended Mill Hill School and went on to study history at St John's College, Oxford. After graduating, he worked as a journalist on a variety of magazines, including the *Times Education Supplement*, *New Statesman* and *Boxing News*, before publishing his first novel *The Monkey King* in 1978. His novels explore archetypal themes of post-colonial fiction – globalisation, decolonisation, migrancy and cultural hybridity – with a wry humour, scabrous wit and often biting satire. Like Salman Rushdie, he is preoccupied with the displaced and the exiled and his characters are usually those of mixed Asian race who find themselves in societies that are not their own. Three times shortlisted for the Booker Prize, this writer who writes about outsiders has for the last ten years exiled himself from the literary scene that originally embraced him. He now lives mostly in the Philippines, and publishes his books under his own Paddleless Press imprint.

The Monkey King is a wry comedy of manners set in post-war Hong Kong. The main character is Wallace Nolasco, a part Portuguese, part Chinese man from Macao who marries into an affluent Chinese family, the Poons. He lives with his in-laws and has to suffer their rules and endure hectoring from the tight-fisted patriarch Mr Poon (a character modelled on Mo's own grandfather – 'the only person I ever put absolutely from life in a novel', as he once described him). Nolasco tries various ways of wrestling free from Poon's control. He attempts to get his new nephews on his side and later steals Mr Poon's prized watch, pawning it for cash. No matter how blatant his rebellion becomes, he's plagued by guilt and, it is finally clear, has become just as bound to the family and its honour as the Poons are, but simply in different ways. Widely compared to early Naipaul, *The Monkey King*, so-called because of an ongoing allusion to the classic Chinese stories of the mischievous trickster hero 'Monkey', is subtly ironic in the way it pokes fun at families and mocks the cultural and racial snobbery of the Chinese, Macao, British and even Indian inhabitants of Hong Kong.

Mo's second novel, *Sour Sweet*, shortlisted for the Booker Prize in 1982, is another ironic tale of cultural misunderstandings but this time the subject is the plight of a Chinese immigrant family struggling to make a living in London during the 1960s. Chen, his wife Lily, young son Man Kee and his wife's sister Mui live in NW9. Chen works in a Chinese restaurant in Gerrard Street, Soho, the Ho Ho (Excellence). Mo makes great comic play with cultural misinterpretation and incomprehension on both sides. (Chen is bemused by the restaurant's English patrons and their curious habit of stirring all the food together and drowning it in soy sauce. Lily later believes the terrapin at her son's school is an instrument of discipline – a terror pin.) But there is a darker reality to *Sour Sweet* than to Mo's first novel. When Chen needs money to help his father with legal and medical fees at home in Hong Kong, a colleague takes him gambling and later arranges a deal with the dubious triads, who rustle up some cash and organise a sanatorium for the old man.

Chen is soon out of his depth and, wanting to be out of sight and mind, he lets Lily and Mui persuade him to set up a restaurant of their own in darkest South London. Called the Dah Ling, after the girls' native village (which causes much amusement to the customers), the restaurant becomes a success. This, however, only attracts the renewed attention of the triads. Chen disappears. The book comes to an open-ended conclusion, with the reader left to make interpretations that Mo makes no attempt to impose. Mui marries and she and her new husband set up a fish and chip shop. Lily seems resigned to her fate – a small amount of cash arrives every month from Amsterdam, which she concludes is from Chen, who has been dragged into the drug trade there by the triads – and she settles on looking after her son, now succeeding at school but also taking lessons in Chinese. *Sour Sweet* tackles weighty themes of assimilation, identity and organised crime without ever losing a surprisingly light touch.

With his third and fourth novels, *An Insular Possession* (1986) and *The Redundancy of Courage* (1991), Mo moved from the smaller scale to the larger canvas with epic stories of imperialism in the Far East, the interaction of East and West and the long-term fall-out from historical events. Mo has been quoted as saying that he 'was not prepared to be kept in a box as the author of quaint ethnic vignettes', and these two novels show his determination to avoid the stereotyping that he felt was being imposed on him. Set in the 1830s and 1840s, during the First Opium War and the founding of the British colony at Hong

Kong, *An Insular Possession* views the march of history from the slightly off-centre perspectives of two American traders, Gideon Chase and Walter Eastman. Filled with a large cast of characters, the book echoes the narrative values of old-fashioned historical fiction while subverting the moral and political assumptions on which that fiction is built.

Shortlisted for the Booker Prize in 1991, *The Redundancy of Courage* is in many ways the pivotal novel in Mo's career so far. It is the first of his books to be narrated in the first person. It is the first of his books to take an angry, polemical stance towards the politics and corruption of contemporary Asia while simultaneously celebrating the richness, abundance and vitality of the Far East. Its publication marked the beginning of Mo's increasingly jaundiced view of the limitations and lack of ambition he saw in British publishing and British fiction. The book chronicles the guerrilla struggle in a fictionalised East Timor, reinvented as the island of Danu, north of Australia, invaded by the 'Malai' from the surrounding archipelago. The story, which opens on the day of the invasion, is told by Adolph Ng, a Chinese-Danuese hotel owner, whose sense of self-preservation guides him through what becomes a tangled web of changing allegiances, betrayals and battles. An archetypal survivor, Ng embodies the truth encapsulated in the title — that in any contemporary political upheaval the ancient value of courage has become redundant, an irrelevance in an increasingly impersonal world.

Mo's latest two novels have both been set primarily in the Philippines — where he himself now lives — and, like their predecessors, revel in a large canvas, a wide-ranging, multi-ethnic dramatis personae and the desire to put the macrocosmic conflicts of modern politics as well as the microcosmic dramas of individuals on the page. *Brownout on Breadfruit Boulevard* (1995) is perhaps the most controversial of Mo's novels. It was self-published by his own Paddleless Press imprint after arguments about advances and demands for editorial cuts with his regular publisher led to an irreconcilable split. A vivid and often very funny portrait of the melting pot of Philippine society, it opens with a truly Swiftian, scatological moment — the sinister Professor Pfeidwengeler is exhorting a prostitute, Sunshine, to defecate on his stomach — and the same, no-holds-barred satire characterises the rest of the book. Politics — academic, sexual and social as well as international — animates the wide cast of characters who bring to life Mo's neon-lit vision of Manila as a battleground between East and West. Moving from the Philippine capital to Macau and further afield to Japan and New York, the plot is as hyperactive and charged as many of its characters.

'I was just too weird a mouthful . . . I guess I made the shortlist a lot more interesting but I was never gonna make the final cut.' Rey, the narrator of Mo's most recent novel, *Renegade or Halo2* (1999), is referring to his failure to be admitted to the priesthood, but construing this remark as an authorial aside about his own position in the literary world seems appropriate enough. Renegade Rey is Rey Archimedes Blondel Castro, a.k.a. Sugar, an illegitimate half-American, half-Filipino 'nigger', and the story he relates is a multicultural, multilayered one. Halo2, pronounced 'hallow-hallow', is a dessert made of incompatible ingredients that prove surprisingly delicious in combination, a suitable metaphor for the mixed cast list of the book. The novel is peopled with refugees, outcasts, racial hallow-hallows, legal and illegal immigrants, *Gastarbeiter*, boat people – the hotchpotch of humanity that makes up the marginal population of most post-colonial cities. As the plot zigzags between delight and disaster, *Renegade or Halo2* becomes a celebration of the vitality that Mo sees in the worlds he has chosen to portray in his fiction over the last decade.

Mo's major works

The Monkey King, Andre Deutsch, 1978.
Sour Sweet, Andre Deutsch, 1982.
An Insular Possession, Chatto & Windus, 1986.
The Redundancy of Courage, Chatto & Windus, 1991.
Brownout on Breadfruit Boulevard, Paddleless Press, 1995.
Renegade or Halo2, Paddleless Press, 1999.

JULIE MYERSON (born 1960)

Few novelists in the period since the early 1990s have written about damaged lives and destructive, often obsessive relationships with the same mixture of intensity and psychological insight as Julie Myerson. Her five novels have all been very different and varied but they have all shared a mercilessly close and unflinching observation of love-starved lives and the lengths to which people will go to escape the power of their pasts and embrace their ideas of what their futures might be. Many of Myerson's characters are haunted by what has happened to them and, indeed, the supernatural lurks in the shadows of much of her fiction. Apparitions and ghosts cross her pages, spooks that might be real or might only be projections of the characters' emotions and states of mind.

Born in Nottingham in 1960, Julie Myerson studied at Bristol University and then worked as a publicist in publishing and in the theatre before her first novel, *Sleepwalking*, was published in 1994. Since then Myerson has published four more novels and has become a regular reviewer, arts journalist and broadcaster. With her partner, the writer and drama producer Jonathan Myerson, and their three children, she lives in London.

Sleepwalking's central character, Susan, is the first of the unhappy women, traumatised by their pasts and by their emotional history, who inhabit the pages of Myerson's fiction. In the last months of pregnancy Susan feels distanced and remote from her husband and from everyone else around her. Metaphorically sleepwalking through her life – the metaphor is later seen to reflect reality in the life of another character – Susan suffers still from the damage inflicted on her by her upbringing. She is haunted, emotionally and mentally, by her past relationship with her father, a petty sadist and domestic tyrant, and, after his suicide, reality again overwhelms metaphor when he appears as a ghost – the ghost of his forlorn boyhood. He, in his turn, has been damaged by his mother, Susan's grandmother Queenie. In Myerson's fiction man very definitely hands on misery to man, and the complex relationships between the characters in *Sleepwalking*, their family links subtly revealed as the narrative unfolds, are her first examples of intergenerational unhappiness. The blossoming sense of possibility briefly embodied in the love between Susan and the artist Lenny seems perfunctorily described but the ongoing traumas of Susan's family are brought very powerfully to life.

Two further novels exploring dysfunctional lives and damaged relationships followed. *The Touch* (1996) approaches the mysteries of religious faith and the potential limits of scepticism through the story of Frank, a charismatic down-and-out who enters the lives of two sisters. Mugged in a London park, Frank is rescued by the sisters and taken to hospital, an act of charity that rebounds on them. The younger of the two sisters, Donna, suffers from disabling pain that has shaped her life and those of her lover, Will, and her sister, Gayle. Frank appears to hold the key to healing her, his unsophisticated faith the source of the cure he offers. Paradoxically, Donna's new lease of life takes her further away from Will rather than closer. The hidden attraction between him and Gayle becomes clear and Frank once again acts as catalyst for a change in the interlinked relationships. *The Touch* plays with all the ambiguous meanings present in its title. Frank's touch heals Donna but is he 'touched' by God or 'touched' by insanity? Does he think of the three young people as an 'easy touch'? How emotionally 'touching' are the assorted relationships into which the novel's characters fall?

In *Me and the Fat Man* (1998) the central character, Amy, is another of Myerson's twenty-something emotional sleepwalkers. Married but remote from her husband, she seeks erotic thrills through brief, anonymous encounters that simultaneously excite and repel her. Her childhood and her mother, drowned when Amy was six, are vague memories, disturbing ripples beneath the surface of her life. When she meets a mysterious man called Harris who claims to remember her mother, she is intrigued and prepared to accept much from him, even the unsettling way in which he pushes her towards a sexual relationship with another of his younger protégés, the fat man of the title. Surprisingly, Amy and fat man Gary become true lovers, but secrets from the past still need to be unearthed and, for both of them, they involve Harris, the Greek island where Amy's mother died and the deadening power of unacknowledged memories. Both *The Touch* and *Me and the Fat Man* move the reader expertly towards narrative revelations and tell slightly outlandish stories which echo fable or fairy tale (the outsider-magus with mysterious powers, the dispossessed orphan with a hidden past) in the prose of social realism.

Many recent novelists, from genre crime writers to Sarah Waters, have turned to the Victorian era for setting and characters. In the past decade few have looked back with such an absence of nostalgia and such an unblinkered freedom from the clichés of costume drama and the heritage industry as Myerson does in her fourth novel, *Laura Blundy* (2000). As the novel opens and we meet the eponymous central character, she has just killed her husband, beating him to death. It's a bloody death and the disabled Laura has used every weapon that comes to hand: 'In the end I use my crutches as well. I don't stop till he's down and twitching, till he's stopped shouting and screaming, till he's down'. She and her much younger lover, a sewer labourer called Billy, work to dispose of the body, and the novel moves back, in a series of interwoven flashbacks, through Laura Blundy's personal history. The past life revealed could have come straight from the pages of a period melodrama – the fall from rich upbringing into sudden destitution, the brutish life on the streets, the disfiguring accident, the unlikely redeemer in the shape of the surgeon who operates on her, the passion for the younger Billy – yet Myerson's skill lies in the way she transmutes this material into a story that has the ring of emotional and psychological truth. Told in Laura's own voice, the novel is unsqueamish in the way it displays, even revels in, the physical horrors it describes. The dismemberment of Laura's husband, the sinking of the parts in the river, the continued floating of the head and its eventual burning in a bonfire – these are all shown to the reader in a prose that is a strange mixture of clinical detachment and grisly relish. Both Gothic horror story (complete with a devastating surprise revelation in its final pages) and acute psychological drama, *Laura Blundy* shows the sophisticated authorial control that Myerson has learnt to exert over her material.

So too did her next novel, the very different *Something Might Happen* (2003), which centres on the impact a seemingly random murder has on a small Suffolk seaside town. The victim is a young mother, Lennie. From the outset Myerson underlines the contrast between the brutality of the crime and its setting. 'This town really is a safe place', the narrator comments, 'everyone knows that. Even in winter, even after dark, it's a place where, once kids know how to cross a road sensibly, they can pretty much go around alone'. This narrator and the focus of the novel is Lennie's friend and neighbour Tess. The unfolding of the narrative reveals the extent to which no town is really 'safe', no life as mundane as it might appear superficially. Tess's own marriage has long been less idyllic than it appears, overshadowed by the gulf of communication between her and her husband. She is drawn into an affair with the stolidly reassuring Ted Lacey, a family liaison officer who comes to the town after the murder.

Something Might Happen has many of the stylistic characteristics of Myerson's earlier work: evocative and lyrical prose used to describe both the everyday and the grotesque; the intrusion of the supernatural when two of Tess's children claim to have seen Lennie's ghost. It also draws on the conventions of certain types of crime fiction – the workaday routines of the standard police procedural, the emphasis on individual psychology shown by writers like Nicci French and Minette Walters. Yet the emphasis in Myerson's work is not of the kind that would exist in a genre novel. There is no move towards a solution to the crime and no sense that a revelation about the identity of the murderer would provide narrative closure and an effective denouement. (Indeed the crime is never explicitly solved.) Myerson's interest is in the psychological impact of abnormal events on the unfolding of everyday life, and the murder provides the most effective example of the abnormal erupting into normality.

The title of Myerson's most recent novel could stand as a description of all her fiction. In the world that she creates something might indeed happen and that something is likely to be unpleasant. Myerson excels in the depiction of the frailty and fragility of the everyday. Behind the façades of ordinary lives ghosts of all kinds lurk, and Myerson's particular skill lies in the way she gradually brings these to the surface.

Myerson's major works

Sleepwalking, Picador, 1994.
The Touch, Picador, 1996.
Me and the Fat Man, Fourth Estate, 1998.
Laura Blundy, Fourth Estate, 2000.
Something Might Happen, Cape, 2003.
Home, HarperCollins, 2004 (memoir).

LAWRENCE NORFOLK (born 1963)

Norfolk has written only three novels in his career so far, but his first, *Lemprière's Dictionary*, was sufficiently startling in its assurance and originality to win him a place on the 1993 *Granta* list of Best Young British Novelists and all have marked him out as one of the most restlessly inventive writers of his generation. *Lemprière's Dictionary* (1991) and Norfolk's second novel, *The Pope's Rhinoceros* (1996), are reminiscent of Umberto Eco's fiction in the way in which they present the reader with a big, baggy amalgam of history, mythology and tall tales. The two books are filled with a kind of half-deranged erudition that is both genuine and tongue in cheek. When Norfolk insists, as he has done in interviews, that, for instance, 'all the weather is accurate in *Lemprière's Dictionary*' and that he scoured ship's records and contemporary newspapers to determine whether or not it was raining on any given day in his narrative, are we to believe him? Or are we to accept his equally mischievous remark, also made in several interviews, that everything that appears plausible in the book is invented and that everything that seems unlikely is historically accurate? The result, if not always the intent, is to break down the barriers between narrative as history and narrative as fiction.

Some novelists want to pare the language and the events of their narratives down to the bare essentials. Norfolk stands at the opposite pole, as *Lemprière's Dictionary* clearly demonstrated. This is a book that is crammed to overflowing with action, characters, description, colour and life. The novel is, ostensibly, the story of the eighteenth-century classical scholar John Lemprière, author of a dictionary of classical literature and the classical world that was for a long time a standard work. However, Norfolk creates an imaginary life for Lemprière, blending historical reality, classical allusions, fantasy and improbable conspiracy theories into a huge fictional extravaganza. Stories from ancient mythology jostle for the reader's attention with rich evocations of the street life of Georgian London; Lemprière's Huguenot ancestry is shown to have strange connections with the rise to wealth and power of the East India Company; pirates, plotters, assassins and revolutionaries stalk the book's pages. Zigzagging back and forth through the centuries, Norfolk produces one of the more overwhelming debut novels of recent years.

The Pope's Rhinoceros is set in the sixteenth century. A new world has been discovered in the west and two great maritime powers – Spain and Portugal – are competing to gain a monopoly of its riches. In Rome the pope holds the key to the division of the spoils. The pope is Leo X, a man with an obsessive interest in the collection of marvels and prodigies from around a world that is rapidly expanding as Europeans journey into the unknown territory of other continents. He has an elephant but he has read of even stranger beasts in classical literature. Representatives of Spain and Portugal enter a race to provide the pope with what he wants. The book's heroes are two archetypally picaresque characters, Salvestro and Bernardo. Together Salvestro and Bernardo have tramped the length and breadth of a Europe disintegrating into bloody chaos under the impact of new religious ideas before they are duped into heading for West Africa to evade the trouble that seems to seek them out in Rome. Norfolk's novel is, however, a book that, like *Lemprière's Dictionary*, defies précis. The search for the 'Beast' (never actually named as a rhinoceros except in the book's title) is the hook upon which Norfolk can hang his stories within stories, his digressions, his weirdly offbeat knowledge. The religious wars that were ravaging Europe at the time, the existence of a Baltic Atlantis known as Vineta, the thought processes of herring, conspiracies at the papal court, the Medici family – all find a place in Norfolk's flamboyant, generous book.

His third novel, *In the Shape of a Boar* (2000), begins with Norfolk's retelling of a story from Greek mythology. The goddess Artemis, slighted by the country's ruler, has sent a boar 'of surpassing size and ferocity' to ravage the kingdom of Kalydon and terrorise its inhabitants. A band of heroes – plus the virgin huntress Atalanta – gathers to hunt down the boar and free the country from its reign of terror. Norfolk's enigmatic, allusive account of the hunt is accompanied by lengthy, erudite footnotes which cite an enormous range of classical sources to question and undermine the narrative. His intention in using these footnotes seems to be a mixture of the same kind of playful mockery of over-elaborate scholarship that can be found in his earlier books and an attempt to undermine the firm foundations of any narrative. Any story, Norfolk seems to be saying, has endless possible variants. Only later in *In the Shape of a Boar* do we realise that the footnotes have another role to play as well.

From pre-Homeric Greece, the book fast-forwards to Romania in the late 1930s. Three Jewish teenagers – Sol, Ruth and Jakob – have a particularly close, triangular friendship. The war is approaching, the forces of Fascism threaten Romania and the three are to be torn apart by the suffering of the times. Later in the war Sol, fleeing for his life, finds himself in the same Greek mountains that were the setting for the mythological hunt which is strangely recapitulated and echoed by the tracking down, by Greek partisans, of a Nazi officer. The novel moves forwards in time again – to Paris in the early 1970s. Sol, witness to the killing of the Nazi, is now a writer with a European reputation. His most famous work is a poem which has reworked his experiences and linked them with the myth. A film is to be made of the poem and during the making of it Ruth re-emerges from the past. So too do the truths which Sol has disguised and hidden. *In the Shape of a Boar* is the most carefully structured of Norfolk's novels, meticulously interlinking the present, the imagined past, historical reality and the realm of mythology. If it lacks a lot of the sheer ebullience of his first two novels, it makes up for it in the skill with which it leads the reader slowly into the heart of darkness at its centre.

In all three of his books Lawrence Norfolk is a novelist who makes demands of his readers. He expects them to pay attention, to have something approaching the same interest in the minutiae of life in the past that he has, to be prepared to work at the overflowing texts he provides for them. In return he offers some of the most rewarding fiction of the past ten years – large, meaty narratives that are so bursting with energy and vigour that they can make most other contemporary novels seem fairly thin gruel in comparison.

Norfolk's major works

Lemprière's Dictionary, Sinclair-Stevenson, 1991.
The Pope's Rhinoceros, Sinclair-Stevenson, 1996.
In the Shape of a Boar, Weidenfeld & Nicolson, 2000.

CARYL PHILLIPS (born 1958)

Phillips was born on the island of St Kitts in the West Indies in 1958 but moved to Britain with his family when he was still a baby, growing up in Leeds. He studied at Oxford and, after graduating, worked in the theatre. He has since pursued a dual career as writer and university teacher. His first novel, *The Final Passage*, was published in 1985 and it has been followed by a very varied body of work, which has ranged from five further novels to an anthology of writings on tennis, from TV scripts to books like *The European Tribe* (1987) and *The Atlantic Sound* (2000), which fuse travel writing with historical and cultural meditation.

Several of Phillips's novel are set in the Caribbean and feature characters who directly struggle with the dark legacy of colonialism and the crises of identity that it can engender. He has said in an interview:

> The reason I write about the Caribbean is that the Caribbean contains both Europe and Africa, as I do.... The Caribbean is an artificial society created by the massacre of its inhabitants, the Caribs and Arawak Indians. It is where Africa met Europe on somebody else's soil and that juxtaposition of Africa and Europe in the Americas is very important for me.

Even when the setting of his fiction is not the Caribbean and the plot is not overtly driven by post-colonial concerns, themes of displacement and alienation, of physical and psychological exile, haunt his work.

Phillips's first novel *The Final Passage* fictionalises the experiences of his parents and thousands like them who left the West Indies in the 1950s to travel to Britain in the story of Leila Preston and her husband Michael. In the poverty-stricken backwater of their small West Indian village, Britain – always presented to them as a nurturing 'Mother Country' – offers hope of a new and better life. When they do emigrate, they discover that image and reality are very different and that a new sense of cultural belonging is not easy to attain. Bertram Francis, in *A State of Independence* (1986), Phillips's second novel, reverses the journey made by the Prestons in *The Final Passage*. Francis has spent twenty years in Britain and returns to St Kitts, expecting to feel 'at home' in a way that he has not done for a long time. In a narrative that is both shrewdly observant and delicately comic, Phillips charts Francis's homecoming to a place he no longer recognises, caught as he is between two cultures.

In the two books Phillips explores the ways in which both emigrants' views of their destination and exiles' images of their homeland are fantasies, sometimes sustaining but ultimately disillusioning ones.

Higher Ground (1989) indicated Phillips's ambition to increase the density and complexity of his fiction. Both his first two novels, though well done, are more or less straightforward linear narratives. His third novel is a tryptych, three stories linked by the experience of dislocation and exile. In the first, an elderly African, caught between his own people and the slavers for whom he has been obliged to work, inevitably loses the brief, redemptory hope that his relationship with a young girl brings. The writer of the letters which make up the second is a 1960s prisoner in an American gaol clinging to dignity and self-respect through belief in the potential of the Black Panther movement. In the third, a Polish woman in 1950s Britain, wretchedly scarred by her experiences as a Jew in the Second World War, struggles to retain her sanity and her will to live.

Both of Phillips's next two novels deal overtly with slavery and its legacy. *Cambridge* (1991) uses two very different narrative voices – those of a nineteenth-century Englishwoman sent to visit her father's West Indies sugar plantation and a gifted Christian slave, the eponymous Cambridge – to tell a chilling tale of an island society irredeemably tainted by the inhumanity on which it is built. Life on the plantation and the events which fuel the central plot are seen from the very different perspectives of the two narrators as the book moves towards a murder and a hanging which have the sombre inevitability of a Greek tragedy. As in *The Higher Ground* before it and the two novels which have followed it, *Cambridge* shows Phillips's remarkable ability to make vivid and convincing the imagined voices from the past that he has created.

'I sold my beloved children' is among the opening lines of *Crossing the River* (1993), and the complex, intertwining but brilliantly handled narratives that follow show how the legacy of that transaction between a destitute African father and the English master of a slave ship reverberates through two hundred years of oppression and alienation. In three stories set at three different periods of history, characters who remain in some sense the 'children' of that original transaction struggle with its consequences. An emancipated slave sent to Liberia in the 1830s is unable to reconcile the warring elements within himself of the Christianity to which he subscribes and the Africa which he experiences; a black woman freed after the Civil War journeys westwards in search of the husband and daughter she lost in the slave years; during the Second World War, an Englishwoman, victim of an abusive marriage, finds solace in an affair with a black GI. A fourth narrative, in some ways the most daringly ventriloquist of them all, contrasts the blank amorality of a slave-ship captain in his 'business' with the passion and love he expresses in his letters to his wife. The four separate tales combine to produce a moving, multifaceted picture of the human consequences of the forced diaspora from Africa.

In *The Nature of Blood* (1997) Phillips writes not about slavery and black suffering but about the Holocaust and Jewish suffering. His themes, however, remain the obsessive inhumanity of racism, the ambiguities of 'belonging' and the insistent need to stigmatise others in order to define it, and he retains the kaleidoscopic, interwoven version of historical fiction that he so successfully used in earlier books. The central story is that of Eva Stern, a young woman the reader first meets as a traumatised survivor of the death camps which have taken most of her family. Phillips moves back and forth between this narrative and others. One is that of Eva's uncle, who abandoned wife and children to battle for the creation of a Jewish state in the Middle East. Another is the story of an episode of hysterical anti-Semitism in a medieval Italian town, unleashed by rumours of the ritual murder of a Christian child. A third is the self-narrated story of Shakespeare's Othello – although the character is never explicitly identified as such. Phillips juggles his varying narratives with great skill, gradually bringing them all together in an exceptionally daring conclusion to the book.

Caryl Phillips is one of the most talented of that generation of 'postcolonial' writers (Timothy Mo, Kazuo Ishiguro, Salman Rushdie) who have opened up new subjects for English fiction. Through his carefully crafted but passionate investigations of people painfully uprooted from their selves and their past, he has provided an original perspective on themes of home, exile and memory that have exercised the imaginations of many novelists. He has ranged widely, both geographically and historically, in creating narratives that stretch the boundaries of what readers once expected British fiction to be.

Phillips's major works

The Final Passage, Faber and Faber, 1985.
A State of Independence, Faber and Faber, 1986.
The European Tribe, Faber and Faber, 1987 (travel/history).
Higher Ground, Viking, 1989.
Cambridge, Bloomsbury, 1991.
Crossing the River, Bloomsbury, 1993.
The Nature of Blood, Faber and Faber, 1997.
The Atlantic Sound, Faber and Faber, 2000 (travel/history).
A New World Order: Selected Essays, Secker & Warburg, 2001 (essays).

MICHÈLE ROBERTS (born 1949)

Often described as a feminist novelist, Michèle Roberts has nonetheless been quoted as expressing the hope that eventually there will be 'male writers and female writers, rather than as at present feminist writers and writers'. Certainly her novels deal with themes that can be seen as 'feminist' – female sexuality, the narrow bounds within which male society can limit femininity, religion's (and especially Catholicism's) definitions of womanhood and the often troubling bonds that link mothers and daughters – but they resist, as all good novels do, easy pigeonholing.

Born in 1949, the child of a British father and a French mother, Roberts was raised as a Catholic and was educated in a convent school and at Somerville College, Oxford. Although she has reacted powerfully against her religious upbringing, Catholicism and the language and narratives of religion have continued to play a major role in her writing. After Oxford, Roberts worked as poetry editor of the magazines *Spare Rib* and *City Limits* and as a writer in residence in two London boroughs. During this time she began to publish her own work – fiction, poetry and drama – and soon established a reputation as one of the most daring and inventive novelists of her generation. The winner of several awards for her fiction, including the 1992 W. H. Smith Literary Award, she was also shortlisted for the Booker for *Daughters of the House*, which remains perhaps her best-known novel. Michèle Roberts has been associated, for more than a decade, with the famous creative writing course at the University of East Anglia and she is currently Professor of Creative Writing there.

Her early novels, as well as much of the best of the poetry she was writing at the time, grapple with conflicting images of femininity, both within women's own construction of self and within the wider culture. Both *A Piece of the Night* (1978) and *The Visitation* (1983) have as their central characters women whose sexuality, creativity and drive towards self-realisation battle against the constraints placed on them by convention and upbringing. The theme of women struggling against the expectations of others (mothers, lovers, children) continues throughout her fiction. Like the work of most novelists of her calibre and ambition, Roberts's work has evolved and changed in the course of a career that extends over more than a quarter of a century but certain other themes and the means used to explore them have remained consistent. In interviews she herself has identified her subjects, only slightly tongue in cheek, as, 'food, sex and God'.

Certainly religion has been an ongoing concern. Two of her most successful novels of the 1980s involve joyously imaginative reworkings of biblical stories which succeed in rescuing women's spirituality from the straitjackets imposed by patriarchal narratives. In *The Wild Girl* (1984) a fifth gospel, written by Mary Magdalene, is found in Provence. Allowed her own voice, she retells the story of Christ and his Passion from this unfamiliar perspective. Drawing on Gnostic traditions that told of a sexual relationship between Christ and Mary Magdalene, Roberts refashions the most familiar narrative in Western culture in ways that are both disorienting and rewarding. *The Book of Mrs Noah* (1987) has as its central character a woman visiting Venice who, in its watery ambience, enters a fantasy world in which she is Mrs Noah, in charge of the Ark. Her fellow voyagers on the Ark, repository of human knowledge and experience, include five Sybils and the Gaffer, self-styled 'speaker of the Word of God' and guardian of the male view of creativity ('I'm damned if I'll lie down and hand over my creative function to any pipsqueak thinking that her garrulous confessions or streams of consciousness constitute a proper act of creation'). In opposition to the Gaffer, Roberts uses the voices of the Sibyls and of Mrs Noah, with subversive humour and imagination, to explore different ideas of female creativity and self-expression. Ten years later religious motifs and the spiritual and creative quest seen from a female viewpoint are again at the heart of *Impossible Saints* (1997). The book recounts the life of an imaginary saint, St Josephine, struggling with her own desires (for God, for her father, for her priest-lover, for her own intellectual fulfilment), and intersperses this with other stories of women allowed the debatable privilege of sainthood. Roberts's characteristic historical and mythological imagination and sensual prose are used to summon up the least canonical of saints' lives, from St Peter's daughter, witness to the apostles boozily drowning their sorrows after the crucifixion, to St Thais, condemned to twenty years at the bottom of a well for the delicious sin of sleeping with her father.

Roberts has often shown herself adept at ranging through the centuries in her fiction and using the real lives of genuine historical characters as the jumping-off points for her own narratives. *In the Red Kitchen* (1990) is a collage of overlapping and intertwining stories that move back and forth between ancient Egypt and the present day. At its heart is a nineteenth-century medium, Flora Milk (based on the real Victorian spiritualist Florence Cook), who challenges the 'rationality' of scientific explanations of her communication with the dead and acts as the means through which the earlier story, about an Egyptian

Queen-cum-scribe, and the modern story are linked. Roberts herself, as writer, emerges as the medium through which lost voices can be heard again. She performs similar acts of imaginative resuscitation in *Fair Exchange* (1999) and *The Looking Glass* (2000). *Fair Exchange* opens with a peasant woman in early nineteenth-century France asking her village priest for absolution from the most momentous sin of her life and opens out into a story of sexual passions both acknowledged and unacknowledged. Drawing on incidents in the lives of both Words-worth and Mary Wollstonecraft (both appearing under thin disguise in the book), the novel's emphasis is not on the hunt for historical models for the characters but on the hidden histories of guilt and deceit that the narrative slowly reveals. Both *Fair Exchange* and *The Looking Glass* are filled with the sensuous appreciation of the physical world so characteristic of Michèle Roberts's prose. Roberts and her characters lavish attention upon the tangible and the material. Genevieve Delange, for example, the young servant in nineteenth-century, provincial France who is one of the narrators of *The Looking Glass*, is shown taking pleasure in the brioche she has made ('fresh and spongy, tasting of eggs and salt and butter, a yellowish wedge of lightness, spun holes, in my fingers') and finding evocative memories aroused by such simple things as a 'mottled blue coffee-pot' and the painted surfaces of her room. The plot centres on Genevieve's loss of innocence and on the interrelationships, gradually unveiled by the assorted narrators, between Genevieve, Gerard Colbert, a charming but self-centred poet for whom she goes to work, and the women who love him.

Roberts's two finest novels succeed brilliantly in marrying past and present, in creating intricate webs of connection between their characters' current circumstances and the histories which have led them there. *Daughters of the House* (1992), shortlisted for the Booker Prize, is the story of two cousins, Therese and Léonie, growing up in a small Normandy village in the 1950s. A religious vision – embraced by Therese, eventually rejected by Léonie – shapes their adolescences, as does the wartime secret harboured by their elders. Over the decades the guilty past that gave them their birth emerges when the cousins are reunited after a long estrangement. Mixing lyrical evocation of the Normandy countryside in which the two central characters grow up with the disturbingly dark consequences of collaboration and murder that lurk beneath its surface, *Daughters of the House* weaves its way through a complex plot towards a revelation of the ties that bind Léonie and Therese together. *The Mistressclass* (2003) also looks at two very different women whose familial connection yokes them together in a symbiosis which they may resent but which they can never break.

Both are writers. Both have reached middle age and yet their lives are still shaped by events decades earlier. Catherine is a professor of literature, with a lucrative sideline in pseudonymously published erotica. Her sister Vinny, former lover of Catherine's husband Adam, is a poet, growing increasingly eccentric as she enters her fifties, still mourning the loss of Adam to her sister. Interspersed with the story of this modern love triangle is a sequence of letters written by Charlotte Brontë – Catherine is a Brontë specialist – to the Belgian headmaster, M. Heger, with whom she conducted a painful and largely unrequited love affair. The affair revealed in the letters parallels the long-ago relationship between Catherine and her father-in-law to be, a painter for whom she modelled, and the revelation of this affair, together with the renewed intimacy between Vinny and Adam, drives the plot towards its conclusion. Michèle Roberts's most recent novel revisits the themes of women's needs to create their own voices and identities and the complex interrelationships between love, sexuality and writing that have fuelled her fiction from the late 1970s, but it does so in new and powerful ways.

Roberts's major works

A Piece of the Night, Women's Press, 1978.
The Visitation, Women's Press, 1983.
The Wild Girl, Methuen, 1984.
The Book of Mrs Noah, Methuen, 1987.
In the Red Kitchen, Methuen, 1990.
Daughters of the House, Virago, 1992.
During Mother's Absence, Virago, 1993 (short stories).
Flesh & Blood, Virago, 1994.
All the Selves I Was: New and Selected Poems, Virago, 1995 (poetry).
Impossible Saints, Little, Brown, 1997.
Food, Sex and God: On Inspiration and Writing, Virago, 1998 (criticism).
Fair Exchange, Little, Brown, 1999.
The Looking Glass, Little, Brown, 2000.
Playing Sardines, Virago, 2001 (short stories).
The Mistressclass, Little, Brown, 2003.

JANE ROGERS (born 1952)

Born in London, Jane Rogers was educated at Cambridge and began her career as an English teacher. Her first novels were published in the early 1980s and won immediate critical acclaim and attention. Her second novel, *Her Living Image*, was given the Somerset Maugham Award in 1985. She has published seven novels and has also worked successfully as a writer for both television and radio. (Her TV adaptation of her own novel, *Mr Wroe's Virgins*, screened in 1993, was one of the best television dramas of the 1990s.) She has edited an extensive guide to the novel, *The Good Fiction Guide*, published by Oxford University Press in 2001.

Jane Rogers's most impressive and resonant writing is to be found in her two historical novels, *Mr Wroe's Virgins* (1991) and *Promised Lands* (1995). *Mr Wroe's Virgins*, a humane and intelligent exploration of the mysteries of faith and love, is set in 1830s Lancashire and based on real events from the period. John Wroe is the charismatic prophet of a small sect, the Christian Israelite Church, who announces to his congregation that God has told him he should take seven virgins to live with him 'for comfort and succour'. Members of the congregation present him with their daughters, in accordance with God's word, and the events of the next nine months – before accusations of indecency and a scandalous trial bring the household to grief – are seen through the very different eyes of four of the virgins. Rogers proves very skilful in driving the story forward through the four narrative voices and in distinguishing each voice from the others.

Each of the virgins has very different expectations of her place in the household and of what the future will bring. Leah is no virgin at all. She has secretly given birth to a son, the father has disappeared and her aim is to use her sexuality to attract Wroe's especial notice. 'The Prophet is assailable', she decides; 'He is not all Godliness. There are chinks in his armour, and I have seen them. He will not be able to pretend that I am not there. Or that I am merely one of the women. He must see me. Me. Leah'. Joanna – 'Saint' Joanna, as Leah scornfully calls her – is the most devout of the virgins, a woman for whom religion has become a repressive force, alienating her from self-knowledge. Hannah, intelligent and sceptical about all religious claims, has been led by accident and circumstance into the household. At first she is deeply resentful of Wroe and unimpressed by his status as an alleged visionary. 'I am sure he is a charlatan', she notes, 'but, I suspect, an unknowing one'. She remains a sceptic but, ironically, it is in Hannah that Wroe finds he can confide, and she finds herself drawn to him. The fourth 'virgin' is Martha, brutalised into a near-animal existence by physical and sexual violence shown to her in the past. When we first meet her, she expresses herself only in insistent terms about basic needs: 'Eat. Eat. Stuff hot cold sharp sweet. Much. Cram it in. Tear bread crust eat. Dough soft mouth filling. Yellow cheese crumbling sour. Hard egg slippy white. Dry inside. Eat. Shove in mouth. Chew swallow. Is more'. Her development as a person in the novel is echoed by the development of her language from these inarticulate expressions of immediate desire and pleasure to a more sequential, ordered prose.

The major criticism of *Mr Wroe's Virgins* is that the four virgins who tell the story are too formulaic, their characters too shaped by the author's wish to present four distinct modes of interpreting and interacting with the world. Its great strength, paradoxically, is that Rogers also stands back, tactfully, from imposing judgements on the reader. Is Wroe a charlatan or a visionary? Is religious faith a strength or a weakness? We are left to make our own assessments. In one of their conversations, Wroe asks Hannah, 'You would not exchange this world for a better?' and she replies, 'I would have this one improved'. Rogers's novel acknowledges the power of both these contradictory views of the world and our place in it, in a narrative that is always surprising and engaging.

Two stories, one contemporary and one historical, run in tandem in *Promised Lands*. In the historical story, a young officer arrives with the First Fleet to establish the convict colony in Botany Bay, Australia. William Dawes, a budding astronomer, has instructions to erect an observatory but he soon finds himself caught up as much by the growing pains of the settlement as by any scientific work he may have promised himself. Dawes may know the stars but he is a poor observer of his fellow humans. When he hears of a convict woman who has committed infanticide on the journey from England, he is both appalled and fascinated by her story. After meeting the woman, Molly Hill, he finds it difficult to acknowledge that his increased fascination is as much sexual as humanitarian in origin. He makes love to her, is guilty about his 'sin' and decides that he will salve his conscience by marrying her. In visiting her to propose, he surprises her with another man. Dawes has been unable to empathise sufficiently with Molly to understand the very limited choices her situation allows her and has misinterpreted almost everything that has passed between them. In the same way he is oblivious, until it is too late, to the love felt for him by his cynical, homosexual friend Bradley and wilfully naïve about the relations between convicts, officers and aborigines. Dawes is a kind and well-meaning man but in the circumstances in which he finds himself his good intentions come to little.

The story of Dawes is paralleled by the contemporary story of Stephen Beech and his Polish-born wife, Olla. Beech is a teacher who believes in the power of reform and change to make the world better, even though his own attempts at improving the school where he worked have gone disastrously wrong and he is faced with a wife whom he cannot understand and a severely brain-damaged child he finds it hard to love. Olla, haunted by her childhood experiences, has no faith in the potential goodness of the world and is contemptuous of what she sees as her husband's naïvety. All her energies are focused, with a terrible intensity, on her child.

The links between the two stories are clear enough. Beech, cast out from his teaching job, is struggling to write a historical novel about Dawes and in his need to tell the story he is propelled into a strange, sudden and fatal journey to Australia. Both Beech and Dawes are men who, in some fundamental way, fail to connect with the reality that faces them. Yet there are times when the links fail and the two narratives seem as if they belong in different books. Much the better of the two books would be the historical novel. The contemporary story often feels flat and Beech, too often seen through the distorting mirror of his wife's contempt, is an unconvincing character. The story of Dawes's encounter with a world he cannot grasp is, however, a powerful narrative about idealism and about the consequences of projecting one's own ideas and interpretations of reality on to others.

Before writing these two historical novels, Jane Rogers had published three novels in the 1980s. *Separate Tracks* (1983), a strange semi-parable or allegory about two very different lives which briefly converge, was followed by *Her Living Image* (1984) and *The Ice Is Singing* (1987). The latter book, as original in its format as it is in its prose, is made up of a woman's journal interspersed with a number of short stories she has written. The stories are bleak – a man loses his daughter when he discovers that she is not his biological child, a middle-aged woman loses the focus of her life after the death of the mother for whom she cared – but they provide a strange comfort for their fictional author, Marion. Unlike her own life, in which she can see little narrative pattern, the lives in the stories are hers to shape and structure. The journal records a flight from a life in which her husband and elder daughters have left her and she is struggling to bring up her newly arrived twins. Leaving the babies with an aunt, Marion travels a wintry landscape (both literal and figurative) in search of answers. She doesn't find them, but in a revelatory moment at the end of the novel the melting ice 'sings' and she sees some kind of way of moving forward.

Since *Promised Lands* Jane Rogers published only two full-length novels, *Island* (1999) and *The Voyage Home* (2004). Using the motifs, themes and (at times) even the language of fairy tales, *Island* tells the story of a young woman who was abandoned by her mother at her birth. Furiously resentful at the desertion, Nikki Black has, in her late twenties, decided to track down her mother and kill her in order to 'free myself to fly'. She locates her on an island off the coast of Scotland. The mother is renting rooms and, incognito, Nikki moves in. She finds that she has a strange, slow-witted brother (or half-brother), who finds a link with his sister in the folk tales of the island he knows and shares with her. Through the telling of these tales – often only too relevant to her own personal history of abandonment – Nikki moves towards a new truth about her entry into the world. *The Voyage Home* follows the journey of Anne Harrington, taking ship from Africa to England after the death of her missionary father. Through her reading of her father's journals and through her encounters with fellow travellers on the ship, including two stowaways, she learns more about both the influences that have shaped her and her own relationships with others. Present echoes the past revealed in the missionary's diaries, and her own actions on board the ship, undertaken with the best of intentions, lead to tragedy and death. In these two novels Jane Rogers has returned, particularly in *Island*, to the fable-like narratives of her earlier books but they also share the sharp, unsentimental vision of her two historical novels. They reveal a mature novelist in full control of her material and able to use her flexible and intelligent prose to explore the histories and self-discoveries of her characters.

Rogers's major works

Separate Tracks, Faber and Faber, 1983.
Her Living Image, Faber and Faber, 1984.
The Ice Is Singing, Faber and Faber, 1987.
Mr Wroe's Virgins, Faber and Faber, 1991.
Promised Lands, Faber and Faber, 1995.
Island, Little, Brown, 1999.
The Voyage Home, Little, Brown 2004.

SALMAN RUSHDIE (born 1947)

No modern novelist has been obliged so painfully to bear witness to the ongoing power of narrative to upset and disturb those who resent its open-endedness as Salman Rushdie. Born in Bombay in 1947, the son of a prosperous Muslim businessman, Rushdie was sent for his education to England, where he attended Rugby and then read history at Cambridge. After graduating, he worked as an advertising copywriter for a number of years – reputedly he was responsible for inventing the well-known slogan 'naughty but nice' used in promoting the pleasures of fresh cream cakes – while writing his first two novels. The enormous success of *Midnight's Children* allowed him to write full time. He has since published six further novels as well as collections of short stories and essays. *Midnight's Children* and his third novel, *Shame*, both proved controversial, arousing the wrath of politicians in India and Pakistan, but nothing could have prepared Rushdie for the appalling consequences of his 1988 novel *The Satanic Verses*. Certain passages in the book so infuriated religiously extreme Muslims that a *fatwa* was pronounced against it by Iran's Ayatollah Khomeini, in effect placing on the devout the duty of assassinating its author. Rushdie was obliged to go into hiding under state protection for many years and, although the *fatwa* has now been lifted, his life remains (and presumably always will remain) affected by the impact of his book. He responded to the threats in the most effective way open to him – by continuing to write challenging and imaginative fiction – and Rushdie, now living in the USA, is one of the few British authors to have undisputed, worldwide stature as a novelist.

Rushdie's first novel, *Grimus* (1975), won some critical praise for its imaginative mingling of science fiction, echoes of folk tales and mythology (Eastern, Western, Native American), and sophisticated contemporary ideas about narrative but gained little real attention. In an interview Rushdie himself described the book as 'a fantasy without any roots in the discernible world' and in doing so pinpointed *Grimus*'s major shortcoming. It is a novel of great cleverness and energy but all its inventiveness seems to be taking place in a vacuum. It did, however, lay the foundations for Rushdie's second novel, *Midnight's Children* (1981), a shape-shifting, ever-metamorphosing fantasy that none-theless has its roots firmly in the discernible world. Its story, endlessly inventive in the ways it unfolds, is told by Saleem Sinai, a worker in a Bombay pickle factory, relating to his lover Padma the saga of his own life, which also proves to be a reflection of the history of India and Pakistan in the decades before and since independence. By virtue of his role as one of midnight's children – those born at the exact hour India gained its independence from Britain – Saleem's fortunes and those of his country are inextricably intertwined. His narrative, mixing techniques that echo those of fictional forms as diverse as Hollywood and Bollywood movies, European novels like Grass's *The Tin Drum*, South American magic realism and the folk tales of India, moves back and forth in time. Saleem's confusing ancestry, the result of the tangled mixture of East and West that was the British Raj, is gradually revealed. Telepathically linked with the other midnight's children, all of whom have their own magical powers, he joins with them in a mental unity that proves to have no equivalent in the everyday world. There the promise for India represented by the children disintegrates and the twin nemeses of Mrs Gandhi and Saleem's changeling counterpart, Shiva, work to destroy their potential.

Midnight's Children won the Booker Prize in 1981 (it later went on to win the Booker of Bookers, awarded to what the judges believed to be the finest book from the assorted winners in the prize's first twenty-five years) and his third novel was also shortlisted for the prize in the year it was published. *Shame* (1983) is, in most ways, a more direct narrative than its predecessor, often reading as a straightforward political allegory in which a parallel Pakistan is ruined by the competing ambitions of two corrupt rulers, Iskander Harappa and Raza Hyder. Yet, however much the temptation exists to identify Rushdie's characters with real politicians (Harappa with Zulfikar Ali Bhutto, Hyder with General Zia ul-Haq), the novel's narrator insists, sometimes disingenuously, sometimes not, on the book's status as fiction. Fantastical events pepper the narrative. The central character, Omar Khayyam Shakil, is born to three sisters, sequestered from the world, who all share both the experience of giving birth and the upbringing of the child. Sufiya Zenobia, daughter of Raza Hyder and eventually Omar's wife, is a child in a woman's body who embodies, both metaphorically and physically, the 'shame' that gives the book its title. The state that the novel describes, burdened by its own shame and the shamelessness of those who rule it, is both Pakistan and a parallel nation of Rushdie's imagining.

At one point in *Shame*, Rushdie's narrator, tongue in cheek, remarks that 'nobody need get upset, or take anything I say too seriously'. Five years passed before Rushdie's next novel was published and, soon after publication, these words gained a cruel, extra irony. It is impossible today to read *The Satanic Verses* (1988) with innocent eyes, to read it without the knowledge of the consequences that writing it had for Rushdie. Yet in many ways it was not a radical departure for Rushdie. It follows the patterns and techniques established in his earlier works. The fantastic and the realistic jostle for position on the page, as do narratives drawn from, or reflecting, 'high' culture and popular culture, Eastern mythology and Western politics (and vice versa), the serious and the playful. All come together in a fiction that begins with two characters, Gibreel Farishta and Saladin Chamcha, falling to earth in Britain after the mid-air explosion of a passenger plane. Shape-shifting into angel and devil, Gibreel and Saladin become the means by which Rushdie can explore his characteristic ideas about the flexibility of identity and the contingencies of history and politics. The specific passages which most outraged conservative Muslims are those which make playful use of an ancient legend in which the devil smuggles certain verses into the Koran by impersonating the angel Gabriel, but the entire book is, like all of Rushdie's fiction, a repudiation of any ideology or narrative that tries to lay claim to a monolithic certainty.

Despite the terrible constraints imposed on his life after the *fatwa* Rushdie continued to write. And his writing inevitably reflected both his own uniquely confining circumstances and his continuing faith in the power of fiction. *Haroun and the Sea of Stories* (1990), a kind of post-modern fable in which Rushdie, defying the *fatwa*, celebrated the open-endedness of narrative, begins when Haroun, son of the storyteller Rashid, inadvertently freezes his father's imagination. The well of storytelling dries up and the book follows Haroun's search for the means of restoring his father's gift. A collection of short stories, *East, West*, appeared in 1994. The long-anticipated major novel *The Moor's Last Sigh* was published the following year. The book is narrated by Moraes 'Moor' Zogoiby, looking back on his life and the tribulations of his family from what, it emerges towards the end of the book, are bizarrely imprisoning circumstances. Moor, suffering from accelerated ageing (at twenty he appears forty), is haunted by the ghosts of his extraordinary multi-ethnic clan and, particularly, by the imposing shadow cast by his mother, an artist of extraordinary fame, forcefulness and beauty. From her story and those of his other relatives, Moor builds a many-layered narrative that explores exile and belonging and celebrates the vibrant pluralism of India and, especially, Bombay. With its highly coloured carnival of wordplay, jokes, low farce and serious drama, and its unquenchable conviction that if one story is good, then many stories are better, *The Moor's Last Sigh* represents Rushdie's continuing belief in the life-affirming qualities of fiction and, together with *Midnight's Children*, is his most accomplished and satisfying work.

Since *The Moor's Last Sigh* Rushdie has published two novels and, although both have provided the kind of linguistic verve and imaginative energies that Rushdie's admirers have come to expect, both have also seemed overly determined by the structure he is intent on imposing on them and overly laden with rhetoric and hyperbole. In *The Ground Beneath Her Feet* (1999) Rushdie daringly attempts to fuse the images of mythologies East and West with the contemporary iconography of rock music in a story that begins in the melting-pot Bombay which has provided the setting for much of Rushdie's best work and expands into the global village created by popular culture. The narrator is a photographer, Rai Merchant, who watches the rise and rise of his childhood friends Ormus Cama and Vina Apsara from their complicated family backgrounds to joint apotheosis as legendary rock stars. The novel takes place in a world that seems to be our own, but small hints – Kennedy survives the Dallas assassination, the British take part in the Vietnam War, famous songs are reassigned to different singers – lead us to the realisation that we are in some kind of parallel reality. (The technique is one that has been used by science fiction writers, most effectively by Philip K. Dick.) Messages from other parallel realities begin to reach Ormus as he enters reclusive middle age and apocalyptic dreams of colliding worlds trouble his waking and sleeping mind. Vina dies in an earthquake but her posthumous fame goes on to exceed her earthly glory. Ormus, an Orpheus for a post-modern world, attempts to rescue his lost love through a lookalike replacement but eventually meets his death at the hands of a mysterious assassin, possibly a revenant Vina, come to take him down to the underworld. Rai, a rueful everyman obliged to report on the lives and tragedies of two friends propelled into modern mythology, is left an impotent observer of their fates. The book is rich in Rushdie's hyperactive linguistic invention and, in its use of the motif of parallel worlds, renews his commitment to the potential of fiction and stories to renew possibilities and rewrite history. Yet it remains, despite its seemingly packed plot, paradoxically short on narrative. Ormus and Vina too often seem characters created only to embody the mythological parallels Rushdie demands. Readers are forced to take their rock-god status on trust, and their dramas, like those of the Greek tragedies occasionally invoked, take place off page.

In *Fury* (2001) the central character is driven by forces with similarly mythological resonance: 'Fury – sexual, Oedipal, political, magical, brutal – drives us to our finest heights and coarsest depths.... The Furies pursue us; Shiva dances his furious dance to create and also to destroy'. Malik Solanka is a philosophy professor turned TV intellectual who has become fabulously wealthy through his unlikely creation, a doll called 'Little Brain' that becomes a worldwide, cross-media brand. Pursued by his own furies, Malik flees London for New York. There he is pitched into what Saul Bellow called 'the moronic inferno' of American culture, forced to exorcise his demons or be devoured by them. *Fury* has all the elements that make Rushdie's fiction so memorable – the dazzling wordplay and satiric verbal gymnastics, the co-opting of references from high and low culture, the seamless interweaving of the comic and the tragic – but, like *The*

Ground Beneath Her Feet, it is both shaped and undermined by the limitations of its chief character. In the final analysis, Malik Solanka, for all the venomous outrage of his rants and tirades against the excesses of America, consumerism and the derangement of everyday life in a media-drenched world, seems too inadequate a vehicle to carry the weight of significance Rushdie wishes to place on his shoulders, and his existential angst perilously close to fretful self-indulgence.

In the course of his career Rushdie has had to bear a weight of responsibility for his imagined worlds unlike that of any other modern novelist. He has continued to use his fiction as a means by which to express his faith in the importance and regenerative power of stories and the imagination. 'I love story, and comedy, and dreams', he once said; 'And newness; the novel, as its name suggests, is about the creation of the new'. In his best work – in *Midnight's Children* and in *The Moor's Last Sigh*, most notably – he has done much to make modern fiction new and exciting and emancipating.

Rushdie's major works

Grimus, Gollancz, 1975.
Midnight's Children, Cape, 1981.
Shame, Cape, 1983.
The Jaguar Smile, Picador, 1987 (travel/politics).
The Satanic Verses, Viking, 1988.
Haroun and the Sea of Stories, Granta, 1990.
Imaginary Homelands: Essays and Criticism 1981–1991, Granta, 1991 (essays).
East, West, Cape, 1994 (short stories).
The Moor's Last Sigh, Cape, 1995.
The Ground Beneath Her Feet, Cape, 1999.
Fury, Cape, 2001.
Step Across This Line: Collected Non-fiction 1992–2002, Cape, 2002 (non-fiction).

WILL SELF (born 1962)

Most writers don't have to worry that their public persona will come between the reader and their work. Most writers have little or no public persona. They are not household names anywhere other than in their own household. Will Self has a significantly higher public profile than the majority of 'literary' novelists. His reputation as some kind of *enfant terrible* of contemporary fiction reached an apogee in 1997 when he was accused of taking heroin on John Major's election campaign plane. The *Observer*, whose special election correspondent he was, sacked him and his face was all over the front pages of other newspapers for the next few days. Self's attitude to his non-literary fame has been deeply ambivalent. In essays and interviews he has derided contemporary obsession with personality rather than achievement but he has also made appearances as a team captain on the Reeves and Mortimer television show *Shooting Stars*. He has denied being overly concerned with publicity and yet he had few qualms about recreating himself as a living exhibit in a London art gallery in the run-up to the publication of one of his books.

There is also an ambivalence at the heart of his literary career. He is sometimes presented as a bad-boy outsider, writing, like the Americans William Burroughs or Hubert Selby Jnr, about sex, drugs and violence in a very direct way. Yet he is not some class warrior storming the citadel of the literary establishment from the outside but an Oxford-educated, middle-class metropolitan who, despite his protestations to the contrary in interviews, is about as much at the heart of that establishment as you can get, a place he has occupied almost from the start of his career.

Self first came to notice with a collection of short stories, *The Quantity Theory of Insanity* (1991). These already showed his characteristic verbal pyrotechnics in full flight – the self-consciously dazzling wordplay, the enjoyment of assonance, alliteration and allusion, the promiscuous mingling of mandarin vocabulary (thesaurus and dictionary are required reference works for the reader) and the language of the street and the drugs world. He followed the short stories with two linked novellas, *Cock and Bull* (1992), which were ingenious, explicit fantasies of gender-bending and the transmogrification of sexual roles. In 'Cock' a downtrodden housewife grows a penis and the nature of her sexuality begins to change until, finally, she ends by raping her husband. In 'Bull' the average Englishman John Bull awakes one day to find that he has a vagina between his calf and knee. This realisation (unsurprisingly) changes his perspective. The city becomes a new place to him:

> Doors, windows, garage forecourts, railway tunnels, even bus shelters. All struck at him with forceful, imagistic reso-nance.... It's all openings and entrances and doorways.... It was patently absurd to describe the city's architecture...as 'phallic'. The church spires, the war memorials, the clock towers, the skyscrapers...were all terminally irrelevant, ultimately spare pricks. The real lifeblood of the city, Bull now saw, was transported in and out of quintillions of vaginas.

Seduced by a male doctor, Bull finds himself in the submissive, needy role conventionally associated with femininity rather in the robust, macho role he has previously assumed. All the strange, metamorphosed couplings Self imagines – and describes in un-squeamish detail – might be considered pornographic but are played as black farce.

So too is the violence and sexuality in his first novel, *My Idea of Fun* (1993). The narrator/anti-hero is Ian Wharton, a man who possesses, or imagines that he possesses, the ability to look into others' minds. As a child, Wharton was schooled in magic and murder by the Mephistophelean figure of Mr Broadhurst, also known as 'the Fat Controller'; as an adult he has become a marketeer, scaling the corporate ladder, but 'the Fat Controller' returns in the shape of a devilish tycoon who seduces him into further murder. In *My Idea of Fun*, Self plays relentless games with the reader, who is constantly left wondering what is reality and what is fantasy. Are Wharton's graphically described exercises in violence and necrophilia 'real' or are they imagined? Is 'the Fat Controller' a projection of elements in Wharton's subconscious? Is Wharton who he claims to be? The atmosphere in the book is one of fervid surreality, of 'dreams that operated within dreams and dreams that were themselves fragmentary evidence of some long-lost hypnagogia'. In the end the book, despite its wit and intelligence, remains unsatisfactory – both because Self's control over the ambiguities of his narrative often seems to slip and because lurking behind the baroque descriptions of nastiness the reader can always sense a slightly sophomoric desire to do no more than shock, a wish to see just how far he can go to make our flesh creep. *My Idea of Fun* is astonishingly clever in its use of language but it has little of the satiric power of Self's later fiction.

This later fiction very often takes off from a single idea or conceit. Both his best novels can be summarised in a short sentence. *Great Apes* (1997) tells of a man who wakes one morning to find that he and the rest of the city's inhabitants have been transmuted into chimpanzees. *How the Dead Live* (2000) reveals that in the afterlife London's dead simply move to duller and more remote parts of the city. However, Self takes his basic premises and spins out the consequences with such invention and energy that the reader is pulled into the alternative worlds he has created. In *Great Apes*, artist Simon Dykes awakes from a particularly exhausting night of drink- and drug-fuelled debauch to find that his girlfriend has been transformed into an ape. Indeed the world is now one populated by apes and the only humans are to be found in zoos. Unwilling to accept this brave new world, Simon eventually finds himself hospitalised, attended by chimp nurses and primate psychiatrists intent on ridding him of the delusion of his humanity. The narrative manages to sustain both a larkish delight in the possibilities of man-to-chimp transformations and a savage, visceral satire that emerges from the turning upside down of the world. There is a relentless succession of enjoyably 'bad' puns and jokes – apes go 'humanshit' with rage etc. – but also a tremendously powerful sense of disgust with the body and with physicality – with the carnal animality that we share with our chimp cousins.

One of the short stories in *The Quantity Theory of Insanity*, 'The North London Book of the Dead', tells of a grieving son who finds that his dead mother is, in fact, in Crouch End, where her life continues much as it did before her demise. Nearly ten years after the publication of that story Self returned to the idea in *How the Dead Live*. In the full-length novel he creates an entire geography of the dead. His narrator is Lily Bloom (one of the more obvious of the many literary and cultural allusions in the book), an elderly, cantankerous Jewish-American woman who no sooner dies in a London hospital than she finds herself being shepherded across town by an aboriginal spirit guide so that she can take up residence, south of the river, in a basement flat in Dulston. Death provides just as many problems as life did. The next-door flat is inhabited by Lily's former fat selves – she has been a lifelong dieter and body obsessive – who mock and taunt her; she is haunted by the ghost of a child killed in a car accident; the community of the dead sleeps around and is as screwed up as the community of the living. Self's vision of London as a land of the still-living dead is remarkably, recklessly inventive and *How the Dead Live* shows him harnessing his invention to a coherent satiric vision in a way that only *Great Apes*, of his previous fiction, can match.

Will Self's most recent novel also launches into complicated flights of satiric imagination from a simple, one-line idea. What would a contemporary version of Wilde's *The Picture of Dorian Gray* be like? *Dorian: An Imitation* (2002) is Self's answer. It follows Wilde's plot closely. The original portrait is transformed into a video installation but the characters, situations and London settings are all there, shifted a hundred years into the future and our present. Dorian makes his amoral journey through another *fin-de-siècle*, the history of which enables Self to weave two contemporary realities into his narrative. One is the media mythology that came to surround Princess Diana – the book's events march side by side with the events of Diana's life – and the other is the terrible progress of the AIDS epidemic. The picture of the new Dorian accumulates all the ravages that the archetypal late twentieth-century disease can inflict. Like all of Self's fiction, *Dorian: An Imitation* is witty, brutally frank in its descriptions of drugs, sex and violence, and it continues to demonstrate that its author is the most savage and wide-ranging satirist among contemporary novelists.

Self's major works

The Quantity Theory of Insanity, Bloomsbury, 1991 (short stories).
Cock and Bull, Bloomsbury, 1992.
My Idea of Fun, Bloomsbury, 1993.
Grey Area, Bloomsbury, 1994 (short stories).
Junk Mail, Bloomsbury, 1995 (essays and reviews).
Great Apes, Bloomsbury, 1997.
Tough, Tough Toys for Tough, Tough Boys, Bloomsbury, 1998 (short stories).
How the Dead Live, Bloomsbury, 2000.
Feeding Frenzy, Viking, 2001 (essays and reviews).
Dorian: An Imitation, Viking, 2002.
Dr Mukti and Other Tales of Woe, Bloomsbury, 2004 (short stories).

IAIN SINCLAIR (born 1943)

More than any other contemporary novelist – more even than Peter Ackroyd – Iain Sinclair builds his fiction around his ideas about London and its history. Like Ackroyd, he spins endless, numinous connections between the city's past and its present, mystical recurrences of event and character which shape the inventions of his fiction. More than Ackroyd, his imaginative sympathy goes out to the marginalised – those whom history and politics have pushed aside, ignored, misrepresented. And all of this is encompassed in a fantastic, highly wrought, allusive and demanding prose that is utterly unlike any other used in fiction in the last twenty years.

Iain Sinclair was born, not in London, but in Wales in 1943 and was educated at Trinity College, Dublin, and at the Courtauld Institute. From the late 1960s onwards he worked (at various times) as a dealer in rare books and as a gardener in the public parks of East London, developing that obsession with the city that has been so marked a characteristic of his fiction. Throughout the 1970s he was also involved in a number of small-press ventures which published his own poetry and that of poets he admired, such as Brian Catling. His first significant London publication was *Lud Heat* in 1975. This was an unusual *mélange* of poetry and prose pieces which ranged from reflections on the churches designed by the architect Nicholas

Hawksmoor and their presumed psychic power to diary entries and thoughts on a movie by the underground filmmaker Stan Brakhage. It was weird, original and passed almost unnoticed by critics and readers alike (although not by Peter Ackroyd, who obviously drew inspiration from it for his novel *Hawksmoor*). It was followed by another unclassifiable work, *Suicide Bridge* (1979), which mingled prose and poetry and drew on everything from the mysticism of Emmanuel Swedenborg to the gangland mythology of the Krays in its visionary remapping of London.

White Chappell, Scarlet Tracings (1987), Sinclair's first novel, revisits all the themes that had been rehearsed in the poems and prose pieces scattered through the small-press publications of the 1970s and early 1980s. Urban blight, the decay of 1960s ideals, the burgeoning selfishness of the era, the interest in those whom life and the literary canon have bypassed, the byways of London history. Indeed Sinclair specifically refers to the book as closing the 'triad' begun with *Lud Heat* and *Suicide Bridge*. The novel, originally published by a tiny independent publisher and only republished by one of the major firms when Sinclair's literary star began to rise, is an extraordinary yoking together of two storylines. One revisits and reimagines the Jack the Ripper murders in Whitechapel, peering again at the darker fantasies of both the Victorians and ourselves. The other is a picaresque story of a group of lowlife book dealers in search of obscure tomes to buy and sell. The link between the two stories – or one of the links, for nothing is ever simple in Sinclair's fiction – is a rare variant edition of Conan Doyle's *A Study in Scarlet* (first published at the time of the Ripper murders) that the dealers, Dryfeld and Nicholas Lane, come across. However, as in Sinclair's other fiction, plot (in any conventional sense) isn't the driving force behind the novel. Sinclair doesn't 'do' plot with any great enthusiasm or conviction. What drives *White Chappell, Scarlet Tracings* is the exceptional, manic energy of the prose. The critic James Wood has called Sinclair 'a demented magus of the sentence' and said that 'anyone who cares about English prose cares about Iain Sinclair'. Although Wood was writing a decade after the publication of *White Chappell, Scarlet Tracings*, the quality that he pinpoints in the later novels was there from the fictional debut.

White Chappell, Scarlet Tracings was followed by Sinclair's greatest achievement so far, *Downriver* (1991). Possessed of more structure than his other novels, it is built up of twelve interconnecting narratives centred on the Thames and its riverbank. 'I wanted to unwind congeries of narrative in the form of a novel', Sinclair has said, 'to travel backwards down a changed and changing river'. There may be more structure in *Downriver*, but it is also the culmination of Sinclair's endlessly digressive, excursive fictional journeys through the capital. The novel takes as its connecting thread the story of a film crew making a documentary about the blight and ruination inflicted on the riverside by the changes of history and politics, especially the policies of the Thatcher years. But the real centre of the book is the Thames itself and the histories it holds. *Downriver* teems with characters and stories. Stephen Hawking, Lewis Carroll, Victorian boatmen, aboriginal cricketers, 1960s gangsters, wide-boy dealers and a thousand other unlikely figures people its pages. Sinclair's recurring obsessions – forgotten writers from his alternative canon of English literature, Jack the Ripper, David Rodinsky and the Princelet Street synagogue, strange psycho-geographical connections between different parts of the city, the churches of Nicholas Hawksmoor – all have a role to play. Like the city it reflects, the novel contains multitudes. And, as always, there's the dense, rich and rewarding prose in which Sinclair writes. Ezra Pound said that poetry was language 'packed with meaning to the maximum possible extent'. If that is the case, then Sinclair's prose aspires to the status of poetry. Elaborate, allusive, self-consciously attention-seeking, often very funny, Sinclair's language is unique in modern fiction and *Downriver*, a vast compendium of lives and stories past and present, contains his most monumental vision of the city that has inspired his work.

Throughout the 1990s Sinclair showed as much interest in non-fiction as fiction, as great an eagerness to collaborate with other, sympathetic artists as to publish work on his own. He produced a third novel, *Radon Daughters*, in 1994. Its central character, Todd Sileen (who appeared briefly in *Downriver*) is one of Sinclair's familiar literary lowlifes, a writer with an addiction to x-rays. Caught in the fantasies of the mysterious policeman-cum-secret serviceman, Drage-Bell, Sileen is led not only through the contemporary wastelands of East London but into a series of mad pilgrimages to Oxford, Cambridge and Ireland in search of an elusive manuscript alleged to be a sequel to *The House on the Borderland*, a horror novel by the early twentieth-century writer William Hope Hodgson. The book is as strange as this brief précis suggests, but it is once again powered by the relentless invention and vigour of Sinclair's style.

In the seven years after *Radon Daughters* Sinclair concentrated on non-fiction. *Lights Out for the Territory* is a collection of unsurprisingly idiosyncratic excursions through London's topography and history. He worked with the artist Rachel Lichtenstein on *Rodinsky's Room* and with the photographer Marc Atkins on *Liquid City*. *Slow Chocolate*

Autopsy, a graphic novel on which he collaborated with Dave McKean, is another vision of London conjured up through the time travelling of its central character. A fourth novel was finally published in 2001. In *Landor's Tower* Sinclair, who has always sailed perilously close to the reefs of self-parody and pretentiousness, sometimes seems to have struck them. He also is in great danger of repeating himself, as themes and motifs familiar from his past career resurface and float freely through the text. Ironically, this is his first book in quarter of a century that doesn't have London, his great subject, at its centre. Not only that, but Sinclair, one of the most self-conscious of modern novelists, is aware of the difficulties and even attempts to pre-empt criticism by providing it himself. His narrator, a writer commissioned to produce a book on the nineteenth-century author Walter Savage Landor, is castigated by another character for the predictability of his work:

> 'Don't you have any imagination?', the Brummie droned . . . .
> 'Every novel starts with a stalled car, a squabble of
> bookdealers . . . . What's with this three-part structure? One:
> lowlifes running around, getting nowhere. Two: a baggy
> central section investigating "place", faking at poetry, genre
> tricks and a spurious narrative which proves incapable of
> resolution. Three: Quelle surprise. A walk in the wilderness.
> What a cop-out, man.'

Whether passages like this (actually a concise if unfair précis of Sinclair's novels) ward off the criticism they are anticipating or not is doubtful. Certainly *Landor's Tower* seems the least successful of Sinclair's novels. The extraordinary verbal fireworks light up the night sky once more but the landscape they illuminate (the borderlands of Wales and the South West) seems to interest Sinclair, and consequently the reader, less than the familiar cityscapes of London. A further novel has been long announced, placed in the more Sinclair-like setting of Hackney. In the meantime his admirers have been given another of his non-fiction excursions into weird terrain – *London Orbital* (2002) records his journey, haunted by many familiar figures from Sinclair's personal pantheon of writers, filmmakers and visionaries, around the edges of the M25 – and a fictional journey that enters territory just as strange in *Dining on Stones* (2004). Sinclair's extended project, in which he lavishes his 'demented magus's' prose on the forgotten and the marginalised, continues.

Sinclair's major works

Lud Heat, Albion Village Press, 1975 (poetry and prose).
Suicide Bridge, Albion Village Press, 1979 (poetry and prose).
White Chappell, Scarlet Tracings, Goldmark, 1987.
Downriver, Paladin, 1991.
Radon Daughters, Cape, 1994.
Lights Out for the Territory, Granta, 1997 (non-fiction).
Slow Chocolate Autopsy, Phoenix House, 1997 (graphic novel).
Rodinsky's Room (with Rachel Lichtenstein), Granta, 1999 (non-fiction).
Landor's Tower, Granta, 2001.
London Orbital, Granta, 2002 (non-fiction).
Dining on Stones, Hamish Hamilton, 2004.

GRAHAM SWIFT (born 1949)

With seven novels in nearly a quarter of a century, Graham Swift has not been the most prolific of recent British novelists but he is one of the most respected. All his fiction has explored the ways in which the past, both personal and public, continues to reverberate in the present. The Second World War and its legacy is a recurring theme in Swift's work, as is the conflict between different generations with different views of the past and its relative importance.

Swift was born in London in 1949 and educated at Dulwich, Queens' College, Cambridge, and York University. Until his third novel, *Waterland*, became such a success he combined writing with teaching English part time at a number of London colleges, but he has since worked solely as a novelist and short-story writer. He has won many awards for his fiction, including the Booker Prize in 1996 for *Last Orders*. Swift's first novel was *The Sweet Shop Owner* (1980), the story of an apparently unremarkable man – Willy Chapman, the sweet-shop owner in a London suburb – who has lived a life that, superficially at least, seems narrow and constricted. Swift's achievement in the book, remarkable in a debut novelist, is that he draws the reader into an apparently ordinary life and reveals, through the skilful use of flashback, that, like all lives, it is far from ordinary. Willy's relationships with his demanding late wife, with his daughter and with his employees all unfold as the one day that is the focus for the narrative opens up to tell the story.

Swift's second novel, *Shuttlecock* (1981), moves from a contemporary narrative to a story of espionage and intrigue in the Second World War in order to explore its themes of heroism, guilt and intergenerational conflict. Prentis, its central character, is the chief clerk in an obscure government department investigating unsolved and 'dead' crimes. At odds with his family, resentful of his job and his overbearing supervisor, he is haunted by his relationship with his father. Prentis senior is a catatonic mute committed to an institution, but in the war he was an agent working with the Resistance in occupied France. His code name was 'Shuttlecock' and, after the war, he published an account of his experiences under that name. Swift's book alternates between the younger Prentis's narrative and the older one's memoir, as it unfolds its story of a troubled man searching for a route to redemption through an understanding of the sources of his father's apparent heroism.

Still Swift's most impressive achievement to date, *Waterland* (1983), is a *tour de force* of storytelling, interweaving past and present, landscape and character, in its tale of a history teacher at the end of his tether who is haunted by the power of the subject he has spent his life studying. Set in the Fenlands, the ambiguous landscape where earth and water meet and mingle, the novel focuses on the teacher, Tom Crick, as he attempts, for the last time, to persuade his pupils of the importance of the past for the present. One student, Price, is particularly resistant, unconvinced that the study of history is anything more than an evasion of the responsibility to shape a better future. Crick tells Price:

> 'I believed, perhaps like you, that history was a myth. Until the Here and Now, gripping me by the arm, slapping my face and telling me to take a good look at the mess I was in, informed me that history was no invention but indeed existed – and I had become a part of it.

Waterland's shifting narrative is, in effect, the working out and explication of the meaning behind Crick's commitment to the significance of the past. The book consists of the intertwining stories which tell of Crick's implication in history, moving back into his family's past over several generations and into a death by drowning which occurred forty years before but which lives on, not least in Crick's memory.

Waterland is an extraordinarily labyrinthine but brilliantly organised narrative – or series of narratives – that manages to encompass the history of a changing landscape, the history of a family, the incursions of the wider world into a smaller community, incest, murder, madness and guilt. Swift weaves all his stories into a book that, finally, is a compelling defence of storytelling as a human (and humane) essential. 'It's all a struggle to make things not seem meaningless', Crick says at one point in the novel, 'It's all a fight against fear. . . . I don't care what you call it – explaining, evading the facts, making up meanings, taking a larger perspective, dodging the here and now, education, history, fairy-tales – it helps eliminate fear'.

Swift waited five years before publishing another novel after *Waterland*. *Out of this World* (1988) tells the story of the Beech family and how its experiences reflect and embody the world-changing events of the twentieth century. Harry Beech is a renowned photojournalist who has covered most of the trouble spots of the world since the Second World War. Harry's father, Robert, fought (and lost an arm) in the First World War and was an arms manufacturer, eventually killed (with double-dealing irony) in a terrorist attack perpetrated while his son was in Belfast in pursuit of photographs of the IRA. Harry's daughter, Sophie, has been estranged from her father for many years and lives in New York, where unresolved guilt and anger from her past have driven her to the analyst's couch. The story of a family blighted across the generations by violence and a refusal to communicate is told in a parallel narrative by father and daughter. 'Life', Sophie's analyst remarks aphoristically, 'is a tug of war between memory and forgetting. . . . It's telling that reconciles memory and forgetting'. In the telling of their two stories Harry and Sophie do achieve some kind of hard-won redemption and reconciliation.

The central character in *Ever After* (1992) is a death-haunted academic, Bill Unwin. In a short time Unwin has lost his wife to cancer, his mother and his stepfather. He is struggling to regain a purpose in life after a failed suicide attempt. Researching the papers of a nineteenth-century ancestor, Matthew Pearce, he finds parallels for his own loss of identity in Pearce's anguished internal debate between his religious and his scientific beliefs. *Ever After* revisits many of the themes and motifs of Swift's earlier books. There is the same interest in the interaction of past and present and the inevitable conflicts and failures of understanding between the generations. The book's interweaving of stories from Unwin's life, his father's and Matthew Pearce's echoes the serpentine narratives of *Waterland*. It is often hard, when reading it, to banish the thought that Swift has trod this ground before and done so more successfully. Yet *Ever After* does have its own considerable virtues – most notably the central character and the voice Swift gives him. Painfully intelligent and aware of language and its ambiguous potential, often very witty and funny, Bill Unwin is a memorable narrator in search of what matters in life and an explanation of why it does.

The Booker Prize-winning *Last Orders* (1996) is, in its basic plotting, a straightforward, even banal, narrative. A London butcher, Jack Dodds, has died and left instructions that he wants his ashes scattered in the sea off Margate Pier. Three of his friends and his adopted son, Vince, meet in a pub and begin the pilgrimage to the south coast to carry out his wishes. The novel follows their journey to carry out Jack's 'last orders'. (Without labouring the point, Swift makes significant play with the various meanings implicit in the phrase that gives the novel its title, from the simple call for time in a pub to ideas about the 'ordering' and value of one's life in the face of death.) Told in chapters which alternate the narrative voice from one man to the next (together with brief contributions from Jack's wife and Vince's wife) the book slowly reveals uncomfortable truths which force the main characters into reassessments of their lives and relationships. The prose Swift uses to tell his story is deliberately unshowy, an unpatronising reflection of London working-class speech in its rhythms and cadences. Yet, from an apparently very basic story told without any of the writerly flamboyance that other novelists might have been tempted to use, Swift creates a book that is a moving, often funny revelation of how lives interconnect and what friendship, love and the rites of death, the 'last orders', mean.

The Light of Day, a story that combines elements of detective fiction with characteristically Swiftian ideas and motifs, was published in the spring of 2003. The novel focuses on one day in the life of the narrator, George Webb, a policeman turned private investigator, as he visits a former client, Sarah Nash, currently imprisoned for the murder of her husband. As the mundane events of the day unfold, Webb returns in his mind to his past relationships, to the chain of circumstances which involved him in Sarah's life and to his own complex feelings for her. As in *Last Orders*, Swift's prose is the reverse of flamboyant but its carefully controlled 'ordinariness' has a cumulative power as the pieces of his narrative slowly slot together. Swift again waited a long time – seven years in this instance – between novels. One reason is not hard to find. Swift is a craftsman, passionately committed to the art of the novel and to the importance of storytelling, and novels as sophisticated and cunningly structured as his are take time to create. In *Waterland* he has written one of the indisputably great novels of the last thirty years, and all his fiction, in its compelling exploration of how history shapes individuals, is worth reading.

Swift's major works

The Sweet Shop Owner, Allen Lane, 1980.
Shuttlecock, Allen Lane, 1981.
Learning to Swim and Other Stories, London Magazine Editions, 1982 (short stories).
Waterland, Heinemann, 1983.
Out of this World, Viking, 1988.
Ever After, Picador, 1992.
Last Orders, Picador, 1996.
The Light of Day, Hamish Hamilton, 2003.

ADAM THORPE (born 1956)

One of the most difficult tasks for a contemporary English novelist is to investigate what constitutes Englishness. The images offered by political parties or the media are banal and unconvincing. The glib formulations of politicians and journalists are embarrassing rather than enlightening. Warm beer, cricket on the village green and spinsters cycling home from evensong for the nostalgists. Or ill-defined buzzwords like Cool Britannia for those in thrall to fantasies of a new role for the country. There must be a Britishness in general, an Englishness in particular, that can offer better stimulation to imagination and intelligence.

Of recent attempts in fiction to piece together a viable English identity, to situate the present in the larger perspective of the past, few have been as resonant and successful as the work of Adam Thorpe. Perhaps Thorpe's wish to explore the meaning of Englishness was fostered by his own peripatetic upbringing. In an interview he once said, 'My life has been a combination of travelling and attempting to put down roots'. He was born in Paris in 1956 and brought up in India and Cameroon. He went to a traditional English public school, Marlborough, and then on to Oxford to read English. After Oxford he founded his own theatre company, Equinox, and took shows around the villages of Wiltshire and Berkshire. In one of his own poems he describes himself as:

> a long-haired graduate who wrote, and ran
> a little company with puppets, whose dreams were rural
> in an urban century.

Eventually the demands of the urban century drew him to London, where he taught literature and published his first volume of poetry,

Mornings in the Baltic, in 1988. A further collection, *Meeting Montaigne*, followed in 1990. These volumes of verse, as slim as first collections traditionally are, scarcely prepared the reader for the huge ambition, scope and achievement of the fiction on which he was about to embark.

Thorpe published his first novel, *Ulverton*, in 1992. In the book he undertook a multifaceted exploration of English history by means of inventing a village in the South West, the eponymous Ulverton, and by constructing twelve very different, demanding narratives set in the village at different times in its history from 1650 to 1988. 'Friends', set in 1689, is ostensibly a sermon by the Reverend Mr Brazier to his congregation but manages also to be an account of individual tragedies (the deaths of two men in a snowstorm) and a snapshot of English religion caught between established Anglicanism and the increasingly powerful forces of Dissent. In 'Deposition', set in 1830, Thorpe succeeds brilliantly in encapsulating the class tensions of the time in his story of rioting, machine-breaking and the unbridgeable gulf between Ulverton's squire, with his desire to carve a White Horse in a chalky hillside near the village, and impoverished villagers with nothing but contempt for his well-meaning scheme. 'Here', set in 1988, takes the form of a script for a TV documentary about a greedy and unimaginative property developer and his battle with conservationists in Ulverton.

The stories work as individual, involving dramas but they are also, convincingly, chapters in a longer narrative – the story of Ulverton across the centuries. They create a remarkable sense of change and continuity interacting in one particular and very carefully rendered location over more than three hundred years. And Thorpe's subtle adoption of different narrative voices is in itself a bravura performance. 'Stitches', set in 1887, is in many ways the pivotal chapter of the book, in which echoes of stories from the past and stories yet to come can be heard. Thorpe tells it as one long, unpunctuated dialect monologue by an aged farm labourer taking a walk around the village and recalling, often angrily, memories of class conflict and personal tragedy that places and people trigger. It is an extraordinarily bold but successful ploy on Thorpe's part. He forces the reader to work – to decipher the initially confusing language in which the chapter is told – and in forcing that concentration he also creates a recension of many of the other stories in the book. 'Stitches' is the most difficult and demanding chapter in *Ulverton* but it is also the one which holds the key to the whole structure.

In *Ulverton* the poet in Thorpe can be seen in the care and attention paid to the nuances and allusiveness of language and in the inventiveness of the different narrative voices he creates. In his second novel, *Still* (1995), this care and attention, this interest in creating an utterly distinctive voice in which to tell his story are even more apparent. In telling the story of Ricky Thornby, the failed ex-pat film director, and his millennial retrospective on his life, Thorpe draws on every resource of the language. The result is an extraordinary *mélange* of voices from inside Ricky's head, those of dead relations and lost wives, of colleagues on films and of the masters of the cinema whose work he had idolised but not matched. They all spill exuberantly across the pages of *Still*. The stream of Ricky's consciousness is rich, allusive, demanding, often very funny. Ricky's last and best work is the imagined story of his life, which was premiered in a novel some (perhaps overexcited) reviewers compared to Joyce and Anthony Burgess.

In his third novel, Thorpe returned, like his protagonist, to Ulverton. In *Pieces of Light* (1998), Hugh Arkwright is a successful and famous man of the theatre but he is tormented by his past. He cannot forget the disruptions of his early life, when, as a seven-year-old, he was sent from the African colonial outpost where he was born to an England of which he had no experience. His return as an old man to Ulverton, the village where he was lodged with an uncle, himself damaged by First World War memories and obsessed by the prehistoric past and by esoteric ritual, is the catalyst for a narrative which winds slowly and deviously towards a startling revelation. The apparent calm of rural life is shattered by murder and betrayal. The heart of darkness beats in England as in Africa.

Part of Arkwright's quest in *Pieces of Light* is a quest to understand his own Englishness. As a member of a bomber crew in the Second World War, he ponders the question quite overtly:

> What does this 'England' mean? What did Rachael mean by saying I was 'so English'? I never saw England until I was just seven. Everything I knew, everything I loved, was far away. Now I am encased in steel and bolted Perspex, flying through the air to bomb a city, in the name of this England. How did I arrive by this?

Arkwright's childhood in Africa has produced in him a classic colonial schizophrenia. His commitment is required to an England of leafy lanes and quiet copses, the rural idyll that Ulverton sometimes seems, yet his own earliest memories are of the African bush. Rural England and colonial Africa collide continually in his mind. His progress towards an understanding of the terrible secret at the very beginning of his life is also a progress towards a definition of English rural life and Englishness that is obliged to accommodate the horrific as well as the idyllic.

In *Nineteen Twenty-One* (2001) another emotionally traumatised Englishman needs to find a way to allow very polarised feelings to co-exist in his mind. The book is Thorpe's contribution to what has been a thriving sub-genre in recent English fiction – part of a continuing late twentieth-century/early twenty-first-century response to the deaths and dislocation of the First World War. Thorpe has his own characteristically original take on the subject. Where the central characters in novels like Pat Barker's *Regeneration* and Sebastian Faulks's *Birdsong* have been profoundly disturbed by their experiences on the front line, Joseph Monrow, Thorpe's protagonist, is troubled by his failure to get to the front line. Accidentally gassed during a training exercise, Monrow was never in combat. Almost three years after the war has ended, he is living in a cottage in the Chilterns attempting to exorcise his demons by writing a great anti-war novel. Yet his work is stalled and going nowhere. It seems that art – at least Monrow's art – is incapable of encompassing the realities of the war and its aftermath.

Thorpe's most recent novel moves him away from the ongoing examination of Englishness that was such a strong component of his previous fiction. *No Telling* (2003) is the story of Gilles Gobain, an adolescent boy growing up in a Paris suburb in the late 1960s and lost amidst the devious adult realities of his dysfunctional family. Where the book does echo Thorpe's previous novels – *Still*, *Pieces of Light* – is in the way its narrative edges its way obliquely towards the revelation of secrets that shape the life of its central character and others. The book also moves effectively between microcosm and macrocosm. *No Telling* starts with the divisions within Gilles's family and culminates in the larger-scale trauma of a society at war with itself as he and his mother are caught up in the Paris riots of May 1968. It shows, in a different setting, Thorpe's ability, revealed in his other work, to use diverse forms of narrative to direct the reader towards the emotional truths and realities of his characters.

Thorpe's major works

Ulverton, Secker & Warburg, 1992.
Still, Secker & Warburg, 1995.
Pieces of Light, Cape, 1998.
Shifts, Cape, 2000 (short stories).
Nineteen Twenty-One, Cape, 2001.
No Telling, Cape, 2003.

ROSE TREMAIN (born 1943)

Rose Tremain published her first novel in 1976 and was one of
Granta's twenty Best of Young British Writers in 1983, but it was only
in the 1990s that she began to attract the kind of wide readership that
her talents, already recognised by the critics and the list-compilers,
deserved. Most of her fiction has been set in the contemporary world
(or at least in the twentieth century) but it is two historical novels,
Restoration (1989) and *Music and Silence* (1999), which are most familiar
to readers. Tremain was born in London in 1943 and educated at the
University of East Anglia (where she returned in the 1990s to teach on
its prestigious Creative Writing course) and the Sorbonne. As well as
being a novelist, she is also an accomplished short-story writer and
throughout her career has written plays for radio and TV.

Her first novel was *Sadler's Birthday* (1976), a grave, rather
melancholy account of an old man's life that was a surprising book
for a young writer. Tremain avoided the disguised autobiography of
most first novels and has continued to defeat those readers who like
to see direct links between personal history and the novelist's art.
This was followed by *Letter to Sister Benedicta* (1978), in which Ruby
Constant, a middle-aged to elderly widow reflects on her life in a
series of letters addressed to a nun at the convent school in India
she attended many years before. As her confession progresses, more
and more of the secrets (often sexual) of her family and of her
marriage are revealed. The curious thing about Tremain's first two
novels, in view of the expansive narratives and sensuous prose of her
best-known fiction, is their very deliberate restraint and restriction.
They are books that work – often very successfully – on a small
canvas and use a limited palette of colours. It was in her 1981 novel
The Cupboard that Tremain began to widen her fictional horizons.
The book is the story of one woman's long life of literary and
political activity from her childhood in Suffolk through a period of
intense self-discovery in Paris between the wars to an old age ended
by a very deliberately chosen suicide. Her next novel, *The Swimming
Pool Season* (1985), moves between a French village and Oxford as it
tells the story of Larry and Miriam Kendall and their circle. Defeated
by most of the circumstances of his life, Larry comes to see the
building of a swimming pool on his French property as a means of
renewing his sense of himself. Miriam, meanwhile, is tending her
dying mother and reassessing her relationships in the past and
present.

'We're all something else inside', says Mary Ward, the central character in Tremain's 1992 novel *Sacred Country*, and, although this is most dramatically true of Mary, all the people in the book are striving, in their own ways, to reconcile their own inner sense of self with what others and society at large demands of them. The book opens in 1952, during the two-minute silence in honour of the dead King George VI. In a sudden moment of insight the six-year old Mary realises that she should be a boy not a girl and the book follows her decades-long struggle to attain that destiny. Brutally misunderstood by her father, unable to communicate with a mother drifting into mental illness, Mary (or Martin, as she chooses to be) leaves her rural Suffolk home as an adolescent and moves to London to begin the painful process of her reinvention. Ostensibly 'about' transsexuality, *Sacred Country* uses a much wider canvas – particularly the intersecting relationships of the village community in which Mary/Martin grows up – to ask more general questions about identity and individual fulfilment. Tremain's intelligent awareness of the ambiguities of personal identity is evident throughout the book, perhaps most tellingly at the point where surgical intervention becomes a real possibility for her central character, who experiences a sudden realisation that it can be 'easier to believe in the dream of something than in the something itself'.

The Way I Found Her (1997) is a knowing mixture of coming-of-age story and romantic mystery. Tremain is a novelist who can lavish a rich and sensuous prose on the physical world, and it is physicality which her adolescent hero is beginning to appreciate in new and disturbing ways. Lewis Little arrives in Paris with his mother, who has been summoned to work on the English translation of a new book by the best-selling Russian émigré novelist Valentina Gavrilovich. Valentina, exotically alluring and more than twenty-five years his senior, becomes the focus of Lewis's burgeoning erotic fantasies and dreams of love. When she disappears he determines to find her, turning amateur detective in the attempts to track her down. As Tremain unravels her plot, the real adult word of pain and loss impinges cruelly on Lewis, still more than half-rooted in the childhood from which the events of the novel cast him. The book is told in the voice of Lewis himself, struggling between the precocious knowledge that 'things happen in ways you never expect' and confused attempts to analyse himself and interpret others.

Both *Sacred Country* and *The Way I Found Her* are excellent novels, but Tremain's finest work to date consists of her two books set in the seventeenth century, a century which she summons back into life in a rich, descriptive prose that dwells lovingly on clothes, food, drink and the human body the material objects of a vanished world. *Restoration* (1989) is the story of Robert Merivel, a minor courtier attendant on Charles II caught up in the amoral hedonism of the court, only to be cast aside and forced to make his way in the far bleaker world outside its gilded walls. It is a book rich in the fruits of Tremain's historical research – we learn how wigs were worn, how the mad were treated, the path taken by the Great Fire of London through the city streets and much more – but it is not a conventional historical novel. The past is recreated to tell what is in many ways a strikingly modern story of a man torn between the many pleasures of the flesh and a sense of their essential worthlessness, between conspicuous consumption and a desire to root his life in something more meaningful. The Restoration of the title is not only the historical period but the restoration of Merivel to a truer sense of himself. This is, perhaps, to make the book sound rather solemn and it is anything but. Merivel is an enormously appealing and life-affirming character and what the reader finally carries away from the book is the narrative voice that Tremain has created for him – bawdy, vivid, witty and self-tormenting.

Music and Silence (1999) follows Peter Claire, an English lutenist of strikingly angelic good looks, as he travels from his East Anglian home to the very different world of the Danish court. The King is Christian IV, a man who was once energetic and vital, but who has been thrown by circumstances into a melancholy and depression that only music seems to soothe. His wife, Kirsten, is estranged from him, interested only in the sexual prowess and attentions of her German lover. Claire is haunted by memories of his failed love affair with an Irish countess, whose husband was his earlier employer, but is drawn to one of Kirsten's maids, herself a woman in flight from her past and her family. Christian, meanwhile, seizes upon the young Englishman as some kind of potential saviour, the one person who can rescue him and the country from moral and spiritual bankruptcy. Tremain marshals her range of characters and her contrasting motifs of love and egotism, light and dark, music and disharmony with great skill. Told in a number of narrative voices, *Music and Silence* is less highly coloured and less of a bravura performance than *Restoration* but no less convincing and enjoyable as a historical novel in which contemporary themes are echoed and reflected.

Tremain's most recent novel, *The Colour* (2003), is also given a historical setting but one very different from the hedonistic courts of Charles II and Christian IV. The central characters of the book, Harriet and Joseph Blackstone, are English emigrants to New Zealand in the mid-nineteenth century whose dreams of a better life are confronted by the harsh realities of landscape and circumstance. The promise of gold offers another delusive chance of riches and an easier life as Joseph sets off for the goldfields and Harriet is forced eventually to follow him. Tremain's rich prose is used to great effect in describing the unforgiving terrain amidst which the Blackstones' hopes are slowly worn down. Tremain has said that in her fiction she aims to seek out 'the strange, the unfamiliar, even the unknowable', and *The Colour* is a further example of her ability, best seen in her historical novels, to use the strange and the unfamiliar to illuminate the more mundane.

Tremain's major works

Sadler's Birthday, Macdonald, 1976.
Letter to Sister Benedicta, Macdonald, 1978.
The Cupboard, Macdonald, 1981.
The Colonel's Daughter and Other Stories, Hamish Hamilton, 1984 (short stories).
The Swimming Pool Season, Hamish Hamilton, 1985.
The Garden of the Villa Mollini and Other Stories, Hamish Hamilton, 1987 (short stories).
Restoration, Hamish Hamilton, 1989.
Sacred Country, Sinclair-Stevenson, 1992.
Evangelista's Fan and Other Stories, Sinclair-Stevenson, 1994 (short stories).
Collected Short Stories, Sinclair-Stevenson, 1996 (short stories).
The Way I Found Her, Sinclair-Stevenson, 1997.
Music and Silence, Chatto & Windus, 1999.
The Colour, Chatto & Windus, 2003.

BARRY UNSWORTH (born 1930)

Born in 1930, Barry Unsworth grew up in a Durham mining community and, as he has emphasised in interviews, he was the first in his family to escape the necessary drudgery of the pit. After studying at Manchester University and completing his national service, he spent much of the late 1950s and 1960s working and travelling in Greece and Turkey. He taught English in universities in both countries and both have provided the settings for some of his novels. In the 1980s Unsworth was attached to several universities as visiting fellow or writer in residence. His period at Liverpool University, a time when he was already struggling with the research and writing of his masterpiece on the Atlantic slave trade, *Sacred Hunger*, is reflected in *Sugar and Rum* (1988), which, among other things, is a disquieting study of writer's block. Unsworth now lives in Italy.

Most of Unsworth's early fiction, with exceptions like *The Greeks Have a Word for It* (1967), is set in England. His very first novel, *The*

Partnership (1966), takes place amid the tawdry tourism of 1960s Cornwall and focuses on two men, Foley and Moss, partners in a business catering to tourist tastes, whose alliance begins to crumble under the pressures of hidden desires. *The Hide* (1970), another early novel, is an ominous, disquieting examination of voyeurism, exploitation and class interaction that largely takes place in an English country house and its gardens. Told in two narrative voices – that of the voyeuristic Simon, obsessively digging a network of secret tunnels from which to spy on others, and that of a naïve young gardener on the estate – *The Hide* is a curious, offbeat novel unlike anything else in Unsworth's *oeuvre*.

There is no doubt that Unsworth's fiction of the 1960s and 1970s was competently written and always interesting to read, but there was not much to distinguish him from a host of other young novelists who were publishing their first novels at the time. Occasionally, as in *Mooncranker's Gift* (1973), a story set in Turkey which tells of the anguished falling out of the relationship between a young scholar and his mentor, a man in terminal alcoholic decline, Unsworth suggested further depths to his work. Only the most prescient critics, however, could have guessed at the remarkable extension of Unsworth's range in the 1980s and 1990s and the new ability he showed to marry narratives of past and present into one seamless narrative.

The Ottoman Empire, in its decadent decline, provided Unsworth with the settings for the two novels which announced his new stature. Both take place in the last few years before the outbreak of the First World War, which was to bring Ottoman rule to an end. *Pascali's Island* (1980), set on a Greek island still governed from Constantinople, is the story of an unscrupulous chancer, Basil Pascali, who makes his money as an unacknowledged agent of the authorities. An Englishman, apparently an archaeologist, arrives on Pascali's island and the two men enter into a complex game of bluff and counter-bluff, of love rivalry and treachery. In *The Rage of the Vulture*, published two years later, another Englishman, Robert Markham, is drawn into plots amid the shady diplomatic world of the last sultan's Constantinople and into memories of a massacre he witnessed which cost a former lover her life. Markham's guilt and remorse fuel his actions as he tries to seek redemption where none is available. These two were followed by *Stone Virgin* (1985), set in Venice in the present day but using its motif of the sculpted fifteenth-century *Madonna*, which is being restored by the central character Simon Raikes, as the means by which the story can travel back and forth in time. Possessiveness in art, the possessiveness men feel for women and the possessiveness of murderer for victim are all present in a narrative which moves sinuously between three periods – the era in which the sculpture was created, the eighteenth century and the present, in which Raikes's growing obsession with both the *Madonna* and the enigmatic Chiara Litsov, descendant of the Venetian aristocrats who once owned it, leads him into ambiguous waters.

Sugar and Rum (1988) is Unsworth's response to the Thatcher years, the story of an ageing historical novelist, Clive Benson, who is struggling to write a novel set in the heyday of the Liverpool slave trade. Ostensibly pursuing his research, Benson spends much of his time slouching through the blighted streets of the city and when he meets an old wartime colleague reduced to whisky-sodden homelessness he is forced to confront his own guilt about events in the war. Benson gains new purpose in his life with the planning of an elaborate comeuppance for the arrogant officer under whom he served, now an archetypal representative of the Thatcher plutocracy angling for a knighthood. Part melancholy portrait of the artist as an old dog, part meditation on the respective values of art and action and part indictment of the state of the nation, *Sugar and Rum* is not one of Unsworth's most elegantly structured novels but it is one of the more interesting, if only for any autobiographical hints it may contain about the writing of his masterpiece, *Sacred Hunger* (1992).

Unsworth's major achievements are two works published within a few years of one another in the early 1990s. There could scarcely be two more different novels. *Sacred Hunger* is a sprawling, 600-page saga of the eighteenth-century slave trade, which won the Booker Prize in 1992. At the book's heart is the confrontation between two men. One is Erasmus Kemp, the son of a ruined shipowner striving for wealth and position through the traffic in human beings. The other is his cousin Matthew Paris, a physician forced to witness the horrors of the middle passage at first hand. Matthew is present when the maniacal cruelty of the ship's captain, Thurso, precipitates a revolt and he takes part in the utopian experiment in communal living, isolated on the remote Florida coastline, which follows the mutiny. *Sacred Hunger* is a bleak work in its unrelenting depiction of inhumanity, and the enlightenment values Matthew represents are shown as fatally flawed. Eventually he concludes that 'nothing a man suffers will prevent him from inflicting suffering on others. Indeed, it will teach him the way'. Yet the book, paradoxically, rises above its pessimism in the rich, physical details of eighteenth-century life that Unsworth provides and in the moral intelligence of his investigation of greed, power and the terrible relationship of oppressor and oppressed.

Morality Play (1995), by contrast, is a spare, concisely written book, set in fourteenth-century England, that succeeds in combining elements of a murder mystery and a fable of art and meaning. Its central character, Nicholas Barber, is a priest, bored and restless in the church, who escapes to join a group of travelling players. Plague, physical and spiritual, affects the land. The troupe arrives in a town where a murder has taken place and a woman has been condemned for it. Despairing of an audience for their conventional biblical dramas, the players take the radical step of re-enacting the murder and events surrounding it. Not only is this dangerous morally and aesthetically ('Who plays things that are done in the world?', demands one of the troupe'), but when the re-enactment begins to reveal new truths about the crime it becomes physically threatening. The murderer is not the woman about to hang. The real murderer is still free and the actors' decision to 'play the murder' has placed the murderer under threat.

Nothing in the last decade has matched the twin peaks of these two very different novels but Unsworth has continued to show himself one of the most inventive of contemporary novelists. *After Hannibal* (1996), an uncharacteristic study of expatriate manners and mores in Umbria, was followed by the more substantial *Losing Nelson* (1999). *Losing Nelson* cleverly fuses past, present and the present's interpretation of the past in the story of a man obsessively researching a biography of Nelson. As he struggles to reconcile what he learns with what he wants to believe about the great naval hero, he slowly begins to lose his grip, not only on his idea of Nelson, but on his own sense of self. Torn between his longing to retain an untarnished image of Nelson's heroism and his doubts about one particular episode in the admiral's career, Charles Cleasby eventually travels to Naples in a doomed attempt to save both himself and his view of Nelson. As in other Unsworth novels, the search for truth – about the past, about one's heroes – becomes an ambivalent enterprise.

Unsworth's most recent novel shows the mastery of form and tone that this elder statesman among modern novelists has now achieved. In *The Songs of the Kings* (2002) an invasion fleet is gathered on the shores of eastern Greece and an army awaits its opportunity to set sail for Troy. Only an unprecedented unseasonal wind stands in its way, trapping the ships in the narrow straits at Aulis. Clearly the gods are angry and need to be appeased. Amidst the wrangling of rival priests and the jostling for position of petty chiefs and princes, the daughter of King Agamemnon, Iphigeneia, is summoned from the palace at Mycenae. She is to be the sacrificial offering to Zeus and once her father and his fellow warriors have chosen to shed innocent blood there can be no turning back. Unsworth's ironic and subversive retelling of Greek myth and literature is full of delights. Often very funny in its irreverent portraits of legendary heroes – Nestor is a gabby old fool forever reminiscing about the gory deeds of his youth, Achilles is a vain psychopath and Odysseus a scheming political chancer – this is an old story with very modern echoes. As Agamemnon, almost as much as Iphigeneia, becomes the victim of shameless and cynical political manoeuvring and as the images presented, 'the songs of the kings', become more important than the reality they purport to reflect, we seem to be in a world far more familiar than the historical setting initially suggests.

The Songs of the Kings travels further back in time than Unsworth's other historical fiction but it is as good an example as any of his ability to use stories set in the past to cast a reflected light on contemporary concerns. Over the last twenty years his novels have explored, among many other subjects, the relationship between art and truth (*Morality Play*), the nature of power and justice (*Sacred Hunger*) and the persistence of memory and guilt (*Sugar and Rum*, *The Rage of the Vulture*). In more than a dozen novels he has proved himself a writer who can elegantly combine readability and compelling storytelling with a questioning perspective on significant ideas and the interplay of emotions.

Unsworth's major works

The Partnership, Hutchinson, 1966.
The Greeks Have a Word for It, Hutchinson, 1967.
The Hide, Gollancz, 1970.
Mooncranker's Gift, Allen Lane, 1973.
The Big Day, Michael Joseph, 1976.
Pascali's Island, Michael Joseph, 1980.
The Rage of the Vulture, Granada, 1982.
Stone Virgin, Hamish Hamilton, 1985.
Sugar and Rum, Hamish Hamilton, 1988.
Sacred Hunger, Hamish Hamilton, 1992.
Morality Play, Hamish Hamilton, 1995.
After Hannibal, Hamish Hamilton, 1996.
Losing Nelson, Hamish Hamilton, 1999.
The Songs of the Kings, Hamish Hamilton, 2002.

ALAN WALL (born 1951)

'Repetition and pattern give our lives meaning', Alan Wall wrote in an online exchange with the novelist Michael Moorcock; 'novelty by itself is chaos. If we can't find shared patterns between what we call the past and the present, then there can be no history and nothing can be redeemed'. His career as a novelist has been dedicated to the mapping out of those shared patterns. His characters search, often desperately, for connections between their own histories and those of people (often artists and writers) in the past. With wit and offbeat erudition, Wall charts the progress of individuals pressed by the need to make human sense of themselves and their lives in a larger context than that of the everyday and the mundane.

Wall was born in Bradford in 1951 and read English at Oxford in the early 1970s. In the decades after graduating he had a number of jobs (some reflected in his fiction), from teacher to songwriter to despatch rider. It was only in his forties that Wall became a full-time writer but since the appearance of *Bless the Thief* in 1997 he has published four further novels and a collection of short stories. His reviews and essays have appeared in many newspapers and periodicals and he has returned, after a long absence, to academic life. He now teaches on the Writing Programme at Warwick University.

Bless the Thief is a searching and intelligent investigation of the meaning and value of originality and authenticity, cast in the form of an erudite mystery novel. Anti-hero Tom Lynch, at school in England just after the Second World War, is introduced to the work of the mysterious late nineteenth-century illustrator Alfred Delaquay. Inducted into the Delaquay Society, which looks to protect the artist's hermetic reputation – his work has never been mechanically reproduced and exists only in hand-produced limited editions – Lynch becomes increasingly obsessed. Descending into a drink- and drugs-fuelled chaos that mirrors the rumoured decadence of Delaquay, he turns also to forgery, faking his master's style. The Society expels him but, as Wall moves his novel towards the revelations at which he has been hinting since the beginning, the symbiotic entanglement between Lynch and the long-dead Delaquay continues. Only by understanding himself and unearthing the secrets in his past can Lynch free himself.

Both before and after his ingenious, witty and compelling debut novel, Wall explored the themes it rehearsed – the ambivalent relationship between art and commerce, the interplay of past and present, the place of the individual within a larger tradition – in a number of different literary forms. *Richard Dadd in Bedlam* (1999) is a collection of short stories which range from a title story based on the life of Dadd, the maniacal nineteenth-century painter and parricide who created unnerving 'fairy' pictures in his asylum rooms, to several which make clever and playful use of genre conventions, both those of crime and those of SF. Wall has published collections of poetry (*Chronicle* and *Lenses*) and *Jacob*, a challengingly hybrid work, written in both verse and prose, which won the Hawthornden Prize. Most significantly, he has written a succession of novels which, while varied and imaginative in their narratives and characters, return again and again to his particular, almost obsessively maintained motifs and preoccupations. *Silent Conversations*, his second novel, was something of a disappointment after *Bless the Thief*. The story of an advertising copywriter caught between the demands of the music business and his own preoccupations and obsessions, it drew intriguing parallels between the iconography of contemporary celebrity and that of ancient mythology but Wall found it difficult to sustain his ideas and images throughout his narrative.

The School of Night and *The Lightning Cage*, however, marry narratives of the present to the echoes of the past with greater dexterity and flexibility. In *The School of Night* (2001) Sean Tallow is one of Wall's erudite but ineffectual protagonists, gradually withdrawing further and further from engagement with the everyday world in search of the arcane insights tantalisingly offered by history and literature. From childhood in Yorkshire through education at Oxford to a nocturnal existence as a news editor for the BBC's World Service, Tallow pursues his obsession with the School of Night, a group of Elizabethan philosophers and proto-scientists clustered around the larger-than-life figure of Sir Walter Ralegh. Convinced that the lives and works of these shadowy savants hold the key to the mystery of Shakespeare and his identity, Tallow slowly rids his life of all emotional and personal encumbrances in pursuit of it. The only relationship which he cannot shed is his friendship, dating back to their schooldays, with the charismatic Dan Pagett. Pagett is everything Tallow is not – a man who has engaged with the world rather than withdrawn from it and has amassed a huge fortune in the process. Yet, paradoxically, the novel is narrated retrospectively by Tallow from a point in time where Pagett has withdrawn definitively from the world. 'Dear dead Dan', as Tallow repeatedly refers to him, has (apparently) succumbed to a tumour, leaving his old friend to deal with a complicated inheritance of guilt and responsibility and his long-nurtured love for Dan's widow. *The School of Night* has its faults – the ultimate success of the novel hinges on our belief in the strength of the bond between Tallow and Pagett and too often we have to take this on trust – but Wall brilliantly dovetails the parallel stories separated by the centuries and enlivens both with the intellectual wit and arcane knowledge that characterise all his books.

Wall's interest in the pursuit of visionary states and in the interplay of past and present is once more in evidence in *The Lightning Cage* (1999). The novel's central character, Christopher Bayliss, is, by turns, a seminarian who rejects ordination at the last minute, a graduate student, the employee of a printing firm and the victim of a disabling car crash but, like Sean Tallow in *The School of Night*, he has one overwhelming obsession which runs through his life. His researches into the life of Richard Pelham, an obscure eighteenth-century poet with more than a passing resemblance to Christopher Smart, become not just an exercise in academic resurrection but a means of unearthing his own demons. Was Pelham, renowned for his madness and his alcoholism, literally a man possessed, a genius haunted by spirits that both tormented him and released his creativity? As the novel progresses, the two lives separated by two centuries come to echo one another and Bayliss is forced to confront his own unresolved past.

The recurring themes of Wall's fiction are all present and find their most satisfying vehicle in his most recent novel, *China* (2003). As in his other novels, the values of the commercial and the values of the artist are seen to be in inevitable and irreconcilable conflict. Digby Walton, heir to a Staffordshire pottery firm, confronted this long ago when he attempted to introduce new ideas of design to the company, only to see them fail miserably. Now an ageing recluse in a London flat, he has more personal ghosts from the past to haunt him in memories of his wife Victoria, their Second World War courtship and marriage permanently soured by the shadow of Victoria's other, true love. In the course of the novel his feckless son, Theo, interested only in the jazz music that he creates, is forced to face up to the same conflict and it breaks him. Moving from gig to gig in dodgy London pubs, pursued by debts and disappointed women, he eventually ends up on the south coast, driven into a dead end. Running parallel to the story of Digby and Theo is that of Digby's neighbour Daisy, her ex-husband James and their son Howard. Daisy, a former starlet who appeared in one of Digby's favourite movies, makes some kind of reconciliation with James, a fashion photographer in the 1960s who has taken to snapping quiet country churches, and Howard, absent for much of the novel, appears at its end to hint at new ways of exerting political and artistic pressure.

As in some of his other novels, there is an almost embarrassing richness of material in *China*. Ideas of industrial decay and redundancy jostle with the new critiques of capitalism produced by the internet.

The inevitable estrangement between generations shares the pages with illustrations of the intermittent power of art to heal estrangements. The authentic voices of art and history battle with the 'heritage' industry that debases and destroys them. Throughout the novel Wall's command of this diverse material, however, is more complete, and yet more flexible, than in any of his previous books. His interest in the visionary and in those elements of life that escape the attention of a modern consumerist culture have been present in his fiction since *Bless the Thief* and he has found increasingly successful ways of incorporating that interest into novels with compelling narratives and characters who engage readers emotionally and intellectually.

Wall's major works

Bless the Thief, Secker & Warburg, 1997.
Silent Conversations, Secker & Warburg, 1998.
The Lightning Cage, Secker & Warburg, 1999.
Richard Dadd in Bedlam, Secker & Warburg, 1999 (short stories).
The School of Night, Secker & Warburg, 2001.
China, Secker & Warburg, 2003.

ALAN WARNER (born 1964)

Alan Warner was born in the West of Scotland in 1964 and educated at Glasgow University. In his first novel, *Morvern Callar*, he created a fictional world that was immediately recognisable as uniquely his own: a Scotland at once real and surreal. In the three books that he has published since his debut that world has become increasingly familiar. Often set in an imaginary Scottish town known only as the Port, they feature a ragbag of memorable characters – ex-British Rail trolley-girls, crazed snowboarders, sybaritic members of the aristocracy, weirdly erudite drifters. Warner's writing is uncompromisingly direct, shot through with deviant sexuality and demented humour, but at the heart of his fierce and strange world there is often tenderness, moments of surprising lyrical beauty and a constant sense of a wide-ranging and original imagination.

Morvern Callar (1995) is the story of its eponymous heroine, a low-paid supermarket employee in a remote Highland sea port, who wakes one morning to find her strange boyfriend has committed suicide on the kitchen floor. Her reaction is coolly matter of fact: 'I came back to the scullery then took a running jump over the body. The sink was full of dishes so I had to give them all a good rinse'. The suicide does start Morvern on an odyssey, which takes her from Scotland to hallucinatory Spanish resorts. She hides the body, takes possession of the manuscript of a novel he has been writing and submits it to a publisher. The book is accepted and Morvern uses the advance and the contents of her late boyfriend's bank account in an attempt to escape her dead-end life by travelling to the rave scene of the Mediterranean. She throws herself into a world of casual sex, ecstasy, music and immediate sensual gratification before returning to Scotland, pregnant, to face an uncertain future. Short on plot, *Morvern Callar* comes alive through the memorable first-person narrative voice of its central character. Morvern reacts with deadpan amorality to all that surrounds her yet Warner succeeds both in making her a sympathetic 'heroine' and in suggesting the enormous longings behind her blank exterior. 'No big pleasures for the likes of us, eh?', her stepfather tells her at one point in the novel; 'We who eat from the plate that's largely empty'. Morvern's often grim journey, unflinchingly described, represents her spirited refusal to accept 'the plate that's largely empty'.

These Demented Lands (1997) won the 1998 Encore Award for Best Second Novel and is a kind of eerie, surreal sequel to *Morvern Callar*. Instead of the bleak terrain of depressed port and emptily hedonistic clubland that were the backdrop of the first novel, Warner creates a fantasy landscape on an unnamed island off the Scottish coast where Morvern, most often referred to simply as 'the girl', arrives after a shipwreck. A man known as the Aircrash Investigator roams the island, searching (for his own enigmatic reasons) for wreckage from a plane crash, and John Brotherhood, owner of a hotel for honeymooning couples where 'the girl' enters semi-slavery to pay off her bill, is a sinister presence. Meanwhile, a DJ is trying to organise the rave to end all raves, and Warner's bizarre and bizarrely nicknamed characters – the Argonaut, the Knife Sharpener, the Devil's Advocate – arrive at the Drome Hotel to lose themselves in the drugs and the music. Once again (and more confusingly than in *Morvern Callar*) Warner seems less interested in plot than in just introducing readers, with a kind of 'take it or leave it' panache, to a strange imaginative world. The resulting book is so determinedly, self-consciously and relentlessly 'left-field' that it can become irritating, but there is no mistaking Warner's gifts for atmosphere, quirky dialogue and offbeat characterisation.

With *The Sopranos* (1998) Warner returned to the mainland and to a more conventional fiction, showing again his ability to create young, contemporary female characters who are believable and memorable. The choir from Our Lady of Perpetual Succour School for Girls is travelling to a competition in the big city. Orla, Kylah, (Ra)Chell, Manda and Fionnula (the Cooler) leave behind the grim port town where they live, and the depressing prospects it offers, in search of the bright lights for a day at least. Sex, shoplifting and the consumption of alcohol offer more allure than the competition, which they are determined to lose anyway since they want to be back in their local disco in time to greet the submariners on shore leave who will be invading it. Told largely through the girls' lively dialogue – part teenage slang, part Scots argot – *The Sopranos* is a vivid celebration of their brash exuberance and the vulnerability it masks. Underneath all the garish chatter lies Warner's unsentimental awareness that the exuberance won't last: 'They've youth; they'll walk it out like a favourite pair of trainers. It's a poem this youth and why should they know it, as the five of them move up the empty corridors?'

Warner's most recent novel is *The Man Who Walks* (2002). This is an ambitious, scabrous, drink-soaked odyssey through the Scottish landscape and, peripherally, through Scottish history and literature as the Nephew pursues his uncle, the eponymous Man Who Walks, who has absconded with £27,000 on a kind of deranged pub crawl around the Highlands. Crossing the paths of assorted eccentrics and vagrants, most of them off their heads on drink and drugs, the Nephew finally has a violent reunion with his uncle at the unmistakably symbolic site of Culloden Field. *The Man Who Walks* announces from its first pages Warner's intention to cram it not only with as much outrageous incident as possible but with language as drunkenly over the top as most of its characters. From very early in the book even something as mundane as supermarket detritus can inspire a paragraph of wordy evocation and provide the excuse for casually introduced anecdote:

> It wasn't just during winters the ghost bags came in, rolling over across the dawn-hard fields from distant miles, tumbling for so long on themselves, inside out or inflated, bloated, as when Murdo in the Albannach found the ballooned-up dog, buried just beneath the sand, or, in Gillespie, a living eel emerged from the drowned fisherman's mouth, from its coiled home in his swollen stomach.

Like *These Demented Lands*, *The Man Who Walks* seems sometimes to be compensating for its lack of a sustained and wide-ranging plot by the sheer cornucopia of surreal detail and character that it includes and by the headily extravagant prose in which it is written. Warner's ambition is to be applauded but his most successful books remain

Morvern Callar, with its haunting first-person narration, and *The Sopranos*, for its generous depiction of teenage characters that other writers would have satirised or ignored.

Warner's major works

Morvern Callar, Cape, 1995.
These Demented Lands, Cape, 1997.
The Sopranos, Cape, 1998.
The Man Who Walks, Cape, 2002.

SARAH WATERS (born 1966)

In three novels published in the last five years, Sarah Waters has established herself as one of the most original writers of historical fiction in the country. All three of her novels take the themes and motifs of classic Victorian fiction and overturn or undermine them by introducing the kinds of characters and settings that such literature firmly excluded. Picaresque and Dickensian narratives of the sort familiar to any reader of nineteenth-century fiction are extended to take in lesbian sexuality, transvestism, prostitution and pornography. What remains unspoken or disguised in classic fiction is foregrounded in Waters's novels. Yet her books are much more than pastiche, more than Victorian stories filtered through a post-modern lesbian consciousness.

Born in Pembrokeshire in 1966, Waters studied English literature at the University of Kent and went on to work for a PhD in gay and lesbian historical fiction. It was from her academic work that her fiction emerged as she became fascinated by the hidden lesbian subculture of Victorian London. *Tipping the Velvet* (1998) was the result, a riotous story of self-discovery amid a demi-monde of music-hall entertainers, Sapphic aristos and cross-dressing gender-benders. Waters has published two further novels. She has won the Somerset Maugham Award and has been shortlisted for both the Booker Prize and the Orange Prize. In 2003 she was named as one of Granta's twenty Best of Young British Novelists.

Tipping the Velvet, recently adapted with great brio for TV, is set in the 1890s. Nan Astley, the book's chief protagonist, begins the novel as the respectable daughter of a Whitstable restaurant owner but is propelled into new worlds by her encounter with Kitty Butler, a male impersonator who performs in the local music-hall. As, by turns, Kitty's dresser, lover and partner on stage, Nan moves into the louche theatrical milieu in which her partner works. When Kitty spurns her true sexuality in favour of an opportunist marriage, a heartbroken Nan is forced to find other ways of surviving beyond the music-hall footlights. Her picaresque adventures, cleverly and consciously echoing those of heterosexual heroes and heroines of earlier fiction, from Defoe's Moll Flanders through Tom Jones to David Copperfield, lead her into seedy encounters down dark alleyways, Sapphic games with aristocratic *grandes dames* and an involvement with the fledgling Labour Movement that eventually brings true love and happiness. From its very title (a slang term for cunnilingus), *Tipping the Velvet* is a humorously unabashed and unapologetic celebration of lesbian eroticism and sexual diversity. Waters brings her academic research into the alternative sexual worlds of nineteenth-century England to vivid life and creates a novel that is simultaneously a knowing subversion of older fictions and a lively creation in its own right.

A recurring motif in all three of Waters's books is the disorienting power of female-to-female sexual attraction and its ability to drive her characters either into transgression against the conventions that have previously ruled their lives or into new senses of self and others. For Margaret Prior, the heroine of *Affinity* (1999), her *coup de foudre* takes place in Millbank Prison, the penitentiary that once stood on the site of Tate Britain. It is there, in the 1870s, that, as a prison visitor apparently undertaking the middle-class responsibilities of ministering to the less fortunate, she sees Selina Dawes for the first time. In truth, Margaret Prior has secrets to hide and her voluntary work in the prison is intended to have therapeutic value – she has attempted suicide after a doomed love affair with the woman who is to become her sister-in-law. Selina is a spiritualist and medium whose transactions with the spirit world have ended in disaster and her incarceration for fraud and assault. Yet she persists in proclaiming her belief in the existence of the supernatural and in its power over the ordinary sublunary world. Margaret, initially sceptical, is drawn into acceptance of Selina's claims both by apparent evidence – Selina seems, for example, to have an intimate knowledge of Margaret's past life – and by the force of the growing bond between them. As the novel unfolds and the two women plan an escape from Millbank and a new life together, the metaphorical ghosts of both their pasts continue to haunt them.

Affinity is deftly structured, moving between two separate but interlocking narratives – Margaret's journal, in which the developing relationship between the two women is recorded, and Selina's, in which her past life, leading up to imprisonment, is revealed. Making often brilliant but unobtrusive use of what have clearly been extensive researches into the strange world of Victorian spiritualism, Waters investigates the haunting power of passion and the ways in which what we believe and what we desire are inextricably intertwined. Unlike *Tipping the Velvet*, which, even in its apparently darkest moments, retains the feel of a period romp, a sophisticated lesbian bodice-ripper, *Affinity* moves into genuinely disturbing territory and adds an extra dimension to Waters's writing.

The early scenes of *Fingersmith* (2002), Waters's third novel, take place in the thieves' dens of 1860s Southwark and the book expands into an elaborate story of cross and double-cross centred on what seems to be a suave conman's attempt to use the heroine in a plot to defraud a wealthy heiress. In its very first scene Susan Trinder, the narrator of the opening section, describes being taken, as a small child, to the theatre. The play being performed is a stage adaptation of *Oliver Twist* and Susan recalls her terror of Bill Sikes. This opening scene neatly and economically introduces the two influences – Victorian melodrama and Dickens – which Waters's novel, even more than her previous books, echoes. The novel contains many of the elements of melodrama – the moustache-twirling villain, the innocent orphan and the wicked uncle, the dark shadows of the madhouse and the workhouse – but it uses them for its own more subtle purposes. In the same way that Dickens enjoyed the unsophisticated vigour of the melodrama he saw on the Victorian stage (which finds its way into all his major fiction), so Waters relishes the over-the-top energy that the characters and motifs of melodrama bring to *Fingersmith*. And, just as Dickens gives extra dimensions to the stage's cardboard cruelties and villainies, so too does Waters. *Fingersmith* also carries plenty of more direct reflections and echoes of Dickens's fiction. In particular, the dark mysteries of birth and parentage slowly revealed by the plot parallel the tangled web that surrounds Lady Dedlock in *Bleak House*.

Like *Affinity*, *Fingersmith* makes use of dual narrators, each of whom echoes or undermines the other. In the first part Susan Trinder recounts her journey from the back streets and thieves' dens of the Borough to the rural seclusion of Briar, a country house where she becomes maid to Maud Lilly. Maud lives with her scholarly uncle and Susan supposes her the prospective victim of a plot devised by the novel's villain, the smoothly seductive Richard Rivers. To Susan, Maud is a naïve innocent immured in her country retreat, one destined to be gulled and fooled out of her inheritance. In the second part Maud tells her own story, outlining the horrors of her past, the corrupting tutelage of her selfish uncle and the role she is playing in a plot whose victim she has no intention of becoming. The reader sees some of the same incidents, large and small, from the different perspectives of the two narrators, watching them reveal both gaping chasms of interpretation and also more subtly altered meanings. In the third part narrative duties return to Susan and the two stories twist and turn towards the consummation of the relationship between her and Maud, the redemptive, erotic love that is set against their own earlier greed and that of the other characters.

Fingersmith shows the distance Sarah Waters has travelled in just three novels. All three books have made use of past fictions and have played games with readers' expectations of particular fictional forms, but this playfulness has reached new levels of sophistication. In *Tipping the Velvet* Waters undermined the picaresque tradition to create what remained a relatively straightforward period romp. In *Affinity* she uses the characters and tropes of melodrama and the plot devices of Dickens and other Victorian novelists to fashion a multi-levelled novel which explores, with great skill and complexity, ideas of deception, betrayal and love. In *Fingersmith* she has produced her best novel so far, a book that shares the expansiveness and richness of the Victorian fiction it echoes but which is imbued with the ideas and concerns of the contemporary world.

Waters's major works

Tipping the Velvet, Virago, 1998.
Affinity, Virago, 1999.
Fingersmith, Virago, 2002.

IRVINE WELSH (born 1958)

Few first-time novelists have had as big an impact as Irvine Welsh and fewer still reach a new audience, but *Trainspotting* genuinely did reach out to people who would normally find their artistic needs fulfilled by music or film rather than fiction. Welsh was born in Leith in 1958 (although 1961 and even 1951 have occasionally been quoted as his real years of birth) and left school at sixteen. He had a varied CV over the years as TV repairman, member of assorted bands and even small-time property developer. He was working as a training officer in equal opportunities for Edinburgh Council when *Trainspotting* was published. Since then he has worked as a novelist and short-story writer and his writings have appeared in a wide variety of newspapers and magazines – he has even made an unlikely appearance as a columnist for the conservative *Daily Telegraph*.

Set in the sink estates of an Edinburgh the tourists never see, *Trainspotting* (1993) introduced a group of characters whose lives revolve around drugs. The central character, Renton, is an angrily eloquent smackhead dismissive of what society has to offer him:

> Choose us. Choose life. Choose mortgage payments; choose washing machines; choose cars; choose sitting oan a couch watching mind-numbing and spirit-crushing game shows, stuffing fuckin junk food intae yir mooth.... Choose life. Well, ah choose no tae choose life.

Around Renton and his associates – Sick Boy, Spud, the semi-psychotic Begbie – Welsh builds a portrait of an underclass in determined rebellion against a society that rejects it and in pursuit of a life of hedonism and instant gratification. In a culture which rushes to condemnation, he is refreshingly uninterested in taking any overtly moral stance towards drug use. He simply presents drugs as part and parcel of his characters' everyday lives – sometimes pleasurable, sometimes not. Even his most shocking scenes of casual sex, of even more casual violence and of the unremitting need to score drugs are described with the same black humour. Told in an obscenity-strewn, phonetically rendered Scots demotic, *Trainspotting* was abrasive, energetic and very funny. It succeeded in encompassing material other writers were missing and reached out to an audience which felt alienated by most contemporary fiction.

Of the short stories in the collection *The Acid House* (1994), some were set in territory familiar to readers of *Trainspotting* and others were placed amid more hallucinatory landscapes of fantasy and imagination. They looked forward to Welsh's next novel, *Marabou Stork Nightmares* (1995), which seemed a deliberate attempt on his part to demonstrate that, as a writer, he could move beyond the ground he had staked out so successfully as his own in *Trainspotting*. Roy Strang, comatose in an Edinburgh hospital, replays traumatic events from his past while drifting in and out of hallucinatory fantasies, bizarre parodies of *Boy's Own* imperial adventure stories, in which he hunts down the predatory, flamingo-killing Marabou Stork – 'the personification of all this badness... the badness in me'. The nature of the badness within Strang is slowly revealed as Welsh's plot unwinds. Welsh's ambition in the book is clear but it is not fully realised. The reality of Strang's bleak personal history is always handled with more assurance than the surreal safari in search of the Marabou Stork taking place in his head. The pastiche of a certain style of old-fashioned prose – the memoir of some Edwardian big-game hunter, say – is clumsy and the fantasy itself never carries conviction.

After *Ecstasy* (1996), a collection of novellas subtitled *Three Chemical Romances*, Welsh introduced a character revoltingly compelling, even by his standards, in *Filth* (1998). Detective Sergeant Bruce Robertson is a man who is seemingly without any redeeming qualities at all. Misogynist, racist, violent and homophobic, Robertson is some kind of appalling embodiment of moral corruption, a man given over to the manipulation and degradation of others. Despite the undeniable fascination of the monster at the centre of its often perversely comic narrative, *Filth* is the weakest of Welsh's novels by some way. There is an uncomfortable sense that Welsh has given way to the temptation to manipulate his devoted readers, as much as Robertson does his victims, in the self-conscious descriptions of depravity and violence. There is a weary repetition of themes and language better handled elsewhere, particularly in the rather feeble attempts to explain Robertson's 'badness', which only remind us how much better Welsh did this with Roy Strang in *Marabou Stork Nightmares*. There is sometimes a sense that Welsh is pastiching himself, knows it and doesn't much care.

Glue (2001), however, ranks with *Trainspotting* as his most accomplished novel. The title refers not, as one might expect, to solvent abuse but to the ties that bind the four central characters, whose lives are chronicled across several decades. DJ Carl Ewart, boxer Billy Birrell, addict Andrew Galloway and misogynist womaniser Terry Lawson are the prisms through which we see reflected the 1970s, 1980s and 1990s and each gets the chance to play narrator. The emphasis, as in any Welsh novel, is on the graphically described pleasures and pitfalls of the flesh and immediate gratification. 'Drunk tales, rave tales, fitba mob tales, drug tales, shaggin tales, aw the usual crap that makes life worth living', are told with an energy and verve that Welsh had often lost in his two previous novels. Yet, behind all this, a real sense of time passing and lives changing is evoked. Welsh courts the danger of falling into sentimental laddishness (and occasionally plummets into it only to pull himself out a paragraph or two later), but the 'glue' that holds the characters together remains believable.

In many of Welsh's books ghosts from *Trainspotting* have been glimpsed in walk-on roles, but in his most recent novel Welsh has returned wholeheartedly and unashamedly to the milieu and the characters of his debut book. *Porno* (2002) shows Renton, Sick Boy, Spud and Begbie ten years down the line. Simon 'Sick Boy' Williamson has returned from London to Edinburgh and has decided that the homemade porn industry offers him the chance of riches. His amoral egotism has not been changed by the years. 'You've got two categories', he remarks at one point; 'Category one: me. Category two: the rest of the world. You can divide the others up into two sub-groups: those who do as I say and the superfluous'. He is joined by Renton, drawn back from Amsterdam, where he has been running a nightclub, and by an English film student and part-time sex worker, Nikki Fuller-Smith, in his attempt to use porn as the ultimate scam. In the background are the dementedly violent Begbie and Spud, irredeemably hooked on drugs and falling apart.

Returning years later to the characters of your most successful book is not usually a good career move for a novelist but Welsh's brand of black farce works as well second time around. *Porno* also reveals, particularly in its treatment of the disintegrating Spud, that, beneath the obscenities, the celebration of hedonism and the unsqueamish descriptions of violence and drugs, Welsh has always been a paradoxical moralist at heart. In *Glue* the characters subscribe to a jokey alternative Decalogue (commandments include 'Always back up your mates' and 'Tell them nowt, them being polis, dole, social etc'), and Welsh, too, has his own version of this that is reflected in his fiction. In *Trainspotting* Welsh deliberately and effectively opened up new territory for the novel. That territory has now been visited by many imitators, but his later fiction, particularly *Glue* and *Porno*, shows that no one maps it out with such energy and precision.

Welsh's major works

Trainspotting, Secker & Warburg, 1993.
The Acid House, Cape, 1994 (short stories).
Marabou Stork Nightmares, Cape, 1995.
Ecstasy, Cape, 1996 (novellas).
Filth, Cape, 1998.
Glue, Cape, 2001.
Porno, Cape, 2002.

JEANETTE WINTERSON (born 1959)

It's a commonplace that first novels are often thinly disguised autobiography. In that her first novel told of a sensitive girl growing up in a fundamentalist Christian family and discovering her own lesbian sexuality, Jeanette Winterson seemed typical of the truism, but little in her later literary career has been typical. Winterson has shown an admirable willingness to experiment with form and language in the fiction she has written since her debut, *Oranges Are Not the Only Fruit* in 1985. At first critics applauded the daring of novels like *The Passion* and *Sexing the Cherry* but her recent work has met with more mixed reviews. Yet the same impulse to test the boundaries of fiction, the same refusal to tread comfortable and already well-trodden ground, is apparent in her books of the last few years. Winterson remains a defiantly 'experimental' novelist and most of her experiments yield interesting results.

Jeanette Winterson was born in Manchester in 1959 and adopted by a couple who were fiercely evangelical Pentecostal Christians. She was brought up to believe firmly in her own destiny as a preacher of God's word but at the age of sixteen she had her first lesbian relationship and was rejected by both her family and the church that was at the heart of its life. Leaving home, she supported herself with a series of part-time jobs while simultaneously working to pass A-levels. She went on to read English at Oxford and then worked in the theatre before publishing *Oranges Are Not the Only Fruit*. On the publication of *The Passion* in 1987 she became a full-time writer and has since published five further novels, as well as a collection of short stories, a volume of essays and films for TV.

Oranges Are Not the Only Fruit clearly draws very heavily on Winterson's own experiences. The central character – called Jeanette – is adopted and her adoptive mother is a fundamentalist Christian intent on bringing Jeanette up to spread God's word. The novel recounts Jeanette's intense relationship with her adoptive mother, her difficulties in relating to the world outside the church when she is obliged to go to school and her growing sense of her own individuality. When she reaches her teenage years, her emotional and sexual yearnings are directed towards other girls, particularly towards her friend Melanie. She and Melanie become lovers and eventually, in innocent delight at her own happiness, she confides this to her mother. Mother and church elders respond by attempting to exorcise the demons that have clearly entered Jeanette and she is tormented into a pretence of repentance. Inside herself, however, Jeanette feels no remorse for her love of Melanie. She becomes once again a model evangelist for the church, preaching and teaching in Sunday school. Yet she also begins a new affair with a girl called Katy and when this is discovered she quits the church and is obliged to leave home. Told in the first person, Jeanette's story ranges from near-farcical comedy to the terrifying intolerance of the church's attempt to coerce her.

Yet there is much more going on in *Oranges Are Not the Only Fruit* than a fictional remoulding of autobiographical experience. The book is also the first indication of Winterson's ongoing interest in the very nature of storytelling and its centrality to the way we all struggle to make sense of our lives. The book is shaped so that it becomes the fictional Jeanette's way of reclaiming the Bible and its stories for herself, taking them away from the exclusive, domineering inter-pretation of the church and relating them to her own life and inner experience. Each of the chapters is given the name of a book of the Old Testament, from Genesis (the story of Jeanette's early life) through Exodus (her occasionally traumatic experiences when she ventures out into the world outside home and the church) and on to Ruth (Jeanette's own love for other women reflected in the book in the Bible which most movingly portrays the emotional commitment of one woman to another). Throughout the novel, also, fairy tales and other imaginative fictions are juxtaposed with the apparently straightforward realism with which Jeanette's unusual coming of age is told. The result is a remarkable first novel which uses lots of elements, including the obviously autobiographical ones, to explore the possibilities of love and the dangers of believing that there is only one story to tell.

Boating for Beginners (1985) was published a few months after *Oranges Are Not the Only Fruit* and Winterson, while not disowning the book, tends to be rather dismissive of it, calling it 'a comic book with pictures' on her official website. In fact, *Boating for Beginners* is an enjoyable *jeu d'esprit*, reinventing the story of Noah and the Ark with throwaway wit and cleverness. Winterson's second major novel, though, was *The Passion* (1987). Superficially a historical novel which tells of the love affair between Henri, chicken chef to Napoleon, and a cross-dressing Venetian woman called Villanelle, the book is best read as a fable or fairy tale which uses the historical background as a springboard from which to tell stories in which the ordinary and the extraordinary sit side by side on the page. As Winterson herself says on her website, '*The Passion* isn't a historical novel. It uses history as invented space'. It is a short book which packs much material into its four brief sections. The first is told by Henri and describes his life and the ways it is shaped by war and Napoleon's ambition. In the second the reader is introduced to Villanelle – web-footed, passionate and bisexual – and her life in an extraordinarily vividly evoked Venice (extraordinary not least because Winterson had never been there when she wrote the book). The third shows the two meeting on Napoleon's doomed 1812 campaign in Russia. Henri is still close to his emperor; Villanelle has become a prostitute serving the officers of Napoleon's Grand Army. The two flee and make an epic journey back to Venice. In the fourth section Henri, enlarged and yet broken by his passion for Villanelle ('When passion comes late in life, it is hard to bear', she says of him), takes the blame for the murder of Villanelle's husband and is condemned to a prison asylum. There he goes truly insane, believing that both Napoleon and Villanelle are still with him.

The Passion is filled with what might be called magic realism. Villanelle loses her heart, literally, to another woman, who keeps it in a jar; drunken Irish sentries see twenty miles across country; Henri and Villanelle are both described in androgynous terms and gender seems a flexible concept. All this reflects Winterson's very personal belief, evident in her first novel, of the transformative power of the imagination. 'I'm telling you stories', runs a repeating phrase in *The Passion*; 'Trust me'.

Winterson's use of history as 'invented space' continued with *Sexing the Cherry* (1989). In this novel the space is seventeenth-century England but it is a seventeenth-century England unimagined by most historians. The central characters in the book are Jordan, a foundling rescued as a baby from the waters of the Thames, and his gargantuan protector and mother figure, the Dog Woman. When he grows up, Jordan is apprenticed to the gardener John Tradescant and embarks on a series of journeys around the world in search of exotic plants. The book opens out into dazzlingly concise sequence of stories within stories and journeys within journeys in a vertiginously exhilarating flight through time and space. Linked with all these multi-dimensional travels are reworkings of classic fairy tales and Greek mythology, dream sequences and erotic fables, all intended to undercut and challenge conventional notions of history, gender and the fixed nature of 'reality'.

Written on the Body (1992) opens with the question 'Why is the measure of love loss?', and the novel is, in a sense, a lengthy meditation on that question. It chronicles the narrator's intensely passionate love affair with a married woman, Louise, and its dissolution in the physical dissolution of the body as Louise is diagnosed with leukaemia. The narrator mourns the loss of the dying Louise ('I didn't only want Louise's flesh, I wanted her bones, her blood, her tissues, the sinews that bound her together') in a book that explores the power of erotic love and the desire to transcend the limits of one's own body through vivid and poetic metaphors of sexuality, physicality and the breaking down of the body under disease's assault. Throughout the novel the narrator remains unnamed and ungendered, an ambiguous testament to the visceral power of intense love and its ability both to destroy and to make whole.

In *Art and Lies* (1994) Winterson attempts another of her free-flowing excursions through time and space but produces what is probably her least successful novel, one in which her imaginative gifts too often take second place to the direct statement of beliefs. In her best fiction, her passionately felt beliefs about the importance of erotic love, art and the transformative power of the imagination emerge between the lines of the multiple stories she unfolds. In *Art and Lies* the intertwining stories of her three characters are sometimes lost amidst what can seem like lectures on subjects close to the author's heart. *Art and Lies* was followed by *Gut Symmetries* (1997), arguably the most daringly experimental of all Winterson's works. Experiments, in art or science, run the risk of failure. Some critics were swift to condemn *Gut Symmetries* as disastrously unsuccessful. They missed much of the point of the book. It is difficult (but Winterson intends it to be) and the use of scientific theory (GUT is an acronym for the Grand Unifying Theory of physical forces, which is the Holy Grail for contemporary physics) as a source of metaphor is often laboured. Yet, when so much fiction asks little of its readers beyond an ability to understand nice, simple, straightforward sentences, the ambition that Winterson shows in this book is to be applauded. And, at its simplest level, *Gut Symmetries* is an investigation of that most recurring of fictional themes – the love triangle. Stella, a poet, and her husband, the physicist Jove (short for Giovanni), both have sexual relationships with Alice, another scientist. The novel follows both their tangled attempts to find love and meaning in their lives and Winterson's meditations on the conflict between different ways – artistic and scientific – of interpreting the world and our place in it. Branching out from this central story, as always in Winterson's multifaceted narratives, are the stories of Stella's parents in Nazi Germany, the life of Alice's grandmother and a kaleidoscope of other interconnected tales.

In interviews Winterson has repeatedly expressed her fascination with the imaginative potential of new technologies and she is reported to be working on an internet project for the BBC. *The.PowerBook* (2000) reflects that fascination. The narrator of the book is an online writer, Ali, another of Winterson's indeterminately gendered characters, who fashions and refashions stories for those who request them. 'Slightest accidents open up new worlds', Ali says, and the brief stories and imaginative flights that she conjures up in response to her e-mails and sends back out into cyberspace do indeed open up new worlds. Winterson again plunges recklessly through time and geography, appropriating other writers' stories and retelling them, interpreting fairy tales and contemporary myths with her customary confidence and *élan*. Interwoven with the collage of fictions is the unfolding story of Ali's own love life, centred around another of the emotional and sexual triangles that have featured in Winterson's earlier books. This is much less effective than the myriad fabulations with which it is entwined.

'The point of fiction', Winterson has written, 'is not to mirror real life but to set out from it, to alter our viewing angle and perhaps even the world we are viewing'. This is a statement of artistic intention to which Winterson has remained faithful from her first novel to her most recent, *Lighthousekeeping* (2004). In order to do so she has taken chances and risks (one of her favourite words) which less ambitious writers would have avoided. The results of her risk-taking have not always been uniformly successful – one of the necessary consequences of risk-taking is occasional failure – but her work is always interesting and challenging, provoking readers to re-examine the world they are viewing in ways that most of her contemporaries have not proved capable of imagining.

Winterson's major works

Boating for Beginners, Pandora, 1985.
Oranges Are Not the Only Fruit, Pandora, 1985.
The Passion, Cape, 1987.
Sexing the Cherry, Cape, 1989.
Written on the Body, Cape, 1992.
Art and Lies, Cape, 1994.
Art Objects, Cape, 1995 (essays).
Gut Symmetries, Granta, 1997.
The World and Other Places, Cape, 1998 (short stories).
The.PowerBook, Cape, 2000.
Lighthousekeeping, Fourth Estate, 2004.

INDEX